HARD CANDY

JACK LIVELY

D1727220

GENERAL PROJECTS

...in the darkness, there'll be hidden worlds that shine
When I hold Candy close she makes the hidden worlds mine

-Bruce Springsteen

CHAPTER ONE

The woman in white planted her boots firmly onto the studded yellow safety line of the Kitchewan Landing train station platform. She leaned over the edge to take a good look north. The approaching train was visible, maybe half a mile away and moving slowly. At that speed it would arrive in a couple of minutes, three at most. The train car interior would be warm and cozy and fine if a little dirty from the winter slush coming off boots and shoes. New York City was always going to be a couple of degrees warmer than upstate. They called it an urban heat island.

But the woman in white was wrong and the approaching train wasn't warm.

The conductor was freezing in her little booth. Huddled tight and rubbing her gloved hands together. The heater had failed just after Beacon. Now they were pulling in to Kitchewan Landing, which in addition to being a regular stop was also the principal maintenance facility for the Hudson line. The tracks multiplied on the approach, fanning out to covered repair depots and cleaning huts. The train limped in to the station and the wheels ground to a halt beside the platform.

She leaned forward and pushed the button on the address system with a gloved forefinger. "Kitchewan Landing, final stop on this train. All change at Kitchewan. You gotta get off here folks. The waiting room's warm and comfortable and the next train's coming down the track."

The conductor was cold but relatively happy. She lived in Kitchewan Landing, so this was the end of her day. There might be a few frustrated passengers, but they'd get where they were going, eventually. She looked out the window at the parking lot. Her Jeep Cherokee was parked in the back behind the depot near the trestle, but all she could see was a huge pile of salt, brown and dirty and currently being loaded into the backs of two municipal dump trucks. Equipped with blinking yellow lights and salt sprayers, the trucks were all ready to disperse their loads on the roads once the incoming blizzard hit.

The conductor exited her booth, locked it, and came through the aisle, speaking to the first passenger she saw. "All change here, sir. Train's going into the depot. Once you get up in the waiting room they'll have the schedule." She wasn't apologetic, just delivering information.

The man looked at her evenly and she felt the tug of attraction. He said, "No problem."

The conductor tugged at her zipper and smoothed away any gaps in her protective layers. There was no vanity in her choice of outfit; it was simply a matter of urgent practicalities. Underneath her parka she wore a Metro-North uniform. The name tag was in gold and read, "DeValla."

Tom Keeler watched the conductor move to the doors. He'd been looking at that river for hours now.

Keeler had been on the train since five in the morning, not just this train, a sequence of trains and waiting rooms and coffee kiosks starting out in a remote part of Ontario, Canada, and scheduled to end in less than an hour at Grand Central Station, New York City. It was 4:51 in the afternoon, and Keeler could have used a cup of coffee and a buttered bagel— not that he required these things. They just occurred to him as a desirable mental image over the darkening wastes of the Hudson. Bagels were just one of the things he was looking forward to in New York City.

The doors hissed open. Keeler could see a woman wrapped in a white down coat standing out on the platform and another figure behind her in a black coat. The conductor stepped off the train, arms wide to prevent the waiting passengers from boarding. She spoke, but Keeler could only make out the tone and see the vapor from her open mouth. The tone was informational, tinged with a small amount of performative regret. The woman in white moved uncertainly, first left and then right and was subsumed in the flow of passengers moving off the train and up the platform.

Keeler stood and pulled his backpack from the overhead rack. He exited the car and joined the stream of passengers moving. A small traffic jam was formed by the tight U-turn up the stairs. Keeler shuffled up with everyone else, one stair at a time. He was patient and content, not bothered either by the delay or the cold. He followed the person in front of him, trudging up the covered stairwell. A grimy plexiglass window gave a view onto the platform below. The woman in white was seated on the ground as if she had slipped on ice.

Up in the waiting area, the passengers gathered beneath a set of information screens. The next train was scheduled in

twenty minutes. It would be the express service to Grand
Central Station with only three stops. Keeler moved in the
direction of a kiosk. He could smell the coffee and had already
spotted the individually wrapped bagels.

A couple of minutes later, Keeler finished his buttered
bagel. It had become dark out. Since it was elevated, the waiting
room had a good view of the surrounding terrain. A police car
mounted a rise at the entrance to the parking lot and came down
toward the station, lights on and sirens blaring. Slush and mud
and ice and dirt sprayed from the tires. An ambulance followed
in the cruiser's wake, likewise screaming and blaring with light
and sound.

Keeler observed the passengers in the waiting area: maybe
thirty total, plus the two people working the kiosk, what looked
like an elderly couple. No Metro-North personnel in sight. He
moved to the side that overlooked the tracks. Keeler could just
about see down to the platform. A tight knot of Metro-North
uniforms had gathered around a fallen figure. The woman in
white wasn't sitting anymore. She'd crumpled to the platform,
lying face up on the frozen cement.

The first fat snowflakes drifted through the vapor lights.
The incoming police strobes bounced off the woman's face,
reflecting in sightless eyes trained on the underside of the
stairwell.

CHAPTER TWO

Twenty minutes later, the express train to the city hadn't come, but the snow had, slow and heavy and relentless, drifting and settling and staying put without melting. She hadn't yet received the official word, but DeValla wasn't sure that the train would actually make it, given the meteorological conditions.

She was down on the platform with the medics and the first responder team from the town police. The two paramedics were working hard on the woman in white. DeValla didn't know what the situation was, but it looked serious. The paramedics were communicating by radio with their dispatcher, and she couldn't make out much more than the crackle of radio static, some of which was amplified by the cops.

DeValla knew the local police and had exchanged words and organized for coffee to be brought up from the staff room to the platform. She'd also completed a walkthrough of the debilitated train, looking for lost items and sleeping passengers. The train was just now wheezing back up the track, diverting to the repair depot where the team would be taking a look at the heating system, but not before the morning.

From the south came two powerful horn blasts from a north-bound commuter train as it crossed the trestle. No doubt the driver was aware of the situation and wanted to be safe, warning the responders on the platform that the train was incoming.

DeValla couldn't help herself say the words out loud, "Here comes the money."

One of the cops standing nearby chuckled. "Here it comes."

The phrase was popular with those locals who didn't work in the city. Kitchewan Landing being a commuter town, the money did indeed come up with the northbound trains. Whenever a train came over the trestle, the twin horns blasted loud enough to be heard all over town. More than a few locals would reflexively announce, "Here comes the money."

This one was the express train to Kitchewan Landing, delivering the money fast.

Two more vehicles had supplemented the initial police response. The cops fanned out to block off the site from passengers coming off the northbound train. They'd left the blue lights going on the parked cruisers, because it looked good and serious. The darkness drew closer and the emergency lights bounced off surfaces, lighting up the station area like an actual crime scene.

The northbound express eased to a stop and shuddered. The doors hissed open. DeValla watched impassively as passengers scurried off. Clients, if you could call them that. Whatever condition they'd been in for the morning journey, by end-of-day the commuter crowd was invariably smelly, drunk, and dead tired. Some of the more anxious executive types were still muttering furiously into the air, ears stuffed with remote control hardware, rubbernecking at the emergency scene.

She stood with her back to the paramedic responders, fanning her arm through the air to move the commuters in the direction of the exit. "All right, let's keep it moving here. Go straight up the stairs please."

The train's conductor was the last to exit, a large round man. They knew each other professionally.

He said, "What's going on?"

"Some woman slipped is all I know. Maybe hit her head."

The man was dressed just like she was, peaked conductor's cap and uniform underneath a winter coat. He didn't look half as cold as she'd been. But he didn't look comfortable either.

"Do me a favor and take the walk through for me? I was supposed to pick up the girls from dance class." He tried for a pitiful expression. "We're late and you know Jen's not going to care about why."

She nodded. "No problem, Sal. Go get the girls and say hey from me."

"Thanks, babe. I appreciate that."

DeValla watched Sal move down the platform, following the last of the northbound commuters up into the covered stairwell. She was hungry and thinking of what to do about dinner. She walked down to the end of the platform and stepped onto the last car. Then she walked through the train slowly, looking left and right and crouching to peek beneath the seats. Sometimes there were people sleeping, either because they were tired or drunk or both.

This time there were no people on the train, just a truckload of empty beer cans, potato chip bags, and a laptop bag up on the luggage rack. The conductor pulled the laptop bag down and slung it over her shoulder. She headed off the train and stopped for a moment to report into her radio that the train was now clear of passengers and could be sent up to the depot for the night.

She walked south on the platform, and as she passed the response crew, one of the cops she knew couldn't help himself from commenting. "Too cold out here for your hot ass DeValla?"

She ignored him and continued to the lost and found.

But the guy at the lost and found wasn't at his desk. He'd already padlocked the cage protecting a wall of numbered cubbies and was about to do the same for the front door. He noticed her, and glanced down at the laptop bag in her hand.

"That all you got? You want me to open up again? I'll turn on the computer."

The blizzard was coming in now and the roads would be dangerous once the snow settled. It was best to get going. "Nah, forget about it." DeValla turned away and let the man off the hook.

The laptop bag was black with a rough texture, made of some kind of durable polyester and almost identical to the thousands of similar bags carried by Metro-North customers working in the city. DeValla had a choice. With the lost and found closed, she could either take the bag up to the main office, or take it home with her and bring it in on her next shift. The lost and found office was close to her parked Cherokee. The main office was back up the platform through the driving snow and past the gathered cops and paramedics.

Which pretty much answered the question. The conductor went next door to the staff room. She had some paperwork to finish up and then she was out of there.

CHAPTER THREE

U p in the waiting area, Tom Keeler crushed a cardboard coffee cup in his gloved fist and let it drop into the mouth of a garbage can. It was his second cup. The police and paramedics had accessed the platform from a second passenger bridge, maybe forty yards down. Now they were hustling in the other direction making tracks in the gathering snow. The woman was strapped onto a stretcher breathing out of an oxygen mask. The paramedics moved her into the mouth of the covered stairwell, where they disappeared for a time, reappearing by the parking lot on the other side. The emergency team moved in a protective knot around the woman, now a small figure with the mask over her face.

The information screens displayed a grid of scheduled train departures for the coming hour. On the left side, the train direction: either down to Grand Central, or up to Poughkeepsie. On the right, the word *delayed* blinked in all four rows. Express and local trains both in and out of the city were going nowhere. The blizzard and the emergency, two fine reasons for a delayed schedule.

An hour later the situation was the same but different.

Somebody knew somebody and word had filtered up from the platform to the waiting room. The woman in white was alive and was being moved to Phelps Memorial Hospital. Nobody knew exactly what the deal was, and neither were they speculating. The rumors were idle and vague. Alive was better than dead, and less worthy of conjecture.

Keeler's fellow passengers had stopped staring idly into their phones and had started actively using them, stabbing ungloved forefingers into screens, swiping, stabbing more, with thumbs, and finally holding the slim rectangles out in front of them delicately, like cocktail party hors d'oeuvres to be verbalized rather than ingested. Keeler didn't have a phone as a matter of principle. And if he did have one, he wouldn't have been using it. Instead, he was observing his surroundings.

He watched the emergency vehicles return up the hill to the station exit and disappear over the rise and around the corner. Two police cruisers escorted the ambulance. A few moments later the flashing lights reappeared as the small convoy turned onto the highway ramp and then got up to speed and disappeared all over again.

An hour after that Keeler was alone in the waiting room.

The phone work had been successful, and stranded passengers hadn't hesitated to find a solution to the issue at hand. He'd watched as they filtered down from the waiting room, picked up by relatives, or disappearing into waiting taxi cabs. Whatever the mode of transportation, they'd all made the run up the hill and out of the station.

Keeler found himself thinking about what was going to happen next.

It was after 7 p.m. and the situation didn't look good. The computer screens were now dominated by the word *canceled*. Snowfall blanketed the tracks in a soft white carpet that was only going to grow thicker. Keeler didn't know anything about trains, and there was no one in sight to interrogate, except for the couple who ran the kiosk and they were on their way out. The woman reached up and pulled down the rolling steel curtain with a satisfying rumble and thunk. Her partner leaned in to operate the heavy padlock. She straightened up and seemed vaguely alarmed as she noticed Keeler coming.

He said, "Excuse me ma'am, I was wondering if you'd be able to recommend a place to eat supper in the area?"

"We call it dinner here. Only place I can guarantee open tonight would be the diner." She pointed toward the parking lot exit. "Up the ramp there and go under the highway, make a left at the light. Then you take Riverside down past the duck pond, and you can't miss it." The woman regarded him with tired eyes. "Maybe a five-minute drive."

The station entrance wasn't fancy, just cold and plain. There was a soda machine and a brick wall between two covered staircases going up to the waiting area and the platforms. Across the way was a taxi stand with five spots, four empty and one taken. A man was leaned against the hood of a perfectly preserved Pontiac station wagon from the 1980s, with the wood siding and a taxi light on the roof. Keeler's eyes took in the vehicle and the passengers inside, waiting for the driver. There were three commuters packed into the backseat. The front passenger seat was empty.

Keeler jogged across the road. The driver hardly noticed, his attention elsewhere.

"I'm going to the diner. Mind if I squeeze in?"

The driver swiveled his head. "Car's full, buddy. Where did you wanna sit, on my lap?" His head swiveled back to the station platform, eyes interested and searching.

Keeler said, "There's space in the passenger seat."

"I'm waiting on a guy. Car's full, believe me."

A chain link fence ran the length of the tracks, from the

station entrance to the second passenger bridge forty yards down. A man emerged. He was relatively short and well-built and wore a wool hat and a parka.

The driver said, "There he is." He walked toward the man and they met halfway.

Keeler watched the two come together and conduct a short intense conversation. They knew each other, clearly. Maybe they'd gone to high school together. The driver did the initial speaking and then stood impatiently listening to the other guy respond. They came back to the Pontiac, ignoring Keeler, who watched the driver and passenger open the car doors and climb inside. The suspension sagged and squeaked. The passenger and driver secured their seat belts.

Keeler watched the station wagon cruise out of the parking spot and up the little hill at the exit. The company name was Kitchewan Old Cars, painted in gold and black script. The taxis were now gone for good, packed full of passengers with more expensive destinations than the diner. Keeler didn't figure they'd be back for an empty train station on a canceled line. If the cabs returned it would be the next day, after breakfast, provided the municipal salt trucks and snow plows performed their function and cleared the roads.

The woman had said the diner was a five-minute drive. The snow was coming thick and fast, getting in his eyes if he looked up. Keeler made a rough calculation. Given the traffic lights, snow coming down, and all the other things that would prevent a car from moving, he figured the diner was about a mile away. He'd walk that in fifteen minutes.

CHAPTER FOUR

DeValla, the train conductor, sat in the driver's seat of her Cherokee letting the engine run. The snow was settling, but the wipers were doing a good job of getting it out of the way. The rear defroster was on and the truck was heating up. She flipped the dial on her stereo system and caught the tail end of a classic rock song that she recognized but couldn't name.

By the time she got the vehicle moving, DeValla had it, Jackson Browne, "Running on Empty." By the time she made the left on Riverside she was humming along to Led Zeppelin doing "Dazed and Confused", live in 1969.

She recognized the big guy up ahead, trudging through the blizzard. He'd been on the train and stuck out from the crowd because he was dressed like a lumberjack. Plaid wool coat, wool hat, and big old hiking boots. Like a guy from the backwoods. Kitchewan Landing was a suburb of New York City. A far suburb maybe, with a hell of a lot of woods, a huge reservoir, and the famous Kitchewan dam, but not exactly the backwoods. The guy didn't look like he was from either the suburbs or the city.

On a whim and without thinking about it really, DeValla turned the volume down and pulled her truck to the curb fifteen yards in front of the guy. She lowered the window and waited for him to come abreast. He stepped into the frame and looked at her with intelligent and searching eyes.

She said, "Remember me?" He didn't say anything, just looked at her with those eyes. She resisted the urge to look away. "Where you headed?"

"The diner."

"Hop in, I'll give you a ride." She leaned over to the passenger seat and removed the laptop bag and the three hard-back children's books from the library that had been in the car for a week. She tossed the books and the laptop into the backseat.

The guy loaded himself in. The window hummed closed. He glanced at DeValla. She still had her Metro-North conductor's cap on her head. Something about the searching look made DeValla self-conscious and she removed the hat. A heavy mess of brown hair shook loose and tumbled onto her shoulders and cascaded much lower than shoulder height.

She glanced at the guy and saw that he was looking at her. DeValla sometimes used her hair to impress and didn't know exactly why she was doing it just then. Four and a half minutes later she pulled the truck into a sparsely occupied parking lot alongside the diner building. She executed a neat K-turn, ending with the vehicle pointed at the exit. She put the shifter forward into park. "All right, this is you."

The guy sat back and watched the snow moving through the yellow light of a streetlamp. "What time do you think the trains will start running again?"

"My guess is they'll start back up in the morning. First fast train's 5:02 in the a.m." He didn't respond and DeValla was reminded that he wasn't going to be home in a warm bed after dinner. "The diner's open until ten, take your time eating and you can stretch it until they close. After that you can head back to the station. At least it'll be warm in the waiting room."

He said, "Or I could buy you dinner plus dessert and coffee. Then you could drop me off at the station. I'll relax there while my metabolism does the heavy lifting."

"Oh really, you think?" She twisted curls around a finger.

"Why not? You look hungry. Don't tell me you haven't been thinking about dinner." He jerked his chin at the backseat. "Unless you've got to get back to the kids."

DeValla laughed. "They're at their dad's." She shifted the Cherokee into reverse and executed a flawless curving maneuver into a parking spot at a good clip, which would have been awkward or downright dangerous for a lesser driver. She shifted into park and turned off the ignition. "I don't refuse free food."

CHAPTER FIVE

K eeler kept pace just behind the conductor, letting her lead the way up the stairs into a vestibule with a gumball machine and a waiting bench and a wall of pamphlets. She blew through into the diner. The man behind the cashier's desk nodded at her passing. "Hey, Mini."

She ignored the man and moved through to the fifth booth in from the entrance. She took off her coat and balled it into the corner before sitting. Keeler slid into the booth opposite her.

The conductor eyed him and chin pointed at the guy behind the cashier desk. "Look, man, don't call me Mini, okay? I went to school with that prick so he gets a pass. You try it and you don't get a pass."

"Roger that. What do I call you?"

She glared at him once beneath the long eyelashes. "Why would you need to call me?"

Keeler matched her stare. "The other part of your name is attached to your chest, if I need to, I'll call you that, in case there's a danger of confusion."

She kept a straight face. "Yes, in case of an event in which you couldn't possibly catch my attention any other way you may use the name DeValla. What name should I use in the event of a natural disaster, a stampede, or an active-shooter situation?"

He said, "I'm Tom Keeler. Use whatever part of it you like, DeValla."

He watched her smile finally. She said, "Keeler. Like the way a French person would say the word *killer*."

The maître d' brought over two large and ornately bound tomes. Keeler flipped open the heavy padded and gold-embossed cover and was quickly lost in at least a dozen pages of laminated menu text. He closed the binder. "What do you get here?"

She said, "I'd advise a newcomer to get breakfast or get Greek."

"Not the burger."

"Get the burger if you want."

"I'm buying, you could get something fancy."

"I'm planning on it. Yankee Pot Roast with the mixed vegetables. Comes with appetizer and dessert. I'm getting the clam chowder and the cherry cheesecake."

"Thought you said to get breakfast or get Greek."

"That's advice for the out-of-towners." She looked up, not in any kind of a humorous way. "The menu's too crowded for granular advice. Follow me or go Greek or get breakfast. That's my advice."

Keeler said nothing and went back into the menu for a while, eventually coming up in sync with the waitress's arrival. She had an order pad out front and a black apron with pens and a bulging phone rectangle that she ran her thumb over like a charm. "Hey, Mini."

DeValla acknowledged the waitress and ordered. Keeler ordered the same thing as the conductor. None of them commented on the symmetry since it made sense. New guy comes to the diner for the first time, it's only prudent to follow the example of a local. If you're there a second time you can get experimental. Common sense prevailed all around and the waitress left satisfied.

The diner was well heated and cozy. Keeler leaned back against the cushioned vinyl. The busboy unloaded two large glasses of ice water onto the table and pulled napkins and cutlery from his apron, setting them down neatly. DeValla looked at Keeler. "So where are you coming from?"

"I was up in Canada, dogsledding." He examined DeValla, who resented her nickname. She was a few years older than him, maybe early forties. She had a gap between her two front teeth, and he thought that she was certainly the best-looking train conductor he'd ever seen.

DeValla lifted an ice cube out of her glass and popped it into her mouth. She spoke around it. "You're kidding right?"

"Not kidding, no."

She indicated his balled up wool coat. "They give you that lumberjack coat up there?"

"They did, I arrived underdressed."

DeValla crushed the ice cube between her teeth. "Seriously. You aren't messing with me?"

Keeler shook his head, trying to appear serious. "A buddy of mine started a dogsledding business. I went up there to help him build the sauna, ended up staying a while. Nice place, nice dogs, but it's tourist season now, so I had to leave to make room for paying customers."

She nodded. "You an expert now, pro dog driver?"

"It's called mushing, and no, definitely not any kind of expert."

DeValla smiled. "Mushing, yes, that's what they call it." Her eyes shifted from Keeler to something behind him, which flattened out her expression and pursed her lips. She brought her gaze back to him. "You don't look like you're from the city."

"I'm not. Figured I'd take a week or ten days in New York City, maybe eat some Chinese food in Chinatown." Keeler shrugged.

"Oh yeah, and then what?"

"You mean after New York? I was thinking Puerto Rico or Mexico."

DeValla crushed another ice cube. She was distracted by something behind him.

Keeler was aware of what lay behind him. The counter and the bathroom entrance. The counter was set up for single eaters with a platter of individually wrapped chocolate chip cookies at the corner. There was a drinks fountain behind it for soda and water. Behind that was a wall holding up a section of steel shelving and a glass-fronted refrigerator. Below the steel shelving was a milkshake machine and an ice cream topping unit with several closed pots that Keeler assumed contained things like hot fudge, sprinkles, and maybe fruit chopped into quarters and nuts chopped into small pieces.

When they'd walked in, Keeler had noticed all of that plus the man sitting at the counter, plus the busboy organizing glasses onto the steel shelving. Therefore, Keeler assumed that the object of Mini DeValla's gaze was the individual eater. He said, "What's up, DeValla?"

"That guy was on the train." She corrected herself. "Not on the train, on the platform. He was going to come on the train, but I told him he couldn't get on."

Keeler twisted around and looked behind him. The man sat at the counter, hunched over a plate with both hands up and occupied in front of him. The two raised hands indicated that the demolition of a sandwich was underway. The counter eater hadn't removed his coat, which was hooded and black and bulky. He had removed his hat. From the angle at which Keeler viewed the man it was only possible to see the top half of his head and the rear quarter of his face, comprising ear, neck, some cheek, and some of the right eyebrow. His hair was brown with no sign of graying at the temples.

"You recognized his face?"

She said, "No. I recognized him because he's wearing the same coat as my ex."

Keeler swiveled back to DeValla. "How can you tell it's the same coat?"

"It's in the details. Look at the shoulder thing and the hood."

Keeler turned. The coat had an epaulette, like a pseudo-military affectation. In addition, the hood had a faux-fur trim attached by a zipper. The counter eater set his sandwich down and reached for a fistful of napkins.

"Detachable fur trim. You bought that for your ex-husband?"

DeValla said, "No, stupid, of course not. The only thing I'd buy him is a one-way ticket to another planet. He bought the coat for himself at Sears. I know this because we share the kids."

The rear wall behind the counter was a steel sheet, relatively dull but nonetheless reflective. The individual eater swiveled his stool and looked at Keeler with alert eyes, powerful jaws chewing. Keeler met the gaze and turned back to the conductor. He raised his eyebrows, she lowered her face and hid a grin, protected from view by Keeler's broad figure. DeValla looked up again and flushed.

"Shit, he's coming over."

The man was finishing a mouthful and brushing his fingers with a paper napkin. He had brown hair cropped short and moved in an athletic way, balanced with legs bent, giving him a slightly simian aspect. He arrived at their booth smiling with his mouth, not his eyes.

"You two are making me feel a little uncomfortable. Am I funny or something?"

Keeler experienced a flicker of recognition when he looked at the man's face directly, although he couldn't place it. The face was not special, a regular oval with soft brown eyes and brown hair combed into a neat side part. He had the kind of face that could be described as familiar, a white bread Midwestern kind of American face. Keeler looked at DeValla. She matched the man's smile with her own professional conductor's version. "No, of course not. I recognized you from the train is all."

The man rotated his eyes to the name tag on DeValla's Metro-North uniform and lingered for a long moment before switching back to her face. His expression hadn't changed, the smile remained stapled on.

"I wasn't on any train."

"Not the train, the platform." DeValla waved dismissively. "Either way it doesn't matter. Sorry to bother you."

The man's gaze shifted to Keeler and then returned to the conductor. His eyes blinked once, slowly. "I have no idea what you're talking about, but that's okay. Have a big dinner, Miss DeValla." He walked back to the counter without waiting for a response.

Keeler and DeValla shared a glance. She mouthed the words *big dinner*.

Keeler said, "I thought I recognized him as well. Maybe he just has a familiar face."

"Not just the face. I definitely saw him on the platform. The way he's built, plus the coat. He was there. Why would he deny it?" She looked at Keeler with her eyes open in an exaggerated manner. Keeler shrugged. People do all kinds of weird stuff.

The clam chowder arrived. Two thick ceramic bowls and two spoons along with two plastic sachets of shell-shaped croutons and a basket of garlic bread.

CHAPTER SIX

K eeler finished everything that was put in front of him, but DeValla required a take-out bag for half of her pot roast and the whole of the cherry cheesecake slice. She said it was for her sister, a big fan of cherry cheesecake. When they left, the man with the familiar face was still at the counter. He had a phone propped against a sugar dispenser and was scrolling through it with his left forefinger and eating apple pie with ice cream at the same time.

Outside, the snow was still falling and accumulating on the roads, now magical twisting white paths in the dark gloom. DeValla started the Cherokee and let the engine idle for a while to warm up. Her phone tinkled inside of her purse, not a call, a message. She looked at it and cursed under her breath. Keeler didn't comment. DeValla glared into the falling snow. "Early shift tomorrow dammit. Sal called in sick, after I covered for him just now. What a prick." She looked at her passenger. "I'm only venting. Sal's problems are bigger than most of ours."

Keeler said, "You were planning on sleeping in tomorrow."

She shook her head. "I haven't slept in for years. I'm supposed to pick up the kids from my ex in the morning and take them to school. Now I'm going to owe him one or get my sister to help, in which case I'll owe her one, which could be worse."

Keeler said nothing. The interior of DeValla's Cherokee was getting warm. He wasn't exactly looking forward to the train station waiting room, but he wasn't not looking forward either. If waiting was an art, Keeler figured he'd be close to a master, or at least an experienced professional. Waiting wasn't any kind of a problem.

DeValla put the truck in gear and started up the hill past the duck pond. Her mood had shifted and Keeler figured she had a complicated situation with the kids and the ex-husband. He didn't disturb her with small talk, just sank back into himself and watched the silhouettes of the trees and the falling snow. Winter was a beautiful wonderland of clean white, softening the imperfections of the landscape, including the noise of mechanized life.

DeValla broke the silence. "Well, it's your lucky night, since I need to be back at the station before five." She glanced over at him. "I don't have a guest room, but I've got a decent sofa bed in the living room if you want it. That's going to beat the waiting room hands down."

"You sure that's all right?"

"Yeah, of course it is." DeValla gave Keeler another look. "You're not a complete stranger anymore. We broke bread, you paid. It wasn't a terrible experience."

"I appreciate that."

She nodded and made a left at the light instead of going straight.

"Gotta warn you though, I'm not going to be much good at hanging out tonight. Just pulled a double shift, and all I can really focus on is getting into bed and crashing out."

"No problem."

There were no other vehicles on the road. The Cherokee was handling the snow, but DeValla was a cautious driver and slowed the vehicle considerably before turning. Ten minutes later she piloted into a narrow driveway running up a steep incline, white with snow accumulation. She said, "Cross your fingers there isn't ice yet."

Keeler didn't need to cross his fingers. He knew that the ice hadn't formed yet. In order to do so the snow would have to first melt some and that hadn't happened. The four-wheel drive transmission dealt with the thick snow and the tires found purchase on the asphalt. A half minute later DeValla hit the button on the remote unit clipped to her visor. A small house came into focus with a garage door rising to envelope and welcome them in from the cold.

DeValla's house was a cozy mess but the sofa bed was large and soft with sagging springs and a decent enough mattress. Keeler set up the bed while DeValla made mint tea. They sat around the kitchen table for an hour or so before DeValla begged off for an early bedtime. She'd been up since five in the morning and she needed to be up early again for the next day.

Keeler lay under the comforter with his head supported by a clean pillow that wasn't too soft or too hard. He heard DeValla making phone calls behind the closed kitchen door. He figured she had a busy working mom's life and was touching base with her support network of family and friends. This was her hometown.

Keeler hadn't really grown up anywhere, since the small family had simply tagged along with his mother, moving every year or two. Mom had been a geophysicist, working in the energy industry. The big money people always wanted to know what was under the ground, and if drilling into it would be a good idea or a waste of time and resources. Keeler's mother would present them with options and advice about that, and then move on to the next project. Consequently, he'd had no hometown, no place where he could call upon a tight network of supportive people.

Keeler stared at the ceiling and thought about the woman in white who'd collapsed earlier at the train station. He was curious about the medical emergency. Not in a gossipy kind of way, curious because he was an experienced combat medic. It isn't uncommon for a person to faint. The woman might have experienced a simple drop in blood pressure. That would be something she'd easily recover from. On the other hand she might have suffered a seizure or a stroke, or some kind of cardiac event, which would be worse and could lead to death or a long-term, life-changing outcome.

CHAPTER SEVEN

K eeler woke at four, well rested and feeling excellent. It was still dark out, but the snow had stopped falling. He heard the sounds of an automatic coffee machine from the kitchen. It was the expensive kind with a timer and an integrated grinder. He dressed and made up the sofa before gravitating to the smell of brewing coffee.

The kitchen had a screen door leading on to a wood deck. Keeler stepped out, letting the thick fresh snow compress under his bare feet. The air was clean and dry after the stifling coziness of DeValla's sofa bed. Beyond the patio railing, the woods were dark, but he could make out an incline at the end of a yard. The gentle sound of running water broke through the quiet. The moon had come out, and Keeler saw the dark imprints of deer tracks in the snow.

DeValla spoke from the doorway. "Got a little river down there. Runs from the reservoir to the Hudson." She wore the Metro-North uniform again, looking fresh with the crazy hair under control. DeValla looked down at Keeler's bare feet. "Practicing for a winter challenge?"

Keeler looked at his feet and back at DeValla. He said nothing. Bagels popped from the toaster in the kitchen.

They ate toasted sesame bagels with scallion cream cheese and drank mugs of freshly brewed coffee. After breakfast, Keeler was sent out to shovel the driveway. He took it as an opportunity to get a little workout. Start at the top, work your way to the bottom. It wasn't the first time he'd shoveled snow, not even the hundredth time, but probably the first time he'd shoveled a driveway by moonlight.

Ten minutes later, Keeler was finishing up the last strip before the road, plowed and salted during the night. He shoveled off the last edge at the bottom and found his eyes drawn to a spot about twenty yards away and across the road.

A rectangle had formed in the snow, about the size of a large car. Keeler walked over and crouched close to the impression. The snow accumulation there was several inches shallower than the surrounding white blanket, meaning the vehicle had been parked for hours but not all night. The irregular shadows on the snowy surface were visible in the hard moonlight. He could even see where the exhaust pipe heat had melted the snow down to asphalt at the back.

The blizzard had stopped while the car had been parked, engine on to keep the heat going, no doubt.

DeValla was warming up the Cherokee in the garage. Keeler didn't mention what he'd found and leaned the shovel against the garage wall without comment. It could have been anything, or nothing. Maybe a driver had simply pulled over to wait out the blizzard, which would be an understandable safety measure.

Keeler slid into the passenger seat. DeValla backed the vehicle out of the garage and performed a tight K-turn in the driveway. She negotiated the steep incline without any ice-related issues. At the bottom she paused to adjust her seat belt, which had been twisted when fastened. Keeler got another look at the shape in the snow.

Down at the train station, DeValla parked the Cherokee near the trestle at the back of the lot. Keeler followed her along the footpath by the fence to the station entrance and up the covered stairwell. The entrance area and stairs had been salted and cleared of snow. It was still very early and dark, and the commuters hadn't yet arrived to tramp ice and snow all over the place.

At the top was a wide vestibule with a ticket counter and information screens and several automated ticket machines. DeValla abruptly stopped moving. She was facing the window looking south over the tracks.

"Shit."

Keeler came around. "What?"

She turned with a finger bit between white teeth. "I forgot something at home. A bag that a customer left on the train I cleared. The lost and found was closing, you know, the blizzard. I was supposed to bring it to work."

"You can't go back and get it?"

Behind the conductor was an opening between the ticket area and the waiting area. Past her, Keeler could see a man sitting, nursing a cup of coffee. It was the man with the familiar face from the diner the night before. The one whom she had recognized. Keeler made brief eye contact and the man turned away.

DeValla shook her head at Keeler's question. "No time. My shift starts in a couple of minutes. I'll be lucky to grab a cup of coffee."

"I can swing by your house and pick it up for you, make the train after. I'm not in a rush."

"Next fast train's at 5:32. Then there's a slow train just before six. You'd do that?"

"Sure."

She examined him for a moment, maybe looking for some other reason he was offering to go out of his way for her. DeValla dug out her keys and held them out, like rosary beads. "That's above and beyond, Keeler. I appreciate that. It's a black laptop bag. I think it's on the little table just inside from the garage door." She pointed south, out the window. "There's a lost and found office over the tracks by the second passenger bridge. One story brick building. You can also leave him my car keys. I'll pick them up after work."

Keeler took the keys. "All right."

"Think you can remember where my house is?"

"I'll find it."

"You sure?"

"One hundred percent. Don't worry about it and don't be late."

"Okay, thank you." DeValla looked at her phone. "I have to go."

Keeler watched her walk through the waiting area and out the other side. Presumably there was an office over there. The guy from the diner with the familiar face was no longer sitting where he had been. Keeler started back for the Cherokee.

CHAPTER EIGHT

The Cherokee rolled over the salted roads, the town still dark, streetlamps making pools of light on the snow. It's engine was still warm, and the radio turned out boomer music at the proper emotional level for five in the morning. Keeler felt like he was inhabiting someone else's life, in someone else's town. Like he was an eternal stranger and the world was always going to be new and fresh and exciting.

Keeler recalled the route to DeValla's house. He felt for a second like he was going home to a new life. Take a right out of the train station under the highway. Left at the light onto Riverside. Keeler was a natural at navigation and always had been. He'd been first in his training group coming through the Pararescue and Recovery course up in the mountainous area east of Kirtland AFB, New Mexico. Once he got a sniff of how the land lay it all just felt familiar.

Keeler parked across the street from DeValla's house. He hiked up the freshly cleared asphalt rise, looking for spots that he'd missed and kicking the most egregious into the edge with his boot. DeValla's key ring was heavy with jangling metal. The car key, plus the house key, plus all kinds of other keys, plus a large fuzzy thing in rainbow colors.

The little table by the garage door had no laptop bag.

Keeler didn't have to search far, the laptop bag was on a chair, tucked under the kitchen table. DeValla must have forgotten the bag after breakfast. The sky was now turning colors, the sun not yet up but getting close, over the horizon. The trees were stripped of leaves, making dark silhouettes spidering the growing backlight. Keeler opened the sliding door to the deck and went to the railing, placing his hands on the snow covered wood, feeling the frozen surface and inhaling cold and fresh air.

The yard was flat and open for about twenty yards and then abruptly descended toward the river below. Keeler liked the crystalline sound of water running under and around ice. The deer tracks were preserved in last night's snow, shallow impressions just beginning to take light. Keeler gazed directly down from the deck to another set of tracks, these ones human and sunk deeper, coming from around the side of the house.

Keeler came back through to the front and locked the house. The tracks came through a stand of trees bordering the property. His own boot was more or less the same size as the intruder's, so he assumed it was a man. The approach had been made halfway back to the rear, when the intruder had stepped out of cover to a basement window. There he had stopped for a while, evidenced by the mess his boots had made in the snow. After that he had come around the back, but had not mounted the stairs to the deck.

Keeler followed the man's path through the area of growth and back to the road, precisely across the street from where the car had been parked. He walked over to look once more at the vehicle's mark. Near where the driver's window would have been was a small pile of cigarette butts. Keeler counted a dozen of them, burned right down to the yellowed filter. He examined one, white with a double gold band, no brand name.

He leaned against the Cherokee. The vehicle's hood was warm and smelled like fuel and oil and transmission fluid. He had smoked cigarettes at one time, when he had first joined the military and before that when he was just a kid trying to get the hell away from home. His mother was a high achiever with a PhD. Keeler had rebelled, going in the other direction.

His sister had been the academic one, following in her mother's footsteps, though pursuing not hard science, but social science, if that was actually a science. Eventually Keeler had found a world in which showing initiative and thinking counter-intuitively actually paid off. He'd been a natural in the tactical arts, and a high pain threshold hadn't hurt.

He felt the buzz now, leaned up against the Cherokee, looking at the place where a vehicle had parked overnight. Its occupant had crept around DeValla's house. Maybe it was just her ex-husband, but she'd said the ex was with the kids, so why would he be out there stalking her house?

Could be another local man stalking her. She was damned good-looking, and it wouldn't be a surprise if her beauty attracted creeps.

From behind the Cherokee came the growl of a large motor, turning onto DeValla's street from the corner. Keeler pivoted and watched the dark shape of a pickup truck approach behind two bright headlights. The tires crunched over the salted road, and the engine had a throaty sound to it.

The driver hadn't noticed Keeler. He was hunched down and gazing through the passenger side window at DeValla's house. Prowling and peeping. Keeler watched as the driver's head swiveled to the front and did a double take, seeing Keeler in his peripheral vision. He stomped on the brake. He was in his forties with a rough goatee beard and a baseball cap pushed down over his eyes.

The man's eyes flicked first to the Cherokee, then to Keeler and travelled down to the laptop bag hanging from his shoulder. He looked up at Keeler's face again. "Who the hell are you?"

Keeler said nothing.

The driver revealed a mouth full of bad teeth. "I just came up from the train station. Lost and found guy said that Mini DeValla's got this laptop bag and isn't on shift today." He pointed at the laptop bag hanging from Keeler's shoulder. "That wouldn't be the bag in question would it, brother?"

DeValla was on shift, but maybe she hadn't been scheduled. She'd received the message last night after dinner.

Keeler felt the weight of the bag, tugging at his shoulder. "This is your bag?"

"Friend of mine's. Left it on the train last night. I'll save you the hassle and take it off of you." He looked hopefully at Keeler.

At first, Keeler was inclined to hand the bag to the man. Why not? The story was plausible enough. Something about the guy though turned him off. Keeler looked at the man and saw eagerness and the impatience of someone who'd much rather snatch than ask. That was it, Keeler thought, the guy didn't like asking.

The man said, "What do you think, brother, you want to give that to me? My buddy needs to do some computer type of shit with that, you know what I mean? Said he's going to get in trouble if he doesn't log in or whatever."

Keeler looked at the sky. He determined it to be close to six in the morning. A little early for a friendly visit. Improbable verging on highly unlikely.

He looked at the guy. "You're in a rush for an early bird."

"I got to go to work, and I'm doing my friend a favor. Believe you me, I'd rather be tucked into those flannel sheets."

Keeler opened the door to the Cherokee and tossed the laptop bag into the passenger seat. "I'm going down to the lost and found. You can pick it up from there if you like, once it gets registered and everything."

The driver's eyes turned dull and he adjusted the ball cap on his head. Loose hairs poked out from under the bill. "Ah, man, why'd you want to do it like that, it could have been so simple."

Keeler nodded. "That's true, but sometimes things have to go the hard way."

He climbed in and fired up the Cherokee and let the engine run, waiting for the pickup truck to get out of the street. The truck stayed put for a minute, before the driver spat out the open window and closed it. The big engine growled and the truck moved off. Keeler looked again at the spot where a vehicle had waited during the blizzard. The marks in the snow were hard to make out, but the shape looked a little narrower and longer than the pickup truck.

A few minutes later, Keeler was cruising along a two-way boulevard split by a wide snowy strip. In the rearview mirror he saw the pickup truck turning off a side street and falling into place behind him. Keeler watched it for a second and wondered what the hell was going on.

The truck followed him all the way to the train station. Rush hour was just beginning, and a traffic cop was stationed up on the road. It was early, the sun barely coming up over the hills and woods to the east. The freshly plowed parking lot glowed with the faint light of dawn.

Keeler glanced at the laptop bag next to him. The guy in the truck had been really hot and heavy for whatever was inside.

CHAPTER NINE

K eeler made an executive decision.

He pulled open the Velcro flap from the laptop bag beside him and slid the computer out of the bag and onto his lap. The three children's books were in the backseat, a bit of a stretch, but they'd do. The books went in the laptop bag. Keeler lifted the bag from the seat. The weight substitution was acceptable.

He parked the Cherokee in DeValla's spot, thinking that the train conductor would want the vehicle where she usually kept it. The pickup truck pulled close behind him and then swung out and around next to the municipal depot. Before, Keeler hadn't been able to tell what color it was exactly. Now, in the growing light, he reckoned the truck was steel blue, or blue steel, whatever the terminology was. It was a Ford, but a midsize version.

Keeler pushed the laptop into his backpack where it would ride snug against his spine. With the backpack slung over one shoulder and the laptop bag carried by its handle, he left the Cherokee and locked it with DeValla's key fob. The footpath by the cyclone fence had been cleared but still bore the residue of snow with patches of it remaining where the asphalt was uneven. The driver came out of the truck when Keeler approached. Keeler watched him, bemused and curious, but without expectation. What was going to happen would take place regardless of expectation. The less specific a person's expectations, the less likely they'll be surprised or disappointed by what ends up happening.

The driver leaned against the side of the truck and scowled. Keeler smiled at him pleasantly.

The man spoke around a mouth full of chewing gum. "Not going to make this easier for me, huh?"

Keeler came close, so that he was standing in the man's personal space. "If tough shit happens to you often, you may want to consider a change in lifestyle, or maybe therapy."

The driver's face remained in its scowl. "Like what exactly, digging into my subconscious?"

Keeler examined him with his curious eyes. "I like mine to stay where it is—underneath, hidden. That's why they call it sub, like the subway."

Keeler walked to the sidewalk and took a lingering glance back. The pickup truck had a New Jersey license plate, and Keeler memorized it as a matter of course. He walked past the municipal depot building, and soon he was walking up the stairs to the waiting area.

The woman at the ticket desk pointed the way to the lost and found: platform three all the way to the end and down a set of steel stairs to a low brick building. The office was dark with a single dirty window facing north. There was a waiting area featuring three blue plastic bucket chairs and a tourist poster of Sicily from the 1960s. A scarred wooden counter divided the space in half, and behind that was a steel cage. Behind that were cubby holes where lost items waited to be found.

The guy at the counter was doing a newspaper crossword

puzzle, gnawing on a pencil. He looked up and Keeler couldn't help but notice how the single lamp hanging from the ceiling so perfectly illuminated the man's cranium, bare but for a half dozen wispy strands that had once been brown, but now had no color to speak of. Keeler set the laptop bag on the counter.

"Dropping this off for Miss DeValla, the train conductor."

The man spoke like a pedant. "And did she ask you to bring it here?"

"She did, along with these." Keeler let the heavy bunch of keys fall to the wood surface. "Said she'd pick them up from you after her shift."

"I didn't know she was working today." The man put his hand over the keys and slid the bunch toward him. "I'll take these." He pointed at the laptop bag. "The customer came for that last night, middle of the blizzard. I'd already closed up but he was an insistent little guy and found me in the staff room. I told him that the conductor of the train had brought it home, because of the blizzard situation. Told him she'd bring it in the morning. Told him it was because of the snow."

Keeler said, "Did you recognize the customer?"

The man looked up with an annoyed expression. "A passenger, from the train. The customer who this belongs to."

"But you gave him her name and address."

The man looked up quickly. "No, of course I didn't." He was frowning at the crossword puzzle in front of him, tapping his pencil. "Prey-prehending claw." He looked up at Keeler, hopeful.

"How many letters?"

"Five."

Keeler thought for a moment. The man in the pickup truck hadn't been the customer. He'd been a local man who knew DeValla. Which meant that the customer had told the man in the pickup truck that DeValla had the bag, then the man in the pickup truck had inquired about which specific conductor had taken the bag home. Quite a lot of investigating for an overnight lost bag situation.

Keeler said, "Talon."

The man nodded. "Oh, yes, thank you." He filled in the word with the pencil and slid his newspaper to the side. He raised his hand, palm down. "The guy who came for that computer bag. Kind of blond, yay high."

The palm was raised, but not high. It might have been five and a half feet off the ground.

Keeler said, "Short guy."

"That's right. About my height." The man rose, stoop shouldered. "I used to be five seven, now I'm like five six, maybe. I don't know. The guy was like me, but younger. Maybe forty."

"How do they prove the items are theirs?"

"They aren't required to. Anyway, the customer showed up straight off the train. He'd gotten confused because of some brouhaha last night on the platform. Said he accidentally left his bag on the rack coming off the northbound fast train. Why, I shouldn't believe him?"

Keeler shrugged. "That's your call."

The man watched him, gauging Keeler's reaction, ready to be demonstrative if insulted, but not finding any reason. He turned to the laptop bag and put a hand over it. "I've got this now. I'll take care of Mini's keys, too, so you don't need to worry about it."

"What time do you figure she'll be done with work?"

"I guess she's on the first shift, ends at two."

Keeler nodded. "Appreciate it, have a good day."

"You too, fella."

CHAPTER TEN

K eeler returned along the platform and climbed the stairs to the waiting room. He went to the wide set of windows looking out over the parking lot near the ticket counter. The pickup truck was gone. The driver had been pretty anxious to get that bag. No doubt he'd be picking it up from the lost and found soon. Probably waiting until Keeler was out of the way.

He could feel the hard rectangular contours of the laptop riding flat against his back. It would be a good idea tactically to take the laptop out of circulation for a while, see how everything settled, and then take it from there. DeValla would be done at two, he'd be waiting for her at the station, and they could talk about it. She needed to know about the guy outside of her house the night before.

Chances were there wasn't an issue, and the guy with the pickup truck was just an asshole. But that was only one possibility and better safe than sorry. If the customer got his laptop a couple hours later it wouldn't be tragic, and if it was tragic it was just too bad. Shouldn't have left it on the train in the first place.

It occurred to Keeler that he had another reason for sticking around and giving a shit, a reason named Mini DeValla. He quickly tucked that thought out of the way.

Keeler went to the ticket desk and asked about luggage storage. The answer was simple, no luggage storage at the Kitchewan Landing train station. Keeler wanted to know if there was a solution to be found, maybe outside of the station, maybe nearby. The young guy behind the counter looked at him blankly, unable to imagine a possibility beyond the current context, uninterested in creative solutions, a static thinker. A woman came from the back with a puffy pale face and light eyes behind thick glasses. She had the answer, however, and delivered it in a monotone, UPS Store down by ShopRite opens at eight. Maybe they'd be able to help.

Which was helpful and a decent enough idea except it wasn't yet eight.

The information screen reported that the time was six a.m. and change. Slightly less than eight hours to go before DeValla's shift finished. Keeler drifted to the coffee kiosk, attracted by the scent of a fresh brew. The man from the diner with the familiar face was up front, ordering a cup of coffee and some variation of cake with a crumbly top that looked pretty good. Keeler recognized him from behind, thanks to the Sears coat.

Why hadn't he left on the first train to the city?

He let the man finish the order and walk away, two fists occupied with coffee and cake. When Keeler approached the kiosk the same woman from the night before looked at him expectantly.

"Medium coffee black and a slice of whatever that cake is."

"The coffee cake?" She pointed at a tray of square slices.

"That's right."

The woman used a spatula to remove and pack the coffee cake into a paper bag. The bag got folded closed and a napkin was wrapped around it. She doubled up on the paper cups and apologized. "Ran out of coffee cup sleeves."

Keeler got his hands around both items and turned away. Rush hour had begun and the waiting area was filling with commuters jostling for a spot on the coffee line. He focused on the objects in his hands, concentrating on the task of not bumping into anyone. Once clear of the crowd around the kiosk, Keeler found himself in direct eye contact with the man from the diner. The guy had seen him first. For the second time, Keeler felt a strong intuition about the man. The face was both regular and familiar, but the connection was not being made.

The man broke eye contact and turned to the stairs leading to platform one. The information screen said that the southbound local train for the city was due in a minute.

Keeler wasn't a great believer in coincidence. The woman in white on the platform the night before. The guy at the diner who'd denied being on the train. The familiar face. All that stuff about the laptop that morning.

He had time to kill. Why not follow the man and see where he goes? There was no downside. Worst case the man goes somewhere boring. Best case he goes to Chinatown. Keeler hadn't been to New York City for about a decade. Maybe he'd get to eat lunch in Chinatown, make it back in time to catch DeValla when she got off work, tell her about the laptop and the pickup truck driver and the vehicle parked at her house last night.

He waited for the man to go down the stairs to the platform before he made a move. The wind was biting out there by the river, a patchwork of ice stretching out far into the distant cliffs on the other side. The train pulled in like a mechanical worm blocking the river view.

CHAPTER ELEVEN

The landscape went by to the local train's chugging rhythm, what DeValla had called the slow train. Local meant that the train stopped at river towns between Kitchewan Landing and the city. Places like Ossining, Tarrytown, Irvington, and Dobbs Ferry.

The view was bleak and monochrome but moving forward relentlessly like a movie worth watching. The conductor came by for the tickets and Keeler had to pay extra because he hadn't paid in advance, par for the course, the kind of thing that happened to him all the time. If there was going to be a life tax for not planning in advance, Keeler figured it was worth it.

He was in the same car as the man with the familiar face, who sat up in the front section past the doors. The coffee cake was satisfying, moist and buttery and sugary and spiced with cinnamon. Keeler wondered if it could be considered regional cuisine, maybe specific to New York City and its suburbs. After Yonkers, the conductor announced the next stop, Ludlow. The man with the familiar face came out of his seat and made his way to the exit.

Keeler watched his reflection in the window. Why here,

why now, why Ludlow? He'd expected Grand Central Station and the high domed ceiling with the astrological signs and the constellations. Ludlow looked denuded of life, a windswept landscape of warehouses and industrial buildings, on either side of the tracks.

None of that mattered. The pressing issue wasn't so much the diminishing likelihood of lunch in Chinatown; it was the question of how to get off the train without the guy noticing him.

The doors separating Keeler's car from the one behind him banged open and a large-framed woman came through, squeezing past his seat. Keeler took his opportunity and spun out behind her, using her body as a screen. He got through into the next car and kept going until he had two lengths separating himself from the mark.

In the exit vestibule he removed his coat and pushed it into the backpack. He put on his hat, hoping that with the coat off, the adjustment would be enough. The laptop was there, packed into the bag, a hard black plastic rectangle. The doors opened and Keeler stepped onto the platform. He'd have to lead the guy rather than follow. He could switch up and follow once they were out of the station.

Ludlow wasn't much of a station. There was no waiting area, no bathrooms, no coffee kiosk, no ticket desk, and no Metro-North personnel. Only the platform and a steel-framed staircase to a road over the tracks. Maybe there had been a lonely ticket office once, but they'd installed self-service ticket machines on the bridge, with a roof to cover them.

Off the bridge was a wholesale baking supply business sunk back from the road. It was suitable for Keeler's needs. The door opened and an electronic bell went *brrrring*. The store was overheated, hot dry air pushing in from ducts in the ceiling. A humidifier steamed in front of the checkout counter, trying to compensate. The place smelled like kitty litter. Keeler stood by the glass door looking out. A few people coming off the train walked by. The man from the diner wasn't among them.

A woman's voice called from the back of the store, hassled and busy. "Just one second."

Keeler kept his eyes out the glass door and called back. "Take your time."

The man with the familiar face walked past, eyes fixed to the phone in his hand. Keeler almost had him then, the identity and memory of the man tangible, yet not coming through. Like a sneeze that wouldn't come.

He counted to thirty and left the baking supply store. The guy was a block away on the other side of the street. A couple blocks later, the neighborhood changed and became residential with stores and apartment buildings. It started to look more like New York City, even though it wasn't. From the signage and city buses, Keeler knew that he was in Yonkers, bordering the North Bronx.

The man with the familiar face walked straight east for ten minutes and then stopped cold in front of a bookstore, as if he'd seen a really interesting new release in the display case. Keeler kept going to the next corner and turned south. There was a pretzel kiosk and he went right in and asked for a fresh one.

The man stopping at the bookstore window was playing it straight out of the counter surveillance playbook. Alarm bells rang in Keeler's mind. The window reflection providing an opportunity to study surrounding bodies. A trained operator could pick out and memorize qualities of the people around him, what they were wearing, height and age, and ethnicity and gender. Then he would stop at another spot, what they called a checkpoint, and see if the same people were following, maybe get eye contact.

The question on Keeler's mind was whether the bookstore

was the first checkpoint, or he'd already been identified. Because he'd be easy to spot, since the man had seen him last night at the diner. One thing that Keeler hadn't anticipated was the possibility that the man with the familiar face would be some kind of a professional, which made everything all the more interesting.

The first bite of the pretzel was good, hot and salty with a smoky mineral taste from the crust. The man with the familiar face crossed the street, continuing his journey. Keeler didn't look directly at him, but saw him in his peripheral vision. Something about the way the guy moved triggered a tingling feeling up his spine.

The man running the pretzel kiosk was looking at him strangely.

Keeler spoke around a mouthful. "What?"

"Nothing. Only, I was thinking you look like that guy in the movies. Take a gun and shoot all the bad people. The old movies, what's-his-name."

"I don't know what his name is." Keeler stayed behind the kiosk, waiting for the man with the familiar face to get halfway down the block before following again.

The kiosk man was still looking at him with a thousand-yard stare. "The guy looks like he could kill, but the ladies like that. Maybe they like you too."

He ignored the pretzel guy, turning away with just a slight nod to show that he'd heard the man. He took a packet of mustard from the dispenser and tore it open with his teeth. He half watched the man moving away down the block and spread mustard on the remainder of his pretzel.

The feeling was back, of knowing the guy's gait. Keeler shelved it for later and got on with the project of following him. He was reminded that tailing someone is a job for at least three operators, not one guy alone. He kept back, considering abandoning the pursuit as he finished the pretzel. The bookstore checkpoint had been obvious; there might have been less obvious points.

During his service, Keeler had been one of the pararescue operators selected for clandestine training. As a PJ, his job was extraction and rescue on the battlefield. These days, the battlefield was a blurry designation. He'd spent a high percentage of his last couple of years in military service working undercover. Keeler knew there was a good reason why they'd taught him not to conduct surveillance alone, but he had already committed.

Furthermore, he wasn't in the military anymore, not subject to discipline and hierarchy. Now nobody was going to tell him what he could or could not do.

CHAPTER TWELVE

A half hour later they were in a neighborhood called Riverdale. Banners on a couple of light posts announced it. Riverdale was fancier than Ludlow, that was for sure. The man walked west to the river and entered a busy public park, a stark wintry esplanade with open spaces and nowhere to hide.

The man with the familiar face moved south. Keeler bought coffee from another kiosk, fitting in with the early morning walkers. He watched the man up ahead, slowing to look at his phone, leading Keeler to where the park ended in a dramatic overlook. Beyond the waist-high stone wall, the land sloped down to where the water split off from the Hudson into a creek. A rail bridge spanned the gap, which Keeler figured separated Manhattan island from the continental mass.

The early light painted the bridge a bright orange. Keeler read the plaque on the wall, Spuyten Duyvil Creek, leading to the Harlem river.

Twenty yards east, two joggers huddled together holding coffee cups. Both of them had ears stuffed with hardware, which was normal for people out jogging, but not normal for joggers out talking. Usually, people take the ear buds out before having a conversation. Keeler couldn't help but smile to himself. He was enjoying this.

He crushed the cardboard cup in his fist and looked for a garbage can to throw it in. He swiveled his head in a semicircle and found the can, but also found the man with the familiar face, looking right at him, eye contact and everything. Keeler felt the hairs on the back of his neck stand and the thrilling rush of adrenaline. The game was up. The two joggers were watching, no longer casual. It was pure clarity, like a standoff.

He bounced the crushed cup in his hand and went up to the garbage can. The man with the familiar face stood his ground. Keeler tossed the cup into the can from ten feet away. He said, "Three points."

The man said nothing, just stared, boring his eyes into Keeler's. The two joggers kept their position, and Keeler realized it was up to him to make a move. Either he took it further, or he turned away. At the moment he had nowhere to take it. This had been a fishing expedition, not an actual mission.

So he turned away, coming back to the stone wall overlooking the Spuyten Duyvil rail bridge.

Keeler looked out over the river for a while, knowing that the joggers and the man would be gone by the time he turned around. They'd caught him following and had wanted to warn him off. If they'd had more wicked intentions they wouldn't have been so obvious. Now, he was going to have to run a security route of his own just to be sure he wasn't being tailed. So much for lunch in Chinatown.

Keeler turned around and leaned against the stone wall to face the park, his back to the view. Commuters hustled across the esplanade on their way to work or school or whatever civilians did with their days. He didn't know because he hadn't even begun to think about himself as a civilian yet, despite having been discharged from the military a couple years ago. He thought about the train conductor instead, Mini DeValla. Weird how the little things can turn out to be important. In the diner she'd recognized the man. At the time, it hadn't meant anything, but now this.

Keeler had made the connection in that last moment, making eye contact with the man. He'd met the guy before, a decade back at least. Met him three or four times, in fact. He also understood why the face had been tough to recall. Two reasons, really. The man must have had some work done to his face—the nose had been altered and maybe the chin and cheek-bones. Possibly they'd tried to make a face that would withstand facial recognition technologies. The other thing was, the man must have been wearing contact lenses to disguise his eye color, because the person Keeler had known way back when didn't have two brown eyes, he had one brown and one blue, what they call heterochromia.

The man's name was Vince Farrell.

CHAPTER THIRTEEN

K eeler had run into Farrell for the first time in a suburb of Baghdad, in a schoolyard to be specific. Not exactly an active schoolyard, but recognizable anyway. The yard had come into view at the top of a sewage runoff ditch, an incline running alongside a fence alive in the heat with fluttering plastic bags and junk picked up by the wind and stuck there.

It was a chore to walk even a hundred yards in close to a hundred and twenty Fahrenheit. Keeler and his team humped fifty pounds of gear each and had already walked about a half mile. There was a concern about sniper fire hitting the helicopters. They'd need to take out the shooter if they didn't want to walk back.

Keeler crested the hill first, climbing out of the runoff ditch onto the flat schoolyard. He saw a line of Iraqi men kneeling in the sun and a small cluster of Americans gathered in the shade. He signaled to his men and they all came up out of the ditch.

The five Iraqis knelt by the wall with filthy bags over their heads, clothed in a collection of dusty sweatpants and tracksuit tops with sweat and blood stains. On their feet were cheap sneakers without socks, or else plastic shower slippers.

The school was on a rise, no point in town overlooked the yard, which is why Keeler's team was staging there. They loped in single file, keeping to the shade and cover of a second building off to the side of the main school. One of the captured insurgents was shaking uncontrollably and Keeler could hear his teeth rattling. He wore a yellow striped sweater, improbable in the insane heat. A growing patch of dark wetness grew on the front of the man's sweatpants and evaporated immediately.

Off in the shade stood five private military contractors in nonregulation combat gear, black tactical webbing and baseball hats and gym-bred biceps thick with ink. The insurgents were their prisoners, and it was coincidental that this business intersected with Keeler's. For the most part, PMCs were combat veterans who had decided to come back for money. These specific PMCs were Americans on contract with the Vincelli Corporation, muscle for deniable operations. Keeler knew this as it had been part of the operational briefing.

He didn't know Vince Farrell yet, but the different-colored eyes made him stand out from his buddies, that and his commanding presence: the man was powerfully built in a simian fashion, all taut muscle and rangy limbs, like a natural predator. He was clearly in charge. He didn't come forward, but waited for Keeler and his team to do the work and get there. It was better standing in the shade. What Keeler remembered was not simply the weird color of the man's eyes, but the calm craziness that was almost instantly recognizable. He'd seen it once in a while in men who enjoyed killing for the sake of killing.

Farrell turned his weird eyes on Keeler as he approached. He jerked his thumb at the school building. "Other side of this shit. Go get 'em, champ."

Keeler said nothing and only observed that the contractors didn't seem interested in helping an American patrol in jeopardy. Keeler spat into the dust and ignored Farrell. There was actual business to attend to.

Down the hill on the other side of the school was an army patrol trapped on the road by an IED sandwich. Keeler had seen footage from the reconnaissance drone. One Bradley destroyed and upside-down, the other immobilized with both tracks busted. Currently there was a standoff, the insurgents in and among the ruined buildings, with at least one sniper taking out whatever moved.

Intermittent small-arms fire rattled, and smoke from the Bradley drifted over the low school building, smelling like diesel and human hair. The high-velocity punch of .50 caliber sniper fire banged out sporadically. The shooter was doing the lion's share of keeping the guys pinned down. At least one man was badly wounded and would most likely bleed out before they could suppress the fire.

Keeler was assigned to the Air Force's Expeditionary Rescue Squadron in Iraq. It was up to himself and the four other men to figure out how to extract the patrol. Two hours later Keeler stood over the Iraqi sniper tucked deep into what had once been a hotel room. The enemy combatant had been hit by a single round that had gone through the wall and nicked his femoral artery. Keeler watched the man's life leak freely into the dust until he was dead.

The team ended up evacuating a dozen Americans including two who had lost limbs and three who'd lost their lives. The schoolyard was the extraction point for the helicopter dust off. The Pave Hawk lifted away. Keeler sat on the edge of the opening, looking down at the yellow schoolyard. The drainage ditch came into view below him and he saw the bodies. The sacks had been removed from the captured men's heads, but he recognized the yellow striped sweater. Keeler's gut dropped as the helicopter lurched upward. He had seen that each of the captured men had been shot once in the back of the neck and a second time in the head. They'd all had the same wound patterns.

That was the first time he'd seen Vince Farrell.

CHAPTER FOURTEEN

Now Farrell was in New York.

The operational assumption had to be that a thread connected recent events. Woman in white, Farrell with the new eyes and altered face, the prowler outside of DeValla's house, and the laptop. Farrell was a mercenary, a big word that covered a lot of different activities. Basically, a human weapon for hire.

Hiring a guy like Farrell is a drastic measure. You'd need money, first of all. Which would mean that there were high stakes and a good reason. In Keeler's experience the reasons people hired mercenaries fell into two categories: protection and elimination. If the woman in white had been the target of an elimination, maybe Farrell's job was over, or maybe not.

The other question was: Had Farrell recognized him?

Now that the memories were filtering back to him, Keeler didn't see how Farrell could have looked at him like that and not recognized him. They'd had significant interactions after the run-in at the schoolyard.

Keeler remembered Farrell at the diner, looking at DeValla's Metro-North uniform and name tag. *Have a big dinner Miss DeValla*, is what Farrell had said. Which meant that Farrell had memorized the name and filed it away. It would be no bother at all to connect that name with an address, given that she was a Metro-North conductor.

DeValla had seen Farrell on the train platform just before the woman in white had gone down. Taken to its logical conclusion, this meant that there was a good chance DeValla was in serious danger and didn't know it.

Regardless, Keeler needed to put the questions behind him and get himself clean. It took almost three hours to run a security route and be certain that nobody was following him.

By then it was brunch time and he was deep in Brooklyn at a Russian restaurant near the boardwalk. Three kinds of pancakes were involved in the breakfast menu and Keeler had them all put in front of him. Cottage cheese and cherries competed for his attention with smoked salmon and chives and scrambled eggs with red caviar and sour cream. The restaurant was a welcome respite from the freezing streets. The blinis were warm and comforting, and the repetitive process of eating helped him think.

Keeler thought about the order of things. He'd need to get in touch with someone from the old days and run some queries about Farrell. But getting up to Kitchewan Landing and securing DeValla was the current priority. Which meant Keeler had things to do and places to go. In between, Keeler was going to need to do some shopping.

It was Keeler's first time in Brooklyn, and he liked what he was seeing. The place was a sprawling urban disaster zone. A vast spill of residential neighborhoods, industrial areas, and pockets of more organized municipalities, like the downtown part where the subway had first spit him onto the Brooklyn streets.

He had no clear image of what he was facing, but the little he did know allowed him to draw a few initial conclusions. The most important were about security and safety. Hope for the best, prepare for the worst.

Best case, he'd get back to the suburbs and find DeValla having dinner with her kids. Worst case they'd all be dead.

First up were clothes, the lumberjack coat was too distinctive. At the army surplus store, he found an old heavy-duty winter Carhartt jacket that looked like it could manage anything the New York winter might throw at him. Keeler left the lumberjack coat on a hook in the changing room, like an offering. His friend in Canada had given it to him for free, and he was happy to give back.

He already had jeans and boots and a hat and gloves and a backpack. Keeler picked up a fresh roll of duct tape and a survival knife with a can opener attachment at the hilt and waterproof matches packed into the grip. If, in the end, there was nothing to stab or cut, he could always open up a can of ravioli, or beans and have lunch around a campfire.

At the register, old milk crates were filled with impulse purchase items like flashlights and key rings and baseball hats. The guy at the counter was large with pronounced biceps and an overly developed chest. He'd have trouble running and slipping into tight spaces; even working a cash register might be a challenge.

"You have any decent impact weapons?" Keeler asked.

"Like what exactly?"

"Not too long and not too heavy, but well balanced and maybe with some lead in there or a spring to make it snap."

The big man reached under the counter and brought out a scarred hardwood billy club the length of Keeler's forearm. "Illegal in New York state, double bad in the city. Drop me a twenty and you can pick this up off the counter like you just found it there. Lead tip so be careful you don't go too hard with it."

Keeler dropped the twenty, liking this part of the city. Off the tourist beat, the deep part of Brooklyn where the heart was located. He thought, *But what if I want to go hard with it and saw Vince Farrell's face?* And realized that he was up for this, big-time.

Another thing he noticed about Brooklyn: in terms of fashion, there were no rules. People were walking around wearing literally anything. Halloween in Brooklyn could either be the most frightening experience of a person's life, or a hell of a lot of fun, depending on disposition.

Across the street from the army surplus was a Best Buy, a renovated storefront with the yellow letters. The man inside sold him a prepaid smartphone for thirty bucks. Keeler put another twenty onto the SIM card, and he was good to go. Outside the Best Buy, Keeler backed against the wall and looked around.

The howling wind was whipping freezing air and icy particles down the wide avenue. Civilians staggered, hunched against it in their coats and hats. The heavy duty canvas jacket was doing a great job of allowing Keeler to ignore all of that. He was snug as a bug and feeling just fine. What he needed now was a ride, preferably unconnected to him by any kind of a paper trail.

CHAPTER FIFTEEN

After a couple hours of reconnaissance, Keeler felt qualified to write a tactical manual for illicit drug operations in Brooklyn. The same patterns were repeated in the areas that he'd previously scouted. Drug dealing wasn't casual here, it was an organized business designed to look casual to the casual observer. To Keeler's eyes it was a lucrative and therefore competitive activity, given the paranoid security measures that he was seeing.

Corners were held by military-aged males between sixteen and twenty-five years of age. He hadn't seen any weapons, but didn't doubt that they were armed. These soldiers served dual roles as muscle to hold the territory and the initial contact with the customer. Once contact was made, the soldier on the corner would make a hand signal, which served to notify a colleague that the sale was on.

The soldiers didn't touch either cash or drugs. The next level of operations was conducted in and around the surrounding apartment buildings. A second layer of workers handled the actual transaction. Cash and the drugs were never handled by the same person. Both were tucked back in abandoned or requisitioned apartments.

Every half an hour, a vehicle rolled up and pulled to the curb with its engine running. In each case a worker egressed from the stash house and a transaction took place through the passenger side window of the vehicle. After watching the third one Keeler knew they were cash pickups, the vehicles on constant rotation, touring the organization's territory and collecting accumulated earnings.

Which made tactical sense, if the police came in for arrests, or a rival gang attacked, only a half hour's worth of operations would be impacted.

Keeler sat on a stoop in the middle of a block of abandoned row houses. It wasn't the best part of the city, but nobody was messing with the big guy who wasn't afraid to make eye contact. He was watching a Toyota sedan make the money drop. The Toyota rolled off the corner only to pull in again farther up the street. Keeler watched it for a while, wondering why they'd pulled over and then realized that it was lunchtime and the driver and passenger might be taking a break.

Which made this the opportunity that he'd been waiting for. Keeler got off the stoop and began to stroll up the street to the corner. Even though his breath made a thick cloud of vapor in the freezing air, he was warm and cozy and feeling just right.

The car itself was low-key, but the tinted windows and loud music weren't. Keeler approached and the music just got louder. He could respect the dexterous verbalizing of some rappers, but he wasn't a fan of electronic beats. He hadn't come to this view all by himself. Keeler's musical education had been just one result of a month-long assignment in Estonia, stuck in a safe house providing operational services to a fifty-year-old CIA case officer and jazz fanatic with a PhD in anthropology. That's how Keeler knew that drum beats are culturally modeled after the vital thumping of a human heart, which in the CIA man's view was best kept organic and animal. Heartbeats can be regular, he insisted, but they aren't fixed. If they were, life would be boring, the same being true for music.

In the end, Keeler had agreed with the man.

A hand emerged from the passenger side window, well-formed and elegant in its bone structure, a masculine wrist adorned by a gold watch, fingers holding an empty soda bottle subsequently dropped into the gutter. That was followed by two empty potato chip bags and a wadded-up foil wrapper. Keeler disapproved, his eyes narrowing some. He considered littering more than just sloppy, it was unsocial and generally disrespectful of public space. Besides the bad musical choices, littering helped provide the moral justification for what he was about to do.

The vehicle's windows were tinted so that it wasn't possible to see inside. The street was deserted, which Keeler found curious. Maybe people just stay inside when the known drug dealers are around. It wouldn't be stupid to feel intimidated by young men with a casual approach to violence. If that was so, then it would also be true that the locals were aware of the vehicle's presence and significance. It followed that at least some of the locals were standing at their windows peeking out through cracks in closed curtains.

Which meant that Keeler's tactical plan should be to shift any action away from prying eyes. Now he was at the other side of the corner and approaching fast. A candy bar wrapper was dropped from the passenger window and fluttered to the curb. So far, there hadn't been any sign of a back-seat passenger. The Toyota was silver, unremarkable and perfectly suited to his needs.

When he was two cars' lengths away, Keeler let the backpack slip off to the ground and knelt between two cars. He removed the billy club and held it by his leg as he walked the distance to the Toyota. He saw nothing in the side mirror and visualized the driver, biting into a Big Mac or a chicken leg.

Keeler pulled the handle on the rear door and it opened smoothly. He slipped into the empty backseat and pulled the door closed behind him. The passenger turned with an aggravated expression and began to verbalize something. He got about two syllables into an angry outburst before the lead tipped club clipped him on the temple. Keeler leaned over the front seat and snapped the kid's head hard into the dashboard, letting his unconscious body slump out of sight.

The driver struggled to see what was going on. His first instinct was to exit the vehicle, but Keeler's left fist pounded the lock shut, trapping him. Keeler threaded his left arm around the driver's head and pulled him tightly in, while fastening a rock-solid right forearm against the back of the man's neck. The driver struggled mutely. Keeler leaned over the seat to use his weight. He watched the driver's face in the rearview, shocked and struggling, fighting for life but losing. Keeler adjusted his hold as the driver weakened. After half a minute the technique worked and the blood flow to the driver's brain had been sufficiently halted to make the guy unconscious.

He slipped out of the vehicle and retrieved the backpack. He pushed the driver out of the way, against his companion, and got behind the wheel. The car was still running. The windshield was tinted enough that a casual witness would only have seen him entering the Toyota, and maybe a little rocking of the vehicle on its springs.

Keeler got the car moving. He leaned over and checked the glove compartment. A 9mm handgun was inside. Keeler removed it and dropped it into a storm drain on a street corner. He found another handgun taped under the driver's seat and disposed of it the same way. The men were regaining consciousness and keeping quiet, which was smart. Keeler had the club on his lap and used it as a prod to maintain discipline.

It took him fifteen minutes to find a dead end butting up to something called Newtown Creek, which looked less like a creek and more like a toxic waste site. All around were low industrial buildings and frigid air. Nobody was out on the streets, and nothing was moving except discarded garbage tossed by the wind.

Keeler got the two men out of the Toyota and had them sit against a cement wall holding up the rusted remains of a corrugated steel panel. Neither of them was carrying a weapon, both had thick leather wallets. Keeler stacked the wallets on the hood of the Toyota.

He knelt down in front of the men. The driver was shooting him looks to kill, but Keeler was used to that. He said, "I'm going to borrow the car. Maybe you'll get it back, maybe not."

The driver rolled his eyes. "It's my uncle's car. He won't be happy. He'll find you and chop your fucking head off."

Keeler thought about it for a second. Possible, but improbable. He slipped the cash and two New York state driver licenses out of the wallets and tossed the empty leather at them. "I'll keep these for reference. You don't want me coming back to find you." He looked at the driver's identification. The word *veteran* was printed on the top left corner. Any qualified service member can request to have the status on their identification. Maybe the guy thought it would help if he was stopped by the police.

Keeler looked up. "Alphonso, thank you for your service."

The driver scowled. Keeler smiled.

CHAPTER SIXTEEN

The Toyota had a built-in GPS and Keeler fed it the name of his destination, Kitchewan Landing. Arrows and curving lines appeared on the screen, along with a satisfying bleep as the destination triangulated with the satellites. He turned his attention to the music, flipped through the program buttons on the Toyota's stereo system until he found a station playing something appropriate. Once the real guitars and drums of "Like a Hurricane" started filtering through the speakers, Keeler began to have warm feelings for the drug dealer. The stereo system was excellent and he rolled down the windows, let in the cold air and howled along with Neil Young's shaky voice and guitar.

The fuel gauge was low. A few miles up he turned into a rest area with a gas station. Keeler filled the tank and checked the oil and antifreeze, in case the drug dealer's uncle wasn't good with maintenance. He paid in cash at the office and walked back to the Toyota, parked at pump number four. Taking a cop's point of view, the vehicle looked suspicious with those tinted windows. Wouldn't be a good idea to get caught with contraband; better to do a thorough search.

The hidden compartment was behind the heating vent serving the backseat. The ducts had been sealed and the vent cover popped off giving access to a spacious drop box. Keeler flipped through the first bundle of cash. There were several bundles in there. He figured it was in the area of ten grand, along with a small quantity of cannabis. Keeler tossed the weed into the trash can and got the car back on the road.

Coming off the exit ramp from route 9A and into the town of Kitchewan Landing, the elevated ShopRite sign commanded attention. Keeler turned right and passed beneath a series of underpasses, cold concrete with the powdery white bleakness of winter. Two right turns and the Toyota was moving downhill. To the left was a shopping complex built around the ShopRite supermarket chain. There was the UPS storefront, a recognizable logo among a cluster of nondescript businesses.

He parked in the middle of the lot and killed the ignition. Didn't figure he'd be able to just open up the laptop and see what was on it, but he wasn't about to leave it in storage until he took a look at the thing. As expected, the computer wasn't accessible, but that wasn't because it was password protected. The laptop wouldn't turn on, like the battery was drained.

He watched the people walking in and out of stores and cars. They wore bulky parkas and wool hats and moved slowly against the wind. A wide-framed man in red and black plaid wool pushed an older woman in a wheelchair. The man wore no hat and his blond hair moved in the wind.

The UPS Store didn't have luggage storage. What they did have were mailboxes to rent by the month. The issue was that the mailboxes were too small for the laptop.

The woman behind the counter was wearing the store

uniform and rectangular black-rimmed eyeglasses. She was looking at Keeler, waiting for him to have an idea, unwilling to offer any of her own. Keeler was looking back at her, wondering what she was thinking, if there was thought going on in there.

He said, "What happens if you receive a package for me that doesn't fit the mailbox?"

"We hold packages for two weeks sir."

"Uh huh."

Behind the woman was a peg board display showing cardboard boxes in three sizes. Keeler pulled the laptop from his backpack and held it up for her to see. "I'll take one of those boxes, something that fits this." He set the computer on the counter. "I can rent the mailbox, then send this to myself, then you'll hold it for a couple of weeks, is that correct ma'am?"

She nodded slowly, her eyes fixed on his, the pupils roving pinpoints behind the lenses of her spectacles. "I don't know why you would want to do that sir, but technically it would be possible. You would have to rent the mailbox first. After that had gone into the system, we can do next-day delivery, or five business days."

Keeler took a step back and considered. Did he need to go through this? What he didn't know was what he was going to find up at DeValla's house. Maybe everything was going to be fine, and then again maybe it wasn't. If the laptop was some kind of a hot object it would be an operational priority to get it safe.

Decision confirmed.

The process of renting a mailbox required ID and he used the New York state driver's license pilfered from the drug dealing driver of the Toyota. The dealer was a different ethnicity and ten years younger, but the woman at the counter didn't seem to even look at the photograph.

When the computer was all packed away, he asked the

woman behind the desk the question on his mind. "You're really going to put this into the delivery system, even though you know it's just coming back here?"

She looked up at him warily, like she was dealing with a tricky and annoying customer. "Sir. You paid for next-day delivery." She glanced at the clock above the counter and nodded. "It'll be here tomorrow by nine."

Keeler said nothing and completed the transaction. The clock above the UPS desk said 4:05 p.m.

Keeler drove the Toyota down into the train station parking lot. DeValla's shift was over, but he wanted to be sure she wasn't still at work. The parking spot was empty. Keeler pulled into it and parked. Through the windshield, he was looking at the train station and the municipal depot. He got the phone out of his pocket.

It was time to make the call to Blomstein.

CHAPTER SEVENTEEN

B lomstein, special operations intelligence officer based out of RAF Mildenhall, England. At least he had been, a couple years ago. The other thing Keeler remembered was that Blomstein was from somewhere in Brooklyn. They had history together that wouldn't fit into any kind of a book. Blomstein had come out of Delta and transitioned to intel officer, an unusual change from ACE operator to a guy sitting behind a computer, but the guy was inclined that way.

Keeler got the phone up and tapped in the number he'd memorized long ago and used a handful of times. The number was free and operational from anywhere on earth and maybe from space as well. Didn't matter where you made the call; it got funneled to the airbase at Mildenhall, an unsurprisingly flat part of England somewhere between Cambridge and Norfolk. The call center serviced operators who needed information but weren't on regular missions with regular intel support.

The arrangement wasn't supposed to include retired Air Force Special Operations captains like Keeler. But, in the past he'd been able to get Blomstein on the line, eventually. This time it wasn't like that. No Blomstein, no joke. Only a hard assed lieutenant with no sense of humor and no clue who Keeler was talking about.

Keeler let the phone fall into his lap and tried to remember actual personal facts about Blomstein. The man was on the upper side of six foot four and looked like a GI Joe action figure with improbably light-blond hair, and he was from Brooklyn.

The prepaid SIM card included data and the phone had an internet browser. It wasn't easy or fast or cheap, but it was the internet. Five long minutes later, Keeler was looking at five listings for landline phone numbers in Brooklyn in the name of Blomstein. These would be established residences, since hardly anyone got a new landline anymore.

Five addresses, four phone numbers. The first number was disconnected, the second try, a woman's voice answered, the throaty voice of an elderly smoker, somewhere between a croak and the sound of sandpaper on concrete. "Yeah."

Keeler asked to speak to Blomstein, recognizing that he'd never learned his buddy's first name. The woman on the other side of the line coughed sincerely and asked him which one.

He managed to make light of it. "The one who was my buddy in the military ma'am."

"Hold."

Two minutes later, the croak returned. "Yakov is up in two oh three with the radiator. When he's done I'll tell him you called."

Yakov? It had always just been Blomstein. He'd been Keeler. Nobody did first names. Some guys got stuck with a bad nickname, which started to bring some sense to the issue. Guy name of Yakov would keep that to himself. Which reminded Keeler that Blomstein had said his family was in real estate, owned a building with a bunch of rental units. He imagined Blomstein hunched under the old radiator, fiddling with wrenches and screwdrivers.

"Ma'am, I'm an old buddy from the military. My name is Keeler. I really need to speak with him now, if you don't mind."

The woman drew from a cigarette. "Well Mr. Keeler, take a ticket and wait on line. I have no idea how long. Could be five minutes, could be an hour. Maybe if they had taught him more practical skills in the military, he'd be faster. You want to leave me a number he can call?"

Keeler was about to speak, when he heard a commotion on the line. A male voice and then the sound of the phone being set down. Then the woman coughing and speaking to somebody else, in a strange language.

Blomstein came on the line. "Keeler." All casual, even though it had been at least a year.

"Blomstein."

"What's up?"

"Remember that guy Farrell, Vince Farrell, from the sandpit?"

"Yeah. Scumbag. You run into him?"

"I did."

The woman's voice was haranguing Blomstein on the other side. Speaking fast and intermittently coughing. She sounded like a rough customer.

"What do you need, I'm a little tied up, man."

Keeler smiled. "You didn't fix the radiator?"

"Need to get a part from the hardware store before it closes."

"Roger that. I need to know what Farrell's doing now. Remember that thing that went down with Vincelli? You have a way of running a search, see if he's still with them?"

"I can make a call or two. I'll get back to you on this number."

"Copy that, brother."

"Later."

Blomstein ended the call and Keeler was left with only one reality, the train station and the closing winter dusk. He thought about Blomstein and how they were pretty close, in topographical terms. Brooklyn wasn't far from Chinatown.

Keeler navigated up the hill, onto Riverside, then another right off Riverside where DeValla had made the left from the diner after asking if he wanted to stay over. From there he let muscle memory guide him until he found the base of DeValla's driveway.

He parked the Toyota just past where he'd seen the impression of a surveilling vehicle in the snow. The mark had been swept into indistinction by the wind. Keeler walked up the driveway and to the house. Lights were on inside and as he approached, he heard the sound of children.

Looked like DeValla was home eating dinner with her kids, which was the optimistic version of the outcomes modeled in his mind during the drive up from the city. Better alive than dead, that was for damned sure. Now the job was to verify the situation and make sure it stayed that way. Maybe Blomstein would get back to him and Keeler could get on down to Mexico or wherever he was going to spend the winter.

He rehearsed an excuse for being at DeValla's house, but rang the doorbell before he had it all figured out.

One ring and then waiting on the door step. DeValla was taking her time getting to the door, probably expecting nobody and likely involved in some kind of a child related tangle, maybe involving spaghetti, maybe not. The door opened. A woman looked at him, a version of DeValla from a time machine. Same person, just ten years younger, equally beautiful but in a very different way.

Snap out of it, he told himself. Take a reading of the situation. The woman was hassled, most likely by kids. It wasn't the DeValla he'd met, obviously, but the little sister. Little sister had no idea who Keeler was, but she exuded apprehension. It was visible in the tightness around her jaw and eyes and in the way she hugged herself in the doorway, although that could be a result of the freezing polar vortex.

"Yeah?"

Keeler said, "I'm a friend of Mini's, is she home?" Knowing she wasn't, needing to ask that question anyway.

The younger DeValla shivered and stood for a moment with her mouth slightly open, the question being, what are you about to tell me about my big sister. Instead she said, "A friend from where?"

"From the train."

"From the train how, like today or like in general, from the train."

"From last night. The train got canceled and she let me stay on her sofa." Keeler pointed in the direction of that piece of furniture.

"She's still at work."

He assumed the sister was there taking care of the kids. Maybe she'd even picked up the kids from the ex-husband. Maybe she did that often. Which suggested availability, a student, or unemployed perhaps. Or maybe she had a flexible job that she could do from anywhere, like a poet or an online Pilates instructor, or maybe she worked nights. Or, maybe she was there at the request of another family member, the mother for example.

He said, "I was just down at the train station and her car isn't there. I've got concerns."

The woman paused, looked at him and Keeler saw that she

was worried. She said, "Yeah but Mini could have parked in a different spot."

Keeler didn't say that he'd been the one who'd parked the car in the morning. He said, "Cut the shit. She doesn't usually stay late at work, or go out after if you've got the kids, unless she warns you right?"

"Not usually, no. She comes straight home; she's like that." The sister looked at Keeler. "Why, what's going on?" Her arms were getting goose bumps from the cold, hands rubbing at the opposite elbows. She was wearing socks and jeans and a pink sweater. Her hair was long and dark brown and done up in a ponytail. She had a faint dusting of freckles and blue eyes that were dark and infinite.

"Did you call your sister?"

The woman nodded, like it was a relief to talk about it. "Yeah, I called her a bunch of times."

"No answer, or is her phone just turned off?"

"It rings for a while and then goes to voice mail. Who are you?"

Keeler said nothing. The phone wasn't off, it was unattended.

"How do you know I'm her sister?"

"You look like her is how. I'm Keeler. What's your name?"

"Candy."

"Okay. Maybe we should talk inside."

Candy stood shivering in the doorway. She looked left and right and beyond Keeler down the driveway. "It's colder than a witch's tit out here."

CHAPTER EIGHTEEN

K eeler followed Candy back to the kitchen where two children were making a mess at the Formica table. An older woman came into view as Keeler was guided through the house. Candy spoke to her. "Ma, there's a guy here, friend of Minerva. I'm going to talk to him out in the living room all right?"

The woman in the kitchen glanced at him, worry written on her face in equal measure to a kind of pulverized patience that had been installed. Keeler lifted a hand. "Ma'am."

Candy fired off a rapid sequence of words in Italian. Her mother nodded and glanced again at Keeler. They made eye contact. Candy closed the kitchen door and looked at him. "Ma'am? I think that's the first time anyone ever said that to her."

"Do you think she liked it?" Keeler was looking around, wondering what he was doing there, if there would be a benefit to coming in the house.

Candy ran a hand over the back of the sofa. "Ma probably didn't notice, to tell you the truth."

She pointed to the sofa. "Sit down. I was making coffee if you want some."

"Sure."

She went into the kitchen and closed the door, leaving Keeler alone in the living room. He sat on the sofa where he'd slept the night before, looking at a low shelf full of paperback books. Candy kept him waiting for five long minutes.

She came out of the kitchen, shutting the door behind her. "Sorry, the kids." Candy handed him a mug and took a seat on the armchair facing the sofa. She took an initial sip of her coffee and looked over expectantly. "So what's up?"

Keeler indicated an old framed photograph on the mantle, a beautiful young woman and a handsome guy who looked like he was wearing a suit for the first time. "Your parents?"

Candy nodded. "Wedding photograph."

Keeler looked at Candy, and spent two seconds considering what he was looking at. Before, at the door, he'd thought she was hassled by the kids. Now, he knew the kids were under control. The worry was her big sister, which meant Keeler and her had something in common. Still, he was hesitant to jump in with the whole story about the woman in white and Vince Farrell and the laptop.

Keeler decided to drop just a few crumbs. "Your sister drove me to the train station in the morning. When we got there, she realized that she'd forgotten something at the house, a laptop that someone had left on the train. I came back here to fetch it for her, took her truck. I brought the truck back to the station and left the laptop bag and her car keys at the lost and found."

"Okay, and?" Candy's eyes flicked to the window behind Keeler.

"Thing is, someone was at her house looking for the laptop." He gestured out the window. "Drives a blue Ford pickup truck, Jersey plates. Does that ring a bell for you, Candy?"

"Not off the top of my head, no. He was here at the house?"

"After I got the laptop bag out of the house and was about to go back to the station, he showed up. Very eager to get his hands on the laptop. He didn't even know I was here at first. I think he expected Mini to be home."

"Did you give it to him?"

"I didn't, I gave it to the lost and found just like your sister asked. The guy in the pickup truck wasn't happy about that."

"And you think that's got something to do with the fact that Mini's kind of AWOL at the moment." Candy's gaze again shifted to the window and Keeler began to realize that she'd asked her mother to call someone, when she'd spoken Italian earlier. Now she was just delaying him, probably not even listening to what he was saying.

Keeler said, "I don't know. Maybe."

Her eyes came lazily back to him. "So, bottom line is you don't know what's holding my sister up."

He said nothing.

Candy looked at him without expression for a moment. She was tapping her knee with the nails of her left hand. Like a staccato rap. He saw her, thinking and calculating and coming to some conclusions that she wasn't happy with.

She said, "You take a cab here from the station, just now?"

"Drove."

She tilted her head. "Which is strange since you were on the train this morning." Candy began to tap her leg with a pointed finger. "So you take the train this morning down to the city and then here you are again this evening with a car."

Keeler leaned forward, close to her. "I just want you to know that I'm not here for any other reason than concern for your sister." He got her to lock eyes with him. "Did you call the police yet?" he asked.

Candy shrugged. "Kind of."

"Uh huh."

She looked away. The beams from a powerful set of head-lights cut into the room through the front window. A vehicle mounted the driveway and pulled to a stop outside: a large cruiser with a Kitchewan Town Police logo.

She said, "It's Frankie, Mini's ex. He's deputy chief, which gets him his own cop car." She leaned back in her chair. "No hard feelings, but I don't know you from Adam."

"Do you like Frankie?"

"Nobody likes Frankie; he's a dick. He's gonna give you a hard time."

"He can try, but none of that's going to help your sister."

She shrugged. "He's a cop. Just tell him the same thing you told me. No harm in telling the truth right?"

Which was funny enough to make Keeler smile broadly, with all of his teeth.

Candy was still watching him when the front door opened. She was biting at the ends of her ponytail, and the two of them shared a long look. The policeman coming in the door was wearing civilian clothing and was extra-large sized with a belly and a red face framed by a brushed helmet of red hair going gray. Something bulged in his cheek, like a wad of tobacco and he didn't look happy. Frankie's coat had shoulder straps, military style but fake. The hood had faux-fur trim. Same coat as Vince Farrell. Keeler wondered if Farrell had actually gone to Sears to buy it himself.

Frankie came in the door and pointed straight at Keeler. "You stay right there." His words coming out slightly slurred and a pained look on his face.

Keeler looked at Candy and raised his eyebrows. He didn't blame her for calling the police. Here she was worried about her sister not coming home and then a strange man comes to the door says he knows Minerva. No harm, no foul. Candy's eyes widened a little and the beginnings of a smile creased the corners of her perfectly symmetrical mouth. The big policeman strode into the living room and looked first at Keeler, then at Candy. "This is the guy?" He glared at Keeler.

Candy unfolded herself from the armchair. "Sit down, Francis." She walked back behind the sofa, speaking to Keeler. "Why don't you tell him the story you told me." She turned to her sister's ex. "Frankie, you want a beer or a Coke?"

"No. I can't eat or drink anything. Just got my goddamned wisdom tooth removed and I'm still bleeding." Frankie sat down in the armchair and extracted a bloody wad of gauze from his mouth. He looked off into space, probably feeling around with his tongue. Cursed under his breath and put it back in place. He looked impatiently at Keeler. "Go ahead. What's your story?"

Keeler looked at him with a flat stare and said exactly nothing. Frank's red face was a permanent feature, not a function of the cold or the tooth. He had bushy red eyebrows and bloodshot blue eyes. A two-way radio bleeped at his hip.

He lifted the handset. "Go ahead."

A compressed voice crackled and gargled down the line, not easy to decipher, but evidently speaking some kind of police language. There was a name in the transmission, easily comprehensible. Alphonso Jesus Jackson.

Frankie grunted at the end of it. "Okay, stand by."

Keeler realized that Frankie's colleagues were down at the Toyota and had run the plate number. Frankie spoke aggressively. "What did you say your name was?"

"I didn't."

"Let me see your ID."

Keeler produced his driver's license and handed it to Frankie. The large man examined the document, flicking eyes back to Keeler and again to the license. "You live in Hawaii?"

"No, I just go there to drive once in a while."

Frankie registered the joke as a disrespectful comment. He stood up. "Okay, wise guy, we can talk about it down at the station."

Keeler remained seated. "Is it illegal to drive a friend's car in New York state?"

The policeman looked at him. "I don't know. Is it? I'm not a lawyer."

Frankie was standing. Keeler looked the policeman in the eyes for the first time. "Why don't you sit down, Frank. The car's not important. You can run the plates and get my friend on the phone, whatever you want. I don't care about that. I'm here about your ex-wife."

Frankie didn't sit down. He leaned over Keeler. "What is it you think I want to hear about my ex-wife from your mouth?"

Keeler stood up slowly, which couldn't help but create a physical presence. Frankie backed off, an involuntary step to relative safety. Keeler examined the man in front of him with the hard belly and the expression of stupidity and anger. Candy was shifting from one socked foot to the other. She hadn't stopped gnawing at her hair ends.

Keeler spoke to her. "I'll probably see you later."

The response came out of her mouth instantly, seemingly without reflection. "Okay."

CHAPTER NINETEEN

Candy stood, pinned like a deer in the headlights by Keeler's direct address and his physical proximity, all of which had become weirdly intimate. She hadn't realized how confident the man was, until she saw him move in the same space as Frankie, the brash cop whom people generally took to be a model of masculinity. The Keeler guy made Frankie seem weak and off balance. Keeler looked like he'd be impossible to push off balance, like he had a special relationship with gravity.

She watched Keeler turn on Frankie, giving him instructions. "It would help if you could find information about the woman who got sent to the hospital last night. Also, you should get in touch with the Metro-North people. Maybe they have cameras down there."

Frankie's red face was growing a deeper shade of crimson. "You telling me how to do my job?"

Candy had her hair out of her mouth. She was experiencing a sinking regret about calling Frankie. She watched Keeler's broad back as he went out the front door and into the cold.

Frankie stood in the center of the living room, looking lost. She turned on him. "What the fuck, Frankie?"

Frankie was flustered. Candy stepped into his path, preventing him from going out the door and doing something stupid. "Frankie, you go out there and be constructive. She's the mother of your children; that's the important thing. Forget about your pride. I think that guy came because he was legitimately worried about Mini."

"So why'd you call me?"

"I don't know. I probably shouldn't have but I was worried about Mini."

"You don't just think she's gone shopping or something?"

Candy shook her head. "Not anymore I don't, no."

Frankie gazed at her, trying to look stern. Candy went to the door and saw Keeler, moving past Frankie's police vehicle and to the bottom of the driveway. There were a couple of Frankie's guys in uniform standing around it. Keeler didn't look too bothered about the police.

He walked straight to the car with only the briefest of nods at the two uniforms standing around it bouncing on their toes to keep warm. Both cops turned to look at the house. Frankie was next to her and she nudged him with an elbow. He glanced at her and gave a shrug to the uniforms, which meant, leave the guy alone. Still, one of the guys couldn't help himself.

Candy heard him ask, "Is that your vehicle, sir?"

The guy ignored the question and got into the car. He fired up the engine. The cops stepped away and the Toyota pulled out of the spot.

Keeler sat at the counter in the diner and ate breakfast. Two eggs over easy with rye toast, bacon, home fries, and coffee. He had asked for the home fries well-done, a request received with a curt nod and an "of course." He was thinking that it didn't look good for Mini DeValla.

What was he looking at? A contract killing of the woman in white, gone wrong in two ways. First, she hadn't died, second, the blizzard had scuppered the getaway. Farrell as the would-be killer, stranded by the blizzard and then recognized by a train conductor, which was the primary reason it wasn't looking good for Mini DeValla. DeValla had done nothing wrong. She'd behaved in a perfectly normal way, it simply hadn't been her lucky night.

Keeler ate and sipped his coffee, a good strong blend hitting the correct notes. An old guy with a big loose face slid onto the stool next to him. "You mind?"

"Not at all."

The old guy unpacked himself from several deep layers and finally settled. He unrolled a newspaper and smoothed it on the counter. Keeler glanced at it. The *Kitchewan Gazette*. The blizzard took the headline spot, in big bold letters above a picture of kids sledding. Farther down was a smaller headline. *Woman in Critical Condition after Incident at Kitchewan Landing Train Station.*

He scanned the first paragraph, which divulged nothing more enlightening than the headline itself. The man with the big face saw Keeler staring.

He shrugged. "Crazy shit."

Keeler looked at him. Brown eyes set into a creased and floppy face. A fleshy mouth and the big red nose of a drinker. The man had a bush of silver hair.

"Do they have a name for her?" Keeler asked.

"Haven't read it yet." The man slid the paper over to Keeler and reached for a menu. "Knock yourself out."

The text of the article was fit around a black-and-white photograph of the scene from last night. A crowd of Metro-

North staff and police, backlit by emergency lights from the parked cruisers. The article didn't name the woman, but they gave her an age, fifty-two.

The man looked over at Keeler. "They got a name? Maybe I know her."

"No name."

The guy made a face. "Probably haven't notified next of kin." He looked into Keeler's eyes. "That's how it works right? Got to notify next of kin or else you run the danger of her husband or mother or sister or daughter learning about it before they've been properly told."

Keeler was reading the byline for the article. The journalist's name was Tim Burke. He looked up at the man. "No, that wouldn't do."

The guy laughed. "Not at all. Got to maintain standards, even here in Kitchewan Landing." He pointed at the menu. "What am I getting here? Been here ten thousand times and can never figure it out. Menu's too damn long."

Keeler slid the paper back to the man. "I heard you either get breakfast or you go Greek."

"So you got breakfast."

"Right."

"I had breakfast this morning. Guess I'll go Greek."

Keeler flipped the paper to the front page, which supplied him with an address, 25 Brook Street. He paid and nodded to the man, who hadn't yet figured out what kind of Greek he was going to order.

CHAPTER TWENTY

Twenty-Five Brook Street was a couple of blocks down from the municipal building and the police station. The *Gazette* occupied a solid brown brick and cement building from the forties, repurposed into offices. The newspaper was on the second floor, above an attorney's office, and windows glowed with warm electric light.

A middle-aged woman wearing horn-rimmed glasses sat in the center of a large room, surrounded by computers and desks laden with paper. Now that Keeler was standing in the door, she looked at him. He knocked.

"Good evening, ma'am," Keeler said.

"Hello." The woman picked up a pencil and twirled it while her chair swiveled left and right. "How can I help you?"

"Looking for Tim Burke. Is he around?"

Eyebrows lifted. "Do you have an appointment with Tim?"

"No. I wanted to ask him about an article he wrote. The woman from the train station. I was there last night on the train. A guy at the diner had your paper, so I read the article. I'm curious is all."

Keeler left that hanging, hoping that being there last night gave him the legitimacy to be interested, to ask further questions. Apparently it did, since the woman blinked twice slowly and settled her pencil onto the desk in front of her, as if to mark a decision.

"Nothing wrong with being curious." The woman swiveled her chair again in both directions, looking relaxed and casual. "I could probably answer your questions, if you want." She coughed. "Not like Tim knows anything that I don't. I was just going out for a smoke. Come keep me company."

Keeler waited for her to suit up. Her smoking spot was just outside the front door on top of the fancy stoop. She leaned back against the wrought-iron railing and lit up. "Okay, shoot. What do you want to know?"

"I was curious. They didn't give her a name in the article."

She blew a set of smoke rings, which worked since there was no wind. "She's not doing great, apparently. In a coma or something. They haven't been able to notify her family yet. Not ideal, but I wanted to get the article out before our competition does. You know, get out ahead of the news cycle." She puffed on her cigarette and looked up from the glowing tip. "You know, if there's one thing we've got going for us it's the quality. Got to maintain that advantage."

"There's another paper in town?"

"Corporate conglomerate. They open up local papers and consolidate the reporting across the county. It's a nationwide corporation. We're being pushed out—not very slowly either." She tapped her ash. "Good old diner. I think about half our sales come from there, outside of subscribers. Then we have a couple of delis and the train station. Getting an internet person soon. Maybe that'll help."

Keeler examined the woman in front of him. She looked like a person who enjoyed her work. Dedicated. He said, "It's only you isn't it? There is no Tim Burke. That's just bullshit so you don't look like a one-woman show."

The woman laughed, coughing out smoke. "Oh shit. Is it that obvious?"

"No desk up there for Tim."

"Oh, an observant one." She pulled on the cigarette and did this thing where she spoke while letting the smoke seep through her teeth. "Tim's my favorite avatar. We used to be a team of four, but now it's me, hanging on by a thread. Best thing about good old Tim is how he can always be counted on to take the blame when someone doesn't like what's in the paper."

Keeler wanted to get the conversation back on track, but he didn't want to be pushy. He let her lead. The woman chewed on her lip and blew smoke and coughed again. "You seem all right, whatever your name is. You also look like you're trying to look patient, when in fact for some reason, you're dying to know this woman's name. She had ID on her. Her name is Irma Rosenbaum."

"Source in the police department or the hospital?"

"I'm not going to divulge my source." She gave a short laugh. "The only reason I'm talking to you is because I'd like to know why you're interested. If you knew Rosenbaum, you wouldn't need to speak to me. The fact that you're here asking about her, without knowing her, makes me think there might be something more to know about her." She raised her eyebrows. "So tell me, should I be interested?"

Keeler laughed. "I'm usually the guy who asks that question. "I was there last night, on the train. Saw the woman down on the platform. Tonight I saw the article."

He didn't want to mention Farrell, open up the can of worms.

"And, what, you're like a curious bystander? Bullshit."

She was looking at him, smoking and observing. Keeler knew that this was one of those moments: let her in, or not.

He said, "Where did you work before this place?"

"What, before this? I was an international editor at the *Times*. You know, last couple of years before I got out. This is retirement." She let out a throaty laugh. "So tell me, mister mystery man, what is so curious about this woman's unfortunate circumstances?"

He didn't want to mention Mini DeValla yet. "Look, I'm not going into details right now. I'll tell you this, I have a good reason to think that whatever happened to that woman, Rosenbaum, isn't totally kosher. That's all I have for you. You should look into who she is, in my opinion. That's what I'd be doing if I wanted to stay a step ahead of the competition."

She looked at him for a moment and smoked. Looked away. "Okay, so you don't want to tell me anything real, or you can't tell me." Smoke blew through pursed lips. "I'm all for sharing, but I'll want you to share as well." Eyes returned to Keeler, glinting from the streetlight.

Keeler looked into the night. "I can't tell you about it now, but I could use your help in learning more. In exchange, maybe I'll give you a call at some point, tell you something that nobody else knows."

She blew out smoke. "I don't have a ton of information. I have sources among the police, the paramedics, and the hospital. It's the benefit of actually being from here. Rosenbaum isn't local. She was up at Copenhagen House. I guess they're trying to get in touch with the family. What happened to her, it's touch and go. They have no idea what's wrong, just that she's barely alive. Supposedly they're running toxicology tests that take a little time."

"What does that mean, up at Copenhagen House?"

The woman drew on her cigarette. "You aren't from around here."

"No."

"Copenhagen House is an estate, up past Dyer Bridge." She pointed northeast. "It's an old manor, like an aristocratic European home, now run as a residency program for a think tank. Something like that." She blew smoke and Keeler saw that behind the horn-rimmed glasses, her eyes were lively and intelligent.

Keeler looked across the road at the darkness and the row of houses clad in aluminum siding. "Did you try to learn anything about Rosenbaum, who she is?"

The woman took a moment to respond. "Actually, I didn't." She took a last puff. "But I will now. Didn't even consider there'd be a real story, to be honest." She crushed the butt into an empty flower pot that was having a second life as an ashtray. "Shit, you're trying to tell me that she may not be just a person who had an accident." The gloved hand was extended. The nicotine hit was making the woman gregarious. "I'm Julie Everard by the way."

Keeler took the hand and they shook. He wasn't going to give his name to the journalist. He said, "Ron Darling." He'd always liked the fact that the former Mets player was from Hawaii, and since this was New York, it seemed fitting to use his name.

Everard's hand was bony beneath the fleece padding of her glove. Keeler's mind drifted to other things, like toxicology, syringes, and the various means of killing somebody with modern poisons. If the police don't suspect foul play, there isn't usually any kind of postmortem investigation. Cardiac arrest happens all the time. Minuscule punctures of the epidermis are hard to spot, and investigating death requires time and energy and most importantly, suspicion. He was also wondering about the place. Killing her on the train would have been preferable since the assassin could then have hopped off at any stop and been conveniently distant when the body was found. But whatever they'd done to her hadn't completely worked out, Rosenbaum was still in the land of the living.

He said, "Will you let me know if you find anything else?"

Everard produced a business card from her phone holder and handed it to Keeler. She was watching him carefully. "So you aren't just a guy who was on the train?"

He regarded the cool set of eyes examining him and shook his head. "For now I'm just a guy who was on the train. Tomorrow I might be a different guy, we'll see."

"All right then, Ron." She indicated the card. "That's my personal number. Call it right now, I'll have your number. That way I can let you know if I find anything interesting about Irma Rosenbaum."

Keeler slid out his phone and tapped in her number, called it so that she had it on her phone.

Everard said, "I'm going back inside to finish up and then skedaddle back home for dinner. He's making shepherd's pie tonight, and I do love me a good shepherd's pie." She pointed at the business card, still in Keeler's hand. "I'll look into this again tomorrow.

Keeler watched Everard enter the building and make her way up the stairs. He had no traction on the situation. Everard had given him a clue, something to look forward to, a location even, which meant a destination. Who knew, maybe something could come of a visit to Copenhagen House.

He came down off the stoop with a sense of relief and even something like anticipation. Copenhagen House sounded both fancy and old and mysterious, in equal measure. He was looking forward to creeping around the place and seeing what he could shake up. If nothing came of it that was all right too. He could go back to DeValla's house and see if she had come home, or not.

He'd take it from there, one step at a time.

CHAPTER TWENTY-ONE

Mini had not come home, and her sister, Candy, was worried.

The kids were in bed and she sat with her mother in Mini's kitchen eating a grilled cheese and tomato sandwich her mom had prepared. Mom didn't eat, just busied herself around the kitchen, reorganizing it into some kind of an ideal image, despite its not being her house. If she was in a kitchen, that kitchen was going to be organized.

Candy ignored her mom. She was pissed off at Frankie. He was a ham-fisted idiot, like most of the Kitchewan Landing police force. Minerva had projected attributes onto Frank that were more her own fantasy than anything possessed by the actual Francis Robert O'Leary. It wasn't only Candy who had been surprised by the marriage; pretty much the whole town had been a little surprised, including Frankie himself.

Candy hadn't been surprised by the divorce, only that it'd taken so long for Mini to figure out that he wasn't the guy she thought he was, that Frankie wasn't going to suddenly grow a brain. She bit down on the last corner of the grilled cheese and had what she liked to call a *brain fart*.

The computer.

Candy rose from the table and went into Mini's bedroom. On the dresser was a laptop computer. She brought it back to the kitchen and set it on the table. Her sister's password was an amalgamation of the kids' names and dates of birth. The laptop was the same brand as Mini's phone. Candy opened an app for finding lost phones. The computer demanded another password and luckily Minerva had used the same one for everything. The computer whirred and a little wheel spun and fifteen seconds later a map was forming on the screen. There were more things to click and select before a little blinking blue dot appeared.

Mini's phone was at the golf course.

Candy spoke to her mother. "Ma, you okay here? I'm going out for a bit. Give me a call if Mini comes back."

Her mother was busy finding a new home for the cheese grater and shooed her away. Candy went to the door to get her boots on. She was feeling trepidacious but excited.

The golf course was up in the hills north of town. It was accessed by a long winding driveway, but by then everything had been plowed, and driving steep hills wasn't so much of an issue. Candy was pretty certain that nobody played golf in the winter, at least not in New York state. The parking lot was a nighttime teen hangout spot in the summer, but she'd never been to the actual club and didn't know anybody who had. That said, she understood that golf clubs were clubby, in the sense that hanging out in them was part of the deal. Maybe more so than actually playing a round of golf.

Candy steered her old Subaru up the incline. At the end of the driveway she came to the parking lot. On the other side of that was the clubhouse, a sprawling stone structure that wasn't very old, but was made to look it. The lighting helped, recessed spots highlighting angular gray stone. The entire place was snowed over, but the walkways and the lot were cleanly shoveled, plowed, swept, and lit.

There was light coming from the clubhouse and cars in the lot.

Candy parked and kept the Subaru running. She had her sister's laptop, and used her own cellular device as a hot spot to get Mini's phone location activated again. It took a while to do that, but the phone once more appeared as a blinking blue dot on the map. It was in the same place as before, but now Candy zoomed in on the location. The dot wasn't just at the golf course; it was in the parking lot.

Candy swept her eyes from left to right. There were maybe fifteen parked cars besides her own. None of them were vehicles she immediately recognized. The actual blinking dot seemed to be on an empty area of the lot. Candy got out of the car with the laptop balanced in one hand. She walked to where she thought the dot was located, and saw nothing but wet and cold asphalt.

Weird.

For a second she didn't know what to do, but then she figured out the best course of action.

Candy switched off the ignition on her little Subaru. She kept the laptop open for fear of losing the signal and walked up the clean path of stepping stones to the entrance. The interior of the club was hermetically sealed by a two-door system with a space between the doors the size of one great big step. Candy was five foot nine, which is tall enough for a woman, but didn't make her any kind of a giant. She crossed the threshold in a step and a half. Through the second door, she experienced an atmosphere change, like the cold was sucked out of her and replaced by a cozy warmth. Inside the foyer was a solid oak concierge desk with a young guy sitting behind it eating with both hands.

When Candy approached she was able to identify the object in his hands as a club sandwich. He looked up at her and did a double take. For a moment the boy looked silly, staring at Candy with elements of the sandwich visible inside of his open mouth. Candy was used to seeing the reaction her appearance produced on men's faces. She tried not to judge them for it. The kid closed his mouth and finished his bite. Candy set the laptop down on the counter and rotated it around for him to see. The kid was in his teens, maybe the son of a member who was working nights at the club for pocket money and free food. He wiped his fingers on a napkin and composed himself.

She spoke slowly and articulated her words well. "This computer is telling me that my phone is at your club. Do you see that?"

The kid leaned in and examined the screen. Candy saw that his eyes flicked over the interface elements comfortably, like he'd seen that kind of thing before and knew what it was. "Yeah. It's in the parking lot."

She pointed at the blinking blue dot. "But it isn't exactly there. That spot is empty asphalt."

The kid nodded. "They don't give an exact spot. Margin of fifteen to twenty yards or something like that. It's probably in one of the cars. You know anybody at the club?"

"No, I don't."

The kid stared at her blankly. "So how did your phone get into one of the member's cars?"

"It's my sister's phone, and I have no idea. I guess we should check the cars."

He shrugged and she saw indifference in his eyes. "You can go ahead and look into the cars, but don't go opening the doors or anything, that's private property. Where's your sister?"

"That's the point. I don't know where she is and I figured I might find her phone with this." She tapped the laptop. "Now I found the phone, and it's at your club. We need to find out whose car the phone is in and then speak to the vehicle's registered owner."

The kid didn't like the direction this conversation was taking. "I don't know. It's a private club. But if you find the phone, come back and let me know. I'll ask."

Which pissed Candy off. "There are like, fifteen cars out there. I bet they're all having dinner with each other or playing poker or something. What else would they be doing?"

The boy shrugged. "I don't know. Hold on a second and I'll ask. What's your sister's name?"

"Minerva DeValla."

The kid was back inside of three minutes. He shook his head. "Nobody's heard of her. Nobody has her phone."

Candy went back outside into the cold. She roamed the parking lot, looking into the vehicles. Ten minutes later she had gazed deeply into the interior of fifteen automobiles without a glimpse of her sister's phone, or any phone for that matter. Thirteen out of the fifteen in the lot could be described as SUVs, the remaining two were luxury sedans. One was a silver Jaguar with tinted windows that she couldn't see into. The dot on the laptop screen kept on blinking stupidly.

Candy drew two conclusions from this. One was related to the vehicles. The Jaguar had been hidden behind a large Chevy Tahoe and she hadn't noticed it initially. The Jag belonged to Bob Tsipiras, the owner of the diner. Everyone knew his car. The second conclusion was related to the kid inside. He wasn't going to help her open up all of those vehicles. She also knew that it would be a pain to get the members to cooperate.

So she called Frankie again. At least that meathead was good for breaking things, if for nothing else.

CHAPTER TWENTY-TWO

K eeler was good at a lot of things, including breaking and entering.

He was sitting twenty feet in from the road in the snow with his back against a tree. In terms of public access, and the view from across the road, Copenhagen House presented as a stone wall with a tall white wooden gate. The wall was high enough to dissuade casual entry, but low enough to be unremarkable. As far as Keeler could make out, the gate was under observation from two cameras.

The woods were quiet. There were not many sounds louder than his own breathing and the occasional crackle of ice and snow adjusting. Just a trickle of water from the river off in the distance. The estate boundary ran along the narrow road that he'd taken up. The property occupied a plateau above the steep valley. The river was most likely the same one he'd heard behind DeValla's house, except he was now on the other side of it and farther to the northwest. It was peaceful and beautiful; heavy clouds covered the moon, which made it even more picturesque.

A car came up the road from the valley below. The sound of tires on asphalt preceded the appearance of headlight beams. Once the vehicle rushed along the straight stretch of road before him and disappeared around the bend, the winter silence reasserted itself.

Keeler got up and moved through the woods, parallel to the stone wall on the other side of the road. Every step plunged his boots into the thick snow. He paused several times to examine the wall. There were no surveillance devices as far as he could make out. Just the two cameras at the gate. The wall turned after about a quarter of a mile, running directly away from Keeler's position.

Maybe there was surveillance from the inside, but he'd have to get up on the wall to check. Doing so required little more than scaling the narrow trunk of a tree, then stepping onto one of the stone slabs which topped the barrier.

Keeler crouched there, well balanced, hidden by branches. He had a view across a meadow. In the dark, the fresh layer of snow looked like a white blanket laid atop the flat area, with soft mounds that he figured were buried boulders or hedges. There weren't any buildings in sight—only the meadow, a dividing line of trees, and traces of white beyond signaling another open area.

Keeler stayed up top for a good three minutes, thinking and waiting and watching and listening. He wasn't tired, and he wasn't hungry. He was alive and invigorated and curious enough to get in there and see what was going on.

He slid down the other side of the wall, slowing himself with a hand against a tree trunk, his feet stepping and slipping down the stone face. At the base of the wall, he crouched and watched for a minute before moving northeast along the inside of the wall until he arrived at the edge of the meadow.

He cut into the overgrown spit dividing the open area from another just like it and stayed in the trees until the end of the wooded section. On the other side of the second meadow was the building, three sides of a giant rectangle surrounding a courtyard. The external walls had a line of windows, some of which were lit, illuminating plant beds hosting a mix of evergreen and deciduous trees and shrubs.

To get closer to the building, Keeler would have to cross open space. He was stranded on the thin peninsula of wooded cover, like standing on the forked tongue of a giant serpent. Nothing was moving out there. Inside the building was warmth and light. He could see movement in one of the windows, and the hot glow of a fireplace.

Keeler detached from the trees and slipped across the white meadow. The snow was thick and his boots sank deep. The crossing was slow going and it took all of a minute and a half to get into the shrubbery close to the building. Then he was at the window, looking in. The walls were lined with bookcases. Everything wood paneled and wood floored, with high oak beams crossing an A-frame ceiling. The fireplace was glowing and a silver-haired man sat on a velvet sofa with his back to Keeler.

The guy's head wasn't doing anything except nodding every once in a while, which made Keeler think there might be someone else in the room he couldn't see. He shuffled over to the next window about fifteen feet away. From there he had a new angle into the room.

Instead of looking at the room however, he was looking directly at a woman standing in the window gazing out. The woman had silver hair cut in a bob and a plaid dress beneath a gray cashmere sweater. The floor she stood on was about a foot and a half above the ground, which brought her head about level with Keeler's.

It took her a half second to focus on Keeler's face, then she dropped her scotch glass and screamed with everything she had.

Except, Keeler couldn't hear her scream, or the sound of her heavy glass hitting the floor. The windows were perfectly soundproofed. For a long second he stood watching her face do contortions. In the background, the man leaped up off the sofa, eyes gaping.

CHAPTER TWENTY-THREE

K eeler slid away from the window. He still couldn't hear anything but the pure winter silence. What would happen next? They'd call security, if there was any. If not maybe they'd call the police. Keeler let that thought sit there for a moment and examined it. Maybe they'd send big Frankie up. On the other hand, if someone came out from the estate to check the grounds, they'd simultaneously open up the place for Keeler to get in.

He slid along the wall to his right, which was back toward the entrance. He had the germ of an idea and sprinted close along the side of the building where the snow hadn't accumulated, staying just inside the shrubs. He wasn't going to be making any more tracks in the open meadow, that was for sure. If he went out that way he'd go back on his own steps. Twenty seconds later the wall stopped being straight and jutted out in a semicircle. Keeler followed the curve around and stopped behind the cover of an evergreen hedge. He was looking at the entrance, the opening in the three-sided rectangle.

Just inside that was a guardhouse, also made of stone with a single window looking out.

About five yards from Keeler's position was a footpath that had been cleared of snow. The path connected to a plowed driveway area directly in front of the entrance. Consequently, the removed snow formed a pile several feet high along the edge of the cleared gravel. Keeler stepped across the footpath to the snow bank and rolled himself over the other side of it. Behind cover he lay still and waited.

A minute later a door opened. Two men were speaking. The first voice was low and deep and sounded like the voice of a Black guy. "It's mainly a difference in crust. That's what she said."

The second voice was almost an octave higher and was inflected with the lilting vocalization of a native Hispanic man. "Why did she think it was important?"

"Because there's old crust and new crust and she likes the old better. Which is why we can't go eat there anymore."

"I guess that's too bad for her. It's what you call a her problem."

The voices were accompanied by footsteps. The steps weren't crunching into snow, they were the steps of boots on stone, with a little gravel or salt between sole and surface.

The first guy sighed, like he was exasperated. "Okay, so you need to understand that before you guys showed up, pizza was made by Italian people."

"And?"

"And they paid more attention to the thickness of the crust is all I'm saying. Don't take it the wrong way, but Mexican crust is thicker."

"They aren't Mexican; they're from Ecuador. That's like the difference between Texas and Connecticut. Anyway, maybe in Ecuador they've got different pizza priorities."

"You mean, like, maybe they need the extra calories from the extra crust."

Keeler pictured the other guy shrugging, even if he didn't see that happen.

He was facing the other direction, out to the meadow. The flash of an errant Maglite beam played over the snow. The footsteps started to crunch snow and the voices fell off into murmurs. Keeler waited for a minute, then rolled up so his head poked out from behind the snow bank.

There were cameras covering the entrance and the guardhouse, but he knew, dollar to a dime, there wasn't anybody there to see what they recorded.

Keeler knew a little about closed-circuit security systems. In civilian applications, they are like baby pacifiers, installed to make people feel better, more secure. Many people like to imagine that security camera footage gets seen by security people. The truth is that the images are hardly ever viewed. When they are, it's from the comfort of the future trying to reconstruct the past.

Keeler walked in through the entrance with his head down and opened the guardhouse door.

The guardhouse comprised a small room with surveillance camera monitor grids taking up all of the real estate on a single large screen. A desk ran the length of the room. There was a computer keyboard and mouse and the remains of a large pizza, a can of Coke, and a can of orange soda. The other piece of hardware was an office telephone, the old kind that has a cable going into the wall. A plain white keycard was placed at an angle, in front of the telephone, the kind of card they use for hotel rooms.

Keeler slipped the card into his hip pocket.

Twenty yards into the horseshoe-shaped courtyard was a door on the left. The lock was a sleek steel and wood piece of hardware that fit in with the environment. A red glow winked from a discreet recess. Keeler presented the white card and was rewarded with a solid green glow and a satisfying thunk as the bolt receded.

He walked through into a cold and dark kitchen, clean and tidy with a foil-covered oven dish standing lonesome on a wood topped kitchen island. The foil had the shape of a roasted chicken. Keeler took three steps up through an archway, finding himself facing a long corridor. He stood close to the wall and could see warm light at the end. There was distant music and the faint muttering of conversation.

He figured he'd go explore, try to find out whatever it was people did up there at Copenhagen House.

CHAPTER TWENTY-FOUR

The golf course was three miles from Copenhagen House as the crow flies, across the valley and up a different set of hills.

Candy DeValla was frustrated because Frankie wasn't going to come. He didn't care that she'd had a breakthrough with the phone-finding thing on Mini's computer. He didn't attach any importance to it, and didn't even seem worried that his ex-wife was missing. He'd said that people go missing all the time and that usually it's not a big deal because they come back. Candy had insisted and Frankie had insisted back at her, you can't even force an adult to go un-missing. If the police were to find her, legally, they'd need Mini's permission to inform her little sister.

Plus, Frankie had a couple days off work after his dental surgery, which was going to make it even harder to convince him. It all made Candy extremely pissed off.

She was sitting in her car, her phone on the passenger seat, warm from recent use, useless to her for anything but as a Wi-Fi hot spot for the laptop, also on the passenger seat, the little blue dot blinking idiotically from the area around Bob Tsipiras's

Jaguar. She'd been able to look into the other vehicles, but Tsipiras had felt it important to tint his windows to keep prying eyes out. DeValla's suspicions intuitively gravitated to the hidden interior of the Jaguar.

She pictured Bob in her mind, around sixty-five years old, a Greek guy who'd made it big with the diner. He still ran the place himself and was always hustling around, making sure everything was up to scratch. She could go back into the golf club and try to convince that kid to get Tsipiras from out of whatever poker game he was currently involved with, but it wasn't an appealing idea. Candy didn't like to beg or ask favors. Speaking to Frankie had been enough. She felt herself getting angry, and her mind blanked as she got out of her car.

Enough thinking, it was time for action.

In the center of the parking lot was a little landscaped area which, in the spring, would smell of wood chips and bristle with lush leafy bushes, but was now a lumpy snow carpet. Candy hunted around and dug out a good-size rock from the snow. Carried it over to Tsipiras's Jaguar and found her range. Her two gloved hands lifted the rock up over her head and sent it hurtling into the tinted passenger side window. The rock hit with an ugly click that made Candy wince. It bounced off the glass, thunking onto the asphalt.

She stood there looking at the window, still intact. Shit.

Candy picked the rock up again and tried to find a more direct angle, this time from farther back and harder. Same thing, the rock hit and made a white mark in the glass, but it didn't go through.

She tried it again, for the third time. The rock was the size of a child's head, but it just bounced off the glass. It occurred to her that maybe Bob Tsipiras had armored windows on his Jaguar.

It was frustrating and lonely up there in the freezing

parking lot, all by herself with nobody else to turn to. She thought of the guy who had come for her sister back at the house, Keeler, and wished that he was here with her now, but she didn't even have a way of getting in touch with him, so what was she going to do about it, cry?

Candy went back to her car and looked again into the laptop screen. The battery was running down but the blue dot was still blinking in a regular pattern. Mini wouldn't just abandon her phone, that would never happen. She'd never abandon her family either, something even less plausible than the phone.

Which meant she was missing for real, and this was an emergency.

Candy picked up her phone and called her mom. No, Mini hadn't come back or called, but the kitchen was totally reorganized. Yes, the kids were in bed and sleeping, and she didn't need Candy's help; everything was under control. Which made Candy feel a little bit relieved and also made her realize that she desperately wanted a slice of cherry cheesecake from the diner, with a cup of coffee with two sugars and two creamers, please. Candy laughed to herself, a short giggle. Trying to break Bob Tsipiras's window had been borderline insane. Good thing it hadn't worked.

The engine turned over with a stutter and a grumble. Candy got her hand on the shifter, all set to make the move from park into reverse and then get down into town for some of that cherry cheesecake populating her mind. She was reaching hard for comfort in the face of the impending tragedy. A tear fell from her eye onto her cheek. Candy knew that she wasn't yet willing to accept the situation, but she felt helpless.

What the hell could she do?

The thought came to her, so obvious, immediately making sense, *Call Mini's phone again from up here, see if it rings, and then find it by the sound of the ringtone.* She switched off the ignition and plucked her phone off the passenger seat. After a couple of pecks and flicks on the screen her sister's phone number was up and ringing.

Candy stepped out of her car, phone held in her hand. The parking lot was the same lonely place that it had been before, but this time she could hear each and every little sound that made up the winter silence. The whipping of wind in the trees, the sound of snow being blown across the asphalt, the lonesome whistle of a train from down by the river, carried by its bass frequencies up into the hills.

Here comes the money.

Candy heard something else, muffled and distant but easy to place, her sister's ringtone, which was the opening of "Johnny B. Goode." Candy got super alert as she approached the Jaguar. The Chuck Berry jingle looped for the second time, but she seemed to be getting farther away from it. She turned to her right and moved toward a row of parked vehicles clustered together on the way to the club house. The jingle looped for the third time, closer. Candy slowed down and tried to identify its source. Not the first vehicle, or the second. She passed the third vehicle as the jingle came around for the fourth time. At the fourth car Candy realized that she was moving away from the sound.

She turned back and looked at the third vehicle in the row. A silver Dodge SUV, not the big luxury model, but a small stubby well-used runner, wheel wells crusted with winter residue of mud and road salt. Now that she saw it, Candy realized that the Dodge stuck out from the group of parked cars. This wasn't a luxury car like the others, it was a base model a decade old and didn't belong up at the golf course, as much a stranger as Candy's own plucky little Subaru.

The jingle stopped. Minerva's prerecorded voice came from

Candy's phone. "Hi there, thanks for calling. Leave a message and I'll get back to you."

Not the most original message in the world, but a practical one. That was her sister, pragmatic and good.

Candy approached the stubby Dodge. She'd already looked in and hadn't seen a phone. Candy rubbed at the grimy hatchback with her gloved hand and her sleeve until she could see inside. It was dark in there, the parking lot lighting barely penetrating. She removed her glove and got her phone into flashlight mode. Candy pressed the light to the window and the back of the Dodge SUV lit up. A red and blue plaid blanket was thrown over something.

She stared at the lumpy blanket, the shape of it impossible to accept as her sister's body. Candy stepped away for a moment, unsure of how to continue, disoriented. She breathed deep and came back, peered straight down near the inside of the hatchback door. and passed the light from her phone over the contours of the blanket. Candy staggered back.

Great heaving sobs came from deep inside, incapacitating her. After a minute, she got her breath back. She went to pick up the rock that she had used on Tsipiras's Jaguar. But then her wits came back and she knew that she couldn't break the window on the Dodge; the police would need to investigate, and she couldn't disturb the scene.

She gave a great heaving gasp and stifled the keening cry that was attempting to come out of her throat.

The rock thudded into the cold asphalt at her feet. She took her phone in trembling fingers and called Mini's number again. The Chuck Berry guitar riff looped again, four times before Mini's voice answered.

"Hi there, thanks for calling. Leave a message and I'll get back to you."

Her next call was to Frankie. This time he wasn't able to

raise any arguments against coming up to the golf course, although she could tell by his voice that the misogynist prick still didn't believe her. Candy looked into the back of the Dodge, at the form under the blanket. She'd decided that it wasn't Mini's body in there until she saw it. Only when she saw it herself would she allow that feeling of vertigo to take her down.

CHAPTER TWENTY-FIVE

Keeler took a couple of steps out of the kitchen to stand at the intersection of two corridors. The part up ahead Keeler had already seen, because he'd been right outside of it, looking in the window at the frightened woman and the guy.

Keeler made the left. The ceilings were high with exposed oak beams. He came to a door with the number five on it, and a hotel-style locking mechanism. He touched the keycard to the door and watched the green light wink at him, accompanied by a whir and a click. He pushed the door open an inch to see that the room was dark, then let it swing shut on its own weight. He kept on walking until he hit the middle of the curve, from there he was able see down to where the corridor opened up into a larger room. Looked like the front of the place, maybe the reception, lively and warmly lit, animated by moving bodies too far away to distinguish. The dinging of glassware and tinkling laughter indicated a little alcoholic social lubrication.

Keeler stood a moment looking down the way and then reversed in the other direction. Story of his life, when people engage in a group activity, do exactly the opposite. Except there was a good practical reason for it in this case: if everyone was at the party, their rooms would be available to search. He had the master key.

Up ahead around the curve a man coughed and a woman's voice asked if he was okay. They sounded older, maybe the couple he'd disturbed before. It wouldn't be optimal if the woman recognized him. Keeler backtracked to the closed door in the center of the curved corridor, number five, and touched the keycard to the lock. A whirr and a click and the light winked green. The door snicked shut behind him and the voices cut out immediately. Top-notch sound proofing.

The room was pitch-black. After a while he was able to make out the faint outline of blackout curtains. Keeler moved to the window and drew a section of curtain. Despite the lack of light, the white field of snow pulsated with an internal lumines-cence. Against that, he made out two silhouettes swinging flash-lights as they trudged through the knee-deep snow.

The two security guards didn't look very concerned, prob-ably still discussing the geopolitics of pizza. The night table lamp was in reach, and Keeler pressed the button and got noth-ing. He crossed the room to put his keycard into the slot by the door, activating the electricity. The lamp hummed and Keeler turned to its warm glow. The lamp shade was a glowing pyra-mid, behind it the cream wall paper had a barely visible vertical gold stripe every couple of inches.

The suite featured a king-size bed and a section of sofa facing an armchair, with a coffee table between them. The windows were lined with natural wood benches. A modern armoire took up most of the wall space opposite the bed. Inside the open armoire hung five men's suits wrapped in cellophane. Next to the suits were shelves stacked with clothing. Whoever was in the room was male with a taste in clothing that ranged from baggy sweatpants and hoodies to jeans and a wool turtleneck. Keeler inspected the paper tag around the hanger of one of the suits: "Jim's Formal Wear, Peekskill, New York."

The suit was dark gray, approaching black. The tag had no measurements, only a number. The one that he was looking at was number five. The others had identical tags, different numbers. Keeler lifted number four from the rack and looked at it critically. In the Air Force there had been uniform regulations. It had been important to know the measurements of nameplate, braid, chevron, and ribbon—and the distance of each element from seam, edge of sleeve, and elbow, among other points.

As far as Keeler could tell, these suits wouldn't fit him, not even close.

The door lock whirred and clicked. Keeler had the cellophane wrapped suit held between himself and the door.

A woman's voice, slightly out of breath. "You're back. I saw the light on." The door closed and Keeler hung the suit on the rack and saw a woman, leaned back against the closed door. If she was surprised to see him, she didn't show it. She was slim, midforties with silver-streaked dark hair and wore a sweater tucked into a medium gray wool skirt. "Oh. You're early. Who gave you the key to his room?"

CHAPTER TWENTY-SIX

K eeler looked back at her, seemingly calm while his mind whirred and tumbled, sorting information and data points. The woman was comfortable to be inside the room with him, alone, which suggested that she knew him, but clearly not as an individual person. She knew him as a person who was early, meaning someone who was scheduled to show up.

He took a stab in the dark. "I got the keycard from the guy at the front desk."

She blinked once, slowly. "He wasn't supposed to give you anything."

"Part of my skill set, the art of suggestion. I used to be a magician."

"Really?"

Keeler said, "Sure."

She blinked once again. "Far as I know Jerry's waiting on you down at the station. Should I call and tell him you made your own way?"

"Good idea."

"What about the others?"

Keeler took another stab in the dark. "Not coming, it's just me." She opened her mouth to speak, but nothing came out. He jerked a thumb at the suits. "For me?"

The woman was manipulating a phone, eyes down and concentrated. She threw a single glance at Keeler, and he knew he'd screwed up. It was clearly not for him. This was somebody else's room, the person that she had expected to find. She held the phone in one hand, the same way people hold canapés at cocktail parties, right before popping them into a waiting mouth, or so Keeler had heard.

The phone was on speaker, a man's gruff voice answered. "Yeah."

The woman spoke slowly, looking into Keeler's eyes. "Jerry the guy showed up, he said you can come back because he's already here. Got in early I guess."

Jerry said, "A guy? I asked for a team."

"Evidently it's a team of one, hopefully the A-Team." Her eyelids had settled low, eyelashes heavy with mascara.

On the other end of the line was silence, finally broken by Jerry. "Did you call them without me? We already had this discussion."

"No. I didn't call them. The guy showed up, one guy. He said they just sent him. Don't blame me, Jerry."

"All right, don't yell at me either."

The woman hung up the phone and slipped it into the waist band of her skirt. She shook a few strands of hair out of her eyes and looked up at Keeler. "Why do men always think a woman's yelling when she's only telling the man he's wrong?"

Keeler said nothing. She filled the empty space.

"I wanted one very good man for security, but Jerry wanted a team. He's into teams. Like football versus tennis. I'm more of a tennis person than a football person." She shrugged as if it was fate that had decided in the end. "Where did they get you, ex-military?"

Keeler didn't know what the correct answer would be, so he decided to continue the nonresponsiveness. He looked at her, eyes to eyes. What was she thinking?

She looked away. "If you're hungry, I've left a chicken out in the kitchen." Mascara thickened lashes lifted to observe his reaction.

"I already ate."

"You did, where?"

"The diner."

"All roads lead to the diner." The woman sat on the edge of the bed.

Keeler said, "So, this is his room."

"Correct. The protagonist's room."

"What do you mean, the protagonist?"

She said, "Codename. When we're talking about a high-value person, we use that, because there's always the danger of someone overhearing the name."

"Which wouldn't be a good thing."

"No, it wouldn't." She observed him. "You're new to this."

Keeler shrugged. "I'm quite experienced actually, just not so experienced in the civilized aspects."

"Well, it's like with the president and the secret service. They don't use their actual names, they use code names." She bunched her fist and raised her finger. "Trump was Mogul. Obama was Renegade. Clinton was Eagle." She ticked the names off and then opened up her hand, flexing it. "Here we're just using the protagonist because Jerry used to be in theater back in the day. We've never done this, to be completely honest."

"Used a codename."

"Never needed to provide security for a protagonist."

Keeler jerked his thumb at the collection of suits. "These all his, the protagonist's?"

A shrug. "Never know what's going to fit and I heard he doesn't stand for measurements, so I got five of them. Looking at the pictures he's a skinny little thing, so the thin and tall one should fit."

He sat beside her on the bed and looked at the woman. "Kind of old-fashioned, wearing a suit."

She said, "I don't think he'll wear it."

"What kinds of threats are you expecting? Why get protection up here now, if the guy's been here for a while already?"

She looked at him, her gaze making an evaluation. "They didn't brief you at all?"

"Humor me."

When she opened her mouth to speak, she made a slight smacking sound. "Okay, well, I'm not the client. The conference organizer insisted." She studied him. "Until now it's been real small scale, just him and a couple of others working on stuff. We run residency programs where people can do research together in a nice environment. The conference starts tomorrow: two days and organized and paid for by a different foundation." She gestured to Keeler. "Hence the security requests. It's open to the general public. Maybe they figured it's best to have someone like you on hand. You never know."

"That's for damned sure. So you're what, his manager?"

"No." She laughed and shook her head. "These people don't have managers. They kind of wander around the world in a haze of wellness," she said, as if describing a wonderful new species. She got into it, using her hands. "Like they're in some kind of a Zen state, a flow state, know what I mean? They meditate and play ping-pong and stuff. They focus on what they eat and get nuts about it. Like one day it's all meat; next day it's like only vegetables the color purple or something. You can't make it up. They spend all their time trying to live forever. Funniest thing is they're all supposed to be workaholics, but nobody ever sees them do it."

"Do what?"

"Work."

"Sounds like you know a couple of billionaires."

"You bet I do. Started off on yachts, then went into massage but there's no longevity in that."

"So what now?"

"Now I'm in events." She spread her arms around, indicating the place, Copenhagen House.

"When does this protagonist show up?"

The woman looked straight ahead, into the mirror, seeing them both there on the bed. Looked like the view sobered her. "He walked out of here, said he wanted to get some air. Hasn't been back since, but I hear that's normal for him. He had camping gear with him. Maybe he's building an igloo. We have a masterclass scheduled for tomorrow at eleven, so we assume he'll make it by then." She put a hand on the bed cover between their knees. "Apparently he does tend to, you know, be a little unpredictable."

Keeler let himself fall back against the mattress. "What else can you tell me about him?"

He pulled himself up, saw the woman looking at him with her lazy eyes, shaking hair out of her face. "Two things you need to know about the protagonist. He might be the richest person in the world, nobody knows. The other thing is he looks like he's sixteen years old, when in fact he's more like thirty."

"How come nobody knows how much money he's got?"

"Because it's not money yet; it's crypto." She patted Keeler's knee. "You're sitting awful close. Sexual tension makes me thirsty. Can we go get a drink? You can meet the crypto people before the protagonist shows up, and you need to get serious."

Keeler laughed. "What's your name?"

"Jill," she said, looking at him with humor in her eyes. "You're really not who I expected they'd send."

He waited for her to ask his name but she didn't, and he realized that there was a reason for that. The guy she was expecting wasn't the kind of guy whose name you want to get to know. Which was fine and everything, but evidently a team of real security men were on their way up. Even if Jerry aborted the train station pickup, they would still arrive.

But that was going to happen in the future. In the present there was only Keeler and Jill and whatever was going on out there in the reception.

CHAPTER TWENTY-SEVEN

Out in the corridor, Keeler kept pace with Jill, who was slightly ahead of him and on his left. Walking slow, looking relaxed and casual in her wool skirt and tucked in sweater. Her eyes, wary and experienced and getting ready for contact with the crypto people. Among the many things that Keeler didn't know, but high up on the list of what he wanted to know, was what any of this had to do with Vince Farrell.

Keeler wondered how long he'd be able to maintain the charade.

Jill surprised him. "So tell me something, how many people have you killed?"

Keeler looked at her, glancing at him, wary and aroused and kind of interested in an answer. He looked away from her, down the hall and kept his voice flat and serious, like a bodyguard. "I never counted."

She didn't respond, just accepted that as an answer. Ran her tongue over dry lips and looked up ahead at the people milling around in the well-lit reception area.

Up at the entrance, two well-dressed men stood just inside the doorway. Young guys in their twenties, well fed and tall with good shoulders and organized hairstyles above chiseled facial geometry. Gatekeepers, both looking at Keeler. They already knew Jill and were sizing up her new companion.

Jill's phone barked, like a dog. It was a ringtone. She stopped walking about ten feet shy of the entrance and turned away to take the call. Keeler waited for her, peeking in at the reception, liking what he was seeing: Informally dressed people with oddball fashion sensibilities, maybe from Brooklyn, looking like they were having a good time. Servers threading through the crowd with silver platters of nibbles in various shades and forms.

Jill was listening intently to her phone, like she couldn't hear properly. Her eyes swiveled to Keeler, looking at him, expression turning horrified and then angry. Which wasn't the kind of reaction Keeler was hoping for. He thought, well there goes that. The charade was over.

She brought the phone down. "Who the hell are you?"

He thought, Jerry figured it out. Or, more likely the train had arrived, unpacking hired muscle to be transported up into the hills. No doubt Jerry and the crew from the city had questions.

Keeler allowed his shoulders to relax and soften, kept his arms at his sides, palms open. In for a dime, in for a dollar. "I'm Irma Rosenbaum's brother."

Jill coughed in a single violent convulsion, glancing at the two guys holding up the door, then back at Keeler. "What kind of an asshole psychopath are you, how could you say that?"

The big men advanced. The one coming from the left spoke. "Is there a problem, ma'am?"

Keeler thought, *Oh man.* He held up his hands, pleading good intentions. "I'm kidding. Did you know Irma Rosenbaum?"

The bouncers were looking at Jill. She was staring at Keeler, open-mouthed. "Throw this man out and make it unpleasant please, Jimmy."

"How unpleasant do you want it, ma'am?"

She was still looking at Keeler but turned away then, with a confused expression. "Just regular."

The phone was in Jill's hand again, and he realized that she'd never hung up. As the two men converged, he heard her talking into the phone, "Okay, we'll talk in a few." Then a pause and she nodded and said yes and returned the phone to her waistband.

The big guy who had spoken gestured toward a recessed opening immediately before the doorway. Three steps down and a foyer led to a courtyard entrance. "If you'll come this way please, sir. It's the shortest way to the exit."

Keeler complied, seeing Jill standing near the door, small but well-proportioned in her classy outfit, and shaking with anger. He wondered what Jerry was like and realized he might be about to find out, since it seemed as if Jerry was due from the station at anytime.

He let the bouncers shadow him out into the cold. The door led to a graveled footpath sunk into large piles of shoveled snow. The two men were looking at him, something glinting in the silent one's eyes as he rubbed his hands together. The other one said, "Sorry but she wanted you to have an unpleasant experience. We'll make it as comfortable as possible. Comfortable for something unpleasant, that is."

Keeler looked at them both, two big men in suits standing there thinking about violence. He said, "How do you intend to do that?"

"Do what?"

"Make something unpleasant into something comfortable."

"Usually we just do it fast and then it's over. That all right with you, sir?"

Keeler felt good standing there in his hiking boots and winter jacket. More than good, he felt invincible. Which these two guys couldn't understand. The grin on Keeler's face was involuntary. The mute guy wasn't liking it, he started to make grumbling noises. The other guy began nodding rhythmically, maybe psyching himself up.

"Look fellas," Keeler said, "it's best if you turn around and go back inside. It's warm in there, and you'll definitely feel more comfortable. Tell Jill you did it and that it was truly unpleasant but still relatively comfortable."

"Then we'd be lying. You saying me and my brother are liars?"

Keeler thought, *Oh boy.*

The mute one came in first, lunging low, aiming to sweep the legs out from under him, dump him onto the gravel. They'd use their feet then, kicking him senseless without putting any strain on their suits or hairstyles. The other one had his feet spread apart, ready to rock once his brother had finished the first part. They'd done it before, maybe often.

Keeler didn't dodge away or anything tricky like that. He stepped into the mute's lunge and met him halfway. The steel-tipped toe of his boot swung up in a tight arc, clicking into the place where jaw and chin meet and bone attaches to skull. The impact made a loud snap, startling the otherwise peaceful winter landscape. The mute brother skidded to the gravel like a bundle of wet rags.

The talkative one looked down at the unconscious body, then up. Keeler said, "Take him in, feed him some of that roast chicken Jill left for the help. He'll be okay."

"What about Jill? I'll have to lie to her."

Keeler shrugged. "I guess so. Not your fault if you think about it. She asked you to do something you can't do, beyond your competency. You never signed up for this, remember that."

Headlights raked the other side of a hedge, and the crunch of tires on gravel ate up the renewed silence. Keeler couldn't see the vehicle through the bush but figured it might be Jerry. The talkative brother was looking at him, mean, like he hadn't heard the warning. It wasn't clear if he was going to accept the recommendation or not. The headlights from the approaching vehicle cut across his face, momentarily blinding him.

Keeler stepped in and punched hard, right into his mouth. The man sat down on the gravel, the shock of it knocking his hair out of place. Keeler crouched in front of him, a hand on his shoulder. "Jimmy, right?" The bouncer nodded, mouth bloody. Strands of hair fell over his eyes, which looked far off still. Keeler smoothed the hair back in place, feeling the gel or whatever he'd put in there. "Good. Hope I don't see you again, know what I mean?"

Jimmy felt his teeth. "I think so."

Keeler stood, knees cracked. Time to get a look at Jerry and the guys.

The hedge was too tall to see over, but it was winter bare and Keeler found a patch where he could look through. The driver was out of the vehicle, a polished black Mercedes S-Class. He was large bellied and tall with the kind of pulled back ponytail balding guys sometimes go for. That was Jerry, sporting a white-streaked goatee to go with the receding ponytail. He carried a small beige dog of indeterminate breeding in his arms. The plate was New York state, and Keeler committed the number to memory. Besides Jerry, hard men wearing comfortable clothes were unpacking themselves from the vehicle, one after the other.

Keeler had half expected to see Vince Farrell come out of the Mercedes. That didn't happen, just men he didn't know. Three of them so far, two carrying small backpacks and one guy with a duffel, enough space for toiletries and a single change of clothes, maximum. They weren't up there for long. A fourth guy emerged from the vehicle with a crew cut and a close-cropped beard to match. The guy was stacked like a rugby player and as languid as a python. Sometimes you see guys like that, impossibly wide and somehow unencumbered by the muscle. He looked like he could kill the other three men just by blowing on them.

Keeler watched him move, thinking if he had to tangle with that guy, it wouldn't be like those two kids he'd just put down. The men shook out stiff legs and rumpled shirts and filed after Jerry to the house. Security men from the city were unlikely to fit in with the crypto nerds, but maybe that was the point, to project a certain look, like extras in a B movie.

Keeler worked his way out of the courtyard and past the guardhouse. In the window, the two security men were still good-naturedly debating something. One of them made eye contact and nodded in a friendly way.

The front gate opened as Keeler approached, motors whirring on command. A camera's impersonal eye winked at him as he passed. The red dot of a laser sensor flicked over his leg and he was out, the gate closing behind.

A minute later it was just as it had been before, when Keeler had arrived at Copenhagen House, cold and silent and quietly beautiful. He studied the surroundings, thinking about the protagonist. There was still a lot to learn, but it was time to check in with the DeValla family, see if the train conductor had been in touch.

CHAPTER TWENTY-EIGHT

Frankie called Candy over. He was leaning his large frame against the stone wall, talking to the diner guy. He didn't have the bloody wad in his mouth anymore. Tsipiras was nodding at Frankie, looking like an evil frog with his weird head of fake hair. Candy had been outside for long enough that she was cold, even with her fancy parka. A light snow drifted in the air, caught by headlights and the clubhouse lamps. Frankie towered over Tsipiras, the little man from Corfu, talking out the corner of his mouth, then looking at her again in his demanding, demeaning way.

"Yo. Come over here, Candy."

Frankie had called one of the on-duty cops up to the golf course. The guy was sitting in his cruiser, staying warm. It was Frankie who'd opened up the Dodge, making the call. They hadn't found Minerva's body in back. What they'd found was her phone under the blanket, which had been thrown over a bunch of clothes.

When Candy had seen that it wasn't her sister's dead body in the back of the shitty Dodge she felt a flood of relief. She'd laughed once, like a kind of embarrassing bark of emotion.

They'd all looked at her with these angry expressions, like she'd rained on someone's parade. She didn't care at all that a whole bunch of people had mobilized. Obviously they were pissed off, but whatever. Her sister wasn't a corpse in the back of a crappy car, so there was still hope.

Candy watched Frankie and Tsipiras, analyzing them, figuring out what they were thinking. Tsipiras was pissed because they'd pulled everyone out of the club just to see who owned the Dodge. He was at the age and position where he expected everything to be for his comfort. Frankie was pissed because he'd been watching his favorite show on TV.

Turned out nobody at the club knew who owned the Dodge.

Candy walked over to the wall. Tsipiras stopped talking and both men looked at her. Frankie's eyes were bloodshot and he smelled of beer. He had Mini's phone in his big hand, extended to Candy.

"Here, take the phone."

Candy said, "Aren't you supposed to be putting that in like, an evidence bag, Frank?"

"Evidence of what?" He leered at Tsipiras, who was expressionless.

"Of whatever. Why was her phone in this car?"

Frankie shook his head, playing the big cop. "It's her phone, Candy. She can do as she likes with it. This is a free country."

Candy was almost mute with frustration. Frankie had agreed to open the vehicle but hadn't done anything further when it had become clear that Mini wasn't in there.

Tsipiras made her think of cherry cheesecake again.

Candy stepped back to get a breath. She inhaled through her nose, four seconds, then out through her mouth for another four seconds. Did a couple of reps and felt better.

Frankie had run the plate number, but wouldn't tell her

who the owner was. Said it was private information. Candy pocketed Mini's phone and used hers to snap a picture of the Dodge's license plate.

"Are they going to give this guy a ticket at least, for parking up here?"

Frankie shrugged. "Private property. I guess someone will give them a ticket eventually, yeah. If they leave that car here. But why would they leave it here forever?"

Tsipiras cleared his throat to speak. "The club manager fired the company that used to do the tickets, because he got a ticket. Nobody comes up here in the winter anyway." He shrugged. "Probably going to hire another company by spring, I guess."

Candy couldn't understand it. "Nobody's even remotely suspicious of this vehicle?"

Frankie looked at Tsipiras, who spoke. "Personally, I've left my car up here at the club when I've had a couple of drinks and someone gives me a ride home." He wiped at his nose. "I get a ride back in the morning and pick up the car. It's safe up here." He looked at Frankie. "I think a lot of people do that."

Candy stared at Frankie. "Is that what you think it is? They left the car up here for convenience?"

Frankie gave her a fatigued and bored look. "Tell you the truth, I do. I think she's with some guy. Met up with him after work." His eyes lit up. "Maybe even *met* him on the train. Maybe they picked up some beers and came up to hang out, or in the woods or something." He looked over at Tsipiras. "Then they decide to go to the guy's place, but the guy's had a few too many, so they leave his car up here and take hers to his place or something. Whatever it is, there was a reason for her being in the guy's car."

Candy couldn't believe it. "You're an asshole, Frankie, you know that?"

"If you say so. I'll just get on back to my three-day vacation, if you don't mind."

"I do say so." She looked at the woods surrounding the golf course, dark and cold and foreboding. They were up in the hills, the forest going for miles and miles to the north and east, only ending at the reservoir. "And you don't think it's prudent to search in the woods? Maybe you're right and they parked here to get into the woods, but not to hang out. It's fucking freezing up here. Why would anyone want to go hang out in the woods?"

She watched Frankie's face and knew that his little mind was calculating how to get rid of her. He was the youngest of four siblings, three of them sisters, which made him kind of dangerous. He said, "You see any footprints in the snow, Candy? You want to tell me how someone gets into the woods from here with an unwilling hostage without stepping on fresh fallen snow, I'm all ears."

The lot was surrounded by meadow, cut neat in the good weather, now a blanket of white. It was too dark to really investigate, plus there was snow falling, which made it harder to see and could have obliterated prints made earlier. Candy wasn't satisfied in any way, shape, or form, but she wasn't going to stand there arguing with the asshole either. She was going down to the diner for coffee and cheesecake, then she'd see.

CHAPTER TWENTY-NINE

The diner was warm and welcoming. Dinnertime, families getting their usuals with all the trappings. The place smelled of garlic bread, marinara sauce, and coffee. Behind the counter a short guy with thick black hair was scooping vanilla ice cream from a tub into the blender. Candy watched him pour in the milk, add some Oreos and chopped nuts from the ice cream topping unit. The blender closed and hummed when the guy activated it. Three pulses was all he needed. The result was poured into a milkshake glass and whipped cream was added.

Candy had eaten half of her cherry cheesecake before turning her attention to the milkshake operation. But something smelled funny, like a campfire. She looked to her left and saw that a guy had taken the stool next to her. She looked at him, but he was not looking at her, instead looking around at everything else. He removed a technical winter parka that looked like it'd been through a couple of wars. The guy wore a tie-dyed t-shirt over thermal underwear and started stuffing his parka under the top flap of a hiker's backpack with a tent and everything strapped to the bottom. He had dirty blond hair in a bushy clump on his head. He was kind of goofy, but when he finally did look at her, his deep-set eyes were bright and lively.

"Hi."

Candy smiled briefly and looked down at the half-eaten cheesecake. The cherries were set into a red glaze: corn starch, sugar, and food coloring with some kind of fake cherry flavor added, she figured. It didn't pay to inquire deeply into the diner's ingredients.

The skinny guy was studying the menu, and she figured it would be neighborly to help out. "Get breakfast or go Greek in here, it's what everyone says."

He looked up slowly. "Really, huh." The words said as a question turned into a statement by the extended *huh*, like isn't that something.

She said, "You can suit yourself and get lost in the menu, but I'm recommending the safe and standard way."

He went back to the menu. "Funny. I was just thinking about that. It's like there's breakfast and there's Greek, and in between you have all kinds of strange and unusual options." The guy flipped to page seven and ran a finger down. "Okay, have you ever in your life tried the hot open-faced turkey sandwich with pan gravy and cranberry sauce?"

"I don't know. Might have. I've been coming here since I was a kid. I wouldn't exclude the possibility that I've had that at some point."

He flipped back a page. "What about grilled American cheese with French fries?"

"A classic. Get it with bacon and get gravy on the fries."

"Oh wow!" He opened his eyes wide and grinned with all of his teeth. She couldn't help but smile in return.

A waitress came to the other side of the counter, rested her hand on the Pyrex cookie platter lid, and addressed the new guy. "What can I get you, hon?"

The guy's smile was relentless. "Hello. I'll have the grilled American cheese with bacon and gravy fries."

She wrote it in her book, looking up to say, "Bacon and gravy are extra, okay?"

"Sure. Coffee also with two sugars and a lot of cream."

"It comes with creamer and the sugar's right here." She indicated the large glass dispenser clustered with the ketchup and mustard in front of him.

"Great, thank you."

He looked at Candy. "Thanks."

"I didn't do anything."

"Okay, well you're here, so thanks anyway."

"Whatever. Are you always this smiley?"

The guy looked up into space. "You're the first person I've spoken to in, uh, say, four days." He looked at her. "And last year I did a laughter retreat, so maybe that's why I'm smiling, in addition to you being the first person I've spoken to in a while."

"What's a laughter retreat?"

"You laugh all day, even if you have to force it. You'd be surprised at how hard that is to sustain over six days."

Candy tried to imagine that, forcing yourself to laugh, basically pretending to be happy, for six days. It sounded like something that people did in California. "That sounds truly terrible, man. You're a glutton for punishment."

The skinny guy's laugh seemed natural. "Truth be told, some of it kind of sucked, but it was interesting too, from a human perspective."

"Sounds to me more like a form of torture."

"I guess the fact that people even *want* to do it is kind of interesting to me." He glanced up at her with his deep-set eyes. "You know, flying out there to India to participate in such an extreme activity. Not only participating, but paying for it."

"No shit. They pay to do that?"

He nodded vigorously. "They do. They pay a shitload of money to be, basically, punished like children."

"People just aren't brought up right anymore, end up paying for their own torture in India."

The guy was looking at her soberly. "You have a point there." He hopped off his stool. "Gonna use the john before the food comes." He grinned at her. "Save my seat!"

Candy watched him go back and around the counter to the bathroom. She realized that he had actually been listening to her, not just talking at her. She liked that. The waitress came and set down his coffee cup. Candy lifted the cup off the saucer and put it down on the counter again with the saucer on top, retaining heat. There was a noise and she looked back at the entrance.

Four hard-looking men had come in, talking loudly amongst themselves, like they didn't care at all what anyone thought. The kind of hard-looking guys who made men focus on their plates in order to avoid eye contact. Exactly the kind of guys Candy detested, like Frankie.

But unlike Frankie, these guys didn't look like they enjoyed slumping on the couch pounding beers. Looked like they got off on pumping iron and doing high-intensity, high-impact work-outs combined with live-fire weapons training.

The diner was crowded, no booths or tables to spare. She saw Bob Tsipiras's son Nick trying to speak to the group calmly, indicating the waiting area.

There were five stools at the counter where Candy sat. Presently, four were unoccupied, but that was only because the new guy was in the bathroom. She felt four sets of eyes on her, knew they were flicking between her body, face, and the empty stools. Candy didn't look at the men directly, feeling them seeking eye contact as they surveilled her.

Candy hated when men searched for eye contact.

CHAPTER THIRTY

After getting out of Copenhagen House, Keeler had walked up the road to the Toyota. He started the engine and let it run for a while to warm up, which got him thinking about Jill and the whole scene up there, the conference for crypto developers and the guy she'd referred to as the protagonist, who was apparently leading a masterclass in the morning.

He thought back to the situation in the room. The fact that she'd immediately assumed he was part of the protection team made Keeler smile, right there in the Toyota by himself.

Then there was crypto. Keeler had seen it before on a computer, the long string of numbers and letters, but he didn't know much about it, other than the basics. There were two of those strings: one public and one private. You didn't keep crypto in a bank; you just memorized your private string and didn't write it down or tell it to anyone because if you did that, you could lose it all in a hot second.

Basically, the idea was that a bank is for someone who doesn't trust her own memory, crypto is for people who do.

Keeler knew that there was more to crypto than that, enough to explain a conference and heavy hitters and protection. What it didn't explain was the connection to the laptop and Farrell. Then there was Irma Rosenbaum, the woman in white. Keeler had thrown the name out to Jill just for the hell of it, a provocation to see what came back. He hadn't gotten much, truth be told, but Jill had seemed to know who Rosenbaum was, which didn't surprise Keeler.

He came out of his thought tunnel and realized it'd been a half hour since he'd started up the engine. Keeler considered his options. Might be a good idea to swing by the *Kitchewan Gazette* offices to see if Julie Everard was still working. She'd have a good computer with a large screen, websites to go to and investigative techniques to use once she got onto those websites. Maybe there was something there about Jill and Jerry connected to Copenhagen House.

Keeler was just coming out of his reflections when the trees ahead were flashed by headlight beams. A vehicle was exiting the gate. He waited half a minute and followed. Keeler recognized Jerry's car. He kept back and let the road twist and turn down into town. A little while later, he watched the big vehicle enter the diner's parking lot.

Keeler drove past and made a u-turn up the hill. He came back to park in the lot, just in time to see the four guys from the city going into the restaurant. He should have guessed, having watched them egress from Jerry's car back at the house, that one roasted chicken wasn't going to do it.

Keeler waited a few minutes and figured they'd be staying to eat. He shifted the Toyota out of park and was just about to give the engine gas when Candy DeValla came skipping down the stairs, followed by a lanky guy with a hiker's backpack slung over one shoulder. They were deep in conversation, focused on each other. The guy's jeans were worn and he had the unkempt look of a person who wasn't too concerned with things like laundry and shower gel.

Keeler put the shifter back into park and watched them for a minute.

The two were high energy, speaking about something in excited tones. The lanky kid had a take-out box in his hand. They came across the lot and stopped in front of a well-used Subaru. Candy was fiddling in her purse for the keys. Keeler put the vehicle into drive but kept the lights off. He cruised across the lot and came up next to them.

The electric window came down, letting in freezing air. "Hey, Candy."

She looked up from her purse, saw him, and her face lit up with recognition. "Hey." She approached his window. "I was just going back to Mini's. What's going on?"

Keeler looked up at her. "Any news?"

She cast her eyes down. "Yes and no. I found her phone up at the golf course. Cops won't do anything about it, not even Frankie." She looked at him. Keeler was looking right back at her. She said, "I know, I shouldn't be surprised about that."

Keeler said, "Where exactly was the phone found?"

"Someone's car."

"Whose?"

"They won't say and they aren't going to investigate."

Keeler considered the new information. "Police don't investigate a missing person until they're gone for a very long time." He thought for a moment. "What was the car doing up at the golf course. Is the owner a member?"

"I don't think so. Didn't look like that kind of a car."

Keeler looked away from her, shifted his gaze to the kid who had opened up the container and was leaning against Candy's Subaru biting into half of a grilled cheese sandwich. He looked comfortable in his expensive technical parka. Keeler said, "If her phone was found in a car, we can at least find out who owns it. Did you get the plate number?"

Candy stared at him for a second and then started digging furiously in her bag. She came up with her phone and showed him the picture she'd taken. Keeler took the phone and examined it. He memorized the plate number and handed the phone back. Looked into Candy's eyes and said, "Bingo."

"What, how does that help us?" she asked.

"Your sister's ex is a cop. What is he, some kind of big guy in the local force?"

"Deputy chief, so what?"

"Deputy chief gets his own vehicle, like you said, which would be parked at his house. Cops have computers in their vehicles. You log on to one of those and you can run the plate."

"Frankie thinks Mini met some guy on the train. Thinks they were fooling around up at the golf course and then took her car to his place."

"What do you think about Frankie's theory?"

"That it's total bullshit. It's a spot for teenagers, but Mini wouldn't go there."

Keeler locked eyes with her again. "Correct. I only met your sister once, and I know it's total bullshit. Let's go break into Frankie's car."

Candy's brow got furrowed quick. "That's illegal. We could get arrested."

Keeler had decided Frankie was a problem. It was entirely possible that Mini DeValla was in serious trouble. If her ex-husband wasn't going to take it seriously, someone else was going to have to step up. Keeler was ready for that.

He said, "Are we at the *I don't give a shit about that* stage yet, Candy?"

Candy gulped and her face took on a grave disposition. "We are, yes."

"All right, then." Keeler glanced at the guy behind her, finishing up the second half of his sandwich. "Who's that?"

She looked behind her. "A friend I just met. You want to follow my car?"

"No. We take this one. Jump in the back."

Candy said something to the lanky kid and opened the rear door of the Toyota. She got in first and the guy followed, lugging his heavy pack. Keeler twisted back in the driver's seat and looked at him, held out a hand.

"Tom Keeler."

The guy's hands were freezing from exposure while eating the sandwich. The take-out box smelled like French fries. The guy was grinning like an idiot but the grip was firm. "I'm Vitalek. Nice to meet you."

Vitalek smelled like a campfire. Keeler examined him for a long moment. Homeless, or insane? He looked at Candy. "You sure you want to bring your friend?"

Candy turned to Vitalek. "Listen, what I didn't tell you is that there's shit going on. We're going to go do something illegal. Come if you want, or not."

Vitalek glanced at Keeler and back to Candy. "Yeah, sure. I'm up for whatever."

Keeler smiled and shook his head. What was obvious, the two were crushing on each other. Which was funny, given the circumstances. Love can be risky, no way of avoiding that.

Keeler flicked on the headlights and put the car into drive. He looked in the rearview. Candy was making eye contact. He nodded at her, like everything was going to be all right. He could see that she was in a fragile psychological state. Half on the edge and confused, which was understandable. She blinked and looked off to the side. Headlight beams slashed over her face and then the light of an Exxon gas station sign illuminated her.

She took the light well. Whatever else this Vitalek was, it seemed like he was a lucky guy.

CHAPTER THIRTY-ONE

K eeler drove and Candy directed.
Headlights pierced the darkness, illuminating the
salt-stained road, curving northwest up into the hills. Trees
whipped by on either side. He watched Vitalek in the rearview,
taking in the scenery, enjoying himself. Saw Vitalek thinking,
obviously intelligent. Then he caught the guy's eye.

Vitalek spoke slowly, drawing out the words as if setting up
a carefully prepared appetizer. "So, what exactly are we going to
be doing? Criminally speaking."

Candy was forthright, no bullshit, just like her sister.
"Breaking into a cop car and checking out a license plate
number."

"Oh."

Keeler's face was a wall, expressionless and calm. He said,
"What do you think, Vitalek?"

The road twisted away from a streetlight, casting the young
man's face into darkness. Vitalek's voice came softly. "In terms
of what exactly?"

"In terms of how-to."

"I see. In that case . . . in terms of how to . . ." Again speaking slowly, he released one word at a time, giving away a lilt to his voice, possible Russian or Greek. "I'm guessing we're going to be trying to access a computer in his car?"

"Correct."

"And that this computer will be connected somehow to an encrypted network."

"Very likely."

Another curve and the streetlight slashed through the darkened cabin. Vitalek grinned when they made eye contact, his eyes gleaming. "Okay I get it. You're thinking there's no way the cop's going to remember his password because the moronic police bureaucracy will force them to use something ridiculous, right?"

"You got it."

"Right, so he'll have his impossible to remember password like, under the visor or something." He giggled.

Candy spoke softly. "Jesus, you two."

Keeler was grinning along with Vitalek, liking him. "So what's the actual challenge here, Vitalek?"

Vitalek snapped his fingers. "Getting into the vehicle without anyone knowing is the challenge. They'll have some kind of security system on it so you can't just break in."

Frankie lived in a small house up in the hills. The street was sparsely populated but there were neighbors. Keeler parked a good distance from the house and they sat in the car looking at it. There were two streetlights between the Toyota and the driveway in question. The deputy chief's Tahoe was parked on the incline, about fifty feet in. Keeler noted that the throw from the closest streetlight didn't cast more than fifteen feet down the drive. The vehicle was in darkness.

He said, "Does he have a dog?"

Candy leaned forward from the back. "I don't think so, no, but I haven't been here for about a year. He got the house when his mom died, moved in when Mini threw the prick out. I go there for the kids' stuff sometimes."

Keeler was thinking that the best and most straightforward plan would be for Candy to go in there and just take the keys. If anything went wrong she'd be able to bluff. He looked at the clock on the Toyota's dashboard. Twenty-two minutes after midnight. "It's late, so hopefully he's sleeping." What he didn't say, Frankie would certainly be armed, but more hesitant to do anything stupid if it was his ex-sister-in-law.

He said, "You good to go in there, Candy?"

She seemed surprised. "Me?"

"Yes. I'll help."

Vitalek said nothing. For a moment there was quiet before Candy shifted in her seat and opened the door. "All right."

Keeler's voice was soft but sharp. "Hold on." Candy paused with one foot out on the ground. He said, "We can decide not to do it. Breaking into anyone's house is risky. For a cop you can double the risk."

Keeler saw Candy chewing on her upper lip and letting it spring back before speaking.

"I have a bad feeling about Mini, so if we can get in there and it'll help find my sister, then I'm all for it. And based on what we know right now, even if this doesn't work I think it's worth trying." She was nodding to herself. "And Frankie's a prick. He kind of deserves this."

Keeler let that lie for a moment. He said, "I'm coming with you. I'll be there. The house might be locked. I'll help you get inside. Vitalek, you're going to stay here. Anything happens that merits alerting us, you honk the horn twice. Beep beep. Okay?"

"Sure."

Keeler liked the fact that this guy hadn't even asked the purpose, what this was all for. Vitalek had made up his mind about Candy DeValla, and to a lesser extent Keeler. Now, he was in for the ride.

Candy went first, because she'd been there before. Keeler followed close behind. They came down the hill through the woods, parallel to the driveway, moving slow. Keeler had said to move together, his big hand on her shoulder. At first it was weird but now, as they got to the house, it was comforting and made her feel safe and strong. Keeler had observed an external light on the porch with a motion sensor, so they'd gone around the side.

For a while they stood at the corner, observing the back. The yard seemed strange and a little different, and she didn't know why exactly. The geography was familiar: a small clearing in the woods with the yard and Frankie's shed over on the other side. Last time had been in the summer, Candy recalled. A birthday party for her nephew. Frankie had an above-ground pool back there where all the kids were splashing. He'd done a belly flop from the roof. Now there was no pool, only a jumble of angular shadows in the moonlight until she realized what it was, some kind of a hillbilly gym that had gotten snowed over because Frankie hadn't bothered to pack it away for the winter.

She broke away from the corner and they moved to the yard, Keeler's hand never leaving her shoulder. Close under the deck was a long vertical pole to stack the weights. Farther out was a man-sized contraption for pull-ups and leg lifts as well as a bench press station, all of it covered in snow.

Keeler guided her to the back porch. No light there, only the same wooden steps up to the old deck. She remembered the red-stained wood, now just pools of black in the night.

The guy moved like a cat and she never even heard him or

felt him overtake her; he was just suddenly at the back door inspecting the doorknob. She couldn't see exactly what he was doing and moved closer. Candy felt a jolt realizing he had a large knife that she hadn't even seem him take out.

There was a soft click and the door inched open. She thought, *Who is this guy?*

CHAPTER THIRTY-TWO

Keeler looked up at her and nodded approval. They'd talked before about the plan. Candy knew where Frankie dropped his keys and wallet at the entrance of the little house. There was a side table right by the front door and he had a bowl for his keys. The wallet was right by it and above that, out of child's reach, was a cabinet where he kept his service weapon.

Keeler had insisted, if the keys weren't in the place she thought they'd be then she would just get out and they'd find another solution or abort.

Candy stepped out of her boots and placed each socked foot over the threshold, one by one. She moved inside, stepping the way Keeler had showed her. Heel first roll down the balls of your feet. It worked, making no sound. It was strange entering that house, where she'd been before, this time in pitch-black darkness. She could close her eyes and it would be no different, although she didn't want to do that because maybe she'd at least be able to make out shapes.

She paused after a couple of steps, remembering what Keeler had said. Map out the place in your mind before moving.

Wait for your eyes to adjust. Even with no light you will still be able to see.

She pictured Frankie's house in her imagination, travelled through it mentally. It wasn't a big place. To her left was the living area in the corner. L-shaped couch with the large-screen TV on the wall. Straight ahead was clear of obstacles until the front door. To her immediate right was the kitchen, an open-plan configuration with counters wrapping around. Up ahead and to the right was the hallway leading to two bedrooms and a bathroom. There was a loft accessed by a ladder at the other side of the living room, where the kids slept when they were at Frankie's.

The refrigerator ticked and there was something else. She held her breath and heard the faint sound of Frankie breathing, which meant his bedroom door was open. The only illumination was the green glow of the oven clock and a red glow from where the TV was plugged into the extension cord by the wall. After a minute this was enough for her to basically see.

Candy started to move.

It took only a few seconds to get to Frankie's keys. They were exactly where she'd said. Her hand slid across the smooth wooden surface until she felt them, a heavy policeman's stack of metal. She fastened her hand around the keys so that they would make no sound, kept her fist tight, and started her retreat. Halfway back she stopped, right in the middle of the house, near the kitchen. Something had changed. She could feel it.

Candy closed her eyes and listened. There was nothing to hear except the ticking of the refrigerator.

She moved again and got to the threshold. The door was closed but not all the way. She figured, Keeler hadn't wanted the cold air to enter the house in case a draft made its way to Frankie. She nudged the door open with a finger and stepped through. Feeling the freezing air once again on her face, Candy felt the tension in her jaw and relaxed it.

She stepped into her boots and bent to tie the laces. Candy stood up and turned to the darkened orifice of Frankie's open back door. Looking into the dark she had a flash realization. What she'd heard, the fridge ticking. What she hadn't heard, Frankie's breathing. What happened in the next three seconds felt like it lasted minutes.

The darkness of Frankie's house boiled in front of her. There was a metallic click. A large shadow came through the door. The moon was still obscured by heavy clouds. She couldn't see that it was Frankie, but she smelled him, that aftershave he wore. He was moving to her, she realized, without knowing who she was. She saw the dull shape of something held in his hand, extended to her and realized too late what it was.

The thought came to her without words, she was going to be shot.

Frankie's shadow expanded suddenly, like the darkness boiling over. There were several hard thuds in rapid succession and the sound of breath suddenly releasing. Something swept down in front of Frankie and the heavy gun fell to the snow-covered deck. There was another surprised grunt, which she knew to be Frankie's, and she heard a cracking sound before being hit by something hard, which catapulted her body against the deck's balustrade off to the side. Candy slipped and smacked her head on the rail. She fell on her ass in the snow. She looked up, saw a shape hurtling away from the house and crashing through the wooden deck railing and heard the wet thud of it landing down below in the yard.

After that, it was silent again.

Keeler had been inside the house. This is what Candy realized as she saw him step into his boots and leap down the deck stairs to the yard below. She got up off her butt and came down after him. The cloud shifted and she could see Keeler crouched over a dark blob on the ground. She came around and saw Frankie's face, pale in the moonlight, eyes open and darting frantically. Frankie's mouth was caught in the shape a child makes when he's surprised, or maybe a fish makes when out of water, trying to figure out what went wrong. He looked stuck and the shape looked wrong. It took Candy a second to understand why it was so wrong. She could see a dark shaft coming from Frankie's chest.

Frankie had impaled himself on the pole his weights were stacked on.

Candy lost it, feeling a sudden pressure, like she was underwater, the atmosphere crushing her to the bottom. In shock, ears ringing with a high-pitch keen, she opened her mouth to scream. Keeler grabbed her arm hard and squeezed. She managed to stifle the scream. Her legs buckled and she fell to her knees, gasping for air. All she could think to do was whisper, "Holy shit." She looked up at Frankie's dark form, right there in front of her and moving spasmodically. "Is he okay?" She felt an embarrassing burn after asking.

Keeler knelt in front of her and put his hand on her shoulder. He spoke very softly. "No."

"What are we going to do?"

"We're going to continue the mission, Candy."

The guy's voice was so damned reassuring, a rock of stability in the sudden nothingness that had opened up beneath her. Candy looked to Keeler, not exactly seeing him but feeling something hard and alien in him. His mission was her mission: find Mini. Frankie hadn't given a shit about her sister, and this guy did after knowing her for less than twenty-four hours. This guy wasn't going to be stopped, even by this. *Continue the mission.* She didn't know precisely how that was going to play out, but she trusted that Keeler did.

Into the abyss.

They watched as Frankie died, panting weakly and making a weird murmuring sound. The thought occurred to Candy that he'd died confused, same as he'd been in life. She felt hardened to it now, sober, seeing things in a new light.

Keeler took her hand in his, warm and dry and strong. She realized her hand was still balled up into a fist around Frankie's keys. She was done with any regret or mixed feelings about what had just happened and she didn't need anyone holding her damned hand. Candy shook free and dropped the keys into Keeler's hand.

She felt him looking at her in the dark, close and knowing. His voice was steady and soft. "Let's go."

CHAPTER THIRTY-THREE

They sat in Frankie's police vehicle, Keeler in the passenger seat and Candy in the driver's. The Tahoe interior was heavily modified. Mobile digital console, plus some other inserts that Keeler wasn't going to think about. The computer unit was touch screen with a row of buttons below the dark rectangle.

Keeler stole a glance at Candy while the system booted up and saw her staring off into space, preoccupied by her own thoughts.

Frankie's death was firmly in the "shit happens" category. It's all fine and good to be an asshole when nothing bad is happening. No real harm, no real foul. But, when the shit hits the fan, the assholes are often the first to get the back splatter.

As if reading his mind, Candy turned from the window. "You know, Frankie was an asshole. Maybe sometimes people get what they deserve."

Keeler said nothing.

He was over Frankie's death, and thinking about how things were different suddenly. Any plate numbers they looked up using Frankie's computer would be on record. Both the search query and the time and place. Once his body was found there would be an investigation. The investigators would review his computer search record as a matter of course. Nobody was going to think that a man impaled in his backyard was a suicide.

"So what happened, exactly?" Candy asked.

"I was watching him tracking you on your way back to the door. He was locked and cocked. There was no indication that he'd identified who you were, and I think he was planning to shoot you. Maybe ask questions later."

"You mean, shoot me without warning."

"You want me to be brutally honest?"

"Please."

"I think he didn't want a dead body bleeding out inside the house, so he was going to do it on the deck." Keeler turned to face her. "Anyway, he didn't shoot you—that's a good thing, right?"

"I meant what happened that made him fly off his damned deck?"

Keeler opened his hands wide. "No idea. He panicked and launched himself off the deck. Hadn't expected a second person behind him in the house, I guess." He shrugged. "The railing was weak." He made eye contact with Candy. "Shit happens."

The screen demanded a password.

Keeler said, "Check under the visor."

Candy flipped hers down and found nothing. Keeler checked the passenger side visor and the glove compartment without success. None of the other compartments elicited any better results.

Keeler said, "Maybe it could be Frankie's birthday, or his kids' birthdays."

Candy said, "I know it's November and April. But I forget the exact days."

Keeler saw her in the light from the instrument panel.

"Maybe it isn't written down here. He might have it somewhere else. Someplace he's liable not to lose it."

"His phone."

"Yes."

"I'll go in and get it."

Keeler said nothing, let her go and get it. She'd have to go past Frankie's corpse, but maybe that would be good for her. Three minutes later Candy climbed back into the vehicle, a little breathless. "It was next to his bed."

She tapped into Frankie's phone and it unlocked with a fake snick sound.

Keeler said, "How'd you do that?"

"Same as my sister's password but reversed. They used to be married."

"There should be some kind of a notes app," Keeler suggested.

"No shit." Candy swiped and tapped and pinched and spread fingers until she had it. "Are you ready? This isn't going to be memorable."

"Ready." Keeler got his fingers hovering over the touch screen keyboard."

Candy read it out. A gibberish of letters, characters, and numbers. Upper cases and lower, all designed to be impossible to remember. The interface was annoying and it took him three tries to tap it into the computer while Candy dictated. Eventually, the lock screen opened.

Front and center was a box into which Keeler entered the plate number from Candy's photo. He tapped a search button and the hit came quickly, the screen transforming into a grid featuring the driver's license image of a thirty-nine-year-old man with sandy hair. The name was Thomas Aldo Santarelli. Keeler turned the screen to her.

"This is the guy owns the Dodge up at the golf course. Know him?"

Candy wasn't sure. "I think so. I think I've seen him down at the station." She squinted. "Oh yeah. He drives a taxi. Everyone calls him Tommy."

Keeler said, "Tommy Santarelli." He was picturing the taxi stand down at the train station. The cab he'd wanted to take and the driver who'd said the last place was taken. Santarelli looked different in the picture, but it could be him, for sure. Keeler took that image and mentally pushed it to the side, compartmentalizing for the moment. "Address is 32 Harrison Street. Can you get us there?"

"Sure."

"Good. I've got a couple of other things to look up."

Keeler's list started with the plate number he'd memorized from Jerry's Mercedes, up at Copenhagen House. He punched in the three letters followed by four numbers and hit the search button. Keeler leaned back in the passenger seat as the results populated the grid.

The vehicle was registered to Jerry Altman with a New York City address. The photograph was from several years ago, when Jerry had been in his forties and had more hair. Now, he was fifty-seven years old. Keeler took a photograph of that screen as well.

Candy was curious. "Who's this guy?"

"Jerry."

"What's Jerry's story?"

"I'm not exactly sure." He looked over at Candy, remembering that she was a local. "He's a guy up at Copenhagen House. You know it?"

"The place up by the dam?"

"Maybe. What's the dam?"

"Kitchewan dam, our local claim to fame. I think it's

supposed to be the third-largest man-made stone structure in the western hemisphere. Something like that."

Keeler shrugged. "Never heard of it." He put a finger to the address. "What part of New York City is that in?"

"Manhattan, near Central Park, which means expensive. Jerry's a rich guy."

Next up was the blue Ford pickup truck. The guy who'd been hot and heavy about that laptop bag. He entered the New Jersey license plate number and hit search. The result was unexpected: not a person, but a limited-liability corporation registered in Delaware.

Keeler read the name off the screen. "Kitchewan Old Cars." He looked at Candy. "That's who Santarelli drives for?"

She looked up into the darkness for a second. "I never paid attention, but it's possible. There's only like one other taxi company in town."

"Right."

"But why is it registered in Delaware?" she asked.

"It's a tax haven."

Keeler was thinking again of the scene at the train station the night before. It was coming back to him in detail, scooped out of the part of his brain where he'd stored it a few minutes earlier. The Pontiac station wagon from the 1980s with the gold decal on the side. Kitchewan Old Cars. Then the other thing, more important; the driver had been distracted, attentively waiting on a passenger who ended up coming down off the second set of stairs crossing the tracks.

The second set of stairs led to the lost and found. The man at the lost and found had told Keeler that a relatively short man had come for the laptop bag. In Keeler's memory it was a short guy with a powerful build, who'd come out of the stairwell and taken his seat in the Pontiac.

Now, the laptop and the cab company were firmly placed as

a cluster in the constellation forming in the front of Keeler's mind.

He turned to Candy. "Okay. We're going to visit Santarelli, see if he's having a good evening."

"What are we going to do with him?"

"Nothing nice, that's for damned sure. I need to deal with your ex-brother-in-law first, though."

"What do you mean, how do we deal with that?"

Keeler had been thinking about it in another part of his mind. He'd concluded that for the moment they were going to buy time. Firstly, because they could. It was below zero outside, so preserving Frankie's body wasn't going to be a huge issue. The issue was going to be getting Frankie off the pole.

Keeler said, "I'll deal with it." He opened the door, looked at Candy, who hadn't moved. "Your job is to put the phone and keys back where you found them. I need to make an adjustment to Frankie's resting place."

At the back, Keeler hunted around for Frankie's weapon and found it under the deck. He gave her the gun and told her to put it by Frankie's bed. Candy took her boots off and went into the house. Keeler examined Frankie's body, spiked onto the pole like a kebab. He figured he could leave the body where it was, provided he was able to source a couple of things from the shed.

Keeler went in there now, prepared to scavenge, but he didn't have to look too hard. He pulled out four sheets of plywood from a stack of a dozen, some rotten, some degraded, but all capable of doing what he needed them to do. Keeler dragged the plywood out one sheet at a time and planted each into the snow around Frankie's body, building a box. Once the box was more or less established, Keeler filled it in with snow he shoveled from the surrounding accumulation, packing it around the corpse. If anything, the temperature was set to drop. Frankie would be fine where he was, preserved like salmon in a fishing boat's slush hatch.

Until someone came down to the house actually looking for him.

Candy sat on the deck steps, wordlessly watching as Keeler finished the job. He showed her how to back out of the area and wipe their boot prints from the snow using a rake he'd found in the shed. They stepped off the driveway into the woods and made their way up the incline, methodically clearing the track behind them.

The forest air was cold. The woods smelled of pine and the faint odor of a wood fire from someone's chimney. Being out in the winter night was invigorating. More so, since Keeler was on the hunt now. The serotonin kick hit him, as it always did after a death. His night vision was better than ever, and his pupils dilated, having increased with the chemical rush.

CHAPTER THIRTY-FOUR

Twenty minutes later they were sitting in the Toyota, Vitalek sleeping in the backseat, Keeler and Candy up front, looking across the road at 32 Harrison Street. Nothing more exciting than a morose porch-fronted, aluminum-sided house with the lights off. The dwelling had been split into apartments and the name *T. Santarelli* had been scribbled in black ballpoint pen on a white piece of card and inserted into a plastic sleeve affixed above one of the mailboxes by the door.

Thirty-two Harrison was among a small grid of streets that constituted the Kitchewan Landing downtown district. What Candy called *town*. Santarelli had the bottom floor. Keeler entered through the back. A window was unlocked, enabling him to slip in through the bathroom. He tumbled headfirst onto the tiled floor, managing to make it relatively noiseless. The place was a one-bedroom apartment with dirty dishes in the sink and an empty refrigerator. Clothes were scattered in piles on the bedroom floor and the bed was empty. The covers were perfectly folded to the right side as if Tommy Santarelli had simply lifted the blankets off himself and rolled out of bed. In any case he wasn't currently inhabiting his apartment.

The living room featured beer cans stacked on the coffee table.

A thirty-nine-year-old teenager with nobody to clean up after him.

Keeler jogged back to the car and got in. He looked over at Candy, awake in the passenger seat. Vitalek was asleep in the back.

"Nobody home."

"So what now?"

Keeler looked out at a few bars and closed store fronts. A dry cleaner and icicles frozen mid-drip from the porch awnings.

He said, "Let's go to the golf course."

Candy nodded and was about to say something, when Keeler's phone rang.

He glanced at her and removed his phone from a pocket, saw the number and stepped out of the car to take the call. His thumb tapped on the green rectangle and the familiar voice came back.

Protocol demanded that the caller announce himself first, unlike the civilian version of a conversation.

"Blomstein."

"Keeler."

Blomstein said, "Word is that Farrell's been working for some newfangled PMC the last three years."

"Unpack that for me. Newfangled as in what?"

"Newfangled as in a new corporate org because the last one got shamed out."

Keeler and Blomstein both knew that private military contractors who got into hot water over bad deeds abroad often simply dissolved the corporate entity and re-upped under another name.

He said, "Like Voltron."

Blomstein grunted. "Yeah, so Farrell got hired as head of

security for Triton Gamma Associates, which is a play on the two founders. Taggart and Grimaldi. Taggart's ex-navy and Grimaldi was some kind of political advisor for some dipshit straphanger in the Obama administration."

"Do you know who exactly?"

"Undersecretary of the undersecretary's underpants, maybe. No, I don't know. The usual clusterfuck corporate bullshit."

Keeler laughed. "Bitter are we?"

"Full of righteous disgust, yes." Blomstein inhaled over the phone, like he was smoking a cigarette. He said, "They ever try to rope you in?"

Keeler said, "You mean to work for a PMC? Sure."

"But you didn't."

"No."

Blomstein inhaled again. Keeler said, "What're you smoking there Blomstein?"

A short laugh. "The guy upstairs tipped me in weed for repairing the radiator."

Keeler smiled to himself, didn't say anything to Blomstein. He steered the conversation back to business. "Triton Gamma. Based out of where?"

"Bicoastal. Grimaldi in New York, Taggart out in San Diego. He's connected across the bay in Coronado."

The Navy Seal base. Keeler said, "Right. Got a New York address?"

"Here it is, 1011 Fifth Avenue, which is on Seventy-Eighth Street."

"Nothing on any specific job."

"No. Now you've got exactly what I have."

"Appreciate that, Blomstein. Catch you later."

"Later."

The line went dead.

Keeler stayed for a moment, savoring the no-bullshit conversation with his buddy . . . Well, almost no bullshit. It was heartwarming to have a brief operational chat once or twice every three years and still be friends. He opened the car door and put himself back into the Toyota. Candy was looking at him, expecting something. He said, "A friend of mine from California. He told me it's warm there now, apparently. He went to the beach today. Why don't people all live in California instead of here?"

"Must have something to do with Californians." Candy shook hair out of her face. "He have anything particularly interesting to say, your friend in California?"

"Interesting, but not exactly earth-shattering."

Candy said, "Fine, so what now?"

He turned the key in the ignition. The engine coughed and the dashboard winked to life.

"Golf course."

CHAPTER THIRTY-FIVE

Thirty-nine miles away, Vince Farrell was leaning forward in an office chair looking at a computer screen on Terry Grimaldi's desk, which was covered in leather the color of an espresso with a drop of cream. Grimaldi ran both hands over the surface, making circles on the soft hide.

The computer screen showed CCTV footage from Copenhagen House, taken that same evening and sent by Jerry Altman in a secure message that read, "Who the fuck is this?"

The camera was mounted high on the wall and had infrared capabilities. The video showed a wide-angle view of the courtyard. Two big men with good hair getting humiliated by a fast-moving athletic guy. Not only did he humiliate them physically, he did it with style. Farrell enjoyed the fight so much that when it was over he grunted involuntarily.

Grimaldi was behind the desk, watching his reaction. He said, "What's that, a laugh or a burp?"

Farrell made his voice even and cool. "I'd say that was more of a grunt, Terry," he said, used the first name strategically. "If I was to have laughed, I wonder how you'd have interpreted that."

Grimaldi lifted his hands from the desk. "Well, what is it to you, Vince?"

"I don't know what it is," Farrell lied.

The query to Clearviz had come back fast. The man beating the shit out of the twins was an outlier, having no social media presence either through his own account or someone else's, like he'd ignored technological fashion for the last ten years. Still, these days there was no escape. The guy's face appeared in two data sets. One derived from a deceased veteran's military memorabilia, uploaded by his widow to an online photo service for a memorial website and subsequently scraped by Clearviz's bots. The photos showed the man, in younger days, crowded around a table somewhere hot and beach related. There were others, all muscular and lean, smiling and military aged and wearing civilian clothing.

The second data set was a trove of documents from Hawaii's department of motor vehicles, uploaded by hackers in a data breach. Now they had a triangulation on the guy. Tom Keeler, thirty-six years old, Honolulu address. Grimaldi's researcher had spent a couple of minutes figuring out that when the widow's husband had been killed he'd been deployed with the 322nd Special Tactics Squadron that had been operating out of Mildenhall, UK.

It was safe to say that Keeler had been only temporarily Hawaiian.

Farrell held the report printout in his hand. It was impressive the way you could triangulate a man's identity so quickly. The whole thing, just one more reminder that Farrell had done the right thing to spend a small fortune in Columbia on facial reconstruction. He sat back in the chair, looking at Keeler's face in the printout. The driver's license picture taken about a decade ago. Farrell knew the man, but wasn't letting Grimaldi know that he knew.

At the diner the night before, he had thought the guy's face was familiar but hadn't been able to place it. Context might have been one reason; he was sitting with that Metro-North train conductor, DeValla, who'd picked him out of the crowd. Farrell couldn't fathom why, since he didn't know her. Maybe it was just one of those things. From now on, he'd wear the mask, even though that wasn't good for situations of extended proximity to other people.

Keeler had an interesting face, Farrell had to admit, somewhere between useful and hard. Yesterday, the face had floated in his memory, like an object stuck in orbit. Even this morning, when Keeler had followed him on the train, the face had been there, the connection escaping him and refusing to click.

Now it clicked, big-time. Unhappy memories, if Farrell was honest with himself and why wouldn't he be? Being honest with himself was the reason he was still alive. Not only was he living, he was thriving. Survive and thrive. He grinned to himself and Grimaldi got upset again.

"What the fuck are you smiling at, Vincent? Is this a problem or not?"

Farrell's eyes got flat, and he threw a look at Grimaldi that he figured was sufficient to make the guy's testicles quiver. Farrell liked to practice looking into the mirror. Grimaldi didn't need to know about the personal connection Farrell had to Keeler. He just needed to be reassured.

Farrell said, "I'm going to get the first train up and take care of it myself."

"You're going up anyway."

"Right, so I'll go up earlier and get this sorted out."

"What are you going to do?"

"Terry, I will see what needs doing and then I will do it. I can tell you more if you'd really like, or I can leave it there, whatever you say."

Grimaldi ignored the thinly disguised rhetorical question. He had his own set of skills and was happy that operational matters were delegated and siloed. He said, "All I can say is don't plant the guy unless it's absolutely necessary. You think Keeler is working for the uh, protagonist?"

"If I had to make a bet."

"Well, nobody seems to know him, so what're you thinking, freelancer?"

Farrell didn't care what the details were. He was just eager to get into this. He deflected. "Who cares what I think. We'll see, then I'll tell you what needs telling, as usual."

Grimaldi looked at him hard and then leaned over to press a button on the communications contraption next to a desk lamp. He spoke into it. "Is Sam Kelly out there?"

A female voice came back. "Yes."

"Send him in."

He leaned back and gazed at Farrell. "Who do you have up there at the house, whatever it's called?"

"Copenhagen House. We've got Milton, James, Fink, and D'Angelo."

A man strode into the room, sleek and refined in an expensive suit and the kind of combed blond hair that allows one to see a clear direction of travel. Kelly was an account manager with the company and Farrell had disliked him from the beginning. The guy was too polished, slicker than grease.

Grimaldi said, "Take a seat." He looked at Farrell and smiled, looked over to Kelly. "Tell him, Sam."

Kelly leaned forward in his chair and cocked an attitude. "Well, apparently the client wants me up there with you. Asked me to keep her posted."

Grimaldi nodded and looked at Farrell, almost in supplication. "Nobody's trying to mess with your team; it's what the client asked for."

Farrell said, "Posted as in how?"

Kelly looked at Farrell directly for the first time. "Honestly, Vince, they're freaking out. She said I need to give her twice-daily updates. Which is why it's best if I'm up there."

Grimaldi said, "We think having Sam up there will demonstrate that we care about the account, you know, that we highly value their business."

Farrell turned to Kelly. "Just as long as you're observing and not doing anything to fuck it up."

Kelly smiled humorlessly. "Sure. That won't be a problem."

"You going up there tomorrow?" Farrell asked.

"I'm driving up immediately," Kelly said. "Car's with the valet. They've got a room for me. Just spoke to what's her name, Jill."

Sponsoring the conference so they could take out the protagonist and his colleague in a controlled fashion had been a smart idea. That had been Kelly's concept, why he was good in client meetings. Nobody ever asked Farrell to interface with clients. Farrell grunted again and stood up in front of the floor-to-ceiling window. A multimillion-dollar view on Central Park at night. A killer view. Farrell thought Grimaldi looked like Frankenstein's monster with his huge square head and pasty face framed by a helmet of gray hair.

Farrell walked out without saying goodbye.

The elevator bank had a reflective wall and he saw his two brown eyes, felt the lenses itching his eyeballs. He wore two contacts, even though it was only the blue eye that needed covering. Better to have a perfect match for color and texture though. His gaze drifted up above his right eye to the dent he carried in his forehead. He was smiling at himself in the mirror, practicing that look. The smile wiped off as soon as he recalled that it was Tom Keeler who'd given him that dent, something he'd managed to avoid thinking about for a long time.

The event was lodged in the back left part of Farrell's memory, where he stored the stuff he really didn't want to remember. But during the elevator ride down from Grimaldi's office, the details dislodged like plaque from teeth.

CHAPTER THIRTY-SIX

Back in the day, Farrell had arranged a situation in south Baghdad. He'd stocked a big apartment with girls in their twenties mostly, not underage. Intelligent and good-looking girls from good middle-class Sunni homes that had been reduced to desperation after the war kicked off.

Because the girls all lived with their families in Sunni west side neighborhoods, the apartment they'd organized had to be on the south side. South in Baghdad meant Shiite and poor. The girls got paid for monthly stints, and because they were across town there wasn't too much danger that their families would find out. The guys got to get laid and hang out with cool girls who were relatively modern and relatable.

In other words, Farrell's team hadn't been doing anything *actually* wrong.

Except, one of the families did find out.

The girl hadn't set it up right. She hadn't told her family she was going away, hadn't told them shit. Just showed up in the apartment and acted all hot to trot. The family freaked out after she'd been gone less than forty-eight hours.

What the Vincelli people didn't know at the time was the uncle was a homicide detective with the Baghdad police, one of the guys who had survived Bremer's purge. The uncle wasn't actually a Baath party member, but simply *being* police in Baghdad meant party connections, which by that time meant a conduit to the insurgency.

What made it worse, the family hadn't always been middle class. They were from a village in the triangle, traditional Sunnis with strong tribal ties and values. So, when they came for the girl, they didn't come intending to save her, they came to bury her. The girl had brought shame onto the family and deserved to die, along with everybody else involved in her humiliation.

They called it *honor killing*, a fairly common event in that part of the world. Farrell didn't blame them for their extreme conservative position. That'd be like blaming the wind for blowing down a fence.

He wasn't even getting laid when the shit hit the fan. He was simply hanging out with a cigar and three fingers of Bushmills in a teacup, leaned back in an armchair talking to a girl named Salma about Paris Hilton's dog. A couple of guys were in the room playing backgammon at a table they'd looted from one of Saddam's palaces. Salma had been an economics major when the invasion hit. Now she was attending a very different school. Not that Farrell was sad about that; he didn't think college counted for much anyway.

The Vincelli company had hired local security: two guys outside and two down on the street. Farrell had his back to the door, looking at Salma. She was talking, gesticulating, the specific conversation about the food that Paris fed her puppy. The memory he had of it was visual, Salma's outfit moving with her gestures, like silk cloth being pulled over a gentle hillside.

Farrell distracted, not even hearing about the dog, mesmerized by the youthful body.

The door blew in. A shock wave rocked the back of his chair, jerking him close to the girl. He had been about a foot away when Salma got the doorknob straight into the center of her face at a thousand miles per hour. The heavy brass knob literally tore her head right off. Behind her, the wall was painted in blood.

Farrell let his chair tip over and rolled out on the carpet with his M4, making it to cover behind the heavy marble table one of his men had already thrown over. Both of the other guys in the room were up and ready, kneeling behind the cool marble ready to rock 'n' roll.

Farrell kept his eyes on the door. Two local men in sweatpants and plastic sliders came in skidding fast, and he ducked his head back behind the table and let the rag heads spray rounds out of their AKs on full auto.

The guys in first were probably the girl's brothers or close cousins, selected to maintain the family's honor. They were spraying ammo hysterically, what they'd do at the girl's wedding, if they weren't doing it to kill her.

Farrell and the two Vincelli guys kept it together behind the marble slab, veterans of the foreign wars, waiting for the idiot boys to empty their magazines. Once the firing stopped, Farrell was up and around the marble with his short-barrel carbine on single. Both of the boys were fussing with hot metal, pumped with adrenaline and fiddling with their magazines. Farrell took them out one at a time, maybe two and a half seconds total. One to each body and one to each head in quick succession, bang-bang, bang-bang, just like that.

But, it wasn't just the two brother or cousins who'd come. The uncle had sent a dozen insurgents to back them up.

Farrell recalled a weird ten-second silence. He heard muffled crying and sobbing from somewhere back in the apartment. The wall to the two adjoining bedrooms had been perforated by the AK fire. He watched Salma's headless corpse slump from the sofa to the floor, the sheer fabric of her lingerie sliding up indecently.

Footsteps pounded out on the stairs. Farrell signaled to the guys behind the table. He knew the layout. To the right of the door was the stair landing. A voice softly called out "Hamed" to one of the boys lying dead on the Persian rug. Smoke and dust hung in the air.

Farrell knew fifteen, maybe twenty words in Arabic. He called back in a whisper. "We killed three. Come."

He looked at the guys. Waited a moment until he could hear the insurgents gathering there and then nodded. He and his buddy emptied clips into the wall. He popped around the doorway and saw a man standing in a Nike t-shirt, gut shot right through the *o* in *Just Do It*, face sallow and peppered with blood. Farrell had his M4 up and pulled. A new flower opened up under the man's right eye, and he slumped to join the three others shredded through the wall.

There was shouting from downstairs followed by three shots and a confused grunt. The body of one security guy lay across the threshold where the door had been. The place didn't smell good. Farrell moved to the window and slipped the curtain open an inch. A cluster of armed men were positioned on the street. Farrell made the decision and picked up the radio to call for help. He was a survivor type and didn't have any choice.

Before he could do that, there was a frenzied shouting in Arabic and five guys literally tore into the apartment shooting. Farrell ducked behind the table, back to the marble. He looked up to see one of his guys get a round to the temple, right by his ear, crumpled like a stringless puppet. He came around and put six rounds into two Hajis and watched as three others made it into the back of the apartment. Farrell radioed for help while listening to shooting and girls screaming from the rear bedrooms.

CHAPTER THIRTY-SEVEN

Normally they might have sent a bunch of marines, or maybe some of the British guys. But the marines and the British guys on standby had been called out for something else, so they sent in the Air Force rescue squad, what they called the Expeditionary Rescue Squadron.

As far as Farrell was concerned, it didn't get more arrogant than Air Force Special Tactics, but back in the sandpit, when you saw the PJs coming, the only thing you felt was relief that they were going to save your ass. Which is what happened and it would have stayed like that if a PJ hadn't gotten himself killed on the mission. Which a lot of people said was on Farrell, being the man in charge. A million-dollar special soldier down because of a bunch of horny PMCs were taking special privileges.

Keeler came for him two days later.

Of all places it had been poolside in the Green Zone, at a sunset cocktail party put on by one of Vincelli's lobbyists to the Coalition Provisional Authority. Farrell had been told to stay out of sight for a week, but he was thirsty, and a new batch of teachers had arrived to try to develop and educate the local

Sunni women. He'd been having a conversation with a pretty grad student from England. She was blond and red faced from her first day in 120-degree weather, excited to discuss her mission of explaining the Turner Prize in contemporary art to a room full of women in burkas.

He hadn't even seen Keeler coming. The guy had appeared out of nowhere and come straight for him without deviation or hesitation. No warning, no words. Farrell experienced the event as a blindingly fast series of confused sensations and involuntary movements that left him floored, bloody, broken, and looking up as the English girl backed off with a horrified expression spoiling her face. When the shock of the attack had worn off and the pain came, Keeler was long gone, still not having said a single word.

Later, someone had explained how it'd gone down.

Keeler had come at him from his blind side and grabbed one of his arms. He'd broken the arm and then the other one and put his fist through Farrell's front teeth. Farrell had gone to his knees, and Keeler had pounded his head into the edge of a table about fifty times, hence the dent. He'd then carefully checked Farrell's vitals and, once satisfied, had broken his left leg. After that, Keeler had grabbed a cloth napkin and a fistful of ice from the wine bucket and walked out the same way he'd come.

Farrell got it, that nobody actually liked him and his guys from Vincelli. But the memory of that evening, floundering there by the pool in his own blood while all those stuck-up assholes stared at him with indifference, barely stopping their conversation, was a humiliation that nobody deserved. Contractors were useful pariahs for the CPA, on the same side.

Not everybody got to play hero.

There had never been any formal explanation, or any kind of an investigation. Keeler hadn't said a word to Farrell, the violence speaking for itself. Command had declined to investigate, and Vincelli didn't want any further action either, given the circumstances.

His CO had said that what happens in South Baghdad stays in South Baghdad, until you call in to be rescued. He asked the guy what he was supposed to have done, die there? The CO hadn't directly responded. Which left Farrell to nurse his wounds back home in a private hospital for a couple of months.

He hadn't seen Keeler again after that, until now.

Farrell came out of the elevator with Tom Keeler's face in his mind, like a target. It was invigorating to have a mission. Not only a professional goal, but a personal one. He decided it was going to be like a correction: he was going to take out Keeler like a typist takes out a typo with the delete key.

CHAPTER THIRTY-EIGHT

M ini DeValla sucked air through the burlap sack they'd put over her head.

The assholes had duct-taped her hands behind her back and her feet to the chair legs. They'd put three smelly blankets over her and left her in the back room of some kind of shack up in the woods with a kerosene heater. She could hear them from the other room, opening beer cans and trying, but failing, to keep quiet.

DeValla had already recognized one of them, Mike Stephanopoulos. He'd been hiding in the back of the Cherokee at the station when she'd gotten off work. She'd heard the voice threatening her from the backseat and knew instantly it was Mike. First thing she'd done was twist in her seat and punch him in the face, before getting the hell out of the vehicle. But that hadn't worked and they'd threatened her kids if she didn't cooperate, so she'd cooperated.

It was about the laptop she'd found on the northbound train during the blizzard.

Keeler had brought it down to the train station, like he'd said he would. Only the laptop hadn't been in the bag. They'd

opened it to find DeValla's overdue library books. Which meant
that the Keeler guy had taken the computer. For a couple of
hours she was paranoid, thinking Keeler had appeared in her
life specifically for that reason, to get to the laptop, but the
explanation made no sense. She was the one who'd picked him
up off the street. He couldn't have planned that, no way.

Which begged the question of why he'd taken the
computer.

Which demanded a follow-up question of why these idiots
thought that kidnapping *her* was going to help *them* get the
laptop back from *him*. She didn't even know the guy.

They'd stood there looking at her in the shed, balaclava
masks on like they were in some kind of a heist movie. What
she'd told them was nothing, zero, nada. She didn't know a thing
and hadn't ever heard of this guy who they said had taken her
Cherokee to the house. What she did know was that she had
been at work, riding the Poughkeepsie train up and back from
the city taking tickets.

DeValla imagined these men without the balaclavas; she
wasn't laughing, but it was still funny. Even with the masks on
they'd looked like a bunch of rejects. Another thing troubled
her: it was tough to put Mike Stephanopoulos and computers
into the same thought. The two things just didn't chime, Mike's
dumb face and a laptop computer.

None of which excused their actions. The morons had
crossed the line and deserved to be punished. She wasn't
kidding herself that they were dumb and dangerous.

Stephanopoulos had made her drive up to the parking lot
behind the old water tower. Someone else in a mask had shoved
the sack over her head and she was put into the back of another
vehicle. She didn't dare use her phone on the ride over. A guy
was in the backseat watching her, or so he said. Still, she'd
managed to leave it in the back of the car when they took her

out. Maybe if she was gone long enough, the police could track the phone and find her.

They'd made her sit on a tarp and dragged her uphill across a bumpy snowy field. She'd been forced to hike blindfolded through the woods after that. Two other guys had been waiting in the shed. Once in the shack they'd taped her to the chair and started asking questions about the laptop.

She'd gone into full denial mode and shut it all down. After that, the kidnappers had kind of milled around, staring dumbly at her and at each other. It was embarrassing. Best they could think to do was to pick her up in the chair and stick her in the back room with the bag over her head again. DeValla had drifted to sleep, exhausted.

Sleep hadn't lasted long though. She'd been jerked awake by a crash from the front room. The door being kicked in and some guy shouting. "Where the fuck is she?"

She was scared then, inside the burlap sack, unsure and unable to see what was going on even a foot away from her. There was more noise, the sound of something being kicked maybe. The sack had been ripped off her head and she'd found herself staring into the face of an ugly middle-aged guy with greasy hair and a goatee. The fact that he wasn't wearing a balaclava was scary. The guy backed off and held up the children's books overdue at the Kitchewan Landing Free Library.

"You don't know where my shit is?"

"No."

"Who's the fucking guy you had go over to your house this morning?"

DeValla said, "I don't know any guy who went to my house."

Because, how could this man verify that she knew Keeler, or what she might have said to him? The guy didn't seem to want verification. He had the children's books held in both hands, his face behind them engorged and furious. Next thing she knew, the stack of books whupped her right on the side of her head. The chair tipped over and DeValla went crashing down to the floor.

Two of the other guys lifted her and set the chair upright again. Her ears were ringing, and a great burning feeling pulsed through her head. Eyes watering, she saw the guy coming again with the books. He fake hit her and laughed.

"Want it again, bitch? Who's the fucking guy?"

DeValla's tongue explored the inside of her mouth and her teeth. The metallic taste of blood was there, a small cut on the inside of her mouth. The teeth were intact, a good thing. She leaned over and spit blood onto the floor. Looked up at the guy and decided to double down.

"You're an asshole, hitting someone who's tied to a chair. You can hit me as much as you like and I still won't know the guy. That's because I don't know any guy. I found the laptop on the train and the lost and found was closed so I brought it home. I didn't look at it or in it. I forgot to bring it to work this morning. That's the end of the story."

The guy was enraged, lips curled back to show his uneven teeth. His eyes were bugging out weirdly. It made her think that maybe the laptop was important to his own survival somehow, making him deranged. The guy pulled the books back to fake hit her again. She flinched. He laughed and walked away, and she heard the front door slamming and him raging outside. "Goddammit!"

Then the sack came down over her head again, and DeValla was left there with a pulsating headache.

She heard them in the other room, the four guys still in there drinking beer and listening to heavy rock at a low volume. DeValla could hear the conversation clearly enough. They seemed to be discussing the merits of bathrooms in local gas stations, a weird topic.

Not the conversation of decision makers, that was for sure; a conversation of losers. She figured the losers were waiting for that crazy guy to make a decision. The most comfortable position was to let herself simply collapse into the constraints. She allowed the duct tape to take all of her weight and five minutes later, she managed to find a thin layer of somnolence to drift on.

CHAPTER THIRTY-NINE

DeValla had never really liked the name her parents had stuck her with, Minerva, Mini. Candy had gotten the cool name and Mini had often felt ripped off in that department. Until one night, when Candy had come home wailing and in tears, her face scratched up and hair torn out by a bigger girl.

Mini hadn't said anything, watching Candy snuffle and whimper in her mom's arms. But something kicked in, inside her. A feeling and a resolve that she hadn't taken notice of before. Mini left the house quietly, making sure the screen door at the back didn't slam. She used the shortcut through the woods, emerging onto the yellow lit streets of Kitchewan Landing, her legs taking her like they already knew where to go.

She knew where the bully would be, out back of the high school, in the football field bleachers. Drinking beer and smoking cigarettes and making the smaller kids scared.

Body in motion, Mini's head felt kind of buzzy and weird, an electric feeling. She was moving with total resolve and zero doubt. She was going to take care of the bully so that Candy wouldn't ever have to worry about that bitch again. The thought came to Mini then, that there were two kinds of candy, the soft chewy kind and the hard kind. The soft kind was easier to eat. With the hard kind, you had to be more patient and break it down over time. Her sister's name might be Candy, but she was soft candy. Mini never said anything about it to anyone, but that night she realized that she was candy too, hard candy.

About ten minutes after falling asleep, DeValla had the subtle sensation of her left wrist slipping maybe a half millimeter in the duct tape. She forced herself awake and tested the bindings. They were strong and tight, maybe it had been a dream. But, after a couple minutes moving her arms up and back, she began to get some play. Ever so slowly, the tape was losing its stickiness.

It occurred to her that the adhesive might be having a reaction to the skin moisturizer Candy had given her for Christmas.

It took DeValla a half hour of slow and focused wriggling to get her left hand free of the duct tape. She did it as if in a hallucinatory daze, a continuous movement like a wave gently lapping at the rocks below a cliff face. The left hand slid out of the binding and she froze for a moment. Problem was, she didn't know if the people in the other room could see her. DeValla had a bag over her head.

She decided to take a chance and removed the hood.

Nobody there, but the door to the other room was right in front of her, about eight feet away. DeValla began using her nails to pick at the tape on her right hand. The edges came up and after a while she was able to unwind the tape. She bent down and did the same with her ankles. It was only when she was free of restraints that she started to think about what to do next.

The room she was in had one door and no windows. On the other side of that door were four men who had deprived her of her freedom. On the other side of them was another door that would get her the hell out of there. What she needed to do: go through them.

DeValla wasn't too scared of the men in the other room, but she had serious concerns about the guy who'd hit her with the books. He'd seemed unhinged. She had only one real memory of Mike Stephanopoulos from high school. He was a couple of years older than her, and she'd once come across him being bullied in the gym. Two guys had been holding him against a wall, while a third burped in his face.

Stupid people did dumb shit each and every day. Once in a while they even killed themselves, or other people. It was statistically improbable, but true nonetheless. DeValla wasn't planning on becoming a statistic. She had to consider the people out there as dangerous menaces that needed to be taken seriously.

She stood up out of the chair, as quietly as possible. Her entire body felt cramped and squeezed. She reached to the ceiling and stretched, trying to get her fingertips up high and her toes down through the floor boards. There were cracks and pops and she shook out her neck, feeling better almost instantaneously. She'd stopped going to Pilates a couple of weeks ago, and Mini decided that after this she'd get back to a healthy routine. The walls were made of wood boards thick and sturdy enough that she wasn't going to be breaking through them easily or quietly.

Mini looked around, what else was in the room? The only light in the room came from the kerosene heater. She'd had the bag over her head, so had not seen inside the other room. The door was solid, with no light coming from under or around it. In the back of the room was a stack of old milk crates. She moved to the crates and looked in the first one.

The objects were dusty and degraded from years of humid summers and freezing winters. Old cassette tapes competed with CDs and stand-up comedy DVDs. There was a tangle of audio wires and a moldy set of guitar strings. The remnants of a teenage boy's room maybe, packed into the back of a shed and left there for twenty years.

DeValla lifted the first crate and set it aside as quietly as possible.

The second crate was filled with a stack of magazines. The cover of the one on top said *Soldier of Fortune*, and had a picture of some guy in military fatigues holding a big machine gun. He was somewhere hot with yellowed grass and a bright blue sky, maybe Africa. Squeezed into the crate besides the magazines was a short chain connected to two other objects. A quiet laugh came involuntarily when DeValla realized that she was looking at a set of nunchucks, martial arts weapons that her older brothers had played with when they were like twelve. She pulled them out by the chain. Solid wood with a weighted core connected by the steel chain. It was all about the fulcrum and lever action of the chain, what made the nunchucks dangerous. She swung them around in the air, making whipping sounds as she got faster.

The problem was, Mini DeValla knew her limits. She could go out there and maybe get one of the guys, like a surprise attack. Mini figured even that would be a lucky hit, and there were four of them. She started feeling around in the crate, getting her fingers below the magazines. She felt something hard and edgy and came up with a throwing star, like something that a preteen ninja would use. Interesting, but not very practical, the star's edges were rusty and she didn't figure it would do any actual damage. She went back to digging and came up with a weighty thing that looked like a blunt steel handle, maybe one inch by five.

The handle pulled apart in two pieces to reveal a blade, steel and maybe seven inches long: a butterfly knife. A latch secured the knife in its open position. She hefted the weapon in her hand and it felt pretty good. Mini felt a fast, tickling sensation crawl up her spine, from the bottom to the top, branching out at her neck and raising the fine hairs. Something in her was aroused.

She considered the door. A round handle that would turn and allow her to come out into the next room. Simple, but complicated. How should she go out, fast and furious, or slow and sneaky? The men in there had been drinking beer. Mini could smell it, which meant that there was enough of it to have dulled their reflexes.

Plus, she knew the guys out there weren't exactly ninjas.

Mini figured she could get close to them with the slow and sneaky method, then go fast and furious, like a ninja. She had two weapons and two hands. To open the door she'd need a hand, which meant the second weapon would need to be temporarily held somewhere else, like between her teeth. She put a hand on the door knob and turned it slightly to feel the mechanism's resistance.

Time to do it.

CHAPTER FORTY

She opened the door at a regular speed, didn't bust right in there, but simply stepped into the other room. Not too fast, not too slow. Mini transferred the butterfly knife from her teeth to her left hand. She did it carefully, making sure she got the grip right. The four guys were sitting around drinking beer out of cans. Two sat on milk crates, one sat on a stool, another on a beanbag. She recognized Mike Stephanopoulos and another guy whose name was escaping her. Beyond them was the door. Balaclavas had been tossed on an upside-down box doing double duty as a coffee table.

She noticed the details, surprising herself with the clarity. The door had no lock, which meant a latch and padlock were needed to secure the shack from outside. Two oil lamps were lit on the floor between the beer drinkers.

It took a second or two for the men in there to notice her, and realize that it wasn't quite correct to see your kidnap victim standing in front of you holding a pair of nunchucks and a butterfly knife. She had the nunchucks with her right hand around one lever, with the other tucked under her arm, keeping the chain under tension and ready to go. In her left hand she had the butterfly knife, open and facing down, cutting side away from her.

Mike Stephanopoulos was closest, sitting on a wooden stool in front and to her left. He turned to look at her, surprise etched onto his face, seeking eye contact. Mini wasn't making eye contact, she was focusing on her target, which was a couple of inches west of the man's right eye. The nunchucks whipped in a fast arc and landed on Stephanopoulos's temple. The impact made a loud crack and he was knocked to the floor. Weirdly, Stephanopoulos's body began to immediately spasm, as if he was a fish out of water. It took Mini a second to pull herself away from the sight of him thrashing on the floor. Maybe it was skull fragments embedding into his brain from the hit?

After that, everything kind of turned into an ear-ringing red blur of frenzied activity. There was another man on the other side of Stephanopoulos's twitching body. He was floundering, and she realized that he had lost his footing in panic after seeing what was going on with Stephanopoulos.

Mini stepped over the twitching body and brought the butterfly knife down into the panicked man's thigh. The blade sank in easily, like the leg was made out of cheese. She pushed it in right to the hilt, where the tip encountered something solid, like bone.

The man made a high pitched scream and tried to push himself back with his other leg. Mini had her hand on the knife's handle and was pulled along with him, tugging at the blade, but unable to get it out of his leg. There was movement in her peripheral vision. Danger.

Mini's mind wasn't making conscious autonomous decisions. There was some kind of partnership going on between brain and nervous system. She was running on intuition, and so far, it was working pretty well. A guy came at her from the left, rising up from whatever he was sitting on and lurching to her.

She saw the man's face, red and suddenly recognizable, but she couldn't place it exactly.

A chubby face, not well fed, but badly fed. Another one of the guys from town she'd seen all her life. Seen without seeing. Mini wanted to strike at him with the nunchucks, but she didn't have the weapon in a good position. The man with the familiar face grabbed her right arm, controlling it. The face appeared close to hers; he was frightened and red, his mouth caught in a rictus.

DeValla stomped on his foot with her boot and his grip slackened. She got her feet into a good position and swung the nunchucks. The man flung up his hands to protect his face and the lead reinforced oak smashed into one of his wrists, making a loud crack, snapping bone. The man went passive and backed away to nurse the injury.

Blood had rushed to DeValla's head and she felt a righteous anger wash over in a wave of hot feeling. She growled at the remaining man backing up to the wall. "Asshole. Who the fuck do you think you are?"

The fourth man was staring at her from a corner of the shack. The tables had turned, now he was trapped. He'd have to get through her to go out the door. DeValla saw him glance to his left, followed his gaze to a firewood axe leaned against the wall to his right. He lurched for it.

DeValla had maybe one second to decide, fight or flight. She found herself rooted to the spot. The man got his meaty hand around the axe shaft and came up snarling. His eyes had changed, from docile and scared, to triumphant and homicidal. She saw that he was actually a very large person, even though much of it was belly. She stepped forward and swung the nunchucks at him. The blow was deflected by his shoulder, and he grunted, grabbing at the nunchuck handle and trying to pull viciously. DeValla let it go just at the moment he yanked and the man fell back against the wall.

She grabbed the closest oil lamp from the floor and threw it at the man. The lamp glanced off his head and exploded against the wall. Flame whooshed. DeValla stepped out of the door and closed it. A padlock hung open on the latch. She closed the latch and clicked the padlock shut and started running as fast as she could. Behind her she heard howling and crashing, but she wasn't looking back.

CHAPTER FORTY-ONE

Candy DeValla was in the passenger seat of Keeler's Toyota. They were winding their way up into the hills again. Streetlights made pools of yellow on the frozen salt-dusted road. The forest was an angular thatch of branch geometry in the sweep of headlights. The temperature had dropped even further. Candy was looking at the window, frosted with a fine network of crystals.

She found Keeler fascinating.

He was an alert predator, feline, quiet, and dangerous. Candy's new friend Vitalek was still asleep, head tucked back in the corner with his backpack for a pillow. Candy liked him. He was cute and snored gently, like a squirrel. Vitalek was intense, but in a goofy funny way. Keeler was intense but different, relaxed at the same time, but not exactly funny and definitely not goofy. No man could be in a room with him and feel a hundred percent in charge.

The kind of guy women fantasize about and who's a little intimidating in person. Vitalek, by contrast, was the kind of guy who made the people around him feel comfortable.

For example, the situation at the diner.

Vitalek was in the bathroom when four hard guys came up
to the counter and took the four stools, as if it wasn't obvious
that one of the seats was already taken. Candy had said something and been ignored. She was gearing up to get aggravated,
when she saw Vitalek coming out of the bathroom. They made
eye contact, her brows knitted, ready for the fight. Vitalek held
her gaze and nodded slightly, respecting her disposition and
offering his own in exchange. He'd understood the situation in
an instant and done exactly the opposite of what she'd expected.
He'd de-escalated without the bullies even noticing and gotten
his grilled cheese to go with an extra pickle.

Vitalek had leaned over and whispered in her ear. "Not
worth it. Let's get out of here."

Her heart had skipped a beat.

Up at the golf course the parking lot was almost empty. Almost,
because the Dodge truck was still there. They'd run the plates
and now knew it was registered to Tommy Santarelli. Keeler
stood next to Candy on the cold asphalt, taking in the surroundings. She watched him sniff at the air. It was freezing up on the
hill. Wind whipping around, making it feel like it was twenty
below.

She said, "What are you looking for?"

Keeler pointed his chin at the night. "Smoke. Do you
smell it?"

Candy sniffed at the air. "It's from the clubhouse." She had
the image in her mind: Bob Tsipiras with a heavy cut-glass
tumbler of bourbon, fireplace roaring in the background. A
bunch of middle-aged guys around the green table, trying to
concentrate on their cards.

"The wind isn't coming from the clubhouse." Keeler
pointed. "The clubhouse is closed."

Candy felt the breeze on her cheek and knew that he was right. She had no time to think because he was striding fast across the lot. She caught up with him. "Frankie said there weren't any tracks in the snow around the property. They'd have had to make tracks if they went into the woods."

Keeler stopped and sniffed the air again. He looked at her. "Not necessarily true. There was some snow earlier, could have masked the tracks. Or they could have used a sled to drag her." He pointed at the dark woods. "I think the smoke's over there. You see it?"

She couldn't make out anything at all over the trees. She saw Keeler's eyes glint in the moonlight.

"You know Candy," Keeler said, "Frankie's no longer any kind of an authority, so let's just forget about whatever he might have said."

"Okay." She nodded, thinking about how Frankie had gotten removed from the alpha male population about a half second after Keeler had come to town.

"What's on the other side of those trees?" Keeler asked, pointing at the woods and looking at her expectantly. She pictured the bird's eye view. The golf course had been built about ten years ago, therefore everyone considered it to still be new. She'd played with a childhood friend in the woods up by Crescent Hill Road, which would be on the other side of the forest. It seemed very far away to her, but that could be her childhood memory.

"I think the woods go on for a couple of miles at least."

Keeler grunted and brought them up to the edge of the lot, on the south side. The golf course plateau ran on an incline from northeast to southwest. Keeler studied the snowpack on the other side of the plowed bank. Candy tried to see what he was looking at.

"What do you see there?" she asked.

He nodded. "Drag marks." Keeler pointed into the snow and dropped to a squat on the other side of the bank.

Candy saw the most imperceptible sign of a linear scratch on the surface. "Mm hmm."

"They took her on a tarp or a blanket or something of that nature." Keeler spread his hands around in an arc. "You can see the indentations. The snowfall covered the tracks they made."

Keeler stepped into the white field and began moving up the hill, keeping a couple of yards to the left of the tracks he followed. She came after him and saw the indentations. Footsteps covered in the light dusting of recent snow. The tracks went up to the tree line. As they walked uphill the scent of smoke grew stronger.

At the tree line Keeler stopped and took a knee. He gestured her down with him.

He spoke very quietly. "We don't know what's out there, so we're going to keep quiet." He waited for Candy to nod. "Good. And you stay right behind me." She nodded once more.

CHAPTER FORTY-TWO

I t wouldn't have been as easy to drag Mini through the trees on the tarp, they'd have had to carry her, or make her walk. Since there hadn't been any real attempt to cover tracks, or to move with much stealth, Keeler assumed that Frankie had chosen not to investigate further simply because he lacked respect for Candy's intuitions and concerns.

Which confirmed him as a dead asshole. So far, Candy's intuitions were right on target.

Keeler entered the forest and moved fast and quiet through the trees, ignoring twigs and branches that scratched at him, letting them bend around and flick back. He made no attempt to ease the way for Candy, coming behind him. She'd figure it out after the first branch in the eye, like everyone else. Intuition is great, but experience makes it operational. He grinned to himself. In for a dime in for a dollar.

Fifty yards in, there were sounds from up ahead. He stopped to listen. Candy caught up and he tugged her down to crouch beside him, a finger at his lips. The sound was difficult to discern. A scratching, which became a faraway crunch and got closer, until it bloomed into what it was, feet running in the snow. Keeler pulled Candy into the cover of a large tree trunk.

He held her arm and made a *you-stay-right-here* gesture. He swung around the tree to face whatever was coming, because he'd already decided that he knew what it was. Mini DeValla, running away from her captors. A gut feeling, something in the cadence, the way a woman's gait was slightly different. That, and the smoke. Something was burning and making a lot more smoke than a fireplace or campfire could produce. He listened to the intensifying footsteps, expecting the crisp sound of boots cutting into snow like fists punching through paper.

What he heard was a muddled audio signature. A close sound layered against one farther back. Two people running out of sync, one behind the other.

He heard Mini's breathing before he saw her coming. She was going flat out, feet pounding through the snow crust and flying out again with a puff. Her breathing pattern ragged, sucking in the air and then blowing it with a loud ahhh. She flew out of the dense woods, her shadow detached from the darkness, limbs a blur.

Keeler had to stop her physically, which required a lot of strength, given her speed and body mass. He caught her and Mini immediately put up a struggle, flailing at him. Her hair wasn't tied back, and there was a lot of it, flying all over the place. Keeler was amused, Mini was strong, fury making her even stronger. He had to pull her tightly to him, immobilizing her, really the only way to do it fast. He put a hand over her mouth and spoke softly, close to her face. "It's me, Keeler. I'm with your sister. Someone's coming after you."

He felt her body against his, muscles coiled for action. Felt it relax as she realized who he was. Keeler could see the whites of her eyes, flashing in the dark. The fine contours of her face outlined by the ambient glow filtering through bare branches. He was paying attention to the darkness of the forest, hearing the second set of boots moving, slower and more chaotic. A man, not running any longer, but walking heavily.

Keeler felt Mini's lips, moving against his palm and looked down. She was calm now and held him tightly with both hands, fingers grabbing at the tough fabric of his jacket. He removed his hand from her mouth. She bit her lip and stared at him, controlling her breathing.

She spoke quietly. "You came back for me."

"Yeah, I did."

"What happened with the laptop?"

Keeler didn't respond, focusing instead on the very large man slowly coming out of the woods. The guy would have heard Mini stop running. Keeler rose and moved toward him, putting his body between the guy and DeValla. The man was holding an axe. Keeler spent exactly half a second wishing he'd have taken the billy club from the Toyota, but he hadn't, so he stopped thinking about it.

The forest behind Keeler was not as dense as in front. He figured the guy could probably see him outlined against the lighter shade.

The man said, "Pat?"

Keeler said nothing and moved forward, putting pressure on the big man to do something.

The big guy took a couple of steps back, uncertain. "Pat?"

Keeler was three strides away, watching the man's shape, a shadow with blurred outlines, but not one that was winding up to swing the axe. How long would it take him to make a swing, to get the leverage and put the weight on the legs to make that axe count? A quarter second.

Keeler closed the distance, covering two strides in a fast

blink. He took control of the axe with his left hand and hooked the guy in the jaw with his right fist. The punch made the man stagger back, but didn't floor him. He struggled for a brief moment, trying to pull the axe away from Keeler's grip. That wasn't going to work. The guy was big, but he hadn't been keeping himself in shape.

Keeler observed the man struggling and decided to end the situation. He kept an iron grip on the axe haft and switched up his footwork. He stamped a heavy boot into the man's knee, eliciting a muted grunt, and kicked the guy down to the forest floor. It was simple then, to get astride him and stab him hard in the throat with stiff fingers. The man released his grip on the axe involuntarily, and Keeler tossed the weapon to the side. He leaned down to the guy and watched him sputter and choke.

Mini DeValla was at his shoulder. She lowered herself to a kneeling position, her breathing more regular. Her hair brushed his face and Keeler could smell her.

Mini said, "There were three others."

"What happened to them?"

"I don't know exactly what happened to them. I think the shed caught on fire."

Keeler handed his smartphone to Mini. "Put the light on him."

She tapped and swiped and a harsh LED came on in bright white. Mini put the light on the guy's face. The man on the ground wriggled and twisted. Keeler clamped a hard hand at his throat, pinning him. In the dark, Mini's face was calm, her silhouette a combination of soft lines and angles. She was looking down at her erstwhile captor.

"I don't think I know him."

The man squirmed. Keeler increased the pressure on his throat. Felt the man's body writhing beneath him. Mini spoke impassively, as if she were assisting in the dissection of a frog. "But I knew two of the guys up there. Mike Stephanopoulos and another one with a fat face, whose name I don't remember. They both drive cabs down at the station."

Keeler said, "Mmm hmm. Let me guess, Kitchewan Old Cars."

The man was trying to say something. Keeler eased up on his throat. The mouth moved, but it was impossible to hear what he said. Because, at the same time as he spoke, Candy called loudly from by the tree where he'd left her. "Someone's running down to the parking lot. They're getting away."

Keeler saw movement, the sound of Candy taking off through the woods. Crashing through the branches in a hot temper, probably so pissed off at her sister's kidnappers that she was oblivious to the danger.

Mini said, "Shit."

Keeler sprang up, releasing his grip on the guy's throat. The man panted, taking large gusts of air into depleted lungs. Keeler felt Mini tug at his arm.

"Come on."

There was no time. Candy had taken off like a spooked deer, blindly chasing her sister's kidnappers. Not a very good idea, given the circumstances. Keeler dropped down and smashed his fist into fat man's throat, immobilizing him. He retrieved the axe, hurling the heavy thing deep into the forest.

Keeler stood over the man, reluctant to leave him behind, but there wasn't much of a choice. Candy was flying down through the snow to the golf club parking lot screaming like a banshee.

Keeler turned and started sprinting down the hill. Mini was already moving. He caught up with her and they both sprinted hard through the woods. Beyond, there was only the sound of Candy howling.

When he got to the edge of the woods, Keeler slowed. The Dodge was skidding out of the parking lot, Candy silhouetted by the taillights, bent over double sucking oxygen. The lights disappeared from view. Mini was at his side, holding on to his arm. Her teeth were chattering. Keeler put his arm around her, figuring any extra warmth would count.

CHAPTER FORTY-THREE

C andy was still blowing hard when they got down to the parking lot. Keeler looked into the Toyota, saw Vitalek in the backseat, sleeping with his mouth open. Anyone who could sleep in places like cars and trains and fast-moving speedboats or freezing mudholes got a lot of credit in Keeler's book.

"The guy up there with the fucking axe I don't know," Mini said to Candy, "but there's another guy I recognized, drives a cab down at the station." She snapped her fingers, eyes angry and wide. "Guy's name is Tommy!"

Candy glanced at Keeler.

Keeler said, "Tommy Santarelli. Drives for Kitchewan Old Cars."

Mini said, "I had to hit Mike Stephanopoulos up there. I was just trying to get away from them. I hit him with a pair of nunchucks. You believe that?" She looked at Keeler, seeking understanding. "I just needed to get away. They could have hurt me."

Candy said, "Nunchucks?"

Mini's voice was tight, constrained. "I don't know but he

looked bad, after I hit him. Like I'd done real damage." She hugged herself.

Keeler said, "Whatever you did up there, you did it for a reason. You had no choice. Getting out of there was the right thing."

She shivered. "They kidnapped me, man. I was scared of what was going on with my babies."

He said, "You did what you had to do Mini. You hadn't done it, you'd still be there, or worse."

Candy stood apart, looking up to the woods.

Keeler squeezed Mini's shoulder. "Let's go up there and take a look. You up for that?"

She nodded, effusive. "Yes. I need to see it."

Keeler knew, first kill was hard. He'd dated an army shrink once who'd told him. Best thing to do for battle trauma is to go back into battle. Go back and see what you did. The military spent tens of millions on video game type simulations of battles to rehabilitate soldiers who couldn't make it past that most exhilarating moment of their lives.

Up in the woods, the axe man was gone. He'd made tracks east. Keeler decided to let him go for now; there were other priorities. They hiked up to where Mini had been held captive.

The light from the fire made it easy to find the shack in the dark. The structure was on a low smolder, embers glowing within. The roof had collapsed, caved in on the far side. The front door had been smashed open by an axe.

Keeler got his phone from Mini and activated the flashlight. The cold beam scanned the smoking ruin. He pushed it inside, saw beer cans and blood traces on the floor. A man's body was resting prone on the floorboards in an ungainly position of tangled limbs. Blood pooled around his head. Keeler darted inside and took a hold of the man's coat collar to drag him out. The flashlight beam swung over to his right and he caught sight of the colorful images adorning the cover of a children's book. Two other books were scattered in the debris behind it.

Keeler pulled the body out and turned the guy over. The face was pale and dead. The side of his head had collapsed. He went back in and retrieved the children's books. No reason Mini should have to pay extra fees for the overdue library books.

Mini stood over the corpse staring at the dead man. "Mike, what the fuck were you thinking."

Keeler watched the emotions play over her face. She was getting perspective, Mini was no shrinking daisy, she was dealing with it. Candy stood a couple of steps back from the burnt shack, biting at the zipper of her parka. She looked like someone who was making calculations. Indeed, her eyes flashed up and found his.

"We can't go to the police, right?"

"Right." Keeler affirmed. He glanced at Mini, saw the frown on her face. He didn't want to say anything to her about Frankie's death. It wasn't the right time and place. He addressed Candy. "What's the best place to go right now and be safe and comfortable. Your place?"

Mini said, "Wait a second. Why can't we go to the police?" She eye stabbed her sister. "Why didn't you call Frankie already?"

Candy shot back. "I called Frankie and he didn't do shit. There's other stuff to tell you but not right now." She gave Keeler a meaningful look. "Plus, Frankie's off work for three days, because of his wisdom teeth."

Keeler understood. There wasn't a great danger of Frankie being missed at work, at least for several days.

Mini said. "Where are the kids?"

Candy came over and put both of her arms on Mini's shoulders, entering into that intimate sisterly space. "Mom's at yours with the kids, Mini. They have no idea what's been happening and they're completely safe and happy. I'll send her a text even though she won't read it until the morning. Let's go to my place." She hugged Mini to her. "This is over."

When they got down to the parking lot again, Candy went over to look at Vitalek, still deeply asleep in the back of the Toyota. Mini came down and looked in to see what her sister was staring at.

Candy half laughed. "I just met this guy at the diner. He's still sleeping. Can you believe it?"

Mini spoke with a small voice. "Great first date, Candy." She gave her sister a wry smile. "Okay, I need to eat something." She held her hands in front of her. "I'm literally shaking, man."

Mini DeValla turned to Keeler and grabbed his hands, burying her own inside of his. Mini's fingers very cold and shivering. He was thinking, could be nutrition, shock, cold, or some combination. Bottom line, get her safe.

She closed her eyes and breathed in. "Your hands are warm." Mini DeValla's eyes opened and looked directly right into his.

CHAPTER FORTY-FOUR

They picked up Candy's car from where she'd left it at the diner. Keeler followed in the Toyota, Vitalek awake now and groggy in the backseat. Candy's place was a walk-up apartment in a red brick development past the town's Little League field. Coming in the door, Candy shot a look over her shoulder to Keeler. "You two get the living room. I'm going to take care of my sister." She head nodded at Vitalek, still half asleep, and dragged his lanky frame up the stairs.

Keeler let the three of them go into the apartment ahead of him, wanting to get a feel for the lay of the land. He leaned his forearms against the banister and gazed out over the parking lot below, peering into the darkness. Candy's apartment was on the second floor of a two-unit building, one up, one down. Each building had three or four of those. Nothing moved out there but the freezing wind. He looked over at where they'd parked. The Toyota right next to Candy's Subaru. Steam rose from both hoods, more from his than from hers. Double the ride. Every other vehicle in the lot was cold, the inhabitants now securely packed into their apartments, snug and sleepy.

The living room had a sofa and an easy chair sharing a plain white rug with a coffee table and a television. Keeler dumped his backpack and threw his jacket on the easy chair. Vitalek had taken the sofa, sprawled there unceremoniously, looking like a conscript after a tough march. Mini was in the kitchen, leaning back in her chair at a small table.

Keeler took a seat and examined Mini's face. "What happened there." He brushed aside a curtain of dark curly hair and pushed it behind her ear. "They hit you."

Mini locked eyes with him. "A guy showed up and wanted to know about you. I didn't tell him anything, so he hit me with the library books you put in the laptop bag."

Candy set down a stack of shot glasses and a bottle of Maker's Mark.

He examined Mini's face. The wound wasn't more than a bruise and a reddening at the cheekbone, where the books had hit. "Candy, can you get me an ice pack and something to clean this?"

"I've got rubbing alcohol and makeup removing pads." Candy focused her attention on Mini. "I'm going to make you rigatoni in red sauce."

Mini poured bourbon from the bottle into three glasses. Keeler slid a glass to Candy, who nodded in appreciation. The three of them touched glasses.

Mini said, "Thanks for coming to get me, you guys."

She knocked the liquor back and rapped the heavy glass onto the table.

Candy sank hers. "It's been quite a night."

Keeler was full of admiration for the attitude. He wondered what their parents were like. He'd seen the mother at the house, but it hadn't been memorable. He figured the mother had more dimension to her than was cosmetically obvious in her grand-motherly outward appearance.

Minerva poured herself and Candy a second round. Keeler

was still sipping the initial shot. Tasting the bourbon and letting it work its way into his system, feeling the alcohol and the warmth that diffused around its passage.

He said, "You didn't need to protect me. Could have told them about me."

Mini shot back, "They didn't deserve to know shit."

"That's true." He pointed at her face. "Might have avoided that."

Mini ignored him, sipped at the bourbon. Candy set a bowl of ice and a kitchen towel on the table, along with rubbing alcohol and cotton pads. Keeler allowed her to move back to the stove before speaking. "The guy who showed up and hit you. Tell me about him. Did he leave after?"

Mini sipped bourbon. "Ugly fuck with a graying goatee and bad teeth. Pink face. Guy was pissed off, kind of hysterical. Shows up, figures out that I'm not telling him anything, that I don't actually *know* anything. Hits me and leaves."

Keeler nodded. He figured it was the same guy with the blue Ford pickup who'd tried to get the laptop from him at Mini's house. "So you didn't know him. Hadn't seen him before."

"No. I recognized Mike Stephanopoulos right off the bat. Then that other guy, Tommy from down at the station." She sipped bourbon. Looked at Keeler with knowing eyes. "These aren't professional kidnappers, man. They're a bunch of local morons caught up in something. I don't know about the goatee guy." She shook her head. "Can't believe Mike Stephanopoulos is dead, what an idiot."

As if he'd died from natural causes, like a falling tree. Keeler looked at her, engaging her eyes, wet with tears. She was beautiful. He didn't say anything, reminded that Mini hadn't yet learned about Frankie's death. He figured it was going to be Candy's job to disclose the information. Preferably in the privacy of a bedroom, sisters huddled into a familiar embrace.

Mini looked at him now, shot glass lifted and whiskey half gone. "So what happened with the laptop? Why did you bring it into the lost and found with books? Where's the computer now?"

Keeler explained it to her, how the guy with the goatee had braced him outside of her house. The footprints in the snow and the car that had been there in the night. How he'd taken the computer and gotten it into the relative safety of the UPS delivery system. How they could pick it up in the morning and deal with it. She listened, sipping on the bourbon and looking down at Candy's kitchen table, nodding once in a while. She looked up when he was finished.

"That was smart." Her eyes bore into his like burning coals.

He had a hard time looking away, so he went to work cleaning up Mini's injury. He applied alcohol to one of the cotton pads and scooted himself close to her. She turned her head slightly, glanced once at him and then looked away, allowing him inside her personal space. Keeler worked the cotton pad around the area on the left side of her face. Her hair brushed his wrists and forearms. He could feel her warmth.

They stayed like that for a few minutes. Keeler taking his time, Mini closing her eyes and relaxing. He had his left hand on the table and she covered it with hers, squeezing hard and then letting her hand just stay there, keeping the warm connection.

Candy had her back turned across the kitchen, heating up leftovers. "This isn't ma's cooking or anything, but it's going to do the job."

Mini looked at Keeler, making eye contact. He drew back. She took her hand off his and picked up the bourbon glass. He got an ice pack going with the kitchen towel and handed it to her. "Keep that on your face for a while and it won't blow up too bad."

She spoke softly. "Thank you."

Candy was ready, two plates of pasta in her two hands. "Come on Min, let's go to my room. These guys can fend for themselves."

The sisters left the kitchen. Keeler got it, Candy wanted alone time with her sister. They had things to discuss. He wasn't hungry, so he cleared up the kitchen and washed out the glasses.

Vitalek was laid out on the sofa, deep in a sleeping bag that he'd pulled out of his pack. The whole room smelled like a camp site. Keeler eased a folded blanket from under Vitalek's sleeping form and took it over to the easy chair. He removed his outer layers, feeling good and airy in boxer shorts. He allowed himself to sink back into the cushions and pulled the blanket over, happy to be reclining in such luxurious conditions.

CHAPTER FORTY-FIVE

Keeler woke to the smell of fresh coffee and the machine-gun-fire tapping of fingers on a keyboard in close proximity. His internal clock was already telling him that it was late in the morning, for him. Maybe ten o'clock. He opened his eyes and found himself looking at Vitalek, stretched out on the couch with a laptop resting on a pillow perched on his belly. He was typing furiously, intent on the screen. Keeler had worked with people who could touch type before. Being able to type blind had its advantages.

Vitalek swung his clear blue eyes over without moving his head. "Sorry if I woke you."

"No problem. How many words per minute?"

"Never counted." He went back to the screen. "I made coffee. They're not awake yet."

Keeler threw the blanket off and sprang up from the chair, stretched his body to the ceiling, and then dropped to a squat before standing up again feeling perfectly ready.

Even better with a cup of fresh-brewed black coffee. Candy had her coffee cups stored in a reasonable location, easy to guess and away from dust accumulation. The cups themselves were divided into two varieties. Mugs with slogans and mugs without slogans. Keeler chose a mug with the words "Sisters Before Misters." He filled it with black coffee from a French press on the kitchen table and brought it back to the easy chair like a prize.

Keeler said, "What do you have there, emails?"

Vitalek nodded. "Haven't looked at my correspondence for a week, the whole time I was up in the woods. I made the mistake of opening the laptop while I was waiting for the coffee." He gazed at Keeler with a smile. "Now, I'm screwed."

Keeler took a slug of coffee and let it run around in his mouth before swallowing. Good coffee, well dosed and strong. He hadn't checked his email account in over a month. He said, "How many spoons of coffee did you use?"

"I don't calculate in spoons."

"What's your method?"

"Ratio of coffee to water, estimate the size of the pot and then make your best calculation. I figure the pot is a liter. I use a liter of water, sixty grams of coffee and then add a couple more for the pot, you know."

"But you ballpark the coffee, unless you've got a scale."

"Yeah, ballpark it."

Keeler took another sip. "Good coffee."

"Grandmother taught me." Vitalek was nodding, still absorbed in his typing. Now he was more intent. He cursed under his breath and executed a wild flurry of clicking and clacking keys, fingers flying over the surface of the keyboard. He glanced at Keeler. "I have to fix this, just give me a second."

Keeler didn't mind. He drank coffee and observed. He'd been around computers quite a bit back in the military. There had always been a couple of geeks assigned to special tactics, like a small on demand nerd force. One thing they all had in common was the ability to type furiously at a million miles per hour. He had no real idea of how the computer stuff worked, but it looked as if coding took a lot of concentration, like playing a musical instrument.

Three minutes later, Vitalek snapped his laptop shut and looked up. "All right, sorry." He lifted a cup that had been perched precariously between his hip and the sofa back. Managed to get it operational and sipped. He kicked his feet and made himself more upright, head back against the arm rest.

Keeler said, "What was that, computer coding?"

Vitalek stared into the ceiling and spoke slowly. Spacing his words and kind of rolling his eyes as if they were also searching for what to say. "Yes, exactly. I had to fix something that a colleague of mine broke a couple of days ago and nobody thought to tell me about."

"A couple of days is a long time in computer world."

"Sure is." Vitalek laughed. "Who knows what could have happened if someone had tried to use the broken part. Might have erased a couple of billion dollars or something. Oops!"

"You have the internet here?"

"Sure." He tapped the side of his laptop, a black plastic nub stuck out with a green light blinking furiously as the data flowed.

Keeler saw what it was, a mobile data key. Convenient. He said, "Let's search something on the internet, if that's okay."

"I love a good old internet search." Vitalek opened the laptop again and put his finger on the keyboard, repositioned his face to the screen. Keeler noticed the security measures. Not just a password. Vitalek had facial recognition and a biometric finger print, in addition to the password. "What are we searching for?"

Keeler said, "Let's find information on a limited liability corporation registered in Delaware, Kitchewan Old Cars. I'd like to know who the owner is, and also run a search relating the company to the name Pat, or Patrick."

Vitalek grunted and got his fingers working on the computer. Keeler remembered how the axe guy had thought he was Pat. He'd called Pat's name, coming out of the woods into the clearing.

Vitalek's furious typing slowed to a crawl and stopped. He drawled. "Okay. Well, Kitchewan Old Cars is a limited liability company registered in Delaware, for tax purposes we assume. I know that you already know that." He darted a look at Keeler. "You want to guess who the company is registered to?"

"Pat."

"Ten points. One Patrick Rooney of Newark, New Jersey."

The blue pickup truck with the Jersey plates.

"Jersey. See if he's got any kind of an address here, in Kitchewan Landing."

"Roger that." Vitalek returned to the internet, looking like he was enjoying the exercise.

Keeler was thinking, if Pat Rooney's got an address here, maybe they'd find Santarelli and the other surviving taxi guys at Rooney's house and wrap it up. Whatever they had gotten into, he didn't care. What he cared about was the safety of the DeValla sisters.

The apartment had a large bathroom on the other side of the sofa. Keeler had already paid it a visit during the night, had seen the shower in there and the towels, stacked up on a steel-framed shelving unit. Fluffy and fragrant, unlike himself. He rose from the easy chair and stretched again. Joints popped and cracked and vertebrae groaned.

Vitalek made a face and looked at him. "Don't tell me you're going to start doing push-ups."

"No. I'm going to take a shower."

He strode barefoot across the carpeted floor in his boxer

shorts, opened the bathroom door with a confident twist, and stepped inside. Mini DeValla was standing on the other side of the bathroom in her bra and panties. There was a connecting door to Candy's bedroom. Mini was turned away from him, examining her bruised face in the mirror. Keeler managed not to stare at her body but caught her eye in the reflection. He wasn't embarrassed and didn't apologize for the mistake, but he was polite. He opened the door again, just enough to step out and close it behind him.

Keeler leaned back against the bathroom door, an after-image of DeValla in his mind, like staring into the sun. She hadn't frowned at his intrusion. Whatever it was, the eye contact, the expression, it had been warm rather than cold. And even though he had managed to avoid staring at her body, he'd seen it anyway and even had the time to read the words tattooed vertically to each of DeValla's perfectly formed calves, *wild* on the left and *kitty* on the right.

Keeler came back to the easy chair and rolled the words around in his mind. Two words, two legs, one remarkable concept. Wild Kitty.

CHAPTER FORTY-SIX

In the meantime, Vitalek had been busy.

He was nodding to himself on the couch, staring into the screen. "Interesting." Each syllable pronounced as if it were a word. "Very, very, interesting."

"What do you have there, an address?"

"Maybe."

Keeler said nothing. Which elicited a look from Vitalek, who seemed impressed with himself.

"I got him through his socials. Look at this." He held his laptop so that Keeler could see.

It was the guy who'd accosted Keeler outside of Mini DeValla's house. The same blue Ford pickup truck registered to Kitchewan Old Cars. The photograph showed the man with unkempt dirty blond hair and a greying goatee set into an unshaven face. The image wasn't flattering. It looked hot out, summer in the Hudson Valley. Rooney, in cutoffs and a Mötley Crüe t-shirt, had a bead of sweat on his lip and was making a face in front of two dogs who were howling and slobbering and chained to the bed of a pickup truck.

Keeler said, "That guy is Pat Rooney, huh?"

"So it seems." Vitalek rattled on the keyboard, and a riot of boxed computer windows flipped and flickered across the screen. Most of them were photos of Rooney engaged in leisure activities. "Got him triangulated through a bunch of social media sites and also, importantly, through other people's socials. People he's friended and stuff." He looked up at Keeler. "You don't use social media."

"No." It occurred to him that Vitalek might have already checked him out while he slept and maybe had even taken a photo of his face and run it through a computer program.

Vitalek nodded, as if what Keeler said had made sense and was important. "Lack of a social media presence is smart but can be read as an indication that you're up to no good. You know that, right?"

"Know what?"

"That keeping up the appearance of a social media presence is one way of deflecting unwanted interest."

"You mean, people with no social media presence are suspicious. You're suggesting that I get on board."

"To certain parties it's suspicious, yes. The conventional wisdom being, what do those people have to hide? You understand, your position is non-conventional, Keeler; you're an outlier. If you really wanted to hide in plain sight you could just have someone post for you, or set up some automation."

Keeler didn't even try to untangle what Vitalek had just said. "We're not interested in me here. Get back to Rooney."

Vitalek did a little duck with his head. "No problem. So this guy, Rooney. He's not simply on all the socials, he's the kind of guy who uses the internet full on without any regard for hygiene." He flipped to a browser window that showed a young woman on a bed. "He's into cam porn and doesn't use a VPN. So, check this out." Vitalek flicked a key to display a window with a black background and a tangle of white text that looked like computer code.

"What's that?"

"IP addresses of visitors to this cam site. Site was hacked a year ago and they data dumped all of this onto some random cloud storage service." He giggled. "I found it after running an IP search for Rooney."

"How'd you get the initial IP address to search?"

Vitalek shrugged. "Once I saw he was an unhygienic cam site dude, I did a reverse image search and got lucky." He found a window and pointed to it. "Rooney uploaded a photograph of himself onto a free image sharing site. See that?"

Rooney was by a lake holding a largemouth bass. Keeler saw it, half knew what Vitalek was talking about. "I see it."

"Image site records IP address of uploader and includes it in the post." Vitalek held up his hands, fingers making quotation marks. "For transparency." Vitalek rolling his eyes. "Duh."

"Did that give you a street address in the real world?"

Vitalek pointed to the pickup truck photo. "Not exactly as simple as that, but I think this is his house." Behind the truck was a house, set back from a small grassy plot with a worn picket fence.

"What makes you think it's his house?"

Vitalek shuttled through several other pictures showing the same house. "I don't know, but it's in a bunch of other photographs, so there's a chance it is."

"Did you geolocate?"

"Of course." He flipped open a map. "Thompson Hill Drive, probably number 68."

"Kitchewan?"

"Kitchewan Landing. About two and a half miles from here."

Vitalek was clearly excited by the chase, enjoying the

facility by which he'd found Rooney's address. Keeler knew people who did that kind of a thing for a living, but they weren't normal people.

"What are you doing here, Vitalek?"

"Doing as in what, here on this couch?"

"As in here in Kitchewan Landing."

"Oh." Vitalek swung his legs over into a sitting position. His toes wriggled on the rug. "I'm supposed to attend a conference some place, I forget the name." He gave a goofy grin. "Maybe someone's house."

"Copenhagen House."

Vitalek snapped his fingers. "That's it. Is that the only possible location for a conference in this town?"

"Could be. Unless you wanted to confer at the diner."

Vitalek perked up. "Speaking of, I'm quite hungry."

Keeler ignored that. He knew who he was looking at, sitting casual on the sofa, the guy Jill from Copenhagen House had talked about, the protagonist. He was having a hard time imagining Vitalek as a crypto king and one of the wealthiest people on the planet.

He said, "Does the name Irma Rosenbaum mean anything to you Vitalek?"

Vitalek's gaze came around slowly to his, something in the eyes gone flatter than before, wiser than he was letting on. "You know who I am."

Not a question, a statement.

CHAPTER FORTY-SEVEN

K eeler decided to put about half of his cards on the table, keep the other half in his pocket. "Rosenbaum is in the hospital; they didn't tell you?"

"What? No. Nobody told me anything. I've been out of touch." Vitalek looked genuinely shocked.

"Because you've been camping."

"Right." Vitalek frowned. "Hold on, what happened with Irma, why is she in the hospital? We're supposed to be on a panel this afternoon. Did they cancel it?"

"I don't know. I was up at Copenhagen House last night." He looked at Vitalek. "It's a little complicated."

Vitalek flipped open his laptop and let fingers fly furiously over the keys. "Irma's usually very responsive." He looked up at Keeler. "What happened to her?"

"Apparently cardiac arrest."

"Let's hear the complicated story, then."

"Night before last there was an incident on the train. A train going to the city. I was on it, so was Mini." He jerked a thumb to the bedroom. "She's a train conductor. Heating system breaks down with a blizzard on the way, the train ends up getting cancelled and I'm stuck. On top of that, a woman had some medical issue. I don't think she was on the train. She was waiting for it, on the platform. Turns out it was your friend Irma Rosenbaum." Keeler indicated the bedroom again. "Mini over there does the walkthrough and finds a laptop computer that someone left behind. Make a long story short, certain people took an unwholesome interest in the laptop. Which is what led to the events last night that you managed to mostly sleep through."

"Uh huh." Vitalek ruminated. "And what does any of that have to do with me or Irma?"

"I don't know. Right now it's the million-dollar question." Keeler leaned back into the easy chair thinking about this guy. Goofy Vitalek was the protagonist. Which meant that he wasn't going to be just a goofy, lanky kid. Nobody got to be the richest guy in the world by being a sheep. Vitalek was more likely to be a wolf in sheep's clothing. Keeler said, "Last night, you missed the party. Were you really asleep in the backseat or was that for deniability."

Vitalek gave him an innocent look, all blue eyes and shaggy hair. "I hung back from whatever you two were getting into. I understood that it was something about her sister being in trouble. In my defense, I truly needed sleep. I've been up in the woods camping for four days."

Keeler figured that meant Vitalek had been out in the woods camping during the blizzard. "What did you do, build an igloo?"

"Uh, something like that. I'm experimenting with heat retention techniques, mostly using plastic wrap." He patted his backpack, as if it was filled with plastic wrap. "Anyway, cryotherapy is supposed to be good for you, like anti-aging and all of that."

"You mean like purposely getting cold, for long periods of time."

"Exactly."

Keeler scrutinized Vitalek, an oddball eccentric billionaire tech guy. "That's your style, you play the bohemian genius. Show up late or whatever from your camping trip and let everyone else kind of work around your schedule. Like you don't really give a shit."

Vitalek looked at him, eyebrows raised, amused. "Something like that. But, I do give a shit. You have to understand, in my weird little world I'm pretty famous." He laughed. "Outside of that little world I'm completely unknown."

"And what?"

"And it kinda sucks to be famous."

"I'm full of sympathy."

Vitalek shook his head. "Ok. It puts a lot of bullshit in your path is what I mean. Dodging bullshit is one of my goals in life. Which is why I don't answer calls or emails or ride in limos or go to Davos or whatever."

Keeler agreed with the sentiment, but he kept the conversation on point. "Is there any reason you can think that anyone would want Rosenbaum out of the way?"

Vitalek said, "Many reasons. Do you know anything about the space?"

"Space?"

"It's what we call the crypto-sphere, the ecosystem of people who work on this stuff."

"I see." Keeler said, "No, I don't know anything about the space. Whatever you think I need to know, make it brief."

Vitalek gave a short laugh and his eyes glazed over. Keeler had the impression that the guy was looking at him without seeing him for a half minute. Vitalek's eyes refocused onto Keeler. "You know what a computer network is."

Keeler nodded. "A bunch of computers connected together."

"Yeah. Connected through software, so they can communicate, right?"

"Right."

"So, a crypto platform is a network. Think of the network as a kind of virtual computer. Like all of the connected computers make it one big computer. In the world of crypto there's something called a hard fork. You duplicate the entire network and then it becomes a whole new thing. The old one remains, but the two are now competing with each other. The same, but different."

"You and Rosenbaum are both forking off in a different direction."

"No. We're not forking, some other people want to fork. They're pissed that we don't agree." He waved a dismissive hand. "There's always that kind of BS going on. I don't really pay attention anymore."

"Rosenbaum's what, your business partner?"

"I've met Irma like, five times. She's a really smart person and a solid developer." Vitalek looked at Keeler under hooded eyes. "We're usually in touch constantly online. She's got a stake in the project, which counts."

"Stake as in a shareholder."

"Well, it's complicated. A better way to put it would be to say that Irma and I have a shared ideological understanding. We're kinda on the same team." Vitalek's eyebrows went up.

"And there's money at stake."

"Uh, yes. I guess so. Those other people are institutional stakeholders, the ones that want to fork. They're always worried about the short-term money thing." He glanced up at Keeler. "I mean, they have houses and families and stuff. It's a job to them. They work for serious institutions. I kind of understand where they're coming from. I just don't want to be them."

"Banks?"

"Not exactly."

Vitalek looked off into space and Keeler got the feeling that money was an abstraction to him, not his main motivating factor. Which dovetailed with Keeler's intuitive feeling for him.

Keeler said, "Off topic for a second. Tell me how you get to be a billionaire who goes on ad-hoc winter camping trips without security."

Vitalek shrugged. "Who said I was a billionaire?"

"Jill up at Copenhagen House."

"Forget about that. I like being out in the woods. I don't like the idea of living with bodyguards. End of story."

Keeler thought, *Either stupid or brave or maybe both. Everyone makes choices.*

He said, "I was up there at Copenhagen House and I got the feeling that things aren't exactly all hearts and bubble bath in the crypto world. I was there at the train station when your friend Rosenbaum was taken down."

"Taken down?"

Keeler didn't want to get into the Vince Farrell situation. "Operational assumption."

Vitalek was nodding, which wasn't surprising. Billionaires aren't the kind of people who can completely ignore security concerns. "You don't need to be so cryptic. Tell me what you're thinking."

"I'm thinking that you need to be careful. They went for Rosenbaum and dollars to donuts they're going to come for you. Only question is: Why haven't they already? I guess it's because you went winter camping."

Vitalek considered him. The blue eyes narrowing. "You know something, I've decided to not worry about that stuff."

"What stuff?"

"Living or dying. I've been under one death threat or

another for a couple of years now." He opened up his arms. "What am I going to do, live in hiding?"

Now it was Keeler's turn to consider the guy in front of him. "Fair enough. So I shouldn't care is what you're saying."

Vitalek shrugged. "I'm touched that you do." His eyes darted to the other room, where the sisters were holed up. He said, "Maybe living for the next couple of days would be worth it though." He smiled. "What do you suggest?"

Keeler grunted. Vitalek was a funny guy. "Since you're mister computer brain with financial clout, I'm assuming that you know people who can help you out with computer security."

Vitalek let a slim smile play over his lips. "Sure. What kind?"

Keeler leaned forward again, getting proximity and getting down to brass tacks. "Four guys just arrived up at Copenhagen House. I figure they're up there either to protect you, or to kill you. Even money at this point. My suggestion is we check them out before you go in there."

Vitalek glanced at his computer. "I'm supposed to be up there today for some kind of workshop. I think also a coffee reception after." He looked back at Keeler. "How do we do that? Check them out?"

Keeler gestured to the bedroom in back. "Honey trap."

A smile played over Vitalek's lips. "Uh huh, like when spies use a beautiful woman to trap the enemy agent."

"Or a good-looking guy, depending."

Vitalek had been looking at Keeler, his deep-set eyes intense and concentrated. The eyes lost their focus, and his gaze drifted upward, to something behind and above Keeler. Keeler almost looked up but didn't, because he could smell her before he saw her. The scent fresh, like spring flowers and incense. Mini

DeValla came up behind him and rested a hand on his bare shoulder.

"The laptop bag wasn't found on the same train you took." She had been listening to their conversation, maybe from the kitchen.

"No?"

"No. You and me were on the southbound train to the city. I don't know if you clocked it, but there was a northbound that came in after that. The conductor asked me to do the walk-through. I found the laptop on the northbound train."

Vitalek and Keeler looked at each other. Keeler said, "I see."

Mini DeValla let her nails slide down from Keeler's shoulder a half inch, making contact with the skin over his pectoral muscle.

"Your turn in the shower, big guy."

The finger slid away, and the perfume receded. Vitalek's eyes held on Keeler's for a beat before traveling down to his backpack on the floor by the couch. He rummaged in the front pocket and pulled out a phone.

"Okay, time to see what's going on in the world."

Keeler got his heartbeat and breathing under control and went to the shower.

Vitalek's phone bleeped in acknowledgment that it had been brought back to life.

CHAPTER FORTY-EIGHT

Keeler took his time in the shower. It had been a while. Candy had at least a dozen products to try, with different scents and foaming capabilities. Some of them had detailed instructions, increasingly difficult to follow as the bathroom steamed up. Eventually he had to quit, having tried out a little more than half of the available options.

He cleared a circle on the mirror and watched himself use a Q-tip in each ear. He hadn't shaved in a while, and maybe a haircut would become something to consider soon. But, not quite yet. There were things to take care of first, more immediate problems.

Keeler came out of the bathroom and dressed. He immediately sensed a change in the psychic atmosphere of Candy's apartment. He found the three of them gathered in the kitchen, the focus on Vitalek, eyes red like he'd been crying. Keeler stayed in the doorway, leaning an elbow against the wall.

"What's up?"

Vitalek looked at him. "Irma's dead. I called the hospital and they said she died last night. I know her family's in Israel. I guess they're trying to get in touch with them before releasing it to the press."

Rosenbaum hadn't made it, which meant that Keeler wasn't going to need to drive down to Phelps Memorial hospital to make sure she wasn't getting dead-checked by the enemy. They'd either let her die of the initial poisoning, or someone had gone into the ward and finished the job. Would have been good to go down there first, but there hadn't been time.

Keeler examined Vitalek. Normal shock reaction to a friend's death.

The thing about death is the sudden absence it creates. A human being or a pet isn't some kind of inanimate object. Life is lived in a shared psychological space. Rosenbaum's death was leaving a gaping hole in Vitalek's experience. Keeler wondered how long it would take the guy to get over it.

Candy was sitting with Vitalek. She had a hand on his arm, a finger playing with his sleeve. Mini was setting up the coffee machine for another round. She caught Keeler's eye and held it for a hot second. The cup he'd been using was on the counter, Mini filled it with the remaining coffee from the last batch and chin pointed at it.

The slogan faced him, Sisters Before Misters.

Keeler moved into the room and threaded a finger through the mug handle. "I'm sorry to hear that." He leaned against the counter and looked sideways at Vitalek. "Now it's time to make sure that doesn't happen to you."

Vitalek nodded. "Yeah." He put his head down to the table. "Man, I can't believe they actually went for it. I thought it was always going to be theoretical, you know?"

Keeler said, "It's always just talk until it isn't." He indicated the sisters. "Have you told them that you're more than a cute hitchhiker from the diner?"

Candy glanced at Keeler. "He told us about the crypto thing, yes."

Vitalek sniffed and wiped his nose on the sleeve of his long underwear. "I'm just me, man, and yes, I told them about what I do, which shouldn't be any more important than what anyone else does."

Mini said, "Only there's the money aspect of it."

"Right. People are greedy; it's so disgusting."

Vitalek was an idealist, a believer in things like democracy and justice and freedom. Keeler liked him. The kid needed to get real and grow up a little, but maybe this experience was going to be good for him, turn him into an adult.

Keeler pulled out a chair and flipped it backwards. He sat down on it and set the mug in front of him. "Whatever. It's time to get that out of your mind and focus on what needs to be done. Mini's right about the money. You're naive if you think you can get above it. They've taken your friend out of the game, and now they're coming for you. What you need to ask yourself is: why they feel like they have the right to do that." Vitalek nodded his head in agreement, but Keeler wasn't done. "And you're not alone, buddy. We're all in the firing line now, so we're going to have to act like a team." Keeler had decided that he'd be the quarterback, calling the plays. He chin pointed at Vitalek. "Remember what I said, about the honey trap?"

"Yeah." The guy's eyes were clearing, vivid and focused in the deeply recessed Slavic sockets.

Keeler said, "Good."

Mini pressed go on the coffee machine and wiped up spilled grounds with a kitchen cloth. "What's a honey trap?" she asked.

Keeler leaned back in the chair and hooked the coffee mug. "You use a beautiful woman to seduce a bad guy. Believe me, it works. We may not have automatic weapons and sniper rifles, but in terms of beauty, our team wins the arms race."

Mini glanced at Candy. "Every girl knows that men are slaves. But, what's the point?"

Vitalek said, "We'll penetrate their communications network. All we need is for one of their guys to click a link on his phone. The rest will be taken care of by software." He nodded his head to Keeler. "I sourced the malware for it. I need like, an hour to set it up, Okay?"

Keeler nodded and pointed at Candy. "You're the one who's going to make the guy feel good about clicking a link on his phone. Are you ready to rock?"

"Me?" she asked, wide-eyed and flushed, getting excited for the mission. "Sure."

"Good." He turned to Mini. "Tell me if I'm wrong, but I'm guessing you'd like to lay eyes on your kids, maybe take them to school, speak with your mom."

She nodded. "It's going to be too late for the school run, but yes, I'd like to just make sure my life still exists. You know, before we go onto other things." Mini gave a short laugh and looked up. "Why do I feel like everything has changed around me?"

Candy lifted her eyes, rolled them around. "Because it has. You can't ignore what just happened to you, Min. And with Frankie, you know."

"Yeah." Mini closed her eyes, shaking her head as if she were gently getting rid of dust. "My car's still gone." She opened her eyes and looked at Candy. "Maybe they just left it up by the old water tower. I need a ride home."

There were two parts to Keeler's plan. The first part Keeler would handle on his own: go to Pat Rooney's house and stage a home invasion. Get in there and see what was going on. Best-case scenario, he'd find Rooney and Santarelli and maybe others, sleeping or eating breakfast. Worst case, nobody would be home.

Meanwhile, Candy would drop her sister off at home and then she and Vitalek were going to go up to Copenhagen house, which is where it would get interesting. Given what they now knew, it was too dangerous for Vitalek to just show up. They didn't know what the enemy had planned. Maybe the order was to kill him on sight. So Candy was going in on a reconnaissance mission. She hadn't yet appeared on the battlefield, which was a good thing for them. But, Keeler warned her, once you show up on the battlefield, you take the consequences.

Candy had nodded slowly and glanced at Vitalek. "I accept."

Keeler already had Candy's phone number. Mini had her phone back and they exchanged contacts. Vitalek got his laptop out and connected to a power source. He had work to do, setting everything up. The rest of them made French toast, with Keeler's job mostly being on the consumption, appreciation, and dishwashing side. After that he decided to make a start on the Rooney project. Once he was done with Rooney, he'd go by the UPS Store. Pick up the laptop, and then get back with Vitalek and Candy.

Keeler suited up and left the apartment.

CHAPTER FORTY-NINE

A little while earlier, Vince Farrell had crossed Bear Mountain Bridge in a rented Kia. He'd picked up the car in Newark using a disposable alias and hoofed it up the Palisades Parkway early, a large cup of coffee securely tucked into the flip-out holder.

The view was incredible from the bridge. The Hudson River choked by snow-covered mountains. Sheer rock cliff faces dropped severely to the ice. A female voice came over the radio, soothing and mature. Another blizzard was expected later in the day. Farrell had a classical music station on. Half the reason was he found the announcer's voice comforting. The other reason was because he felt he was at that stage in his life where he could up his game socially. He'd been trying to get into classical for the three years that he'd been working for T&G Associates and had concluded only that he didn't actively dislike Beethoven. Mozart was terrible, and Bach was weird.

The phone bleeped at him from its magnetic holder attached to the air vent grill. Farrell glanced at his device and saw the notification icon bobbing up and down. He turned down the music and tapped fluently on the glass surface. Dial tone came from the little speaker, followed by bleeps and burps and ringtone.

A woman answered. "I see it too."

Farrell licked his lips. "You have the location? I'm driving."

"I'll send it. Tap it when you get it."

The phone line clicked as she ended the call. Farrell nodded to himself. Another notification bleeped and an icon bounced from the top of his phone screen. He flicked his eyes from the road to the phone and executed a few finger taps. A map appeared with animated arrows and Farrell felt good, like he was on the right path. He turned the music back up a little.

The protagonist had activated his phone, so the tracker was working. The target was in Kitchewan Landing, which boded well. It took Farrell a half hour to drive to the indicated address, a brick apartment complex. He parked next to a Little League field. Farrell fiddled with the phone, hid the map, and got the tracking app up. The protagonist's phone was presented as a red circle with crosshairs.

Farrell navigated the Kia into the development, cruising the patchwork of parking spaces in and among islands of frozen and bare vegetation and the buildings themselves. The development was maybe twenty years old and a little worn looking. He drove carefully, not wanting to call attention to himself. A couple emerged from one of the buildings and made moves to cross the lot. Farrell let them go, watching the bundled forms scurry across. He waved.

The app indicated that the protagonist was in one of the units at the end. Beyond the building was a copse of denuded trees and a rise. There was no way of knowing precisely which unit he was in, because one was on top of the other. Farrell parked back fifty yards.

He reached behind him and got a hold of his kit bag. He pulled out an expensive camera and attached it to a mini tripod, which latched onto the dashboard in front of him with suction cups. With his bare eyes he couldn't see details at that distance, but with the telephoto lens he had an excellent close-up view on the big LCD display whenever he wanted it.

Farrell panned the camera up and over slowly, examining the building's facade. There wasn't anything moving. The curtains were closed on both unit windows. He settled back in the driver's seat. On the way over, he'd secured another cup of coffee, a box of donuts, and an empty water bottle to piss into.

Two donuts and a half cup of coffee later, the door opened on the top unit. Farrell reactivated the camera and adjusted the lens. Someone had come out of the front door and was now walking down the stairs, usefully built onto the outside of the building.

It was Keeler, wearing some kind of outdoor jacket and a wool hat. Guy hadn't given up the life, that was clear already. He looked like a one-man execution squad. Farrell took several photographs of him.

He took his eyes off the LCD display. For a hot second there, it looked like Keeler was coming across the lot right at him, but he veered left and crossed a concrete island. Farrell swiveled the camera on the tripod, watching him walk, the way he strode with a relaxed purpose, face calm but eyes no doubt darting around collecting information. If he was going to take Keeler out, he'd have to be careful.

Which was the problem with following him right that minute, because the tracking device on his phone showed the protagonist was still in the apartment, and the protagonist was the priority target. It was what Grimaldi had said, and what everyone else was thinking.

Keeler was his own little passion project.

Keeler's going out made little sense if the man was providing protection to the protagonist. Protection doesn't go out to fetch breakfast, at least not the kind of protection Keeler would be providing. Maybe there was someone else up there covering for him. All of which meant that it was prudent to not be hasty. Let Keeler leave, Farrell would stay and see what else was going on.

Keeler climbed into a silver Toyota with tinted rear windows, like a drug dealer's car. The vehicle coughed vapor and idled for a minute. Keeler got it in gear and cruised out of the parking lot.

Ten minutes later, Farrell was chewing through his third donut, washing it down with coffee that was still warm. The front door of the apartment opened, and he put the half-eaten donut back into the box, wiped the crumbs off his fingers on the empty passenger seat. The camera was already up and oriented, all he had to do was press a button and the LCD lit up again.

Two women emerged, followed by a man. They descended from the apartment and came across the parking lot toward him. Farrell concentrated on the camera's display. The women were very good-looking, a fact recognizable despite the layers they'd bundled into; they looked like sisters. He recognized the tall, lanky young guy trailing after them, the protagonist.

He concentrated on the protagonist, a total geek, in over his head. These women were way out of his league on any kind of a sexual attraction scale, but then Farrell had to admit, it was hard to quantify charisma. The geek was also insanely rich, which meant his pull could be an order of magnitude greater than it might have been if he didn't have money.

Farrell watched the trio climb into a worn-out Subaru.

Eventually the vehicle pulled out of the spot and the woman driving navigated her way out of the parking lot. Farrell watched and waited, giving it time. He had the protagonist up on his phone screen, the dot blinking at him like a beacon.

CHAPTER FIFTY

Somewhere between his first step out the door and the bottom of the stairs down to the parking lot, Keeler had noticed the Kia. The car sitting in a spot that he'd picked out as a strategically viable observation point. It was somewhere in the region of fifty yards out, in the parking lot of a different apartment building, which made it one of the better spots to watch Candy's building. After noticing the vehicle, he'd walked across the lot to the Toyota. Keeler had discreetly gazed into the vehicle's windshield and detected a very slight movement, ergo, someone in that vehicle was watching Candy's apartment.

Now, Keeler sat in the Toyota looking at a brick wall directly in front of him. The engine idled slightly on the high side. He had backed the car into the apartment complex's garbage disposal area, an asphalt indentation surrounded on all sides by garbage containers. A round convex mirror was up on the wall in front of him, giving a distorted 180-degree view.

Since the watcher didn't come immediately after him, Keeler assumed that he wasn't the target. It was either Vitalek or Mini DeValla—or possibly laptop related. After last night, the Kitchewan Old Cars people would have to be pretty brave or stupid to tangle with the DeValla sisters again. But there was no shortage of stupid and brave out there. He saw movement in the convex mirror: Candy's car, very small in the reflection, was getting bigger and distorting as it approached and passed in front of him. Candy driving, Vitalek in the back and Mini riding shotgun. Even just looking at Mini gesticulating to her sister as the car drove by was doing hormonal and chemical things to Keeler's nervous system.

Welcome distractions.

The watcher was taking his time. The convex mirror empty. The interior of the Toyota getting a little too cozy, made Keeler consider abandoning the position to investigate. He had his hand on the shifter when there was movement in the mirror. Keeler watched the vehicle approach, didn't like the way it was creeping. He decided that he'd terminate this surveillance operation immediately, with extreme prejudice.

The vehicle came from his right. Keeler's foot was ready on the gas pedal, his mind estimating and preparing, his body relaxed and breathing evenly. He felt best in moments like those, calm, with a highly tuned control of nerves and muscles. The body buzzing happily with electric anticipation.

The mirror's distortion made the approaching vehicle look as if it was wrapping around a ball. Keeler waited a beat and hit the gas. The Toyota launched forward, engine whining in high gear. Adrenaline surged, familiar and friendly. He had his mouth closed, teeth together, braced for impact. The car shot into the watcher's front left quarter panel. It was a good, bone-shaking hit, glass exploding and crunching with a drawn-out shriek of metal on metal. The close distance not allowing an impact that could do major damage, but sufficient to immobilize the watcher's car and block it in.

Keeler was out of the driver's seat like lightning on a hot humid night, sliding over the hood with the lead tipped club up and ready. He landed on two feet in front of the driver. Vince Farrell was behind the wheel, currently in a deep grimace. He rated Farrell as condition orange, some level of situational awareness, but a little too stunned to be operational at that moment.

It wasn't exactly what Keeler would call a surprise to see Farrell there, but it hadn't been what he'd expected. Farrell's belt was fastened behind him, a way of a circumventing the annoying seat-belt alarm on newer cars. The Kia's fender had been crushed in, the panel riding up and distorting the driver's side door. Which meant the door might be hard to open. Keeler swung the billy club at the window in a hard diagonal. The glass shattered all over Farrell, who was forced to close his eyes and hold up a protective hand.

Keeler took the club in both hands and stabbed hard between Farrell's upheld hands. The butt end rammed into Farrell's upper lip and drove through the front teeth. Keeler pulled the club back and allowed it to fall from his hands. Farrell was busy with shattered teeth and blood spurting from his lacerated lip, situational awareness further degraded. Keeler saw everything in slow motion.

He leaned in through the window and took hold of Farrell's head, gripping it with two hands under the jawbone. He tore the man's writhing body out through the window. Like Farrell was born again, from a mechanical mother. Once he had him out, Keeler dumped his load onto the asphalt and stepped back, watching him try and scamper to his feet, spitting tooth fragments.

He retrieved the club and gave Farrell a good slap to his knee, refraining from breaking bone or causing a life-changing injury.

"What're you doing here, Farrell?"

Farrell spit blood. "Fuck you."

He put a palm down to push himself upright. Keeler stamped on his hand with a hard boot and ground it into the asphalt. Farrell stifled a howl. Keeler straddled him from behind and got the club under the chin, digging hard into the soft part of his neck.

"Come again, buddy?" Farrell said nothing. He made a strange choked sound. "Come on Farrell, don't draw this out. What's the plan, you really up here to clip the crypto kid?"

Farrell didn't respond. Keeler reached over and put a thumb into his left eye, swiping the contact lens out and flicking it off. A blue eye was revealed, the whites bloodshot and red.

Keeler said, "There we go, showing your true colors now, Farrell, what's to be ashamed of? The face lift kind of worked though, got to admit."

Farrell made his move. He got his right hand dug under Keeler's boot and jerked hard, trying to unbalance him. Keeler was surprised to lose balance on that leg. Hadn't thought Farrell was so strong. He had to hop back a step, compensating with his other leg. In that fragment of a second, Farrell was up and sprang out of the lock Keeler had him in.

Farrell stepped inside the club's reach. He moved like a coiled steel spring, shaping up and delivering a headbutt to Keeler's nose. The heavy skull came through cartilage and bounced off of bone, rebounding while Farrell prepped for another shot. Keeler's head shot back on his neck, almost giving him whiplash. He managed to keep his footing, seeing through blurred vision the man coming at him for the follow-up.

Keeler shook it off and sidestepped. A fist came whispering past his right ear. Farrell's left almost caught him in the solar plexus, burying knuckles into Keeler's chest. Keeler pressed forward, shoving him off. Farrell jumped back and adjusted his feet, hands up in a combat stance. Keeler feigned a left jab and Farrell reacted, half-stepping back and over. Keeler took advan-

tage of the movement. He stepped in and brought the club into
Farrell's temple at a three-quarter angle.

That was it, Farrell went out like a light. He flopped
forward, his face slapping hard into asphalt.

Keeler blew blood and snot through his damaged nose. He
used both hands on either side to crack the cartilage back into a
relatively straight line. He looked around. No civilians yet, but
they'd be coming. Keeler badly wanted to interrogate Farrell.
He figured he'd just take him in the Toyota and extract answers
in a better location. Farrell was still out and the time was right.
Keeler moved forward and got around the guy, dragging him by
the armpits into the vehicle.

Up ahead a car moved out of a parking spot. Keeler let the
unconscious man fall back to the ground. Stepped back out of
sight. Farrell moved. He sat up and put his back against the Kia,
groggy and finding his bearings. Finding himself alive and still
in the game. The vehicle up ahead was slowly moving toward
them.

Keeler went back around to the Toyota. He backed the
vehicle away from the damage, making space for the civilian to
come through, a man in his thirties, rubbernecking. Farrell got to
his feet and waved the guy past. Had to lean in the window and
verbalize. Keeler watched from within the dumpster area. The
vehicle drove out, and Keeler saw his chance.

He'd hit the gas and crush Farrell for good. Rid the earth of
that guy, and at least a couple of the world's problems would be
solved.

Keeler shifted into drive and his foot felt for the gas pedal.
There was movement in the convex mirror. Another civilian on
his way to work. As the vehicle came into view, so did the police
light bar on its roof. Keeler didn't curse, not even under his
breath. He watched the vehicle coming closer, seeing another
one behind it. The second car had no light bar.

Why wouldn't there be police living in the apartment complex, going to work in the morning like everybody else. Farrell would die another day.

He turned out of the dumpster area, toward the exit, window open. Farrell made eye contact, feeling around in his mouth, spoke to Keeler through his open window. "That crown cost a couple of grand, Keeler, just had it done last May. I hate going to the dentist."Keeler smiled as he passed. "Forget about it. You aren't going to need a dentist; you'll need a mortician before we're through."

The Toyota was dented, but nothing major. Maybe fix the headlight, to avoid law enforcement attention if he had to drive at night. Farrell's Kia wasn't really operational. The hood had come up, and it might not be easy to get it down again. First-world problems, like Farrell's teeth.

Keeler drove away, glancing in the rearview mirror. Farrell in the shaky reflection, trying to drag himself upright and slipping on the shattered detritus of his vehicle. The police car was pulling up. The cop probably asking if Farrell needed help. Farrell stood and brushed himself off, making reassuring hand signals. A professional like him would find the right words.

Keeler made the turn out of the development. He pulled into the lot fifty yards away from Candy's apartment complex and parked with a decent observational view of the entrance. The cop came out presently and made a right turn. Farrell's car didn't follow. Keeler remembered the civilian vehicle behind the police cruiser. Maybe Farrell's car was inoperable.

The issue was Vitalek and the sisters, in danger from the maniac. But, he could get them out of danger and still drop Farrell at another time.

Keeler pulled out of the lot and got the Toyota moving. He wondered how Pat Rooney was doing that morning, if maybe Tommy Santarelli was making breakfast, or borrowing a set of

Rooney's clothes. The sky was clear blue. It was cold out, but sunny. He visualized Frankie's body in the snow box, chilled out.

Things were more or less under control. It could be better, but it could be a whole lot worse. Keeler had already been in a fine humor that morning, mostly thanks to the flirtation with Mini DeValla. The scuffle with Farrell had put it over the top, and despite the broken nose, Keeler was now in an excellent mood. He rolled down the window and let the frigid air in, invigorating and healthy. He whistled a line into the rushing air. "Like a Hurricane," the Neil Young tune he'd heard the day before.

Keeler opened his lungs and howled into the morning air. Whatever it was, he was going to figure it out. He was like a quarterback with a great team. Bring it on!

CHAPTER FIFTY-ONE

F arrell watched the civilian drive away. After the cop, the good neighbor had stopped offering all kinds of help. Now he was rolling carefully over crushed glass and plastic detritus, clearing the scene and then accelerating. Farrell raised his hand and waved, barely able to move his arm and keeping his mouth closed so as not to expose the gap where his tooth had been. Inside, he was keeping it together for now. The sole reason he wasn't dead or in prison, the ability to control the beast.

What he'd wanted to do was to kill the man with his bare hands, just beat and squeeze and rub the life out of the nosy neighbor and destroy him. Farrell felt the tug of the other side, a rushing hot wound of a world, where there wasn't any reason to use the human part of your mind. Farrell got to go there some-times, which is why he did what he did.

For now, he needed to get his head straight.

He couldn't even think about Keeler, which was infuriating. He needed to focus on his own security. The Kia was more or less trashed. Farrell managed to force the hood down, bend the metal so that it was out of the way. He stood back, looking criti-cally. Would the law pull him over if he tried to drive that thing?

He didn't have a choice. The last thing he wanted was to stay there and wait for a tow truck.

The vehicle was operational, which was something at least. He had no immediate destination in mind—just get away from there. Farrell got the car moving and turned out of the apartment complex. Past the Little League field he breathed more easily.

He tapped on the phone, miraculously still attached to the magnetic holder on his dashboard. The screen blinked to life and he got the tracking application up. The target symbol was moving along, the protagonist and the sisters traveling south on a road parallel to the river. Blood pooled around Farrell's tongue from the wounded lip. He spit out the open window, a long stream of blood and saliva.

The phone on the dash lit up with Grimaldi's face, requesting a video call. Farrell rejected video and accepted audio.

"Terry, I'm driving."

Grimaldi's voice came through sounding breathless, which meant that he was on the treadmill.

"I saw that he turned his phone on. Did you do it?"

"Not yet Terry, he wasn't alone. I'm going to let him run out the line a little longer. I've got eyes on him."

"Okay Vince, just not up at the conference center."

"Yes, I am aware of that."

"Get it done."

The line clicked off and Farrell cursed again. The menace in Grimaldi's tone was implicit. Get it done, or else. Farrell was cruising down a boulevard with a grassy divider in the middle of it, cute suburban houses on either side. He saw them on fire, like after a Russian invasion. That would be something, bodies scattered everywhere. A conflict where nobody gave a shit, where anything goes.

You walk into some house and do whatever the fuck you want.

He wasn't feeling well, wound up and tense. Farrell needed to get it all out of the system and get straight again. After making the right on red, he turned onto a road running parallel to the highway raised on a mound above town. There weren't any houses on his left side, only the highway. To the right were businesses and the occasional apartment block.

Farrell cut the Kia's wheel to the left, deciding randomly to go through an underpass, beneath the highway, toward the river. The tunnel gave out to an access road along a riverside park with a small marina. A dozen boats were wrapped up for the winter and raised onto jack stands, covered with heavy tarps.

He slowed the Kia to a crawl. There was a single brick building, the marina office probably. One vehicle was parked in front. Other than that and the seagulls there was nothing happening. No sign of life, just ice on the water and a wicked wind coming off the Hudson.

The road dead-ended up ahead. Farrell made a K-turn and came back to park in a diagonal spot next to a worn-out Chevy sedan that had seen far too many winters. He sat in the car for a couple of minutes, getting a feel for his surroundings. The park was a knob jutting out into the Hudson, a white snow field with a couple of trees and a covered pavilion surrounded by barbecues.

He got out of the Kia and popped the trunk. Inside were two duffel bags. Farrell pulled a pair of latex gloves from a side pocket, expertly stretching and fitting them onto his hands and fingers. From another pocket he extracted a silicone mask custom made just for him. Expensive but realistic and very useful. He hadn't imagined that Keeler would have blindsided him like that, or else he'd have taken it out of the trunk earlier. Farrell pulled the mask over his head and stretched and smoothed until it felt good, eye, nose, and mouth holes lined up and operating. The mask transformed him into a Black man in his midfifties.

Farrell entered the park through an open gate in the fence and circled the small marina building, not knowing exactly what he was looking for, but feeling compelled. Cameras were mounted strategically, most of them surveilling the marina.

The door to the building was on the harbor side. Green painted wood, plastered with sailing related stickers. He pushed and it moved, unlocked. There was a camera mounted to observe the building's entrance. The good thing about his mask was it was convincing from even a medium-close distance.

The park was splendidly isolated, cut off from town by the highways, cut off from humanity by the winter. The entrance sported a worn polished wood counter. Behind it was a little desk area for the receptionist with a computer and a chair. There were signs all over for sailing lessons and boat rentals. Farrell heard the sounds of a television from farther in. If anyone was there, they hadn't heard him enter. He took a left after the counter, down a corridor with a low drop ceiling, fluorescent tubes glowing weakly. There was an office on the right side, and the door opened inward.

Farrell stood in the doorway looking at an older guy with a puffed and graying afro. The man was sitting on an ergonomic office chair, watching a game show on a computer. The old guy didn't see him at first, focusing all of his attention on the tall woman with large white teeth and big hair on the screen.

The old guy jumped when he saw Farrell standing in the doorway. "Jesus!" It was like he'd seen a vampire or something. Farrell observed his fear, was surprised as the guy breathed out a sigh of relief. "Man, you scared the shit out of me." The man seemed relieved, which was weird.

Farrell said, "Why are you relieved to see me?"

"I thought you were my boss, when you jumped out." The man took his eyes off Farrell and looked back at the television.

Farrell glanced up the corridor, down the other side. "Is there anyone else here?"

The man chuckled. "You're in the wrong place if you want a boat. Nobody's going sailing until maybe April." He looked up at Farrell without clocking the mask. "I'm the maintenance guy. Winters, I clean up once a week, carpets and dust and stuff. Make sure the boiler's working just because. I watch a little TV sometimes. Make myself coffee. You want coffee?"

There was a mug on the desk in front of the man.

Farrell looked at the old guy again and didn't feel much. The maintenance guy hadn't even remotely clocked that Farrell was wearing a silicone murder mask. Maybe he didn't have good vision. What was the point of having feelings for something as pathetic as that? More than anything, he felt like the old guy needed to be taken out of the game for his own good. A win-win situation all around, since the way he was feeling now, if Farrell didn't kill him, he'd probably end up shooting one of his own men in the back of the head, like accidentally on purpose. Which would mean losing one of his own, plus the others wouldn't be very happy.

He stepped into the small room, crowding into it and getting his gloved hands out front, grabbing with hard fingers. The old guy made a weak attempt at struggling, huffing through his nose and making weird sounds, but it didn't take very long to make him dead. Farrell thought about it like that, like turning off someone's switch. He'd had a dream once, early on, him and a big Rottweiler in the dark on a train line somewhere in the middle of nowhere. The dog and him. Farrell had reached inside the animal's throat and found the switch to just turn him off.

CHAPTER FIFTY-TWO

On his way out, Farrell marveled at the way the whole thing had occurred in a rush of heat and light. He felt a hell of a lot better. Clear and sharp and back on his feet now. He went over to the pavilion by the waterline and sat at a picnic table. The bench was dry, thanks to the pavilion roof. He brought out his phone and tapped and swiped.

Dial tone came out of it and the same woman answered. "Did you get there?"

"Yeah, I got there. What I need now is a team. Who's available?"

"I assume you don't mean the team up at the conference center."

"No, not them. They stay on mission. Did Kelly get there?"

She came back to him fast. "Kelly's there. Right now I've got three who could come up within an hour."

The woman was beginning another sentence, but Farrell cut her off. "You need to go harder. Get me six or seven, not three. And I need the witch. You copy?"

There wasn't a noticeable delay in his command and her

response. She was cold, like steel. Her voice didn't quaver. "The witch, roger that."

"The other thing, my vehicle needs to be evacuated and replaced and I need to eat. Vehicle's at my current location. Confirm."

"Give me a second."

Farrell waited longer than one second, thinking about the witch, a weird guy with some esoteric training in the art of killing people, hence the moniker.

The woman came back on the line. "Got the location. There's a diner nearby. I'll send you the address."

"Outstanding. Just send the guys up to the diner. One hour."

"Is that it?"

Farrell had the image in his mind of the train conductor he'd seen at the diner with Keeler. DeValla had been the name, engraved on a gold tag above her left breast. He knew how his mind worked, let that image stay around for a moment until he figured out why. He got it. One of the women coming out of the apartment with the protagonist. That had been DeValla. Her and Keeler in the diner, coming out of the same apartment this morning.

The woman on the other end of the line was patient. He could hear her breathing while he thought.

Farrell said, "Do me a little research, hun. A woman named DeValla. Probably lives in Kitchewan Landing." He spelled the name. "Metro-North conductor. Find out what you can."

"Sure."

Farrell ended the call and looked out at the frozen river. It wasn't actually one piece of ice, more like a chaotic mosaic of ice floes, jockeying in and around each other for position. Everything was a goddamned competition. His head was feeling weird and buzzy. Farrell shook it, like getting out cobwebs, but they wouldn't come out. He looked up again and suddenly had to tear off the mask. It was suffocating him. For a while he sat there gulping and gasping, letting the cold do its work on his overheated brain.

Things weren't right, and he admitted to himself that he felt uneasy. A vast uncertainty had opened up below him, like he didn't know what was going to happen. Felt like the disorder was sucking him in fast.

CHAPTER FIFTY-THREE

Keeler was in the Toyota across the street from Pat Rooney's house, a two-story set in a hilltop neighborhood sloping down to the river. Rooney's front door had been locked and Keeler wasn't going to break in. It wasn't a question of morality or ethics. From the pedestrian traffic, it would seem that Thompson Hill Drive was a commuter shortcut, a route from up in town to the train station. Every minute or two, someone was walking down the hill carrying a briefcase and bundled up for the walk.

When Keeler was conducting a tour around the house, looking in the windows and checking the back porch, a man had passed through the yard wearing a laptop bag and carrying a refillable coffee cup. Looked like there was a shortcut route between the houses. Through the window, Keeler had seen into the kitchen. Coffee cup and cereal bowl left on the table. No Rooney at home, no friends or relations. Just a single eater who'd taken his breakfast and left.

Through the gap between Rooney's house and the neighbor's he could see the frozen river surface, scarred by long curving lines, snow drifts that had formed on the flat ice. The river looked organized. A self-correcting community of ice types. As he'd learned up in Canada, there are many kinds of ice. Down there on the Hudson it looked mostly like a mixture of frazil and pancake ice.

Keeler broke out of the spell. Looking at the ice and the cliffs over the other side, he'd been thinking about Candy's apartment and the fact that Farrell had been outside in that Kia watching the place. The question was how had Farrell known to be there? The answer to that would have to wait, but Candy's apartment was going to be off-limits until this game was over.

He had Candy on speed dial and thumbed the button. She answered on the second ring. "Yeah."

"I don't want you going back to your place just yet. When you're done up there we can meet at your sister's."

Candy let the words out slowly. "Okay. Why?"

Keeler didn't want to get her anxious about what had just happened with Farrell. She had a mission to accomplish and he needed her calm and collected. At the same time, he wasn't going to negotiate with her.

"Don't bother with the why, just stay away. I'll see you at Mini's later on. Good luck."

Keeler killed the call, wondering if he shouldn't have been more forceful. It was a tough balance. He got the Toyota started and moved off the curb. The drug dealer's car was damaged but still useable. He wasn't worried about the broken headlight; what bothered him were the inconsistencies inhering to the current situation.

For one thing, there wasn't any obvious connection between the taxi company people and the protagonist—and by extension, Farrell. Keeler wasn't even able to mentally put any of them into the same room. Vitalek and some kind of high-end hit job, sure. That was easy to imagine. By Vitalek's own admission the stakes were high, and people will always be prepared to up the game when there's real money involved.

He'd learned to visualize complicated situations as constellations, like the star patterns in the sky. Some stars would fit into a pattern; others wouldn't.

In one constellation you could place Mini DeValla and her sister, Candy, with the locals from Kitchewan Old Cars, Rooney, and the people working for him. They all seemed to know each other to some degree. But when you got on the train, the thread began to fray.

The train connected Kitchewan Landing to the city, and by extension to more constellations. Keeler figured that Copenhagen House had a similar connective role.

If you wanted to put Farrell into a constellation with Vitalek, Rosenbaum, Jill, and Jerry, you'd need to add in the institutions each of them fit into. The crypto project Vitalek and Rosenbaum were involved in, the people Farrell was working for, Triton Gamma Associates.

And behind Triton Gamma, a client who had requested the hits on Vitalek and Rosenbaum. The problem ran deep, and if Keeler was going to pull Vitalek out of the burning oil, it wasn't going to be easy. Take out Farrell, nuke Triton Gamma's offices on both coasts, you'd still have someone with money who wanted Vitalek dead.

Keeler watched the road while he thought. He didn't care where he was driving, aimless was all right. He watched it as an abstraction, lines curving, objects moving around each other, following an invisible order. He thought about Julie Everard, the woman running the *Kitchewan Gazette*. He had the idea that maybe Everard could be useful in the end. Not yet, but later. A win-win situation all around.

Keeler found himself a couple of blocks from Mini DeValla's house, recognizing the street. He hadn't consciously navigated to her house, but there he was. Keeler turned his head slightly to see the children's books taking up space in the backseat, where he'd tossed them.

Why not?

DeValla opened the door and flicked her eyes out past him, as if to see who else was there. Seeing nobody, she opened the door wider. "Come in. What happened to your face?" she asked once she'd gotten a closer look at him.

He ignored the remark about his face—having almost forgotten about the broken nose—and entered, pulling the door shut behind him. "Is your mom here?" Keeler reached up to his nose and felt the swelling. Wasn't too bad.

Mini had a hand up in her mass of curly hair, teasing it out. She closed the door and looked at him strangely. "My mom?" She laughed. "No. There's nobody here. Just me. I have to go to work, unfortunately. Scheduled for the late shift. Can't even pick up the kids from school."

Keeler said nothing. His mind crawled lazily over the various ins and outs of working as a conductor on a commuter train.

She said, "Someone headbutted you in the face."

He grunted. "Something like that."

DeValla looked fantastic. She was wearing a silk robe, maybe getting ready for work. She seemed comfortable just standing there, looking right at him like that. Which was okay with Keeler, he felt good simply looking back at her. Somehow though, his mouth felt like talking.

He offered the library books. "I brought these. No reason you should have to pay overdue fees," he said, a bit unconvincingly, even though it was true in a way.

She took the books from him and tossed them on the hallway table.

"My shift starts in an hour and a half."

Their eyes locked and it was like a threshold had been crossed that couldn't be rowed back. DeValla moved to him and pressed the palm of her right hand against his chest. He brought his hand up and felt the silk slide over her hip, let his hand run back along the curve and his fingers graze the small of her back. With only a few points of contact he had a sense of her as a substantial presence giving off heat and the smell of her skin.

She tugged at his winter jacket. "Get this thing out of the way."

The jacket came off and nobody paid any attention to where it landed. DeValla's lips made contact, and Keeler saw her up close, looking at him. They closed their eyes at the same time, falling into the embrace, letting the magic happen. Both of her hands went up, fingers sliding around to the nape of his neck, pushing through unkempt hair. His right hand remained where it was, against the small of her back, feeling like it was a good place to be, pressing her to him a little and feeling the bump of her body against his. His other hand came up and parted the silk just in front of his chest, fingers finding her skin and getting between her body and the outer wrapper.

CHAPTER FIFTY-FOUR

A fterward, Keeler lay on his back in the bed, DeValla next
to him, running fingers over his chest. He was staring up
and out of her bedroom window, on the upper floor of the
house. The sky was clear blue.

DeValla followed his gaze to the sky. "Hard to believe it's
going to snow again, right? It's so blue. They say it's going to be
another blizzard, like the other one but worse maybe."

Keeler grunted. DeValla blew hair out of her face. "A penny
for your thoughts."

"Thinking about Pat Rooney's house. He wasn't there, so I
was wondering where he might be."

"The Kitchewan Old Cars guy."

"Right."

DeValla shifted herself so that they were facing each other
more comfortably, and he wouldn't have to crane his neck. His
fingers traced her body, from her waist to the contour of her
breast.

She said, "Maybe try the Kitchewan Old Cars office in
town."

"They have an office?"

DeValla moved closer to him, her hair brushing his forehead. He felt her breath on his cheek and her heat. The body, coming to his and making contact, skin on skin. Her hand, brushing over his hip and beyond. The pressure of her thigh against his hip. Her voice, close to his ear and warm. "Yeah, they do."

A half hour later Keeler was examining DeValla's tattooed legs, reading Wild Kitty off her smooth skin. She was facedown on the bed, covers somewhere on the other side of the room. He didn't comment on the tattoos. He asked her if she had any firearms in the house.

Mini got her face out of the pillow, craning her neck. "Frankie made me get a shotgun, back in the day. I've never touched it. Maybe it's in the garage."

Keeler found the weapon, an old Browning A5. There was a box of shells and a cleaning kit. Looked like Frankie's heart had been in the right place, but lacked in the follow-through and maintenance department. DeValla watched him clean the weapon on the kitchen table.

She said, "You know I'm kind of sad for the kids, but I'm surprised that I'm not more sad for Frankie." She touched the Browning's glossy wood forearm. "I'm not a gun person, you're barking up the wrong tree."

"When some guy comes into the house and you don't want him there, you put this up to your shoulder and squeeze the stock hard against your body at the same time as you pull the trigger. Don't hesitate because there won't be a second chance. You got that?"

"Not going to happen."

Keeler examined her and decided that even if she felt that way right now, she wouldn't feel that way when push came to shove. He got up from the kitchen table, went over to the front door, leaned the gun in the corner, and put the box of shells on the little entry table.

"You keep it here near the front door. Once this whole thing's over you can do whatever you want with it."

He'd made her go over the basic operational procedures. The Browning had a tubular magazine that could hold four cartridges, plus the one in the chamber. There were four cartridges left in the box. She watched him at the front door, dealing with the weapon, shaking her head, as if to say, this isn't going to happen.

Keeler said, "Keep the kids at your mother's house for now."

She said, "Yeah, okay, but what if they come over?" DeValla had her arms crossed. She pointed to the gun. "That thing is going into my bedroom closet, capisce?"

He shrugged. "I'm saying keep it available, at least for the next couple of days."

"You mean I won't be seeing you in the next couple of days?"

"That's not what I meant."

She lifted her well-formed eyebrows and moved past Keeler to the door. He watched her pick up the Browning and the box of shells. She brushed past him again, making eye contact, and continued up the stairs to her bedroom.

CHAPTER FIFTY-FIVE

Vitalek said, "Are you sure you're up for this?"

Candy looked at him, seated next to her in the passenger seat of her Subaru. He had a serious expression, as if there were stakes suddenly. She wasn't surprised that behind the bohemian facade, Vitalek was a big-time computer guy. She'd sensed that he had special qualities right from the beginning. Probably, a lot of people thought that his thing was just an act, but she didn't think it was. Vitalek was trying to keep it real, for real.

Now they were parked up the road from Copenhagen House. They'd just talked through the plan again. At breakfast Keeler had laid out his idea and Vitalek had riffed on it. Candy got to play the part of a high-tech business woman. Not that she was completely inexperienced, Candy was currently enrolled at Mercy College in Dobbs Ferry, majoring in Business Management.

She nodded. "I'm up for it, absolutely."

She stepped onto the road and closed the door. It was fresh out, a slight wind with snow falling lightly in a sparse but constant flurry. The walk to the gate took only a couple of minutes, but it was really beautiful up there in the woods, and Candy used the time to calm her nerves. She'd decided to treat this all as a game. Pretend it was for fun or points or whatever and maybe she'd stop being so nervous.

A vehicle was at the gate when she came around the bend in the road, inclining to a gentle curve. The security guy waved the car through. He looked at Candy as she walked up. She turned on her best smile and delivered the line she'd been practicing. "I'm staying just up the road."

The man didn't smile. "For the conference?"

"Yeah."

He nodded and let her through. Candy's boots began crunching gravel. She'd known about Copenhagen House for years but had never been inside the front gate. Copenhagen House. The name itself lent a touch of European class, but from the road it had always looked like some kind of an old age home or something, maybe involving horses. When she came around a set of high evergreen hedges and saw the stone house, she thought it looked impressive.

There were signs with arrows showing the way to a coffee and sandwiches reception. Candy trod the small stones and made the transition to indoors. Two slate steps up and she was inside the door, confronted with a table and two women behind it, smiling. They gave her a name sticker to write on and attach to her sweater. She wrote *Maria* in blue permanent marker. Maria had been her Nonna's name.

There was a rack, but Candy kept her coat folded over her arm.

She hung back a moment and took her time fixing the sticker to her breast. The room was crowded with busy talkative people who all seemed to know each other. They gathered in

groups and clutched cardboard coffee cups and sandwich triangles on paper napkins. Candy's mission was to find the security
detail and get friendly.

Keeler had told her to stay on target. She clocked two Ken
doll–type guys posted behind the buffet table and that was
pretty much it. They were big American boys, milk fed and
broad shouldered with very specific hairstyles. As if they'd
escaped from Cape Cod, or inexplicably come up from
Missouri.

Candy got coffee and a chicken Caesar sandwich from the
buffet table. Two bites into the triangle, one of the twins
stepped away, hailed by a scowling woman in her forties. Candy
saw the opening and moved in. The remaining Ken doll security
guy had his back to the wall and an anxious look about him. He
looked even more pained when he saw Candy approaching.
Refused to make eye contact until the last moment and she saw
a panicked look in his eye, as if he was about to blow a gasket.

The guy had a fat lip and a cut on his mouth. Candy
touched her own mouth. "You get in a fight or something?"

The security guy looked away. "No, ma'am."

"You don't need to ma'am me. I'm just a regular person."
She gave him a million-dollar smile and got nothing back. The
guy was a wet squib, intimidated by her. Candy said, "I'm a
little lost here, don't know anybody. You look important."

The man shifted uncomfortably, getting red. "No, uh, I
work here. I'm security."

"That must be a hard job."

"Not really that hard, just sometimes it's hard."

Like a child.

The man straightened up, like he was seeing something
behind Candy that demanded serious attention. She turned. A
guy was coming across the room. Candy revised that, he was
owning the room as he moved, drawing people's attention with

an impossibly wide frame that looked like pure muscle. The guy wore a button-down Oxford shirt tucked into a pair of jeans, had biceps the size of watermelons and was staring straight at her like he'd seen her before. Candy felt a jolt when she recognized him as one of the men from the diner, the ones who'd stolen Vitalek's seat. She put it together by the time he arrived at the buffet table, breaking off to secure a cup of coffee and a double stack of sandwiches.

One of them disappeared immediately into his close-cut beard, followed by the second triangle. Halfway through it, his inquisitive beady eyes locked on to hers. The guy swallowed. "I've seen you before."

Candy repositioned, facing him and smiling. "The diner, last night."

His face was shiny and red, cropped beard and hair the same length, head like a wedge on top of a muscular neck. "That's right." He pointed a thick finger at her. "You were with some guy at the counter and we took your seats. Goddamn I was hungry. Really sorry about that."

Candy laughed. "That's all right. We were done anyway." She pointed at the third sandwich in his hand. "How do you keep your body-fat ratio correct and eat those things at the same time?"

He shrugged. "I burn it in the gym. Usually think in terms of the worst thing you can eat, like a donut. Takes me five minutes to get rid of a donut, I consider it a good deal."

The guy grunted and winked at her. He used his forefinger to push the third sandwich into his mouth and got busy sourcing more from the open cardboard box. Candy watched him stack six more triangles onto a wad of napkins and walk away, balancing them with two stacked coffee cups. Maybe he'd worked in hospitality before switching to more muscular activities.

He walked across the room to join another man she recognized from the diner. The sandwiches and coffee were distributed between them and the man Candy had spoken with leaned against the wall. She sized them up and decided that she knew who her target was going to be.

CHAPTER FIFTY-SIX

Candy moved around the room, sipping coffee. She managed to make small talk with a woman who looked like a vampire. In the movies, vampires are immortal, frozen at the age they were bitten. If so, this woman had been bitten in her early fifties. Turned out she was the founder of a crypto company developing an application for tallying votes. Candy listened to her detailed technical explanation of consensus rules and managed to drift away gracefully.

She'd spent five minutes getting into the right position to naturally arrive at an angle where she could pass by the sandwich champion guy again.

Candy walked slowly, knowing the way she attracted attention and ignoring the eye contact until the last moment when she turned her head swiftly and caught the guy looking at her. "Hey," she said.

He nodded at her and licked his lips. "How's it going?"

"Fine. I feel out of my depth here."

The guy jacked both thumbs through the belt loops of his jeans. "Oh yeah, why's that?" He had a New York accent,

Bronx or Brooklyn maybe, but it could also have been Long Island.

She decided it was okay to skip the small talk. "What do you do here?"

He had a practical, no bullshit attitude. "We're working here, security consultant."

She raised her eyebrows. "That sounds important."

"Depends on your point of view. Some people don't take security seriously, in the end everyone falls to their lowest level of preparation, what I tell people."

"I like that. Makes it sound so obvious."

He nodded, swallowed the rest of his sandwich and grabbed for another one. "Let me guess what you do, why you say you're out of your depth."

"Sure."

He took a pull from the coffee cup. "I'd guess that you're in marketing."

"Why?"

"Because you're hot. They usually try to stick a pretty girl in marketing."

Candy did her best to blush instead of rolling her eyes and throwing her coffee in his face. "Thank you."

"It's just a fact. So is that right, marketing, why you're weirded out by the geeks?" He jerked his head at the rest of the room.

She made the sound of a buzzer, scrunched her face up. "Wrong. I'm a founder. My start-up is called Bit Zone. We're developing critical blockchain infrastructure for cyber security applications. So, I'm in security too, which is why I felt out of my depth. I'm not a developer."

The guy's eyelids quivered and something resembling a smile tickled his lips. "Fair play. Sounds expensive."

Candy stuck out a hand. "Maria Stephanopoulos." The last

name, blurted out with no conscious thought. She only realized a split second later that Mike Stephanopoulos was the name of a guy who Mini had killed last night.

The security guy gripped carefully. His hand felt like a dry landscape of callus and muscle, enclosing hers. It felt like having your hand inside of a deadly trap just before it springs closed. He said, "I'm Kevin Milton. Pleased to meet you, Maria."

Candy got her hand back. "You guys deal in cyber?"

Milton made a face. "Not me personally, but I work with people who do. Blockchain for cyber security. I've got no idea what any of that means, but it sounds impressive, Maria."

She said, "The tech is super cool, but we aren't yet operational, still testing and getting it all up and ready. Tell you what though, I'm taking note of contractors that we might be interested in partnering with once our next VC round comes through." She brought out her phone, took her time to bring up the email app. "We'll be gearing up for the launch." Candy handed her phone to the guy, gave him the treatment with her eyes. "Just put in your email, Kevin. I'll send you a link to our website. You can take a look and get in touch if you like. I'll take you to lunch in the city or something, talk about security."

Keeler had told her: *You give them your own phone and their defenses drop.*

"Sure." Her phone disappeared into meaty hands. He thumbed and tapped and handed the phone back.

Candy focused on the device. Copying a link Vitalek had given her and pasting it into the email and sending it. "Cool. I sent you the link." Looked up at him. "Check if you got it."

The guy didn't even hesitate. He pulled out his own device and brought his focus to bear. Candy watched as he checked his email and saw the link. He tapped on it. Nothing happened. He tapped again. "Doesn't work." Looked up at her. "Maybe it's the Wi-Fi."

Just like Vitalek said it would go.

"It's probably my fault." Candy re-opened her email and copied and pasted the second link Vitalek had put in her notes app. She sent the email. "I might have gotten one of the characters wrong." She laughed. "Try now, it should work."

He tapped on the second link. A website opened up on his phone like a flower. He gave it two seconds of attention. "Oh yeah, that looks very interesting." A website that Vitalek had put together in ten minutes. Milton put the phone away. "I'll take a look at it when I'm not working."

Candy nodded. "Nice, that's awesome. I'll look out for you if you wish to get in touch, Kevin. We can never be too secure, right?"

She smiled, blinding him with her perfect teeth. Milton looked at her, and Candy turned away, moving off. The man he had been with was now across the room getting more coffee. She allowed herself to drift into an ongoing conversation about video games, asking an inane question and pretending to be interested in the response given by some guy who looked fifteen.

The first link she'd sent was Vitalek's way into the guy's phone. She'd watched Milton tap on the link and seen that nothing had happened, which made her wonder if anything had secretly happened in the background that wasn't visible to the phone's user. Was that it? Were they in now? If that was it, she was impressed and scared in equal measure.

Candy spent the next several minutes chatting with random people and trying to avoid actual conversations. Her phone rang and she answered it, relieved.

"Yeah."

"We're good," Vitalek's said.

"Okay." Candy hung up.

She made for the bathroom but walked past it to a door that led out to the courtyard. She put on her coat and maintained an easy walking pace, telling herself to go nice and slow and to breathe. A couple of minutes later she arrived at the car. Vitalek was stretched out in the backseat with his laptop computer open. The Subaru was running. She got into the driver's seat. Candy turned to the side, facing Vitalek along a diagonal axis.

"You're in?"

"Completely. Got his phone opened up like a gutted fish, checking out his emails." He looked up at her, clearly excited and enjoying himself. "Should be enough for the moment. Now I'm going through the other stuff."

"Wow." Candy felt giddy and buzzed with adrenaline. This was super fun!

Vitalek saw her looking at him that way. "Your first hack?" he asked, a little grin crawling up his face.

"I guess."

He looked at her, eyes shining. Candy understood what it was all about. Like she had just discovered something new and liked it. "So let's go to Mini's."

Vitalek said, "Only one problem."

"What's that?"

He patted the laptop. "Forgot the power cord at your apartment."

CHAPTER FIFTY-SEVEN

Kitchewan Old Cars was squeezed between a Chinese takeout joint and an attorney's office. Just as Mini had said. The words *Kitchewan Old Cars* were painted on the front window in the shiny gold facsimile of an old-timey typeface. Keeler sat in the Toyota, watching the office. On the passenger seat beside him was the roll of duct tape and the survival knife he'd bought in Brooklyn.

He pocketed them both, got out of the car, crossed the street, and got some distance from the office, before crossing again and doubling back to pass right in front. The attorney's next door had fancy vertical blinds, half closed. It was possible to see a woman inside, her bored face done up with makeup and oriented to the bright glow of the internet.

The blue Ford pickup truck was parked out front. Same vehicle with the New Jersey plates. The Kitchewan Old Cars office interior was dark. A very obese person was bouncing a child on his lap at a desk pushed to the back. Keeler walked on until he got to the corner. He made a right and then another right down an alleyway, coming up on the rear of the office. The property was surrounded by a ten-foot-tall unpainted wood fence made from newish treated wood that still smelled strongly of chemicals.

The fence door was locked with a chain. Behind the fence a dog went crazy, barking and growling and making wet noises. A hole had been cut in the door for mail. The dog had a thick tangle of black fur eyeballing him as it lunged against a chain fixed to a buried post. There was a window on each side of a back door, closed and anonymous. Neither special nor surprising.

Keeping a dog tied to a post in the yard has two main draw-backs, in relation to security.

One is the fact that the intruder can just go around it if there is space.

Second is the fact that the dog might bark and growl at everything that goes by, making it a regular occurrence, like a pattern of life. How are you going to know when the dog is barking at an actual threat?

Keeler came to the corner of the yard and pulled himself over the fence. He stood on the other side, examining the canine. The chain's circumference reached to about two feet away from his position. The dog wasn't a trained attack dog. It was a male, neutered, and wary of the new guy in the yard. He approached and the beast backed off to the post. Keeler came forward and observed the dog's tail, inert and rigid but begin-ning to move a little. The dog had floppy ears, one of which was inside out.

He knelt down and put a hand out. "Good little doggy." Keeler hushed and scratched the quieting beast under the chin. A name tag attached to the leather collar read *Arlo*. Arlo rolled onto his back and began to wriggle, rubbing himself against the snow and exposed concrete, showing the dominant dog his submission. Not much of a deterrent.

Keeler eyed the back entrance. A screen door and a solid

wood door behind it. Both were unlocked. He stepped into the rear of the building and began down a narrow hallway composed of tired construction materials. Moldy sheetrock, worn-out paint jobs, and threadbare carpeting that had been cheap even twenty years ago, when it had been new. To his right was an open door, a bathroom that would correspond to the window to the right of the back door. To his left was a closed door. Maybe a back office.

Straight ahead was the front office. A beaded curtain separated front from back. The beads in red, white, and blue, threaded in the flag design, tilted ninety degrees. Keeler approached. The floor was covered in old linoleum, but it wasn't creaking. Through the curtain he had an excellent view of the back of the obese man's head, neck, and shoulders. The man was dressed in a t-shirt and shorts and construction boots, making the chair seem very small. The baby was in a filthy fleece one-piece with a barely discernible leopard skin motif. The baby gurgled happily, a sticky Chinese spare rib held in both of his chubby fists. The man was cooing, holding the baby up with his right hand, while consuming a spare rib with his left.

The big man was operating a radio based dispatch. Kitchewan Old Cars were keeping it real with thirty-year-old technology. A handheld receiver occupied space alongside the bag of Chinese spare ribs. The curly cord travelled to a rack of radio equipment. No computer, no internet, only a telephone and the radio. Old-school.

There didn't seem to be much action on the radio either. Unsurprising, given the events of last night. Kitchewan Old Cars wasn't going to be in business for much longer.

Keeler came through the beaded curtain quietly but directly. The big man sensed him there and stiffened, beginning to turn, but a hard hand on the place where shoulder and neck meet stopped his movement. Keeler took a handful of flesh on the back of the man's neck and squeezed, holding him there. He spoke quietly. "Just keep doing what you're doing."

The baby looked at him with glassy eyes, gurgling his soft mouth around the spare rib.

Keeler slid the brand new survival knife out of its sheath and reached over to cut the cable on the radio handset. He did the same thing with a desk phone. The knife passed easily through the plastic and copper. Keeler saw the big man eyeing the blade.

"Your phone." The man wasted no time and passed a smartphone from his shorts pocket over to Keeler, who pocketed the phone and patted the man on the head. "Good. Stay."

Problem with a knife is always going to be the blood. Keeler snapped it into the sheath and walked on back.

CHAPTER FIFTY-EIGHT

The rear office door was closed, quiet and calm. Keeler kicked it in with a steel-tipped boot, splintering the wood around the jamb and whipping the door back. The swinging door smacked into a man who'd been standing behind it, hit him in the mouth. The guy staggered back and Keeler caught him by the ear with a callused hand. He pushed the man hard to the right, crashing him into a stack of filling cabinets.

The office smelled like dog. Keeler figured it doubled as Arlo's home. Another guy sat at a desk, Rooney, presently fumbling with a drawer, laboriously removing a pistol and looking at it in a panic because he didn't remember what to do exactly.

Because what to do with a pistol isn't completely obvious to the untrained user. The weapon in question was a Glock 17 in 9mm, which Keeler didn't particularly love. He was always going to prefer a 1911 .45. It was all well and good to have a couple of extra shots, but he'd take fewer rounds with more stopping power any day. Rooney fumbled the gun out of his drawer and pointed it more or less in Keeler's direction. He hadn't put a round in the chamber, and Keeler doubted that the weapon would be kept hot, but he wasn't going to take the chance.

He slapped Rooney across the face hard enough that the blow unseated him, launching the guy off his office chair and onto the floor. The side of Rooney's head glanced against the radiator, producing a bell tone. The pistol bounced on the carpet. The other man in the room moved in Keeler's peripheral vision, evidently having recovered from the filing cabinet run-in. Keeler brought the sheathed knife out of his pocket and planted the butt into the man's forehead.

Which had the effect of producing a circular welt in the skin and a thick thud. The man's eyes rolled up and he tumbled to a chair, flipping it and himself into a tangle on the floor. Keeler retrieved the Glock.

He glanced at Rooney, looking bad and unhappy in his corner. Keeler said, "You had this thing hot in your drawer?" He slid back the mechanism and saw nothing in the chamber. "No." Rooney cowered on the floor. Keeler dropped the magazine and checked. It was full of 9mm rounds.

Rooney seemed distracted, trying to move his head. He put a hand to his neck. "I think you broke my neck, man."

Keeler returned the magazine to its place and pocketed the weapon. He shoved the desk aside for easier access and grasped Rooney's head, twisting it back and forth vigorously, making everything a lot worse. "Does that feel better?"

Rooney's face caught in a rictus of pain and shock. His mouth opened, and a long almost-silent cry was emitted like a hiss. Keeler pulled the other man out from the corner to the middle of the carpet. There was a slobber stained tennis ball under the desk. Arlo's property.

Keeler straddled Rooney. He pushed Arlo's tennis ball into his mouth and did a couple of tours around his head with the roll of duct tape. Rooney might have wanted to talk, but Keeler wasn't interested in hearing what he had to say, not yet.

He bound Rooney's hands and feet and arms and legs with almost half of the duct tape roll. The other half of the roll was for the other guy, presumably Tommy Santarelli. When he had them both bound and gagged and able to breathe out of their noses, he positioned them side by side, like hot dogs on a grill. Both men were breathing hard, eyes popping, terrified.

Keeler scooped a bunch of keys from Rooney's desk. He stood over the two bound men, who both looked like they were having a bad day. "I'm coming back in a minute," he said. "Don't do anything. It won't work. Just don't do it."

He stood for a moment, looking at those two. How likely was it that they'd just chill out on the floor? Not very likely. Their choice. Keeler took the Glock from his pocket and chambered a round.

He put the bound men out of his mind and moved down the corridor tactically. Glock up and hot and half expecting the fat man to be waiting for him with a scatter gun. That wasn't the case. The man hadn't moved, still playing with his toddler. The only sign of distress was the fact that the toddler's snot was running freely down the little boy's face. Maybe the fat man hadn't dared fetch tissues? Keeler couldn't know.

The big man was sweating freely. Stains had already expanded from his armpits and the small of his back. Keeler took hold of the man's neck again, put his mouth close to the man's ear.

"That's your son?"

The man nodded. "You're here for Pat?"

"You don't seem surprised."

"No."

Keeler said, "If I were to go around this desk and look at you straight on, you think I'd see someone who'd been playing with an axe last night up at the golf course?"

"I'm sorry. I shouldn't have done what Pat said. I didn't hurt no one. My mom's got a hospital appointment, so I had to bring my son to work."

The child gnawed on his spare rib, which at that point was being used like a lollipop. Keeler wasn't going to start giving advice on nutrition.

He said, "Go on and get."

The man held his breath for a long moment, before letting out a shaking exhale. "You want me to leave?"

"With your son. Just go on and don't turn around, don't come back, don't call anyone. Put this out of your mind for a while and do something else with your time. Come back maybe in a month. Maybe you'll be the only one left here and you can run the company or something."

The man said, "Now?"

Keeler had a thought. "Hold on."

He went back into the yard and untied Arlo from the post. The dog, happy to be free and wagging his tail. Keeler brought Arlo back in and handed the leash to the guy.

"You've got a dog now. Congratulations."

For a very large man, he moved fast and was out of there and gone within a minute.

Keeler went out the front. The keys fit Rooney's pickup truck, and he brought it around to the alley. The bed of the Ford was covered with a tarp, and Keeler undid the snaps, rolling it back.

He found Rooney and Santarelli halfway between the back office and the front room. Rooney was trying to hop to the front, while Santarelli was facedown over the threshold from office to hallway. Keeler wasn't amused. He'd given them clear instructions.

He kicked Rooney's legs out from beneath him and stomped on an ankle, feeling something give beneath his boot. Rooney made a sound, somehow verbalizing behind Arlo's tennis ball. Keeler dragged him out the back and up into the bed of the truck. He came back for Santarelli and slotted him alongside Rooney. The tarp snapped into place, and he backed the Ford out of the alley and onto Grand Street, the main road through town.

CHAPTER FIFTY-NINE

Ten minutes later, Keeler parked the pickup truck in front of the UPS Store. The lot wasn't very busy, given the hour. Probably something to do with the weather, which was beginning to change from sunny to overcast. Anybody out there moving would be doing so in a hurry, making tracks from the vehicle to the store of choice in the shortest possible time frame. Keeler watched the rush of vapor escaping his lips into the winter air. He grinned to himself, patted the buttoned down tarp covering the truck's bed. Got a shuffling sound in return. They were still alive, not yet frozen.

As expected, his package had arrived. The cardboard box had done some kind of an overnight tour, the exact nature of which remained a mystery that could only be guessed at. Maybe a circular drive into New England and back, or perhaps a train ride somewhere out west, like Pennsylvania and then a return trip in the back of a UPS truck. Keeler didn't ask, and he didn't make any jokes about it with the serious woman behind the counter. She looked like she was expecting flack. Keeler played nice, especially since her eyes kept being drawn to his busted nose.

Farrell got a grudging two points for the nose. Not many people were able to get a bony forehead inside the operational circle of Keeler's hands.

The woman handed over the package and Keeler opened it to see the dull black laptop inside. Out in the parking lot, he slid the package into the truck and climbed in. He made a couple of wrong turns getting up into the hills, looking for Frankie's house. Eventually he made the right turns and drove Rooney's truck down the driveway, stopping behind the deputy chief's vehicle.

The sky was clear and bright blue through the bare branches of large trees. The snow had hardened into a frozen crust covering every surface that hadn't been cleared. Keeler dragged Rooney and Santarelli one at a time from the pickup truck to the back of Frankie's house. He deposited them seated together, backs against the improvised ice box he'd made to preserve Frankie's body. Neither of the two were dressed for the outdoors. The time spent in the back of the truck had knocked them both into a state of numb paralysis.

Keeler estimated the temperature at something like twenty degrees Fahrenheit. Not exactly a Minnesota winter but cold enough that un-insulated body temperatures were going to fall, bringing about hypothermia sooner rather than later. He'd seen hypothermia in others and experienced it himself. Part of the training. Bottom line, you start to do dumb things and then you die, unless somebody comes to save you.

Keeler squatted in front of the two bound men. He was having a hard time imagining forgiveness, or mercy, or amnesty. They'd kidnapped Mini DeValla and threatened her children. Things could have gone majorly wrong in a variety of ways. DeValla might have been killed. A quick death was going to be mercy enough. Rooney looked to be in worse physical shape, older and with a drinker's nose. Excessive alcohol consumption doesn't help your chances of survival in the extreme cold.

Keeler had a plan for the current situation, a way of dealing with Rooney and Santarelli, and letting their demise help out with the problem of Frankie's body. However, processes at work in the back of his mind kept spilling over into the front until he could no longer ignore them. Mini had said something early that morning, just before he'd felt the touch of her long fingers grazing his skin with her nails. The skin-to-skin contact had implanted the words uttered a few seconds before:

I found the laptop on the northbound train.

Keeler had been on the southbound train to the city, the same train that the woman in white had been looking to board. Which meant that it was more than likely that Vince Farrell had been right behind her. Mini DeValla had stepped out of the southbound train, waving the passengers back to the waiting room. That must have been the decisive moment for Farrell and Irma Rosenbaum, sealing her fate.

Farrell had wanted to do it on the train, but when the train was cancelled, he'd improvised and done it right then and there. Maybe a needle, or maybe something more up to date. These days they could do it with an aerosol spray, get the poison agent on the skin, and the game's over. The ear is a good vector apparently.

Keeler faced Rooney and Santarelli, who both looked back at him, neither one shaking badly, yet. Neither one capable of moving anything except eyeballs.

He let the UPS package fall to the snow in front of him. "I've got a theory, but I want to hear it from one of you. Blink twice if you're ready for a no-bullshit confession." He brought out the Glock and let it rest against his knee. "I'm not patient. Bullshit gets the bullet."

Santarelli was vibrating a little, maybe slipping into

hypothermia. Rooney blinked twice, the eyelids coming together deliberately. Keeler scooted forward and ripped the duct tape from his mouth. Arlo's ball came out, attached to a long string of saliva, accompanied by a gasping desperate heaving breath.

Keeler removed the laptop from the package. "This computer had no power cord in the bag, which means either it doesn't need one, or we're dealing with a negligent office worker."

Rooney coughed. He wasn't having fun. "Open the battery hatch in the back. I'm freezing man; we need to get warm."

Keeler turned the laptop over in his hands. The battery hatch was secured with a clever latch. He dug a fingernail under it, and the aluminum flipped up. He put a little more pressure on the latch and the cover came off. Inside there weren't any batteries or any computer. The laptop was a plastic shell, the insides of which were stuffed with something enclosed in a plastic bag.

Keeler looked up at Rooney. "Heroin, coke?"

"Dope."

"Which is what, heroin?"

"Yes."

Keeler shook his head. "Bad boy, Rooney. Very, very bad boy." Rooney looked down. Keeler said, "Is that a regular thing for you, pick up the drugs at the train station? Guy brings it up from the city, what, once a week?"

Rooney seemed to be trying to calm his breathing. Like he was on the verge of hyperventilating. He caught his breath. "Yeah, it's a regular run. Only the guy pussied out this time."

What Keeler had suspected for a while was confirmed: these people had nothing at all to do with Vince Farrell and the crypto thing with Vitalek. These were local drug dealers operating Kitchewan Old Cars as a front company for bringing product up from the city.

On the northbound train.

The northbound train had come in later, after the southbound train had been emptied. By then, the platform had already become a brouhaha of police and paramedics dealing with Rosenbaum. And the police presence had spooked the courier on the northbound train, who had left the laptop containing drugs behind him and gotten out of there in a hurry.

"Where's the guy who brought this up from the city?" Keeler asked.

Rooney licked his lips. "He went back to the city, soon as the trains started running again." He twisted his head to look at Santarelli. The younger man had begun to shake. Rooney looked back at Keeler. "You got to get us inside, man. Look at Tommy; he could die."

Keeler wasn't feeling the same vibe. They were not on the same page at all. He said, "Tell me something, Rooney, kidnapping the train conductor, what were you thinking?"

"You were playing it badass, so I figured I'd play it the same way."

"That was a big mistake." Keeler reached forward and ripped the duct tape from Santarelli's mouth. Figured, if he wanted to say something, now would be the right time. He spoke to Rooney. "You remember what I told you yesterday morning, sometimes you need to do things the hard way. If you'd just stopped there and taken my advice, been a little more patient, neither of us would be here. You'd be rolling around selling your heroin and I wouldn't even be in this town. You ever think about that? It's all about your decisions, Rooney, your choices."

Rooney teared up and began to cry. The cold was getting to him, making him emotional.

Keeler said, "Fact is Rooney, you're not a badass. You're just larping as a badass." Rooney sobbed silently. Santarelli wasn't doing well, teeth shaking. Keeler said, "Who do you sell the heroin to?"

Rooney spit saliva all over himself. "Kids. Teenagers mostly and some other people. I work northern Westchester and maybe into Connecticut sometimes. Small-time, man. It's just for the kids to have fun." He slobbered. "Just small-time."

Keeler didn't care about the distinction, small-time or big-time. He didn't approve of heroin dealing as an activity. Pictured Rooney or one of his guys hanging around outside of the high school, selling heroin to teenagers. Weed or psyche-delics were one thing, recreational, fun stuff that people did while listening to music and getting to know each other.

Heroin was something else; it wasn't just a fun thing. People got addicted and died, got their friends addicted, and their friends died. On and on in a miserable chain of negativity.

Normally, Keeler was a live and let live kind of guy, but Rooney had made serious life errors, and it wasn't going to end well for him. Plus, there was the Frankie situation, which needed a resolution. Keeler looked up to the deck by Frankie's back door. The banister had been busted through by the deputy chief's own body weight. Crashed through that and fell onto the pole, impaling himself.

You couldn't make it up.

CHAPTER SIXTY

K eeler thought about how to set the scene. Two drug dealers and the policeman. Mini DeValla shared kids with Frankie. Dead Frankie could go two ways, bad cop or hero cop. Dead and disgraced dad, or dead and heroic dad. Frankie might have been an asshole in life, but Keeler figured it would be for the best if his character improved in death.

Frankie's ghost would be a man that his children could look and live up to, a community hero who fell in the line of duty, protecting and serving. Maybe they'd put a banner for him on the street he grew up on. Mini's kids would love it, they'd be proud.

Keeler felt Rooney watching him. He'd stopped crying and was looking more focused. Rooney was no genius, but it didn't take a genius to look at Keeler and know that this wasn't going to have a happy ending. *Set it up like a home invasion*, Keeler thought. Close to the truth. Except it wasn't Keeler and Candy; it was Rooney and Santarelli. He scooted up to the two men and reapplied the duct tape. Went up to the house, boots off at the door. He came out with Frankie's police-issue Glock 21 Gen4 in .45 caliber. A good weapon for what he had in mind.

The scenario was similar to what had happened. Frankie wakes up to hear the intruders. The question of why they would come into Frankie's house wasn't important, Keeler knew. Cops don't actually care about motive, they care about evidence and confessions. In this case, there weren't going to be any confessions, since the dead don't speak.

He dragged Santarelli up to the deck. The man was experiencing moderate hypothermia, shivering uncontrollably, but not yet violently. Keeler stripped the duct tape from him, mouth, legs, arms, hands, ankles. Balled it up and put the detritus and the UPS box into an unused garbage bag from the roll he'd found in Frankie's kitchen.

He brought Santarelli inside. Stood him up and leaned him against the wall, right by the back door. Santarelli was standing there, shaking and staring. Eyes bugged out and unfocused. Keeler stepped back a couple of paces and checked the distance. Santarelli took a step out into the room, testing his legs. That was perfect, like he'd just come in the house and Frankie had confronted him. Keeler shot Santarelli once in the chest with Frankie's weapon. The .45 caliber round punching through the man's torso, shredding muscle and skin and clothing and embedding in the wall behind him with a splash of red. That put a stop to Santarelli's shakes.

Frankie gets out of bed with his service weapon, enters the living room area and sees the intruder. Keeler reached for the light switch and turned it on. Changed the story. Frankie hears something, turns the lights on, and sees Santarelli. Puts a round into him, dropping Santarelli right there and then. But Frankie's not aware of a second man, Rooney, who's already in the house and comes up behind him.

Keeler turned, facing the bedroom and the front of the house. Okay, so Rooney's been up at the front door. Maybe searching for Frankie's keys and his wallet. Maybe Rooney gets the jump on Frankie and they struggle, which leads to the outdoors part of the story.

Keeler put his boots on and came down for Rooney, whose eyes were bulging out of their sockets. He made moaning sounds, screaming inside, saliva escaping from the dog's tennis ball and the duct tape over his mouth. Keeler figured that it would be best if both Rooney and Frankie came through the banister together, caught up in a tussle, struggling and wrestling.

He carried Rooney all the way up to the house. Removed his boots again and dragged Rooney through the living room, snow and dirt getting all over the floor. He dumped Rooney on the deck and put his boots back on.

Keeler descended again to the ice box he'd improvised around Frankie's corpse.

Rooney watched from above, helplessly as Keeler removed the plywood boards and excavated the corpse. When Rooney saw the deputy chief's body impaled on a pole in the bright cold daylight, his eyes rolled up in his head and he lost consciousness. Keeler went up on the deck and got himself between Rooney and the banister. He shot Rooney twice, once in the thigh, and another time in the face.

Keeler booted Rooney's body off the deck and watched it land against Frankie's impaled corpse. Blood on the deck, and sprayed onto the snow. More of it leaking from Rooney's face into the ice below Frankie.

Keeler came down and tucked the service weapon into Frankie's frozen hand.

None of it would make too much sense to a committed forensic investigator. There were any number of anomalies. But this was a police force with a deputy chief like Frankie. There wasn't going to be any committed forensic investigation. The death of the deputy chief was going to be heroic. They'd be naming a Little League field after him, or at least one of the dugouts. The drugs were going to be found in the intruder's pickup truck and the narrative would take the path of least resistance.

Keeler looked at the sky, overcast and looking like snow. That was going to be fine, the fresh blizzard would come and obliterate any tracks that he might have overlooked.

When he was done setting it up, Keeler walked down the hill to town. He got rid of the garbage bag in a dumpster behind a pizza parlor. He was already thinking of headlines to feed Julie Everard, figuring she could write up a fluff piece about Frankie in the *Kitchewan Gazette*.

Keeler came around to the street, and the smell of freshly baked pizza hit him hard. He was drawn into the small restaurant, past the two four-seater booths and to the counter. A young man in a tank top had his back turned, using a long wooden paddle to extract a steaming hot pizza pie from a wide-mouthed oven. The pizza was bubbling with boiling cheese and red sauce. The crust was thin and scorched in all the right places. The guy at the back shivered the paddle, extracting it and leaving the pizza to steam on a circular aluminum dish. He slid the wooden tool into its place above the oven and turned to Keeler.

"What's up?"

"What's the usual?"

The man laughed. "For you? Two slices of regular and a root beer." He waited for acknowledgement and when it came, sprang into action.

The slicing tool whispered through the pie, dividing it into eight generous slices. Two of them got slapped onto overlapping doubled paper plates. He drew a cup from a stack and glanced at Keeler. "Large?"

"Sure."

Keeler walked back to one of the booths with one hand full

of hot goodness with the other gripping an ice-cold cup of frothing root beer. He ate silently, ravenous. Glanced up at the steamed window every couple of bites before going back in for more. Keeler saved the crusts for the residual oil and sauce, mopping it up in savory, salty mouthfuls, reserving two gulps of root beer for the finale.

When he was done he felt like he'd arrived in New York.

He pulled out the phone and saw that Candy had called three times. She picked up on the first ring. "Yeah."

Keeler said, "Tell me."

Vitalek's voice in the background, saying something to Candy.

Candy said, "We're at my place. Vitalek says you should come here."

"I thought we agreed we weren't going back to your place."

"Yeah, but he left his power cord here. So we're here."

CHAPTER SIXTY-ONE

Keeler didn't want to park inside the complex. There wasn't any road out of it, except for the road into it. Not a tactically sound location. He parked by the Little League field and walked in through the woods, crunching through the snow crust. For a while he squatted at the edge of the tree line, behind Candy's apartment building. He had a decent observational view of the parking lot from there.

Keeler remembered a guy from the Air Force who loved spearfishing. The guy told him once, you go down to the bottom, grab ahold of a rock, and then you wait. The big fish go into hiding as soon as you enter the water. You wait a minute and the big fish come out again.

The guy hadn't elaborated, but Keeler knew. The fish come out again, and then you kill them.

Farrell had been humiliated. Keeler had left the guy shamed and wounded. The little he knew about Farrell was still more than nothing. He knew the history, knew Farrell to be a vicious murderer. A guy who killed for the sake of it, one of those who'd joined up because it allowed him to perform legal murder.

Plus, Farrell wasn't just some ex-operator working for a

buck, he was near the top of the pyramid at Triton Gamma Associates, according to Blomstein. Which pretty much guaranteed that he wouldn't be alone. He'd be able to call in guys to back him up, probably had an assistant on call. Keeler didn't see a situation in which Farrell would leave the battlefield alive. The only situation Keeler could visualize was one in which Farrell stayed locked on to his target, tenacious like a pit bull. The only way to get him off would be to put him down.

Which wasn't a problem. But, Keeler wanted to keep his new friends alive in the meantime. Which is why he wasn't happy.

He'd scrutinized every vehicle in the lot. Candy's Subaru was parked in a conveniently close spot. The only thing of interest was a white panel van that he could barely see due to his position. A vehicle pulled into the lot, a red SUV. It swung into a spot, and a woman got out dressed in a long down coat and a pink hat. She got her shopping out of the back and walked across to one of the buildings. After a while Keeler moved out. He came through a gap between apartment buildings. Candy's building was on his left. He made a right turn across the front of a neighboring block with six apartments, three up and three down. He moved up the stairs to the landing and was able to lean back against the brick wall and get an oblique view of the front of Candy's building.

For a minute he did nothing but watch the parking lot. A couple of crows lifted off from a tree, swooping together through the open space and landing on the roof of Candy's building. Otherwise nothing was happening. Vehicles were static, slotted into designated spots, delimited by painted yellow lines that were no longer visible thanks to the snow.

Keeler pulled the phone and called Candy.

She answered on the first ring. "Yeah."

"You guys come out now."

Candy said, "He's in the shower."

Unbelievable.

Keeler went up the stairs two at a time. Came through the unlocked door without ceremony, his eyes searching. Vitalek was dabbing a towel at the inside of his left ear, sitting at Candy's kitchen table. Candy was in there with him, pouring milk into a glass. They both looked up at Keeler.

Vitalek pointed at his laptop. "I know you don't want us to stay here, but this needs to finish first."

"What needs to finish?"

"It worked, okay? I am inside of this guy's phone, but it takes time to download a copy of it."

Keeler stood in the kitchen door, arms crossed. "How much longer?"

Vitalek shrugged. "Ten minutes? I can explain this to you while we wait. Simple explanation all right?"

The non-operating link that Candy had sent to Milton's email had contained a wicked little piece of malware that allowed Vitalek into the phone operating system, bypassing the security. Vitalek explained that the program was a version of something called Medusa, developed by the Israelis, altered and updated by Latvian hackers so that it was easier to use, and now sold on the black market where Vitalek had paid twenty-six thousand dollars' worth of crypto currency to get it onto his laptop.

The program was powerful, and it gave him a perfect copy of Milton's device, complete with password keychain and a real-time view of the phone's activity. Vitalek's laptop screen was split into two parts, the left side showed the phone's current activity. The right side was a copy that Vitalek could manipulate and explore without the owner cottoning on.

Currently the phone was not in use, most likely it was dormant on the surface of a table, or the inside of a pocket.

Vitalek said, "We can activate the camera and the micro-phone without him knowing." The left side of Vitalek's screen flicked on and all three of them were looking at a shaky shot of a floor. "He's walking right now, doesn't know we're watching."

Keeler recognized the carpet, the hallway at Copenhagen House. "Fascinating," he said. He peered into the top right corner of Vitalek's screen. The battery was charging, currently reading at fifty percent. The download operation was coming close to completion.

Candy leaned back against the Formica counter with her arms crossed. She'd been quiet while Vitalek did his technical explanation. She said, "I'm a little lost. What are we supposed to be doing?"

Keeler said, "First of all, you did a good job up there. Might have saved him." He jerked a thumb at Vitalek. "The people who are trying to rub Vitalek out are major league. You might stop them once, but they'll come back. Worse still, they're hired by someone else. So, even if we do take them out, the people who want him dead can always send a fresh team later on." He pointed his chin to Vitalek, who was listening intently. "This morning when I asked you about the institutional stakeholders you and Rosenbaum were clashing with, I asked if they were banks and you said, not exactly. What are they, if not banks?"

Both of them looked at Vitalek, who looked into space for a moment and then started speaking in his slow manner, spacing out the words. "Banks are usually open to clients. These aren't open to clients. They are funds that pool money from private sources. I know for sure that we're dealing with at least one sovereign wealth fund and a couple of ultra-high-net-worth indi-viduals in the billionaire category." He laughed. "So, yeah. I don't know if they're going to be easily deterred."

Candy said, "How did you piss these people off?"

Vitalek's deep-set eyes were combative. His features were

clearly Slavic and for the first time, Keeler got a sense of his mettle. "They tried a takeover. Wanted to take what I'd created and turn it into a regular money machine for the extreme rich. I'm not letting them get their way just because they're willing to use violence and murder." He looked at Keeler. "Am I just an idiot?"

Keeler shrugged. "That doesn't matter, in terms of the rights and the wrongs. It's okay to be an idiot."

Candy said, "So what's the plan? How do we get him out of this?"

Keeler said, "We take what you got from this guy's phone and hope it has relevant information that can lead us to the client. We give that to a good investigative journalist and take it public. If we can do that, there's a chance that they lay off on Vitalek, at least for a good while. Maybe after a while they decide they aren't so interested in killing you."

Candy said, "Do you know a good journalist?"

"Actually, I do, and she's in town. We're going to her office to lay the whole thing out for her. See what she says." He pointed at the laptop. "We'll have the copy of the phone, right? She'll be able to see for herself what's going on."

Vitalek was staring at Keeler, like he'd found a savior. Candy had nothing to say either. She was nodding in agreement. The computer beeped.

Vitalek said, "It's copied."

Keeler pointed at Candy. "Pack a bag, just in case you can't come back for a while. Warm clothes and toiletries."

"Really?"

"Really." He went to the front door. "I'll wait for you downstairs. Give me a call when you're ready to leave and I'll give you the green light."

❄

Keeler went down the stairs first. His eyes were drawn back to the white panel van. From the new angle and the closer distance he could see new details. It was a contractor's truck, dirty from the salt and the ice. He was able to make out the image of a toilet and the word *septic*. The other vehicles in the lot were either four-door or two-door cars. The septic company van's cockpit was empty.

Four minutes later the phone vibrated. Candy on the line. "We're ready to come out."

Keeler moved to the edge of the balcony and looked out either direction. "What you do is come down the stairs. You take a right and walk back, behind your building."

"I'm parked out front."

He kept his cool. "Listen to me, Candy. What you're not going to do is go to your car. We'll go out back. So tell me what you're going to do."

He heard Candy taking a deep breath. "All right. I'm going out the apartment and down the stairs. I take a right and another right, go back of the building. You'll be there?"

"I will."

"Okay."

Keeler ended the call. There wasn't any more action at the apartment complex than there had been before. He went down the stairs to the ground level and made a right across the building. He waited and saw Candy and Vitalek coming down the stairs, each one carrying a large backpack, like two kids going on a camping trip.

Keeler looked over the other side of the lot at the sound of a brake shrieking. He had to move to see between the parked cars. A gray van was reversing into a spot and parking. Keeler waited for someone to come out of it. It was too far away to actually see a person through the windshield. Maybe the driver was looking at a phone, caught up in some kind of a messaging situation. Or another possibility: hostile combatant just sitting there waiting, with three other men in the back, armed and dangerous.

Hope for the best, prepare for the worst.

Keeler saw Candy at the bottom of the stairs in his peripheral vision, eyes not straying from the van in the parking lot. He beckoned with his hand. "Candy, come over here."

He saw her moving toward him, another twenty yards to go and she'd be with him and they could go back behind the building. Across the lot, the driver's side door of the van opened. Someone came out, slowly. One snow boot down on the ground, another landing beside it. Looked like an old person, possibly female. Perhaps the kind of van an elderly couple might take down to Florida for the winter. It was winter, why weren't they in Florida?

A light flurry of snow was already coming down, drifting slowly, bringing Keeler back to high school, to a Hemingway book they'd had to read. The main character was fighting with the rebels in the Spanish Civil War, up in the mountains. According to his teacher, the snowstorm was symbolic of death and chaos. Keeler looked up at the swirling bits of white, hard to see against the gray sky. He thought, *Bring it on.*

The woman locked the van and began to walk across the lot. Maybe they'd gone down to Florida every winter, but this winter the husband was incapacitated. Something nagged at Keeler and he realized it was the gait, not that of an older person. The woman had her head down, exposed flesh bundled deep into a parka hood.

Candy was at the ground level, looking at him. Vitalek five steps behind her. Keeler held up his hand. "Wait there a second." He wanted to verify the gray van.

CHAPTER SIXTY-TWO

Vitalek cursed. Candy turned, saw that he'd caught his backpack strap on the edge of the banister. She turned again to Keeler and saw him holding his hand up and walking into the parking lot. Maybe he'd said something but she hadn't heard it because of Vitalek's cursing.

Vitalek came up behind her. "Let's go."

She glanced at him. "He said we should go out back."

Vitalek gestured to Keeler's back. "Yeah but he's going that way. Come on."

She began moving out into the parking lot. Keeler was leading, fifteen yards in front. She spotted her Subaru, parked conveniently close to the building. Keeler didn't seem to want the easy option. She supposed he had his reasons.

A forest green sedan entered from their right. Keeler saw the vehicle and stepped back. Candy noticed him keeping the hood of a parked car between himself and the approaching sedan. She saw his right hand down behind his legs, a pistol held with the finger pointed straight along the trigger guard.

Seeing that made Candy's stomach drop.

The green sedan drove by slowly, engine big and growling.

An old Black guy was at the wheel, both hands gripping tight at ten and two of the clock, a careful driver wearing a wool hat and glasses. There was a growing hum from the opposite direction, Candy's immediate left. She turned in time to see a dirty white panel van approaching, coming fast, straight at Vitalek.

Vitalek wasn't seeing it. Candy barked at him. "Move!"

She watched, rooted to the spot. Vitalek saw her speaking, met her eyes, but didn't move. Candy thought maybe he hadn't heard her. It was too late. Behind him, the van came on like it'd run right into him, but it didn't. The driver veered and maneuvered the bumper's edge to knock him hard on the hip, spinning Vitalek to the ground.

Candy wanted to shout something, but it didn't come out of her mouth, because she'd seen two figures weaving athletically among the parked cars, her side of the oncoming van. Men, hunched and moving with guns at their shoulders. Loud clicking sounds cut through the air, accompanied by something that resembled a violent drum roll.

Candy had time to twist around, look for Keeler, but he wasn't there.

Vitalek was sprawled across the parking lot alley. A man bent over him and started pulling him by his backpack toward the van. Candy screamed, cursing and running at the guy. She shoved him off Vitalek, and the man staggered and turned to face her. She backed off because he was goddamned scary looking. Face inscrutable like a demented old man. She felt a dull thud as something collided with her head and she crumpled to the ground.

Keeler was prone, half under a parked station wagon. The asphalt surface was frozen and hard, slick with ice beneath the vehicle. He'd felt the dull hammer blow of a bullet clip the back of his left upper arm. The shot hadn't been a solid hit, but it had been enough to make him lose his balance. The Glock was still in his right hand. Keeler slid the action back, putting one of seventeen rounds into the chamber.

Candy screamed from his left, her voice hoarse and feral. Like the previous night, when she'd gone off chasing those guys.

The clicking sounds had been suppressed semi-automatic fire. He couldn't tell what kind of round had hit him in the arm, but he was guessing at 9mm. He couldn't tell if the suppression was internal or external but was going to go with internal, like maybe an MP5-SD, Heckler & Koch. Luxury weapons made sense for an outfit with funding.

Keeler got up in a crouch and saw the septic company van through the windshield of a parked car, figured out what was going on, and oriented himself. They'd used the green sedan as a diversion and had come from the other direction at the protagonist. The sedan's engine had covered the sound of the other vehicle approaching. The goal had been to separate Keeler from the protagonist, put a wedge between them and pick Vitalek out of the group. Keeler looked to his right through vehicle windows, nothing. Stood up all the way, exposing himself in exchange for a clearer view.

Two men were threading their way among the parked vehicles, coming at him from either side. Aiming to flank him and put a bullet in his head—and Vitalek's and Candy's heads. But that wasn't going to happen.

Keeler got low and sprinted toward the septic van. Triple bursts came simultaneously from behind him, firing out of sync. The result sounded like the clicking of a demented roulette wheel.

The submachine gunfire hammered into vehicles, setting off explosions of car glass and body work, scattering fragments all over, and spraying a fine dust into the chill air. Keeler came up and got off two rounds in the general direction of the shooters and wasn't happy to see that the fire didn't make the enemy combatants dive for cover. They re-oriented and kept coming at him. He saw one of the weapons, confirmed it as an MP5 with internal suppression, since there had been no muzzle flash.

He moved left, in the direction of Candy's outcry. Got down on his belly to look under the van. Two sets of upright feet were visible, widely spaced for balance. Vitalek was being hauled in through the opposite side of the van. Keeler grinned to himself, feeling the adrenaline kick, the familiar exhilaration of combat. So far, the little ambush had been decently planned.

Time to do something about that.

CHAPTER SIXTY-THREE

After a two-second sprint, Keeler came out from between the cars in time to get a glimpse of the septic van's driver. The driver saw him, didn't panic, and hit the gas. The van leapt forward. Keeler had the Glock up, sighting it, the back of his mind churning the variables, anticipating how the rounds would penetrate the van's side panel, travel into the cockpit, and take the driver out of the game.

Oblique targeting, kind of like a parallax view.

He steadied the two-handed grip and squeezed off rounds, keeping the weapon leveled against the recoil. Keeler sent six rounds into the van in quick succession, spreading a wide pattern into the side panel. The vehicle kept going forward. Keeler saw movement in front of him, where Vitalek had been put into the van. There had been two sets of feet, this must be one of them.

Keeler got down between parked cars. Another burst came from the opposite direction, at his back.

He changed direction and crawled toward the new source of fire: the two operators who had been coming through the cars at him. The clattering clicking sound of suppressed MP5 fire came again, the impact of each round louder than the suppressed shot itself. Closer now.

He got down lower and saw two booted feet moving beneath the cars. Keeler crawled forward rapidly, came up on one of the shooters, and sent two rounds into the man's face, not wanting to go for a body shot in case they were wearing armor. The man's expression distorted, the metal rounds transforming his physiognomy and sending the corpse dropping to the pavement like a flesh puppet with strings abruptly severed.

Maybe ten rounds gone, seven left. He hadn't been carefully counting. Certainly not enough ammunition left. Keeler crept toward the downed guy. Saw movement to his left and came up again with the Glock. Bang bang and the slide locked back as the weapon ran out of ammo. He'd the sent last two rounds down the line to the remaining shooter, which bought him time to make a grab for the downed guy's MP5. Keeler stayed cool. He released the slide and pocketed the Glock. It was empty of ammunition, but he'd taken it from Rooney, and he wasn't sure it was a good idea, mixing that into the situation. He had to pry the shooter's dead fingers from around the MP5 grip and didn't manage to avoid looking at what had become of his face, which was no longer a face.

Keeler heard a loud crash behind him and the further click-clacking of suppressed fire making a racket as the bullets vaporized glass and bodywork. Eyes squeezed closed, he withstood a cloud of glass blasted into his face. He crouched and ran back in the direction of the crash. The paneled van had failed to make the turn, rear ending a parked Cadillac SUV. Keeler came around and got the MP5 up, pointed into the driver's cabin. The driver had face planted against the steering wheel, and multiple entry wounds at his back and neck leaked out onto the vinyl seat.

Keeler pulled open the side door. Vitalek was spread-eagled

in the back, shirt, sweater, and jacket rucked up to his armpits. A thin man crouched over him with fingers plunged deep into Vitalek's pale abdomen. Keeler saw it and wasn't sure what was he was looking at. The thin man's fingers spread like steel spider's legs, buried into Vitalek's flesh. Maybe it was a method of killing that made the death look natural. Keeler had no idea, it looked painful. Vitalek's face was caught in frozen agony, eyes bulging and a terrible hiss coming from between his foaming lips. The man bent over him looked up at Keeler, who stared back. There was something weird about his face—the man was wearing a mask, Keeler realized. He moved into the van and punched the MP5's barrel into the man's unprotected chest, sending a single round into him and throwing him against the back door of the van.

It clicked then: they were all wearing masks, latex or silicone, full face masks that looked real until you got close.

Keeler shoved Vitalek. "Get out." Vitalek looked around in wild shock. Keeler slapped him across the face to get his attention. "Get the fuck out." He threw Vitalek out the side of the van. The lanky man scampered to his feet, hardly able to stand. Keeler kicked the backpack after him.

The man who'd planted his fingers into Vitalek's gut was alive. Keeler watched as he pushed himself out of the back of the van, fell on his hands and knees, and began to crawl, face bent to the asphalt. Keeler followed behind him. Saw Candy over the other side of the thin man, lying curled on her side, head beneath a parked vehicle's bumper.

"Candy, get up!" His voice rang out, hard and penetrating. He saw her move and knew she'd been playing dead. Smart girl.

Keeler got up above the thin torturer. Bending to pull the man's mask off. He turned the guy over and found him alive and anonymous, not somebody that he recognized. The man's face was badly scarred, an old wound that looked like an acid attack.

Keeler pressed the MP5's muzzle to his forehead and sent metal into his brain pan.

He spoke calmly to Candy. "Get up and move with me. We're getting out of here."

Keeler stuffed the guy's mask into his pocket, slightly disappointed that it hadn't been Vince Farrell under there. Farrell might have been the one in the green sedan, the old Black guy, wearing a realistic mask, he realized. In his peripheral vision, Keeler saw Vitalek getting his shit together and Candy moving toward them. There was movement up on the left, and Keeler put a triple burst from the MP5 in that direction and saw the shooter moving away, scampering to safety.

He thought about the enemy, how many of them were there? In the septic van there had been a driver and the torturer, plus another guy on foot. Two other men on foot. That was five. Then there was the man in the forest green sedan, maybe Farrell. Keeler replayed it, the old Black guy cutting across in front of him. One of them. A minimum of six men, three of them now dead.

Vitalek wasn't looking so good. Maybe his liver was compromised. Maybe the thin man had managed to do real damage to him in the van. They'd had what, a minute, maybe thirty seconds? That took skill.

Another vehicle moved at the far end of the lot, on the other side of the Toyota. The gray van that Keeler had seen earlier with the old lady. Another diversion. That had never been an old lady, just an operator with one of those hyper-real masks. The gray van was moving slow, drifting through the lot and aiming to corner them. No doubt there were operators in the back or following on foot, unsurprisingly more careful now that three of them were no longer in the land of the living.

Keeler looked behind them and saw a gap between two

apartment buildings with a snow-covered slope behind and the familiar silhouette of a stark, leafless forest.

He grabbed Candy's arm. "Follow me back behind the building. Way it works, I shoot and you run. Do you understand?"

Candy nodded, but Vitalek just stared at him, unsteady on his feet.

"Go." Keeler turned and methodically fired single shots at the gray van.

He could hear the running footsteps from behind him, receding as they got away. He fired two more and then moved out, joined Vitalek and Candy on the other side, putting an entire building between themselves and the shooters. In front of them was nothing but trees and snow. At least the surface of the snow had hardened with the cold. The topography was varied. A slope moving gently north into the hills. To the east a second ridgeline forked off from the initial hill. Keeler's car was parked out by the main road. They'd need to get to it fast, or else choose another means of getting out of there.

All that mess, the cops would be coming in soon. Were probably already on the way.

He looked at Candy and Vitalek. She was excited, meeting his gaze directly with a face flushed and hot. Vitalek wasn't looking so good.

He said, "Candy, get back through the woods to the Little League field. I'll meet you in one of the dugouts."

She nodded. "Which one?"

"Doesn't matter. Whatever you think is best."

"What are you going to do?"

He lifted the MP5. "Need ammunition."

What Keeler didn't say is he wanted to take out another couple of enemy operators before the parking lot became a crime scene with half the law enforcement agencies of New York state crawling all over it, picking up ejected cartridges.

CHAPTER SIXTY-FOUR

Vince Farrell sat in the driver's seat, window down to let the cold air in. He watched as a snowflake landed on his hand and melted almost immediately. The old Black guy mask was sweaty, but it wasn't yet prudent to take it off. Farrell had backed the forest green Ford into a spot up front by the apartment complex's entrance. He had his phone up on the dashboard with a secure line to the remaining three guys. He had just finished ordering them up into the woods. Told them to leave the two vans for the cops to find. The vehicles had been stolen within the last twelve hours. The police wouldn't find anything there.

At this point Farrell was all in, double or nothing. He felt insulated. Nobody up there was going to be able to connect him with anything. The green Ford was clean, and he was no longer carrying a weapon. The only thing was the mask, and he'd be ditching it soon. Thing about an altercation like this, the cops came in hot and bothered. Almost always panicked and excited. All you needed to do was act cool.

He got Milton on the line up at Copenhagen House. Farrell leaned forward and spoke quickly and directly into the phone.

"I need you down here now. I don't care what's going on up there." He tapped and swiped on the phone, sending the GPS coordinates. "You get that?"

Milton's voice was professional and gave nothing away. "Copy. I've got the location. You want us at this position. We don't have a vehicle."

"Take what's his face's car."

"Mister Altman, Jerry."

"Yeah. Get here ASAP."

"Roger that. We're about ten minutes out, boss. Already moving."

Farrell had a momentary vision of Jerry resisting Milton, trying to stop him from taking the car and suffering the consequences. Milton was a fucking animal when he got going. Two police vehicles screamed into sight from behind him. He kept himself calm and followed with his eyes as they entered the complex from the main road, tires squealing around the turn.

Farrell tracked them through the old Black guy mask eye holes. He knew what they were seeing, just a crusty old innocent. Both cruisers ignored him completely, each of them containing two cops, each cop intent on whatever they were going to find a hundred yards in. Which was going to be smashed shit and 9mm cartridges and the corpses of three freelance contractors operating their own business out of unrelated corporate accounts in Delaware. Three out of one and a half million registered corporations in the state.

The police cruisers stopped fifty yards away in a wedge pattern blocking the road into the development. The cops were afraid to enter the battlefield, using any excuse available to avoid heading in to a kill zone.

Farrell had seen it all before, nothing ever changes.

Still, the situation wasn't ideal. Keeler still out there, although now on the run, up in the woods with the protagonist.

Farrell gazed out of the window at the boring winter scene. At least they'd sent him the witch. The witch was dead, but he'd gotten his scary-as-shit fingers into the protagonist, maybe for long enough—which meant there was a good chance the geek was done, and Farrell's mission accomplished.

He hadn't seen Keeler into the grave, but that was a personal project that was going to have to wait. If the protagonist was done, so was he. If the objective was achieved the money people wouldn't care that the job had run into complications, which meant Farrell probably wasn't going to get kneecapped.

The old Black guy mask was almost perfect. Almost, because there was a gap of a couple millimeters between the eye holes and the eyes, which meant that Farrell's peripheral vision was slightly impeded. By the time he saw the guy coming from his left, it was too late to respond in any substantial way.

Farrell tried playing it cool, swiveled his head and saw the witch crouched low and coming at him. Except it wasn't the witch. The witch was skinny as a rail and kind of bent and this guy wasn't skinny. It took him a second to recognize the clothes and come to the sinking realization that he was looking at Tom Keeler wearing the witch's mask.

And then Keeler was at the open window, a cold steel barrel pressing against Farrell's temple.

Farrell said, "What do you want, Keeler?"

Keeler's eyes were cold inside the mask he'd taken from the dead witch. The silicone face expressionless, looking past Farrell to the police cars up the road. Keeler reached in through the window and pulled off Farrell's old guy mask, tossing it aside. Farrell felt the freezing air working on the sweat now beading on his neck, forehead, and upper lip.

Keeler said, "I guess there are two things I want right now. First, I was wondering how many bullets remain in this thing."

He knocked the thick suppressed barrel against Farrell's temple, which hurt. "You want to guess? I've got it on triple."

"No."

"Okay, you're not curious, don't want to guess. The second thing is a negative want, like what I don't want."

Farrell sniffed a compromise. He looked at Keeler directly, for the first time. "And what's that, what do you *not* want?"

Keeler said, "Back splatter."

He stepped back and Farrell saw what was happening, Keeler's finger tightening on the trigger.

Farrell already had the index finger of his left hand curled through the door latch. It didn't take more than a fraction of a second to pull it back and slam his shoulder into the car door, swinging it open. The MP5's barrel was inserted through the open window. The inside edge of the door knocked the gun off its mark.

The barrel spat, something between a loud cough and a harsh click that made him suddenly deaf in his left ear. Farrell happened to have measured the decibel output of an MP5-SD. The stats came back to him, weirdly, given the moment, 130db.

The gas emissions blew into Farrell's face. He felt something tug violently at his throat, a dull thud at his neck. He heard the muffled sound of Keeler squeezing the trigger of an empty weapon. There had only been a single round remaining. Farrell fought shock and got a hand to the open gash, the wound pulsing. He pushed his palm against the blood running freely into the cold air and tried to keep himself from panicking.

Keeler's eyes flicked past him, tracking something through the passenger side. He tossed the MP5 in through the window, hitting Farrell in the mouth with the polymer forearm, adding insult to injury. Farrell's teeth were already busted and sore. He turned his head away instinctively, finding himself facing the cops. Farrell was losing consciousness from blood loss out of the neck wound, but his brain couldn't help but register the two policemen sprinting in his direction, weapons out.

He felt himself falling into a warm dark hole, like the car below him was swallowing him up. Everything resolved to black.

CHAPTER SIXTY-FIVE

Keeler backed off, keeping Farrell's car as a visual obstacle between himself and the police. He ducked behind a garbage dumpster and observed for a minute. The two policemen were coming at the car with pistols drawn, like something out of reality TV. Farrell was either unconscious or dead. Keeler suspected the former, at least for the moment. Which meant the police would be calling in the paramedics. Doing so would give them an activity, waiting. In Keeler's experience, the majority of people in the world would rather wait than insert themselves into the unpredictable dangers of a kinetic situation.

He worked his way around the back of the apartment complex, moving on the inside of a low hedge running north. He quickly oriented himself. The woods began to his left, rising up the incline. Up ahead, maybe fifty yards down, the complex ended in a slightly elevated tree line. The Little League field was about a quarter mile through the woods, to the southeast.

What Keeler wanted to do was loot the dead mercenaries of weaponry and ammunition in the parking lot and get up into the woods before the place was flooded with law enforcement. Sirens and hot engines screamed in from the other side of the building. Keeler listened and counted three separate vehicles. One stayed on the outside, where Farrell's car had stopped. Two others sped into the parking lot.

There was movement at the end of the complex, straight in front of him. Keeler froze. Four figures darted into the woods. Operators with weapons, moving tactically up the incline. They were out of sight within fifteen seconds. They'd gone the wrong way, but Keeler wasn't going to assume that had been an error. Maybe they'd wanted to get up into the woods before doubling back and looking for tracks. Vitalek and Candy would have left plenty of those.

Every operator's assessment: the cops would take hours to get organized, especially if the active shooting seemed to be over.

He heard the sound of vehicle doors slamming and radios crackling. There were more police coming. Time to leave. Keeler turned and walked back, found Vitalek and Candy's tracks in the snow. His feet were bigger than Vitalek's but he didn't think it was going to matter. He walked in the existing boot prints until he got to the trees. The ridgeline ran northwest, with a steep ravine on the other side of it. Keeler walked over to the ridge and saw that the ravine ended in another incline a hundred yards away.

He took out the phone and got a map up. The wooded area began at the apartment complex and extended several miles into the hills with sparsely distributed houses and small roads. There was one road cutting approximately east to west through the woods. The east part of it ended at the Kitchewan dam, which held back a huge reservoir. Keeler traced the road over the dam and saw that it wound east and south, passing near Copenhagen House. The dam and reservoir were the source of the running water he'd heard from the estate. Looking at the east part of the forest, he saw the topography was cut through with steep ravines all running essentially north to south with slight deviations.

The four men had entered the woods about a hundred yards to the north. They'd be doubling back at some point, looking for tracks, hunting. Keeler knew the feeling, the hunter's confidence, the sensation of a weapon in hand and the invincibility of the predator's role. He turned and followed the ridgeline toward the Little League field. The snow flurry had picked up, the flakes heavier now, making it through the trees.

Keeler hadn't gone more than twenty-five yards when he saw someone coming through the trees. He took a step into the ravine and got low enough to be hard to spot. The ravine was steep and its bottom was loaded with detritus from the forest, branches and leaves and stuff blown down from storms and wind. All of it poking out of the snow. If need be he could get down there quietly and hide in the tangle.

That wasn't going to be necessary. Candy had the point, leading Vitalek up the slope. The snow had really started to come down. Keeler got up and waved his arms so that she saw him. He waited for them to come to him.

Candy was breathless. "A bunch of guys saw us in the Little League field. I think they're coming up behind us." She glanced nervously behind her, flushed face and voice a little shaky. "I think it's the men from up at Copenhagen House. The guy whose phone we hacked."

Vitalek looked better. He laughed nervously. "Maybe he's pissed."

Keeler said, "He's not pissed because he doesn't know. He just wants to kill you is all. Probably gets a bonus for doing it, now that we've made it more difficult."

Vitalek laughed again, failing to make it sound relaxed. "Great, thanks for correcting me."

Keeler said, "How're you feeling?"

"Better, still not a hundred percent."

"Good. We'll take fifty percent." The weird guy with his hands in Vitalek's guts hadn't had enough time to do his thing, which was a close call. Unless the effects were supposed to be delayed, in which case they'd have to wait to see if Vitalek survived the night. Keeler looked behind them, trying to penetrate the woods with his naked eye but having a hard time because of the heavy snowfall. He said, "How far back do you think they are?"

Vitalek shrugged and looked at Candy. She said, "I don't know. They spotted us for sure. Stopped their car and just left it there by the road.

Keeler kept his eyes on the forest. "What kind of car?"

"European luxury car. Mercedes I think. Big black one."

Keeler recalled Jerry's black Mercedes S-Class. Nodded to himself. He pointed across the ravine to the other side. "I want you guys to cross this ravine to the other side." He glanced at Candy to make sure she was paying attention. Her eyes narrowed, paying attention. "You'll find another ravine on the other side of that one. Get just below the ridgeline facing us and take a right, uphill. Keep walking up into the woods and stay below the crest. I'm going to be right behind you in a couple of minutes."

Candy said, "Where are you going?"

"I want to see what we've got." He made a gesture. "Get going now."

He waited, watching as Vitalek and Candy struggled down the slope and then up the other side. Keeler looked at the traces their boots made and figured that with the new snowfall would make it hard for the enemy to track them. Once he saw them over the other side of the slope, Keeler started toward the Little League field.

He got about fifty yards down and found a tangle of pricker bushes to get behind. Keeler took a knee and waited.

A minute later, the first guy emerged from behind the curtain of falling snow. Keeler estimated him at fifty yards out, hiking up the hill in regular street clothes. It was one of the guys Keeler had seen, first getting out of Jerry's car up at Copenhagen House, then at the diner. Another became visible behind him and to Keeler's right. They had spaced themselves out and were coming steadily up into the woods, looking confident, though they weren't holding weapons.

Keeler slipped into the ravine and moved rapidly up the other side, screened by the snowfall and trees. He came up over the opposite ridgeline and descended the next indentation a quarter of the way down. Now feeling less exposed, he jogged uphill to where Vitalek and Candy would be. He found them in the lee of a boulder stuck into the steep hillside.

Both of them looked at him with worried faces. Candy said, "Maybe we should call the cops. You think the thing with Frankie . . ." She left the sentence unfinished.

Keeler said, "It's not only the thing with Frankie." He chin pointed at Vitalek. "We need to get them off his back more permanently and to do that we have to exploit the phone you hacked."

Vitalek said, "I have to show you how."

"Right." Keeler turned to Candy. "Also I don't think the police will be helpful, or quick enough." He pointed up the hill and started walking. "Follow me."

He kept the pace high but manageable for the others. From what Keeler had determined, there were men behind them and the four others up in the woods somewhere. The two parties would be in contact, probably over their phones. They'd coordinate a little pincer, try to trap them.

He guided Vitalek and Candy over another ridge and into

yet another ravine. Clearly, the woods up there had once been a series of tributaries flowing into the Hudson, probably before it had been seen by human beings. Consequently, it wasn't a terrible topography for evasion. If they could get far enough northeast, they could move past the four operators and escape the death sandwich. He grinned to himself, liking that terminology.

Twenty minutes later they came to a road, high up on another ridge. They'd been moving uphill the entire time, and Keeler could tell that his two friends were tired, energy sapped and strength flagging. He belly crawled up to the road. It was getting dark out and the snowfall was intense. The road was one-lane asphalt, now covered by an inch of snow accumulation. The woods were silent.

There weren't any houses up there, just the one road slicing through forested hills, winding east. They were halfway up the mountain, about a mile from the dam.

Keeler was about to come out of the tree cover and onto the exposed road, when he noticed a vehicle stopped in a turnout. The car was covered in freshly fallen snow, which is why he hadn't initially seen it. He stared into the windshield glass, trying to figure out what had caught his attention. It happened again, not exactly movement, but something, as if the glass was breathing. It took Keeler a moment to understand what he was looking at, the accumulation of steam on the inside of the windshield. He was watching someone breathing inside the car. The road was being watched.

Keeler slid back down the slope to join the others.

CHAPTER SIXTY-SIX

Vitalek had an idea, find a good place to hole up and build a shelter. He touched his backpack. "Got everything we need right here." There was a gleam in his eye, like he was enjoying himself.

Keeler looked at the snow coming down. Not a bad idea. At the moment there were numerous issues. It wouldn't be a winning move, getting shot by some guy hiding in a bush. The visibility was bad and getting worse as the early winter night fell. If they could find the right spot, they could wait out the storm. Plus, Keeler liked hunting in the dark. He had a visual in his mind. Vitalek and Candy, safe and warm in a shelter. Him out in the night, hunting the enemy.

The wind had picked up with the blizzard. The men following them would have adjusted their tactics. What Keeler would have done was stop trying to actively search, start setting up traps and ambushes.

He nodded at Vitalek. "Let's do that." He pointed at the pack. "What do you have in there?"

Vitalek said, "I've got what we need."

Keeler stood for a moment, thinking. Normally he'd be

tearing down Vitalek's backpack and ripping out its contents, selecting and discarding. Definitely not taking some skinny billionaire's word for it. But, this wasn't a normal situation. He started walking, north and west, away from the guys up on the road.

A half hour later he found a decent spot. A huge set of boulders were coming out of a ravine bottom. The ridge above was all tangled bushes and thick pine. By that time, Keeler was carrying both Vitalek and Candy's packs, the two of them trailing behind, having a bad time making their way through the snow. They were both halfway between exhaustion and hypothermia. Probably sweating inside of their parkas. It was time to get into cover and wait it out.

He set down the packs, stretched, and felt his back crack pleasantly. Keeler swept his hand around the ravine bottom. "Let's pick up some long branches, make a lean-to against the boulder there."

The way the snow was falling now, it'd be less than a half hour before their lean-to was covered. Vitalek and Candy were already sitting down, catching their breath. Keeler began hunting for wood. The bottom of the ravine was full of fallen branches, some of them difficult to extract. It took him fifteen minutes to pull out enough wood for a rudimentary frame. He leaned the branches against the boulder. Up on the ridge was a stand of pine. He figured he'd go strip out some evergreen branches for camouflage. The needles would allow the snow to accumulate.

Keeler climbed the ravine and chose low branches with the widest spread of evergreen needles. He used the knife to strip them from the trees, not too concerned that one of the enemy operators would notice the stripped bark. It was going to be fully dark in a half hour. When he got back down, Candy and Vitalek were hard at work. Vitalek had a large professional catering roll of plastic wrap, slotted onto a stick. Candy was pulling the cling film off the spindle, wrapping it around the outside of a wide teepee made out of the bare branches Keeler had pulled out of the ravine.

He watched them working for a while, liking what he was seeing. The plastic wrap was going to provide rudimentary insulation, the open top and bottom providing good air flow. When the wrapping job was complete, they pushed the structure against the boulder, partially collapsing one side. Keeler got busy on the inside, using the fast dwindling daylight to pull out the larger stones and sticks. The evergreens on the outside caught the falling snow nicely. Keeler stepped back to examine the work. From twenty yards, the shelter was invisible. Vitalek had used a box cutting knife to slice the wrap in the middle, making a door.

The temperature inside was already elevated by body heat alone. Vitalek rooted around in his pack. The glow of an LCD camping light illuminated the shelter. He made an adjustment to the device, setting the light as low as possible. Candy sat cross-legged, head dropped to her chest, half asleep already. Keeler caught Vitalek's eye and winked. The guy smiled.

Keeler said, "I guess you've got dinner planned out as well."

The crypto guy held up a tiny camping stove. "Hope you like freeze-dried tuna casserole."

Candy spoke quietly. "Love tuna casserole."

CHAPTER SIXTY-SEVEN

Farrell became conscious.

First came a bleary confusion, so he didn't bother opening his eyes. It took a while, but he'd been through the training. Settle down and run the diagnostics. Even under mental strain it was possible. Headache the size of a Canadian lentil field. At the same time, he was feeling a little too good, so he opened his eyes to see a tube coming out of his arm and two guys in chairs doing stuff. One, a cop.

Farrell closed his eyes again, having recognized what was going on.

He settled down and listened and explored the sensations. The policeman was running a gunshot residue test on his hands and fingers. The sensation of someone rubbing stuff on his hand, such an alien sensation, led to a minor panic, settled by the morphine. Plus the fact that his hands were clean this time. He hadn't fired anything in a couple of days, since the range in Pennsylvania on the weekend.

Pressure to his neck almost made Farrell do something defensive. The morphine helped again.

Farrell squinted and got a close-up shot of a Black guy's face leaning in and concentrated. A paramedic. The guy's skin was shiny and he wore a face shield, like he was worried about catching Ebola or something. Farrell figured the man was patching him up, which was a minor miracle. Meant that his neck was still intact. He took a deep breath through his nose, got the hit into his lungs and felt relieved that the machinery was functioning.

The other sensation was of movement. He was in the back of an ambulance.

Farrell settled down and focused. It wasn't easy to get past the morphine effects and whatever else they'd put inside him. When he did, he came to the conclusion that he was okay, that Keeler's bullet hadn't put a huge hole in his throat. Must have done something bad, but since he was so heavily medicated he felt good to go.

For some reason, he wasn't handcuffed or bound to the stretcher. Not like he was totally aware of standard police procedures, but if they were certain that he was part of a violent crew who'd shot up the apartment complex parking lot, leaving several dead, they surely would have at least handcuffed him to something solid. They were transporting him to the hospital in the back of an ambulance with a police escort in case the GSR test came out positive.

What had happened was that Keeler had pulled off his mask.

If he'd have been found with the mask on it would've been game over. Farrell felt the warm glow of morphine and the exhilaration of getting away with something. The vehicle he'd been in was clean, no weapons, and they weren't going to find gunshot residue on his hands, only on his face. They were going to classify him as a victim.

Farrell couldn't believe it.

On the other hand he wasn't feeling very stable, emotionally. Past the morphine, things didn't look as good. He felt a sense of imbalance, as if something were wobbly and unsettled. It wasn't only because the vehicle moving either, it was more a question of satisfaction, or the lack of it. Even knowing how lucky he'd been he wasn't feeling good.

He needed to get the fuck out of there, then he'd be able to get clear and back on mission.

He opened his eye a hair and maneuvered himself on the stretcher, snorting and mumbling something, feigning an unconscious man's delirium. The cop was fooling with the GSR kit, not paying attention. He had his weapon holstered to the left hip. A semi-automatic—maybe a Glock. Farrell almost giggled at the thought of finding a round in the chamber and a full magazine—both guarantees since it was a cop's gun. It was almost too easy.

It would have been nice to test himself first, but there wasn't time. Farrell pulled himself to sit up straight. He swung his legs off the stretcher and reached down to the cop's weapon before the guy even registered the movement. Farrell didn't even bother thinking about how he felt. He jammed the barrel into the cop's gut below the vest and squeezed the trigger hard. The cop's ample blubber suppressed the gun shot sound.

Farrell wheeled right around to the paramedic and received a hard fist in his face. He caught a glimpse of the paramedic's hostile expression behind the face shield. The man was getting ready to hit Farrell again, even as his head snapped back from the first punch. Farrell stretched his arms out, pulling the catheter from his vein, and sent two rounds into the paramedic's unprotected chest.

He turned his attention back to the cop, now on the floor of the ambulance, moving around, dying and bleeding—no longer a person, more like a vector for shock and nausea. Farrell pushed the barrel into his temple and blew skull and brains all over the floor. Looked at the weapon, Glock 21 Gen4 in .45. Nice gun, big bullets.

He waited for the driver to stop or at least to slow down, but nothing happened. Farrell popped the back door. They were flying down a dark highway in the middle of a goddamned blizzard. Almost no cars and thick flurries of snow accumulating on the road. Up front was a door into the driver's cabin, off to the right side, looking fancy like something on the inside of a boat. He opened the door and found himself in the cabin. The driver was clueless, concentrating on the road. He noticed Farrell out of the corner of his eye and twitched, almost losing his shit.

Farrell said, "Pull over, right now." The words coming out weak and inaudible. He said it again, louder. "Pull over."

The driver glanced at him and nodded. "Don't do anything stupid okay?"

That made Farrell laugh, kicking off a coughing fit. Nothing stupid. The guy was pulling the ambulance over. Farrell waited for him stop.

"Put it in park."

The paramedic put it in park. Farrell shot him in the right temple, the guy's head slamming into the window and the body slumping over. Farrell got into the cabin properly and angled the rearview mirror to himself. He clicked on the cabin light and examined the reflection. Pretty bad, a little mauled from the spitting hot gunshot gasses, with a good-sized dressing on his neck. He realized that he was naked. They must have cut off his clothes, checking for other wounds.

He went into the back and found his stuff. The clothes were unusable, but incredibly his phone and wallet were there in a plastic basket on the counter. Money and communications, what more could a man want? He stripped the dead cop and got dressed. The uniform was too large, but relatively comfortable. He got his phone up and made a call.

The woman answered. "You know you're supposed to be back. They're freaking out."

"Shut up and get me to the closest hospital. Stand by." He sent his location. "Got it?"

She hesitated to respond. He heard a sigh, something he had never heard before. She said, "I can't help you."

So it had gotten that bad, no medals no glory. He'd either be thrown to the wolves or kneecapped and buried in the North Pole. Farrell looked out at the dark, the snow coming down so relentlessly that it almost had its own agency, like it was alive. He had a sinking feeling of loneliness and let it play for a second, before cutting it out forever. There was no time for that shit, life is too short.

He said, "Come on, Alice, it's the hospital. They can find me there. I need to get help. I might be dying."

She sighed again. "It's Phelps Memorial. I'm not sending you a route. You just need to go straight, and you'll see the sign. Good luck." She clicked off.

Farrell dragged the driver's body into the back and got the vehicle going again. They'd be tracking the ambulance and he was currently in the middle of nowhere. Best place to go was to the hospital, where the vehicle was expected. There would be plenty of transport options at a hospital. He drove and paid attention to the signage. Just like she'd said, Phelps Memorial was indicated a couple of miles up. He pulled off the highway and followed an overpass into the woods. The road went straight for a while, completely devoid of other vehicles until it curved around another slipway, and he saw the medical complex: a cluster of large buildings with lights and a landscaped lawn, now a blank white field of snow.

Farrell parked the ambulance at the back of the complex and locked the doors. It wasn't likely that anyone was going to bother with it, not in the middle of a blizzard at night. Maybe the dispatcher would get curious, but he didn't care. Walking wasn't as hard as he thought it might be. The thing was to avoid any brightly lit places where people could actually see him clearly. He was pretty sure that his appearance was a little shocking. Which made him smile and feel good inside, another effect of the morphine.

The complex had a four-story parking lot. On the ground floor was a loading area with dumpsters. Farrell leaned against the loading dock and looked at his phone, glad also for the cop's overcoat. It was freezing out. He had a dozen missed incoming calls from the office and one text message from an hour ago. The message was from Alice, a long thread of information about the train conductor, DeValla. Farrell read it with concentration bordering on fascination. It was a profile of a person with a life, someone who had things going for herself, stuff that she would miss, people who would miss her.

Minerva Octavia DeValla had been married and divorced, had two kids, and had a good, steady job with Metro-North. She had an address in Kitchewan Landing.

Ten minutes later Farrell shot an Asian woman in the parking lot. He let the body fall to the snow-covered asphalt and took her car, a sturdy Lexus SUV. The only thing he allowed in his head was a mute and routine calculation: he'd used seven rounds out of a seventeen-round magazine, plus the one in the chamber, which meant he had eleven rounds left.

CHAPTER SIXTY-EIGHT

C andy snored softly, curled into fetal position and wearing every single piece of clothing that she'd packed. Keeler saw her by the light of Vitalek's laptop, which had forty-three percent battery remaining. They were huddled together, looking intently at the screen.

Currently, there was no connection to the internet, no mobile phone or satellite signal was penetrating their deep hideaway, so the left side of the screen was a vertical black rectangle. On the right side, Vitalek was exploring the copy of Milton's phone, giving a running commentary as he did so.

"Normally you'd have an issue with end-to-end encryption. Since we've just virtualized the entire phone we don't have to worry about it, because we're in at the front end." He looked at Keeler to see if he was following. "Okay, so I'm supposed to be the *protagonist*, yeah?" the lanky guy's fingers flew. "They run a decently secure comms. Nothing operational over email or on regular SMS chat, so forget about that." He looked at Keeler, letting him in on something. "I got into the emails. He's got invoices. Guy gets paid fifteen grand per month as an independent contractor." Turning once more to Keeler. "That's decent for normal people, no?"

Keeler didn't care how much Milton was paid; he wanted to know what they were all currently doing. Beyond that, he was looking for the next piece of the puzzle: who wanted Vitalek dead, who was the ultimate client. He glanced at the lanky guy and wondered what he was thinking, if it was just a game to him. It was hard to tell. The guy was sometimes completely on point and other times a total space cadet. He wouldn't have lasted five minutes in special tactics.

This guy, Milton, was obsessed with taking photographs of himself and posting them online. He was the kind of operator who moonlighted as a gym bunny with tattoos.

Vitalek stopped scrolling. "There's nothing of interest on here."

Keeler said, "No. We need to get into their communications."

According to Vitalek, the operators were using a proprietary messaging app that had been resistant to virtualization. It came up as a dark purple screen and demanded a password, a fingerprint, and facial recognition. Which would all happen quickly if you were the person using the phone.

Vitalek said, "Well, we need an internet connection and then we need to hope he's communicating so the app's already open."

Keeler said, "Let's go up on the ridge, see if you get a signal." He pointed at the laptop. "At least it's worth trying before you're out of power."

Vitalek was looking at Keeler like, the last thing he wanted to do was go back out there into the blizzard. Keeler reached over and snapped the laptop closed.

"Let's go."

It was no longer a full on blizzard out there, in fact it was beautiful out. The fresh snow cover made everything look completely new and clean in the bright moonlight. They climbed the ravine with difficulty, holding on to small trees growing out of the side as they went. Up on top, Keeler guided them into a copse of pines. Stars were visible, and it was an altogether spectacular evening in the woods.

Vitalek sat cross-legged and got the laptop out of his pack. Soon, he looked up at Keeler and nodded. He was getting a signal. Vitalek spoke quietly. "He's got the app open."

Keeler squatted to join him. "You can copy it now?" he asked.

"No. I can update the copy I've got of everything else, but once he closes this app we're out of it again."

Vitalek started scrolling extremely fast through the secure messaging app threads. Too fast to read.

Keeler said, "Slow down."

Vitalek shook his head. "I'm recording this as a video screen grab. We'll go through it slowly later, since we don't have time now." He looked up at Keeler. "Right?"

"Right."

The battery had slipped to thirty-eight percent. A few minutes later, Vitalek closed the laptop.

"Let's go back and read the messages."

Candy was still fast asleep, curled up. Vitalek ran the video capture through a program that could turn an image into text. They watched it working frame by frame in extremely fast motion. At the same time, they watched the battery percentage diminish, as if each frame processed chewed up its equivalent in power. Keeler figured that nothing came for free.

He said, "Fast machine."

"Yeah."

Seven minutes later, Vitalek had a plain text file and was

running text string searches on it for the term *protagonist*. The searches turned up quite a few hits, highlighted in yellow.

Keeler said, "So?"

Vitalek scrolled through, indicating interesting parts of the messaging with his trackpad pointer. "They've been chatting about the movements of the protagonist, presumably me. Clocked me when I arrived at Copenhagen House. Then again when I left a couple days ago and again when I came out of the woods."

Keeler grunted, looking into the computer. "We already know they were tracking you. What else?"

Vitalek pointed. "You can see. No explicit communication about me, besides them noting my movements out of Copenhagen House. But here's something potentially interesting. Check it out." His fingers fluttered over the keyboard in a rapid staccato. He pointed at the results. "Keyword *Flamenco* comes up quite a bit yesterday and the day before. I think it's Irma." His finger landed on a specific chat thread. "There." Vitalek read it out loud. "Dead check Flamenco." He looked at Keeler. "What's a dead check?"

Keeler said, "It's when you make sure the enemy's dead. For example, when you kick an enemy in the eye to see if he's faking his death. If he moves, you put a bullet in his brain, make sure he's not going to stand up and shoot you in the back."

"This guy was sent to finish Irma off?"

Keeler nodded. "Correct. It means the guy did finish her off. Someone went out there to the hospital and made sure she was dead, maybe this guy Milton."

Vitalek mumbled to himself, letting the fingers fly over the keyboard. "Let's run a search for Flamenco outside of the secure message app. Just in case."

"I thought they were running good security on their comms."

"Just in case, I said."

Keeler said nothing. Vitalek got the main copy of Milton's phone up on the right side of the screen. It looked like a phone screen. All the icons clustered together and unorganized. An anomaly jumped out at Keeler, something that was at first unconscious. He put a hand on Vitalek's arm. "Hold it there."

Vitalek stopped and waited as Keeler stared into the screen, trying to figure out what that intuition had been. His eyes were attracted to one of the phone's icons. He got it. A notification from the regular text message app on the phone. This Milton guy had an insane number of unread messages, a little bubble next to the icon with the number, one thousand three hundred and sixty two. What Keeler remembered in the back of his mind, it had changed. The number had been one thousand three hundred and fifty eight earlier.

He put his finger to the message app icon. "Open that up, he received four messages between the first copy you made of his phone and the update you just did."

Vitalek was looking at him. "Seriously, you noticed that?"

"Open it."

The new messages were all from someone named Sam Kelly. Vitalek opened the first one.

The message thread had a dozen or more entries. The latest message was from a few minutes earlier, an image thumbnail. Vitalek clicked on it. The image grew to fill the screen. It had been taken in the mirror of what looked like a fancy hotel room and showed a man in his mid-thirties—naked and fresh from the shower—flexing his muscles. He had gelled blond hair that perfectly preserved the direction the comb had traveled. The text read, "Wanna show you what's waiting for you up here in number nine big dog. Your room's hot, think I'll sleep with the covers off. Wake me up with a slap please."

Vitalek said, "Jeez, that's vulgar and weird. Isn't it a little early for bed?"

Keeler chin pointed across to Candy, who was currently snoring softly in her fetal position. "Some people go to bed early, particularly in the winter." He pointed at the picture. "Guy looks like a gym bunny. They do all kinds of weird things."

Vitalek agreed. "It's healthy going to bed early. What was it the guy said about that?"

"Early to bed, early to rise, makes a man healthy, wealthy, and wise. Ben Franklin, Protestant work ethic."

"Right."

But Keeler wasn't interested in the guy in the picture, so much as the room he was in.

He put a finger to the photograph. "That's Copenhagen House, don't you recognize it?"

Vitalek concentrated on the image. "Is it?"

"One hundred percent. Look at the wallpaper and look at the night-light. Those things are standardized in places like that."

The night-light lampshade was the same angular pyramid he'd noticed before, what seemed like a long time ago. The wall was relatively far away in the image, but the faint gold stripe on cream wallpaper was visible.

Vitalek nodded. "Sure, maybe."

Keeler moved his finger. "Vertical gold line on the wallpaper."

Vitalek looked at him again. "Actually, I can't tell, but I see that you can. You have impressive pattern recognition."

Vitalek flipped back to the main thread. He opened the previous message, from Milton to Kelly, also an image. This one taken at night, out in the woods with a flash illuminating

Milton's florid and freezing face inside of a wool hat. The accompanying text read, "Fucking freezing my ass off. Make sure that your golden ass is tucked into the silk sheets of room number nine when I get back."

Milton initiating the conversation, the other guy responding with the naked picture. Obviously the two were in a relationship.

Keeler said, "Let's see the previous messages."

Vitalek opened the other messages, scrolling first to the bottom. The correspondence had been going on for three months. It was all similar stuff, aggressively flirtatious jokes and images of the two men in various states of undress, both shots of their entire bodies and close-up shots of body parts. Vitalek made a sound, like a sigh.

"How does this help us?"

Keeler said, "Can you use the virtual copy of his phone?"

"You mean to send a message?"

Keeler nodded.

Vitalek's eyes were opening wide, and Keeler saw him catch his train of thought. "Not on the virtual copy, no. But we can manipulate the phone, for sure."

Keeler said, "This Kelly guy is warm in bed while his boyfriend's out there freezing his ass off and risking his life, which means Kelly's making more than fifteen grand a month." He nudged Vitalek in the ribs. "We're going back up to the ridge. I want you to get your malware into the new phone. Maybe the information gets richer with a higher pay grade."

Vitalek understood the idea: Use Milton's phone to send clickbait to his lover up at Copenhagen House. "What do we send as clickbait?" he asked.

Based on the photo Kelly had sent with his gym muscles and slick hair, Keeler had a pretty good idea the man was vain and therefore insecure. "Send him a message saying something like, 'Check out this photo I took of you sleeping. You look so cute.'"

Vitalek giggled. "Nice."

CHAPTER SIXTY-NINE

Once they were up on the ridge once more, Keeler saw the battery was down to thirty percent.

Vitalek was back on the computer. "Right. This time we don't need to get into the secure messaging app. We're just going regular. So we're good."

Keeler came alongside him. Vitalek accessed the camera on Milton's phone. "Just to see what's going on." The image showed only grainy darkness. He activated the light on Milton's phone for a second, getting a blurred view of the inside of his pocket. "Hopefully he didn't notice the flash."

"Give it a second in case he did." They sat together in silence, giving it the time Milton might take checking his phone. It was cold, but Keeler had experienced much worse. The moon was even brighter than before and the wind was blowing again. Light snow landed on his face and hands. He nodded at Vitalek. "All right."

Vitalek sent the message, just as Keeler had dictated, "*Check out this photo I took of you sleeping. You look so cute.*"

"You think he'll go for it?"

Keeler grunted. "I guess so."

Vitalek said, "Cyber war is a dirty business."

Keeler knew about war, so he ignored the naive statement. He said, "Now we need to get to a power source and exploit the new guy." He was feeling the excitement of hope. They'd get into this guy's communications, Keeler was sure of it. Now they just needed to get out of the woods.

The problem was that Candy was gone.

It took them a while to ascertain this fact, given that there was no light in the shelter. Vitalek flicked on the camping light and they confirmed the absence. No Candy—only a little area where she'd been, next to her empty backpack and a water bottle. Neither Keeler or Vitalek had bothered to check the outside of the shelter when they'd returned. Now Keeler saw the tracks leading away, perfectly conforming to Candy's boot shape and size.

He stood a yard outside of the shelter, looking down the ravine bed. Vitalek was inside kneeling, his head sticking out. They both heard a noise from above, a soft crunch and then silence. It froze Keeler in place, who glanced at Vitalek and saw the guy's eyes wide and staring straight ahead. Again the noise, like a shuffle from above. Could be anything, a deer moving in the night, or a raccoon. Maybe a coyote or an entrepreneurial house cat. Or a team of mercenaries aiming to kill them.

Keeler put his finger to his lips and pointed up. He made a sign for Vitalek to stay inside.

The boulder the shelter was built against was stuck into the sloping end of the ravine, at the bend of a sharp U shape. On either side of the hulking rock was a steep incline. He heard the sound again, this time clearly someone moving stealthily. It sounded like a single person, but Keeler knew it wouldn't be.

The enemy was moving carefully and slowly, one step at a time, walking in sync. The man on point would make the footprints, the other guys stepping into them, making sure it looked like the tracks of a single person.

They were not yet at the top of the boulder, maybe twenty yards out to the east, which, if facing the shelter, would be to Keeler's left. He stepped to the right side of the rock and began inching his way up the incline, each boot step carefully calculated to make no sound. He held himself against the rock face. Zero margin for error.

When he was almost at the top, Keeler tucked himself into a rock crevice. The enemy were closer and the sound they made above was now clear. They were not yet at the boulder, but moving along the ridge. Maybe they'd seen the tracks where he'd been in the pines with Vitalek, not far away.

He scooped a handful of snow and formed it into a ball. Released the survival knife from its sheath. Keeler followed the movement of the men on the ridge and waited until they were directly above the boulder. He tossed the snow ball high, aiming into the gulley. The impact made a soft sound, barely perceptible. The sound above him stopped immediately. He waited. Someone took several steps down into the ravine, maybe trying to get a view. The beam of a strong flashlight cut into the darkness. It came from almost directly above him.

Keeler came out of the crevice, inching around the boulder to his left as the flashlight beam darted about, exploring the gulley. He came around and looked up, saw a man almost directly above him. The gulley was so steep that the man's boot was level with his head. He couldn't see the others, who were still farther up on the ridge waiting for the guy to finish exploring with his flashlight. Keeler took a deep and silent breath. This was it.

He reached up with his left hand and pulled the boot

hard. The man tumbled with a grunt and came sliding fast down the ravine slope. Keeler reached out and pulled the blade of the survival knife hard across the guy's throat, letting gravity do the work as the man fell into the gulley. The wound blossomed in the moonlight. The flashlight's beam went wild, swinging and shaking. A thud and the light stopped.

Keeler was moving fast in the other direction, using his fingers to grab the icy rock, crossing the boulder and coming up on the other side.

A voice called the guy's name. "Josh."

Keeler couldn't see the man down there, but he could hear him making wild sounds. He imagined him thrashing his life out in the gulley. With his throat cut, he was most likely bleeding out. Keeler came around the upper side of the boulder, his boots sinking softly into the snow. Two men were in front of him, both with their backs turned. One closer than the other. The moon was high, making shadows out of branches on the clean white snow.

Keeler came at the man just in front of him, inching up on his back. The tip of the knife went to the back of the neck. He got the steel point a millimeter from the skin in the hollow below where the cranium begins and moved in, taking that last step and getting a strong grip around the guy's chest. In one quick motion, Keeler crushed the man into himself and pushed the knife in at the same time. The blade was still factory sharp. Keeler thrust to the hilt and twisted, feeling the steel edge ripping through tendons and muscle and veins and most importantly the medulla oblongata.

The man's muscular body, taut with shock, went suddenly soft, like he was simply turned off. The weight of the body dropping took Keeler's knife down with it, the blade caught into the bony substance of the man's cranium. Keeler kept his hand on the hilt, going down into a crouch with the corpse and whirling around to his next target.

The second guy stood slightly downhill, up against the boulder where the first guy had been earlier. He was moving fast at Keeler's flank with a handgun coming up to bear. Keeler planted a foot on the dead man's head and pulled the knife, which refused to come out. He had maybe a second and a half to do something. A mantra went off in his head, a mix between a shouting drill sergeant and a bell tolling: *Get in close so the weapon is useless.*

Keeler let gravity work for him, launched himself down the incline to the man, aiming to get on the inside of the raised weapon and knowing it wasn't going to work out. The gun barrel kicked once and Keeler felt the round tearing flesh on his left hip. Keeler slid involuntarily, winding up on the inside of the man's gun arm. He pushed the arm out and made to head-butt him, but the guy moved his head to the side, leaving their faces to touch, up close and personal. Keeler could feel the bristle of cropped beard against his cheek, and he saw an eye in ultra close-up, wide open and staring.

Kevin Milton. Even in the dark, he recognized him from the photograph he'd sent to Kelly. Keeler attacked Milton's nose, adapting to the situation, locking on with his teeth, biting hard and tearing. Feeling the chomp and crunch whipping away and ripping flesh and cartilage and skin, tasting blood. Milton grunted and yanked his head back against the boulder, face a raw mess of exposed flesh. The back of his head snapped into the cold rock and the weapon he'd been holding dropped into the snow.

Both sets of eyes tracked the heavy pistol, landing on the pure white surface and going through the deep snow, disappearing out of sight.

Milton glanced at Keeler, a white-eyed stare of hatred and

fear. Keeler could taste Milton's blood and spit it into the snow, eager for more. Milton glanced at where his gun had vanished. Keeler could guess the thought process, since he had already gone through the possibilities. You go down, looking for the gun. Good chance of finding it on the first try, like eighty to twenty. But will you get it up fast enough, and what about that twenty percent possibility that it's hit the ground under the snow and slid downhill?

Milton's eyes shifted, from where the gun had entered the snow to the abyss. He committed himself to the second option, leaping feetfirst down the ravine, disappearing into the darkness below. Keeler crouched for the weapon, his hand pushing through the snow, not finding the gun, then sweeping in an arc. He gave up and followed.

CHAPTER SEVENTY

K eeler lost his balance, banging the back of his head on the boulder coming down. The rest of the fall was quick and weightless, ending in a soft landing—a little too soft. Keeler scrambled to his feet, realizing he'd landed on a body. The dead man lay at the base of the incline, throat open and the surrounding snow darkened with his blood. The man's eyes turned southwest, unseeing and glassy in the moonlit night.

Vitalek hadn't left the shelter, the opening camouflaged by evergreen branches and snow. Keeler didn't stop to think about that, he got going after Milton, wanting nothing so much as to close in on the kill. His approach was instinctive and predatory. Milton had a head start and was sprinting down the ravine, maybe twenty yards away.

Keeler looked down at his left side, wondering why he hadn't felt the pain yet, and saw that for the second time that day, he'd been lucky. The bullet had just grazed him. There was blood and a deep groove where the round had passed, maybe scraping bone, in which case he'd stiffen up once he stopped moving and the adrenaline was gone.

Do or die, he thought as he pounded through the snow. He

registered Candy's boot prints curving down the ravine and then taking a sharp left toward a rocky outcrop. She was probably hiding behind the rocks. Maybe she'd needed to take a piss, and then it had all kicked off.

Milton's tracks led predictably straight down the ravine, veering to the right after a while. Keeler slowed, choosing not to follow his quarry directly, but to track parallel and try to come up on his flank or rear. He backtracked twenty yards and moved up out of the ravine, taking the direction of the tracks he'd seen. Up over the rise was a flat vista, shining in the moonlight, an open meadow. It was huge, maybe an acre. At the far end of it Milton was crossing into the woods. Keeler judged that to be southwest. He waited for Milton to disappear into the dark, then started sprinting across. Once he got into the trees again there was a new smell in the air, a familiar scent of rotting vegetation and algae. A large body of water was nearby.

He could hear it as he moved southwest, the roaring sound coming from the far side of the woods. Keeler broke through the trees in a hot sprint and almost ran off a cliff. He was standing on a high bluff looking out over a huge reservoir. To his right was a dam. Immediately below the cliff was the spillway, clearly lit in the moonlight. The surface of the reservoir was frozen, but the water was high, spilling out over a stepped wall made of rough stone. The noise was deafening. Thousands of gallons of water rushed over in a continuous roar, frothing white as it cascaded over stone and ice.

Sublime.

Keeler didn't see Milton but figured the man wouldn't be climbing down into the chasm below; he'd be going up top of the dam where a narrow road ran east to west. Keeler followed the edge of the cliff, keeping low, unconcerned about being heard, since the noise was so intense.

To Keeler's left was the deep chasm. He could see the dam's

structure ahead of him. The spillway continued, curving around the side of the dam into a gorge below. The depth was impressive, maybe a hundred yards down. The spill rushing over the rough-hewn stone created a dreamlike mix of fast-moving water and ice formations bubbling up in weird shapes from the stone steps. The immense globules gleamed in the moonlight.

Keeler came up to the road bridge from a narrow cliff edge path below. Looking up over the pavement, he saw Milton crouching by the rear of a glossy Mercedes S-Class, tucked into a parking spot by the woods. He recognized Jerry's car and understood the situation. Milton and his buddies had gone back down for the Mercedes. They'd brought it up to canvas the area of woods above the dam.

The second team might be elsewhere, covering another huge area. Here, there was only Milton, hunting for the key by the wheel well.

Keeler pulled the empty Glock from his pocket, vaulted up to the road, and extended the useless weapon in front of him. Milton wouldn't know the difference, at least not in a hurry. Milton must have heard him. He turned and rose, chest heaving from the run through the woods and the adrenaline of combat. He had a phone in his hand.

Keeler had to shout over the roaring cascade. "Drop the phone."

The phone clattered to the pavement. The man was out of breath. Too much time spent lifting at the gym, not enough time out there moving around.

Milton said, "Let me walk away, okay? We'll end it here. I didn't like this gig from the beginning and I haven't hurt anybody."

Keeler smiled. "You think I'm going to let you walk away?"

"I don't know. But I'll tell you something." He coughed and looked at Keeler, trying to get eye contact and the human empathy machine working. He said, "Woke up this morning, made breakfast for the kids. Waffles with eggs and bacon. Was into my first cup of Joe and the office called so here I am." He waved his arms around. "In this crazy place."

Keeler said, "Where do you live?"

"White Plains."

"A regular guy, huh? Wife and kids and a day job as a murderer." Keeler shook his head, looking at Milton, knowing that was as likely to be an accurate description as not. He said, "Tell me something. You coach Little League too?"

Milton shrugged. "I used to coach the youth football, quit a year ago. Why?"

The way Milton was talking, Keeler believed him. Intuition said, yes, the guy does the family domestic thing, plus he likes to go the other way with boys like Kelly. People's desires are always going to be more complicated than you think. Keeler said, "You're an optimist."

Milton nodded, putting on a haggard expression, like there was no more juice in the tank. Keeler saw the guy was studying him, examining the angles. Trying to evaluate if the bullshit was working, thinking, *Is this guy going to shoot me?* Or, more like thinking, *Why hasn't this guy shot me yet?* Which was pretty much what Keeler would be doing in his shoes.

Milton said, "How can I help you, help make all of this shit go away?"

Keeler watched Milton's eyes darting around until his gaze fixated on the Glock, and Keeler knew what Milton was noticing. Unbelievable, but it looked as if he'd spotted the extractor protruding on the right side of the pistol. Some versions of Glocks have a little tab indicator, letting a user know if there's one in the chamber. The tab sticks out less than a millimeter. You have to feel it with the pad of a thumb or finger. But you can see it if you know what you're looking for.

There was no doubt about it, Milton had seen it, and now he was probably wondering, Did Keeler forget to rack the slide, or is the magazine empty?

It all happened very fast, in the space of three seconds or less. Milton's discovery and his actions. He pushed off with his left foot and launched himself at Keeler, grabbing the Glock by the barrel and twisting. At the same time, he hammered a right hook with zero backswing into Keeler's jaw using body weight alone. The punch hit its target, and Keeler's knees collapsed, making him involuntarily release his grip on the weapon.

CHAPTER SEVENTY-ONE

M ilton stood over him, no longer breathless, no longer a supplicant, his face showing calculated indifference. He pulled back the slide on the Glock and saw the ammunition in the magazine had been cycled through, and there was nothing to keep the slide locked back. Milton's face didn't register panic, it registered competence and professional attention. He moved from using the weapon as a firearm, to using it as a club, rushing at Keeler to pistol whip him.

His face was predatory, teeth bared and eyes hollow and fixed on the target.

Keeler got his feet back and stabilized. He twisted to the outside and caught the blow on his shoulder.

Milton took a step too many, over committing. Keeler was on him in a flash, both legs pushing off. He got behind Milton, threading his left arm around his neck, looking to lock it in with his right and put him to sleep. Milton pushed back hard, using powerful legs to make Keeler stagger back. The mercenary was pure muscle and bone.

Keeler steadied himself, then pushed the other way and tried to complete the hold, Milton writhing in his grasp like a python. The man was quick and hard to get a grip on. Milton dropped all of his weight suddenly, letting gravity do some work, almost slipping out of the hold. Keeler had to move rapidly into him, which is what Milton had been waiting for. He slammed an elbow into Keeler's groin and scored a home run. Keeler bent over, the pain spreading badly, incapacitating him for crucial moments.

Milton whipped around and made contact, slamming hard fists into Keeler's face. The reaction was instinctive. Using pure force and weight to push the guy back and nullify the fists, Keeler had him bent backwards over the guard rail. Milton's fingers scrabbled for soft places to push into. A thumb in Keeler's left eye blinded him, forcing him to put all of his weight into shoving Milton. The guy panicked. Desperate hands grabbed at Keeler's jacket, and Keeler found himself bent over, head pulled down, looking at Milton's feet braced against the iron railing. The man's face turned up to his, straining hard to get Keeler over with him.

Milton roared into Keeler's face, teeth bared and tendons and muscles straining. Keeler felt a wave of vertigo as they went over together, free-falling into the roaring spillway.

It felt like it took a long time, falling like that. Milton was still clutching him by the sleeve. Keeler saw a flash of the man's eyes wide and desperate, mouth agape. The other man's body was directly below him, both of them touching gently in the freezing air. The first impact came as a dull thud. Keeler landed on the other man and spun out into water and a frozen numb blackout. He saw an afterimage, a flash of what his brain had been unable to register when his head had hit the icy surface. The image was Milton's legs cartwheeling away.

Keeler came to, thrashing in the water. He couldn't feel his limbs and had to tell himself they still worked. He grasped desperately at rock, finding only ice, the huge globules formed by the side of the spillway. He spotted a stone area clear of ice and used everything he had to haul himself up. He had landed in a pool on an upper step of the spillway.

Keeler carefully scooted over to the edge and saw the bottom of the gorge far below. Milton's body was down there, his head exploded like a broken watermelon on the frozen rock. There was blood on the ice formations, shining in the moonlight. Keeler lay back and looked into the dark sky, feeling pleasant warm flushes, even as he realized that his body was shaking uncontrollably. The spillway bridge was above, twenty feet up.

The key fob to the Mercedes was in the wheel well, on the other side of where Milton had been searching. Keeler's hands were shaking so hard that he almost failed to hold on to it. He'd fallen into freezing water and could already feel the initial effects of hypothermia. He stripped completely and got in the car. Keeler stepped on the gas pedal with the car in neutral and cranked the heat. Nothing came out but cold air and he began to be a little concerned.

He started feeling his mind drift into incoherence. Had to fight that feeling. The key fob had a trunk button. He pushed it and went back, desperate and shaking. A red and black dog blanket sat neatly folded in the trunk, a little small, but better than nothing. When he got back into the car the heating system had begun to function.

Fifteen minutes later, he was feeling like a human being again. He went back out for his clothing, throwing the wet textile into the backseat. His phone had broken in the fall and was soaked besides. On the positive side, he'd kept the master keycard for Copenhagen House in his jeans pocket. Now, he was looking at it in his hand, wondering if it would work.

Visualizing room number nine.

He got the Mercedes into gear and did a K-turn to bring it around. His mind was clearing, thankfully. His eye was caught by a flashing light. Milton's phone glimmered like a jewel on the ground. Keeler rolled the vehicle forward and opened the driver's side door to retrieve the phone. The ringtone was an electric approximation of a cicada's mating call.

He pushed the talk button. "Yeah."

A male voice, thick, like a man over sixty. "Milton?"

Keeler said, "No."

There was a pause. The man said, "Who's this?"

Keeler said nothing.

The man said, "Is it that guy, what's your name, Keeler?"

Keeler said nothing. The man laughed and sighed. "Well, anyway, it doesn't matter, whoever you are. I was calling Milton, tugging at the leash. I guess he doesn't need a leash anymore. That's too bad. Be that as it may, we're done, so you're done. You understand what I'm saying?"

Keeler wondered if he was speaking to a Triton Gamma Associates principal, Taggart or Grimaldi. Grimaldi maybe, since he was the guy on the East Coast. Taggart was the guy with the Seal connection in San Diego, according to Blomstein.

Keeler didn't care. He ended the call and drove, eyes on the road. Was the guy being honest, telling him they'd pulled back from the hit on Vitalek? With the body count they had right now it was more than likely they'd tactically reassess. Not voluntarily, but because they had to. For one thing, they'd be having a hard time with recruitment. He assessed the situation. Candy and Vitalek up in the shelter, winter camping. Keeler almost laughed since Vitalek seemed to be in his comfort zone up there.

Maybe Candy would get into it too, and they could share a hobby, spend the weekend eating freeze-dried tuna casserole and whatever other delights Vitalek had in his backpack.

One thing was for sure, Keeler wasn't going hiking in the frozen woods with nothing but a dog blanket thrown over his shoulders.

The gates to the estate came up on the right. He pulled the Mercedes into the driveway and waited for the security people to let him in, or not. The gate opened and he drove through. The driveway bifurcated, the main entrance on the right and the side entrance on the left, where he'd seen Jerry park. The Mercedes crunched gravel.

Keeler kept the engine running, waiting to see what would happen. The place looked calm. Warm lights glowed from inside, and there was nobody in sight. Jerry did not emerge to verify that his car was intact. Keeler keyed in Mini DeValla's number to Milton's phone. The call was answered on the third ring.

"Yeah?"

"It's Keeler. Where are you?"

"Finishing up my shift. What's going on?"

He could hear the train sound in the background. Keeler looked down at himself and remembered that he was naked. The wound at his hip was leaking blood onto the leather seat.

He gave a short laugh. "Had to think about that for a second. Not much. I was hoping you'd be up for a little diner action tonight. I think I'm ready to go Greek."

She said, "Tell you what, I'll make dinner at my place. You like spaghetti and meatballs?"

"Absolutely."

He visualized her smile, the cute gap between her front teeth. DeValla's voice became softer, like she was embarrassed speaking to him while at work. She said, "I can't promise we'll make it to dinner, though."

Keeler said, "We'll just play it as it comes."

DeValla said, "Say an hour?"

"See you."

Keeler ended the call. He looked up again at the outside of Copenhagen House. Nobody in there was prepared for a berserker like himself.

CHAPTER SEVENTY-TWO

The clock on the dashboard read eight forty-two, which seemed early, given the darkness and the dense activity of the day. Keeler dialed Julie Everard's personal number. No answer, straight to voicemail. He called again. This time, she answered on the fourth ring and sounded pissed off. "Everard speaking."

"This is Ron Darling. Did I catch you at a bad time?"

She didn't respond immediately. Keeler had the feeling that she was moving through space, maybe getting up out of a chair and making a sign to another person in the room. He heard a door close. "Mr. Darling. I'm eating dinner. Tell me what's going on."

"Good news and bad news, which do you want first?"

Everard took a hit from a cigarette, spoke while exhaling. "I always like the good before the bad."

"Good news is that you're back in business, Everard. The bad is that you're not going to finish dinner. Do you have something to record with?"

Everard said, "Like a voice recorder? Sure. What am I supposed to record?"

"It's going to be worthwhile. Check the batteries and bring that recorder up to Copenhagen House. I'll be in room number nine."

"Now?"

"Immediately."

Everard said, "I'm on my way, Ron."

Keeler ended the call and stepped out of the car. Everard's professional tone filled him with confidence. She hadn't asked the dumb logistical questions, which usually begin with the word *how*. He tried to wrap the dog blanket around his waist but it didn't cover him completely, leaving him to hold it closed out of a sense of propriety.

The keycard opened the side entrance door, and Keeler found himself in a vestibule with an upright piano tucked against a wood-paneled wall with bookshelves. The kitchen was to the left and the hallway leading to reception on his right. Nobody was in sight. The place was warm and comfortable as ever. Maybe Jerry and Jill had packed it in, called the whole thing off and distanced themselves temporarily. Not a terrible idea, given the circumstances.

He walked to the right, up the corridor on the other side of the kitchen. The room numbers began at seven. He stopped in front of room nine and listened. Nothing going on, nothing happening except for the buzz of a faulty bulb and the far-off sound of jazz music. The door behind him opened, room number eight. A woman stepped out and noticed him. She said, "Hi." And walked away.

Keeler watched her go around the curve toward reception. He touched the keycard to room number nine. The lock whirred and clicked discreetly. He stepped inside.

Sam Kelly was propped up in bed reading a book with a silhouetted lion on the cover. He saw Keeler and his face froze in an expression of total confusion. Keeler had seen it before, the shock and paralysis when an enemy is caught defenseless. He took a single stride to the bed and ripped off the covers.

Kelly tried to draw himself up into a protective ball by the headboard, but Keeler got a fist around his ankle and pulled hard and fast, tearing him off the mattress. Kelly's body went airborne, stopped by a hard fist to the face. Blood splashed onto the cream-colored silk sheets. Kelly sputtered, shocked and horrified. Keeler did it again. Another hard fist sent fast into the guy's face. It doesn't take long to make a point when you're ready to break noses and teeth.

He got his fist into Kelly's hair, pulling his head up and speaking into his face. "Here's what's going to happen, you ready?"

Kelly nodded. "You're that guy. Okay, you know it's done, right?"

Keeler ignored him. "How tall are you?"

"What?" Kelly saw that Keeler was going to hit him again and shrank back. "No, stop. I'm six two."

Keeler said, "Good. I need to borrow some clothes."

The guy, thinking that was it, almost laughed with relief and pointed wildly at the armoire in front of the bed. "Take whatever you want."

Keeler dropped him. "Thank you."

He opened the armoire and chose a pair of jeans, a t-shirt, and a sweater. Kelly had high-quality clothing and it fit well. The sweater was cashmere. Keeler couldn't remember the last time he'd worn something so nice, usually cashmere didn't last long on his body. Kelly watched him put on the jeans.

Keeler said, "What are you looking at?"

"That's Japanese denim." Kelly waved a dismissive hand. "Never mind. I was going to tell you how to maintain it." His eyes drifted to a landline phone by the bed.

Keeler shook his head. "No."

Kelly looked down at the floor. "What do you want from me?"

"Milton's not going to be joining you. Neither are the others. It's over now." Keeler sat down next to him on the bed. Kelly avoided eye contact, shivering even though it was warm in the room. Keeler grabbed him by the chin and jerked his head up, slapped him hard across the face. "Look at me when I'm talking to you."

The violence did its work. Kelly's eyes came up, like looking into the eyes of a reprimanded hound. Keeler wasn't trying to make a specific scary face, knowing that an honest look is always more frightening and believable.

Keeler said, "Do you like life, Sam? Do you want to live?"

Kelly began to cry, not daring to look away. Tears formed in his eyes and began to drip onto his cheeks. "Yes, please. I want to live."

Keeler nodded. "Good. I have a friend coming over right now. We're going to have questions. If you answer them honestly and truthfully there might be a light for you at the end of the tunnel. You might have a tough time for a while, Sam, maybe prison time. But you'll live in the end, which is important isn't it?"

Kelly nodded gratefully. "Thank you, yes."

Keeler looked at him hard, knowing the truth of the life and death question. Everyone wants to live, nobody wants to die. Death is going to happen in the end, but very few will give up on life voluntarily. The vast majority of people will take every second they can get.

Everard was on her way over. They'd get what they needed out of Kelly, and she'd publish it in her paper. If everything worked out, the story would go nationwide at the least. Law enforcement would have no choice but to follow up on it, and maybe Vitalek would be safe for a while.

Keeler's mind shifted to more pleasurable thoughts. He pictured Mini DeValla on the train, maybe pulling into Kitchewan Landing. She'd be wearing the uniform with that gold name tag.

CHAPTER SEVENTY-THREE

The Poughkeepsie train was due in to Kitchewan Landing at nine, which was in five minutes. For Mini DeValla that was the end of the day. She was in her little compartment, looking out the tiny window at the night rushing by. It had been dark since four, deep winter. This time the blizzard had been over pretty fast, no cancellations, no deep freeze.

She looked at the phone. Keeler had been popping up in her head all day. She'd had to put him out of it just so that she could keep going. Now that he'd called, her heart was beating a lot faster.

She'd been replaying the last couple of days over in her head, trying to examine what the hell had been going on. It had been completely nuts, but it made sense in a weird way. Mini had the feeling that everything had changed all at once, radically changed. At the same time, nothing seemed very different. Maybe that was because she was at work. Maybe it was going to all come out in a burst this weekend.

She heard the horn and slid open the window, putting her head out into the freezing air. The platform a hundred yards away and she liked to watch it come with the familiar

Kitchewan Landing sign and the platform lights and people waiting for trains.

Mini caught a ride home with a guy from the ticket office who'd also come off shift. Her Cherokee was still missing. The ticket office guy was a little talkative, but she managed to act normal and make small talk on the way home.

Her driveway was blanketed with freshly fallen snow. Mini let herself into the house and turned on the hall light. The coat closet had been left open. She didn't remember leaving it that way, but her mind was still frazzled. She put her coat inside and closed it. The living room and kitchen were dark. She checked her phone again to see if there were messages but saw nothing. She thought, Take a bath, relax. She'd let Keeler figure out the dinner situation. She smiled to herself. Anyway, that would be after, not before.

But first she'd open a bottle of red wine and let it breathe while she got cleaned up.

Mini kicked her shoes off, nudged them into the closet. She took off her socks and the uncomfortable conductor's uniform trousers and flung them over the back of the living room chair. On the way to the kitchen she let her hair down, shaking out the curls, feeling a lot better now that she was home and comfortable.

Mini noticed a weird smell, a second before she entered the kitchen, like medical ointment. She had her hand up to turn on the light and felt a sharp electric shock run up from her toes to the top of the head. She saw the guy in the kitchen, even without the light on. It was too late to turn and run; she was already two steps in. He was sitting there at the table in the dark. He said, "Turn the light on, hun."

She felt the electric shock turn to cold dread, threatening to creep over and control her. She fought it and hit the lights. The guy was dressed in a cop uniform. She felt a huge sense of relief, for a half second. For some reason, the idea came into her head that this was a cop who wanted to talk to her about Frankie's death. But the relief faded fast. The uniform was much too big, the man's face looked chewed up, and he had a medical compress on his neck, which is why her kitchen stank. She wondered if it was Keeler who had done that to him.

"What do you want?" she said.

The guy had a gun in his hand, which was resting on the kitchen table. Not even pointed at her. He looked tired.

"What I want right now is something to eat. Since I don't cook myself, I waited for you. What do you have?"

Mini recognized him. It was the guy from the diner who'd been wearing the same coat as Frankie. Her entire body tensed up, and she was afraid maybe she'd be unable to move. She had to force herself to inhale and exhale, calmly. The guy scared the shit out of her. He had different-colored eyes and looked fucking crazy. The bandage on his neck was leaking blood down the inside his shirt, and he smelled like death.

She tried to act cool. Maybe people like that can sense fear and get drawn to it.

She said, "You like cheesecake?"

He said, "I like it enough, but that's in the dessert category. I need some basic nutrition first, like proteins and carbs and fats and all that good salty shit." He winked. "Then we can talk about sugar."

Mini felt nauseous. Sweat broke out at her hairline and at the small of her back. She went to the fridge. "I'll make you an omelette. Ham on the side and toast. Okay?"

The guy didn't say anything but she felt his eyes on her as she scanned the inside of the refrigerator. There would have been maybe a half chance of getting her hands on the shotgun Keeler had left by the door. But, she'd moved that upstairs, not wanting the gun anywhere near her. Now she was going to have to make an omelette for some psychopath and probably get herself raped and killed for dessert.

She prepared the food, not wanting to turn around and look at him, not wanting to engage. Mini was suddenly angry at the man, the emotions coming from nowhere in a wild swing. She struggled to contain it. Had to stop herself from going for a kitchen knife. This guy was different from the others. He wasn't some joke. He didn't speak much either.

She set a plate down in front of him and backed up against the kitchen counter. The guy said, "You don't want to eat?"

Mini shook her head.

The man ate slowly, watching her while he did so. "You got butter for the toast?" She got the butter out of the fridge. "Grab me the grape jelly you got in there too."

"What else do you need?"

"Ketchup."

She brought out the ketchup and watched him squirt a good amount into his plate. The man chewed his eggs and ham for a while and looked up at her. "It's good, relax."

"That's a little hard right now."

He stopped chewing, looking at her. "Yeah, I guess." Mini felt his eyes appraising her, moving down her bare legs and up again, weird gaze resting where her panties were covered by the untucked conductor's uniform shirt. "Nice outfit you got on."

She said nothing.

When he was finished, the man pushed his plate away. "Now, what about that cheesecake?"

Mini got the take-out container from the fridge and set it in front of him. She got a dessert fork from the drawer and slid it across the table. The man reached out a hand, lightening quick, and grabbed her by the wrist, squeezing hard. He forced her closer, pulling her so that she leaned over the table. Mini tried to hide her pain and fear.

"What do you want from me?" she asked.

The crazy eyes danced, literally moving around. He said, "I wanna know what that means. Wild Kitty. What you got tattooed on those lovely legs."

"Doesn't mean anything."

He nodded. "Okay. You know what I want, I want you to dress up." The man indicated upstairs with his head. "I took the liberty of touring the property. Nice house. Why don't you go up there and put on that little silk dress you got in the bedroom closet? That's what I'd like."

Mini had a silk gown, lingerie that Frankie had bought five years ago and she'd worn for one weekend. He'd bought it for her for Valentine's Day, when they went up to Saratoga Springs for the weekend and stayed in a honeymoon suite with a jacuzzi in the room. She associated that silk gown with the smell of chlorine.

The guy said, "Don't fuck with me now. I know you got kids, where your mother lives. I got it all, hun. Go upstairs to your bedroom and put that silk thing on for me with nothing else. Come back down and we'll see how we're doing then."

Mini DeValla felt a bead of sweat drop down the small of her back.

He said, "Nothing underneath, you hear? I'm gonna enjoy you."

The man let go of her wrist and Mini pulled away. Expressionless as she stood up and left the kitchen. Her arm throbbed from where he'd held her.

CHAPTER SEVENTY-FOUR

DeValla walked up the stairs, thinking about the bedroom closet. If the guy had gone in there and seen the lingerie, he'd have seen the shotgun. She went into the closet, pushed the silk lingerie to the side and saw the blank closet wall behind it— no gun there. So he'd found it. The guy hadn't said anything about the weapon, which was odd.

Something clicked in Mini's mind, and she remembered what had happened earlier. She'd come upstairs to get changed for work. But, she hadn't gone into her bedroom directly. She'd gone into the bathroom to remove her dressing gown and had laid the shotgun across the sink while she peed. She must have forgotten it there in the rush to get ready.

The guy downstairs hadn't mentioned the weapon, but if he'd toured the house, surely he'd have looked into the bathroom. Unless he was wounded so bad he wasn't thinking clearly.

The bathroom was just beside her bedroom. One step into the hallway and she was looking in. From the doorway all you saw was the bathtub and a full-length mirror. The sink was around the other side of the door to the left. Frankie's big gun lay across the double sink counter, completely out of place in the pastel colored bathroom. The box of shells were right beside the cotton swabs. Mini picked up the heavy shotgun, quiet as she could, brought it into the bedroom and set it down on the bed.

Keeler had demonstrated how to pull the slide back and had made her do it a couple of times. She was suddenly afraid that the man would hear her from downstairs. Mini got on her knees beside the bed and pulled back the slide as softly as possible, wincing at the unavoidable snick of steel on steel. The safety button was just behind the trigger guard. She pushed it like Keeler had demonstrated.

Mini came into the kitchen with the Browning's stock pressed tight to her shoulder. The man was slumped with his chin on his chest. He was chewing slowly with the dessert fork clutched in his hand. The pistol was in the middle of the table, just lying there on its side. His eyelids were half closed. When he saw Mini come in with the shotgun he lifted his head.

He slurred his words. "Hey now."

Mini said, "Get your hands up and push yourself away from the table."

He didn't move. "Come on now, I'm just eating dinner. You want me to leave before I finish dessert, that's not a problem."

She laughed nervously, involuntarily. "Okay, sure. Just get back from the table and put your hands up."

The man nodded to her. "Okay."

His hand darted to the pistol and got around the grip, lifting it up. Mini pulled the trigger on the Browning and put a load into his chest, blowing him off the kitchen chair. The recoil staggered her back. The body was inert, folded and crumpled on the floor under the table. Blood and flesh and bone painted the wall behind him. Somehow the guy's face had remained intact. The different colored eyes, uncanny, staring without sight into nothing.

Mini registered movement at the front door, making her jump. She swung the Browning around and a strong hand pushed it away. She fixed her gaze on Keeler's face and let him take the weapon from her. She saw his eyes dart around, collecting visual information. A haze hung in the air.

Keeler laid the gun on the table and put both hands on her shoulders. He looked straight into her eyes. "This is a very bad guy you just put down. I know him. You did good, DeValla, believe it."

She rested her forehead against Keeler's chest. For some reason, he was wearing a cashmere sweater, she noticed. Mini turned her cheek against it. "Yeah."

Keeler held her against him for a long time, letting her dictate the situation. At first DeValla was shaking like a leaf, her body strong and shuddering against his. He could feel her heart pounding until, after a while she settled. When she'd calmed down, she surprised him by burying her face hard into his chest and screaming, a roar really, muffled by his body mass. She pulled herself into him tightly and howled, hot and humid, letting it all go.

She bit hard into Keeler's chest and he almost pulled away involuntarily.

DeValla released him a little and pulled the sweater to her face, wiping herself with it. She stepped back, looking at the place where she'd bitten a hole in Keeler' sweater and potentially his skin. They made eye contact.

"Sorry." She looked critically at the sweater. "You're not the kind of guy who can get away with wearing cashmere."

Keeler didn't understand, having enjoyed the soft feel of the sweater. "Why not?"

Her mouth turned up at the edges slightly. "You need like, canvas or something. I don't know, heavy duty cotton, or just go with fleece. Something durable anyway. That pretty cashmere thing's going to last another day maybe, before it shreds off you by itself."

He said, "Too delicate for me."

"Exactly." DeValla exhaled long and slow. "I need to call the police."

Keeler nodded. "Tell it like it happened."

She looked at the corpse on her kitchen floor. "Except for the part with you in it, right?"

"Might reduce the already existing level of complication."

DeValla's gaze moved up and to the left for a second, "Yeah."

Keeler said, "You good?"

She widened her eyes, as if feeling herself, how she was. DeValla said, "I think so. I'll tell them what happened here, and that's it. Came back from work and this is what I found. Put a load into this psychopath and that's all I know. Which isn't far from the truth. I'll cry and stuff. What're they gonna do?" She held up a hand and looked at it. "Not even shaking anymore."

Keeler had already noticed. He raised his eyebrows. "Too bad you didn't go into the military, you would have been a perfect menace."

She said, "What I am is hard candy."

Keeler looked at her and thought that she was, indeed. He also knew that it was time for him to leave.

He said, "I'll be down in the city for a while. You like Chinese food?"

Mini DeValla pulled her hair into a bun and tied it off loosely. "I like the spicy kind, what do you call it?"

"I call it spicy."

CHAPTER SEVENTY-FIVE

K eeler exchanged Jerry's Mercedes S class for the drug dealer's Toyota, not exactly an equal exchange, but there wasn't really much of a choice. He got the Toyota on the road down to the city. There were two immediate problems, he was wounded and he didn't want to go to a hospital.

But, Keeler wasn't a helpless civilian, so he called Blomstein and gave him a list of pharmaceutical supplies.

It ended up taking almost two weeks for Keeler's wounds to heal completely. The last week was spent helping out around the apartment building. Keeler and Blomstein solved all kinds of domestic problems, mostly involving paint, lubricant, brute force, and the hardware store. The busy schedule of repairs didn't prevent Keeler from following the fallout from recent events up the river at Kitchewan Landing.

Back at Copenhagen House, Sam Kelly had not proven to be a courageous man. Which wasn't a surprise since as an account manager, courage wasn't part of the job description. What an account manager does require is an innate need to please others, combined with a strong streak of pragmatism and in Kelly's line of work, a total disregard for the concept of ethical principles.

When Everard had arrived at Copenhagen House with disheveled hair and a hand-held voice recorder, Kelly had gone straight into confession mode. Keeler and Everard had shared a single surprised glance, before the experienced journalist moved in on her prey. Later on, Everard had been able to corroborate Kelly's verbal testimony with the documents and messages that Vitalek had gleaned from the hacked phones.

The investigative findings were published first in the Kitchewan Gazette as a three part series of in-depth articles. The focus was on Big Finance and the cut-throat war raging behind the scenes for control of the emerging crypto space. It was a universe that most people knew nothing about, since it was complicated and involved math. Still, the big national papers picked up the story soon enough, beaten to the punch by the scrappy local Gazette. There was the alleged hit on Irma Rosenbaum and the attempted assassination of Vitalek, a guy eccentric enough to warrant at least a passing fascination.

One result of Everard's work was that a post-mortem was ordered for Rosenbaum's death. The investigation quickly turned up high levels of Thallium in Rosenbaum's hair follicles, which would account for the previous suspicion of cardiac arrest. The suspected vector for the poison was an aerosol sprayed into her ear canal. Of course no murder weapon was ever found.

Neither did Everard's investigation ever uncover evidence directly linking the big financial players to Rosenbaum's death or any criminal activity at all. But the journalism was compelling enough to make the situation a little too spicy, even for the hard men of Wall Street and Silicon Valley, jockeying for position in a convoluted new world. Whatever issues they had with Vitalek were best left to simmer, at least for the time being.

As for the supposed richest guy in the world, he disappeared off the face of the earth for a long time. There was a whole lot of wild internet gossip. Some said he was trekking in the Himalayas, others were sure they'd seen him in Lapland, following the migration patterns of reindeer herds. Yet others were convinced that Vitalek had fallen in love with a beautiful young woman, married her in a private ceremony, and departed for an extended honeymoon around the African continent.

Keeler and DeValla had lunch one afternoon in Chinatown. They met outside the restaurant and the greeting was easy, no formalities needed. The two of them naturally got along just as they had from the very beginning, when DeValla had uncharacteristically invited him to crash on her sofa, that cold snowy night.

They spoke about many things, animated, happy to see each other. The food was excellent, Sichuan cuisine with three vectors of spice. Hot enough to make the mouth buzz.

Keeler already knew that Frankie's funeral had been attended by police officers and supporters from the tri-state area. He was the first Kitchewan Landing police officer ever to fall in the line of duty. On Veterans Day and the Fourth of July, a hero's banner would be flown, along with banners for the other sons and daughters of Kitchewan Landing, fallen in service to their country.

The thought of Frankie looking heroic and stern on a banner made both DeValla and Keeler smile. It was perhaps the best way for a tragic situation to end. Farrell's attack on Mini DeValla had been officially connected to Frankie's heroic struggle with the local drug dealers, a situation that had spiraled out in a variety of messy deaths over that short period of a few days. The detectives in charge of the case managed to wrap everything up in a dozen pages of logical text, like a gift with a nicely tied bow holding it all together.

Keeler and DeValla each cracked open a fortune cookie when they'd finished lunch. Keeler read his and handed it across the table. DeValla did the same.

She read out loud. "Adversity is the parent of virtue."

Keeler did the same for hers. "Land is always on the mind of a flying bird."

They ate the cookies and discarded the slim paper fortunes into the middle of the table.

The farewell afterwards wasn't awkward, not even a little bit. Two confident people in the prime of their lives, neither one with even the slightest thought about what could have happened. Each firm in their belief that the only pertinent object of reflection was what did happen.

AN EXTRACT FROM
BERSERKER

CHAPTER ONE

A nkara, Turkey. November 16, 2016.

Tom Keeler opened his eyes and saw Calcutti's weathered face looming over him like a desert cliff blocking sunlight. "You're up."

"For what?"

"Canada didn't respond to the ping, so I sent Karim up an hour ago. He says they've pulled the curtain."

Keeler got up on an elbow. *Canada* was the code name for a safe house up in the diplomatic district. "What's the move?"

"I'm switching Karim to overwatch. I want you to do the pass at Canada."

Keeler nodded and swung his feet off the narrow bed to the floor. Calcutti looked at him and walked out. Across the room, another man grunted and rolled onto his side to face the wall. Bratton was up next for a shift, which was why Calcutti had woken Keeler. He put on his boots and stood up, feeling the buzz as his joints cracked pleasantly.

Keeler strapped on a money belt and checked that he had cash inside, plus the passport he'd used to enter Turkey. You never knew what would happen, so it was best to be prepared, even for a training mission.

Five of them were in the apartment, taking rotating four-hour shifts in the ready room. Three guys on duty, two guys in the back bedroom. Keeler had come off shift only two hours before.

He took his jacket from where it hung behind the door and walked into the front room of the apartment. Calcutti was on the sofa with a bag of spicy Turkish potato chips. The window was curtained with a batik sheet held in place by a couple of thumbtacks. The sunlight coming through was orange.

Calcutti pointed a red-powdered crinkle-cut chip at him. "You do your SDR and see if Karim can pick you up in Çankaya." He crunched a handful of chips between powerful jaws. "Mess him up, Keeler, test that kid. Make it hard."

The toilet flushed and Cheevers emerged, looking tired. Keeler noticed that he hadn't washed his hands.

Calcutti said, "Mr. Cheevers, issue Keeler a weapon, please, he's going for the pass at Canada."

Cheevers looked at Keeler, then back at Calcutti, deadpanning. "Just the nine or you want the operational pack too?"

"Just the weapon."

Cheevers shrugged, went to the kitchen, pulled open a panel on the tiled wall, and began rooting around in the cavity. He came up with a plastic-wrapped Yavuz 9mm, the Turkish version of a Beretta 92. Keeler removed the plastic wrap, balled it up, and tossed it in the can. He checked the pistol, inserted one of the magazines, and checked it again before slipping the weapon into his jacket pocket.

He was confused about the combination of training the new guy, name of Karim, and the fact that Canada had missed a ping. He said, "So what's the deal with Canada? Is that for real?"

Calcutti wiped potato chip residue on his jeans. "I don't know. If I did, I'd have told you. Just go up there and check it out. Probably bullshit. Use the opportunity to grind Karim a little."

Keeler said, "I'm asking if they actually missed the ping."

Calcutti nodded slowly and shrugged. "Affirmative."

The three men stood in the apartment's entrance. Keeler pushed earbuds into his ears. The buds looked identical to the civilian version, but were different on the inside. He paired them to an iPhone, also a heavily modded version of the civilian device. Calcutti thumbed a device into his left ear and spoke. "Feel me, bro?"

The voice came through into Keeler's ears, stereo and clear. "Roger that."

He tapped on the earbud and got the electronic click. Tapped twice and got two. Nodded at Calcutti.

Calcutti said, "Switching to channel five." Spoke into the air. "This is Sierra, Charlie, do you copy overwatch?"

Karim's voice came through. "Copy." Something about how the vowel met a consonant gave away Karim's Middle Eastern accent.

Calcutti looked at Cheevers while speaking to Karim on overwatch. "Kitty is leaving Brooklyn."

Keeler left the apartment, another safe house, this one code-named *Brooklyn*.

He rapidly descended three flights of stairs to the street, enjoying the movement. The November air felt clean and crisp, Ankara being a city at a high elevation, almost a thousand meters. Keeler started the steep walk up the hill to Çankaya, where all the embassies were located. The neighborhood quickly turned residential, the shops and restaurants thinning out.

He walked the Surveillance Detection Route, moving the way he'd been taught, unpredictably, switching back on himself and ducking into alleys and street food stalls and generally doing whatever he could to smoke out any mobile squad that might be on him.

The team was on a training mission and Ankara was a great place for it. The capital of Turkey was teeming with spooks, all of them looking out for surveillance, many of them hostile to Americans. If a new guy like Karim could make it in Ankara, everyone would feel a whole lot better about working with him when it wasn't a training mission.

Keeler went up to Çankaya the long way, down the other side and up again through Botanik Park. At the other side of the park he entered Atakule, a shopping mall in the shape of an enormous donut, and took the escalator down three levels to a Lacoste store. He tried on a sweater and flirted with the sales-woman, complimenting her on her English. He bought a latte.

Karim's hoarse voice croaked into Keeler's ears on his way out of the mall.

"This is overwatch. Blue skies." Karim, telling him that he was clean of surveillance and could proceed.

Keeler hadn't seen him and was mildly impressed he'd come in the back way. Keeler tapped twice on the right earbud, confirming receipt of the message. "Good. I didn't clock you." He waited for bravado but it didn't come, which is another reason people liked Karim. "What's the deal with Canada?"

The audio popped in his ear. Karim said, "I went up the back way and the curtain was pulled. I called it in."

"Okay. I'll finish the SDR and take a look. Just stay with me."

The street was pleasant, cafés set back from the road with

patios and outdoor heating. Couples sitting around drinking coffee. A group of friends playing cards. Karim was a local of Turkish and Persian descent who'd been recruited as a street operative able to blend into the environment. So far so good. It had been a while since any of them had managed to screw Karim up; he was coming along nicely.

Hello Friend,

I hope that you have enjoyed this book.

Please consider leaving a review on the book's Amazon page.

I love communicating with readers, and **I send a free Tom Keeler novella to anyone who joins my monthly Newsletter.**

Sign up at jacklively.com

See you there,

Jack Lively

SWITCH BACK

It's been two years since Tom Keeler left the military, but a combat medic never forgets his pilot. So, when he hears that Mallory's got terminal brain cancer, Keeler drops everything to see her one last time. But then he runs into a beautiful journalist, who's trying to escape cartel assassins out to kill her. Keeler's up for the challenge, but he can't get Mallory or her family involved, because the cartels never forget. So he's got to compartmentalize. On one hand there's a woman who's life needs saving. On the other, an old buddy who's life can't be saved. And this is Texas, on the hottest day of the hottest month of the hottest year that anyone can remember.

ALSO BY JACK LIVELY

The Tom Keeler novels can be read in any order.

Straight Shot

Breacher

Impact

Berserker

Badlands

ABOUT THE AUTHOR

Jack Lively is the author of the Tom Keeler series of thriller novels. His writing and interests cover a wide range of topics, genre fiction and narrative, moral philosophy, politics, religion, but more generally focus upon the increasingly dire task of distinguishing an appropriate ethical framework within an increasingly complex and uncertain world.

Follow Jack on BookBub

Hard Candy

ISBN 978-1-0686930-9-0

General Projects Ltd.

London, UK.

www.jacklively.com

Printed in France by Amazon
Brétigny-sur-Orge, FR

22061284R00214